Praise for the novels of Melanie Benjamin

The Autobiography of Mrs. Tom Thumb

"Mercy Lavinia Warren Bump is a big name to live up to, and although she was less than three feet tall, the future Mrs. General Tom Thumb did just that. By turns heartrending and thrilling, this bighearted book recounts a fictionalized life of this most extraordinary of women in prose that is lush and details that are meticulously researched. I loved this book." —Sara Gruen, author of *Ape House* and *Water for Elephants*

"Melanie Benjamin's striking novel about the diminutive Lavinia Warren Bump, one of P. T. Barnum's 'oddities,' shows that love and desire, strength and ambition, come in all sizes. Mrs. Tom Thumb brings out the humanity in all of us."

—Sandra Dallas, author of *Prayers for Sale* and *Whiter Than Snow*

"*The Autobiography of Mrs. Tom Thumb* is a vivid journey of a perfect woman in miniature through the showboats, sideshows, and circuses of rough nineteenth-century America. Under three feet in height, beautiful Vinnie possesses a strong intelligence and sense of humor. As amazing fame is poured upon her for her tiny size, she only wants to be loved for herself—a desire which sadly may never be fulfilled. Melanie Benjamin has created a compelling heroine, whose dramatic and poignant story will capture the reader's heart to the last page."

—Stephanie Cowell,
author of *Claude & Camille: A Novel of Monet* and *Marrying Mozart*

"Vinnie's first-person narration grabs you from the opening pages, providing hints of the absorbing and entertaining story to come. The novel is also a delightful cavalcade of late-nineteenth-century Americana. . . . Those interested in 'behind the scenes' of show business will be equally entranced."
—*Library Journal*

"Small in stature but big in voice and worldview."—*O: The Oprah Magazine*

"A narrative voice that is feisty, intelligent, brave, adventurous, and resourceful."
—*The Boston Globe*

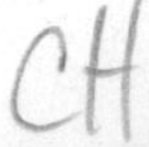

"Lavinia Warren was only thirty-two inches tall, but in Melanie Benjamin's *The Autobiography of Mrs. Tom Thumb* she soars above the tumult of Gilded Age America. Benjamin makes her a woman of courage and refinement with an itch for adventure and ambitions that far outstrip her size. I enjoyed every minute I spent with Vinnie in this exuberant, absorbing, elegantly written novel."

—Carol Wallace, author of *Leaving Van Gogh*

"Benjamin . . . knows how to combine research and readability. And she's given Vinnie such dignity and courage . . . that her heroine commands attention from the first page." —*The Washington Post*

"A remarkable, soaring novel . . . a fascinating story of triumph and tragedy and one person who refused to live a small life. Part biography, with a healthy dollop of artistic liberty, it is a spellbinding tale from the Gilded Age that seems more relevant now than ever." —*BookPage*

"Benjamin handles the era of mid-nineteenth-century America like a native, telling a walloping good story about a tiny person with the soul of a giant. The lovely Lavinia Bump once again comes alive, and we're all the richer because of it."

—Ellen Bryson, author of *The Transformation of Bartholomew Fortuno*

"I absolutely loved it! Vinnie Bump is one of the most engaging characters to come along in a while. Nineteenth-century women had few options; Vinnie had fewer yet. Melanie Benjamin renders her deeply human in a no-nonsense Olive Kitteridge sort of way. Readers will not soon forget her. I know I won't."

—Johanna Moran, author of *The Wives of Henry Oades*

"Vivacious . . . The smart and unyieldingly ladylike Vinnie emerges as an effervescent narrator with a love of life and a grand story worth the price of admission." —*Publishers Weekly*

"Benjamin handles the nineteenth-century material as though she's seeing it all with her own eyes. . . . It's easy to lose yourself in Benjamin's storytelling. . . . Enchanting." —January Magazine

"The true joy of this book is the multifaceted woman at the heart of the story."
—*Chicago Tribune*

"Historical fiction at its very best: extremely well researched as well as entertaining and engaging to read . . . This is a wonderful book, one of the best I've read all year."
—Minneapolis *Star Tribune*

Alice I Have Been

"This is magic! Childhood, sensuality, love, sorrow, and wonder, all bright and complex as the shifting patterns in a kaleidoscope."
—Diana Gabaldon

"Fanciful."
—*The New York Times Book Review*

"Finds glints of genuine magic."
—*Entertainment Weekly*

"This richly imagined novel contains so much—a literary mystery, a royal romance, a vivid portrait of Victorian England, and a poignant story of tragedy and endurance, all pieced together into a glittering whole. A captivating debut."
—Isabel Wolff

"Excellent . . . Benjamin offers a finely wrought portrait of Alice that seamlessly blends fact with fiction. This is book club gold."
—*Publishers Weekly* (starred review)

"The novel doesn't just fill in the blanks of a literary life, but tells the story of someone who was more than a muse; Alice may have been immortalized as a girl but, as Benjamin imagines, she grew up to be a great woman."
—*New York Post*

"A haunting evocation of a long-ago Lolita, richly imagined and deeply felt, that lingers in memory long after the last page is turned."
—Stephanie Barron

"*Alice I Have Been* is a smoky, magical mirror into the life of the real Alice. It's a spellbinding look at another Wonderland: Victorian England. Melanie Benjamin blends the known with the unknown in a seamless tale of love, loss, and myth. It's storytelling at its finest."
—Sarah Addison Allen

By

MELANIE

BENJAMIN

. . . . .

Alice I Have Been

The Autobiography of Mrs. Tom Thumb

The Aviator's Wife

The Swans of Fifth Avenue

Reckless Hearts (short story)

THE AUTOBIOGRAPHY OF

Mrs. Tom Thumb

THE AUTOBIOGRAPHY OF

Mrs. Tom Thumb

[*A Novel*]

MELANIE BENJAMIN

BANTAM BOOKS TRADE PAPERBACKS
NEW YORK

The Autobiography of Mrs. Tom Thumb is a work of fiction. Any references to historical events; to real people, living or dead; or to real locales are intended only to give the fiction a setting in historical reality. Other names, characters, places, and incidents either are the product of the author's imagination or are used fictitiously, and their resemblance, if any, to real-life counterparts is entirely coincidental.

2012 Bantam Books Trade Paperback Edition

Published in the United States by Bantam Books,
an imprint of The Random House Publishing Group,
a division of Random House, Inc., New York.

BANTAM BOOKS and the rooster colophon
are registered trademarks of Random House, Inc.
RANDOM HOUSE READER'S CIRCLE & Design
is a registered trademark of Random House, Inc.

Originally published in hardcover in the United States by Delacorte Press,
an imprint of The Random House Publishing Group,
a division of Random House, Inc., in 2011.

Library of Congress Cataloging-in-Publication Data
Benjamin, Melanie.
The autobiography of Mrs. Tom Thumb: a novel / Melanie Benjamin.
p. cm.
ISBN 978-0-385-34416-6 — ISBN 978-0-345-52757-8 (eBook)
1. Magri, M. Lavinia (Mercy Lavinia), 1841–1919—Fiction.
2. Women circus performers—United States—Fiction.
3. Dwarfs—United States—Fiction. I. Title.
PS3608.A876A94 2011
813'.6—dc22 2010052863

Printed in the United States of America

www.randomhousereaderscircle.com

Frontispiece photograph of Lavinia Warren by Mathew Brady
from the Library of Congress collection

8 10 11 9

Book design by Susan Turner

To Dennis, without whom

From *Harper's New Monthly Magazine,* July 2, 1850

American Vanity

We are not at all surprised at what in this country is most foolishly called the conceit and vanity of the Americans. What people in the world have so fine, so magnificent a country? . . . If ever these magnificent dreams of the American people are realized—and all that is wanted for their realization is that things should only go on as they have been going on for the last two centuries—there will be seated upon that vast continent a population greater than that of all Europe, all speaking the same language, all active-minded, intelligent, and well off.

1885

I SUPPOSE IT WOULD BE FASHIONABLE TO ADMIT TO SOME RESERvations as I undertake to write the History of My Life. Popular memoirs of our time suggest a certain reticence is expected, particularly when the author is a female. We women are timid creatures, after all; we must retire behind a veil of secrecy and allow others to tell our stories.

To that, I can only reply, "Rubbish!" I have let others—one other, in particular—tell my story for far too long. Now is the time to set the record straight, to sort out the humbug from the truth, and vice versa.

Has any other female of our time been written about as much as I have? It was not so very long ago when it was impossible to open a newspaper without reading about my husband or myself! We even preempted the War Between the States during its very darkest days. For a solid week, every newspaper in the land was interested only in our wedding plans—the guest list, the presents we received, my trousseau, in particular, receiving much press. President and Mrs. Lincoln were so eager to make our acquaintance that they put aside their own cares, graciously welcoming us to the White House on our honeymoon journey.

During the elaborate reception in the Blue Room, where we met a number of dignitaries, including many generals who would win themselves Glory on the Field of Battle, I permitted

Mr. Lincoln to kiss me. This was not something I allowed strange men to do as a rule, but felt I had to acquiesce to a presidential request. My husband, however, had no reservations of this sort; without even asking, he rose on tiptoe to bestow his usual happy kiss upon Mrs. Lincoln, who twittered and giggled and blushed a rosy red.

"Mr. Lincoln," she exclaimed with surprise. "The General kisses every bit as nicely as you!"

"Well, why shouldn't he, Molly?" Mr. Lincoln asked with a twinkle in his gray eyes. "I reckon he's had much more practice!"

Everyone laughed appreciatively, and none harder than my husband. I could not join in; it was a sore subject between the two of us already, so early in our marriage.

I determined to mention it to him later that night, when we were preparing for slumber. A more immediate problem, however, soon drove the thought from my mind. The enormous four-poster bed, piled high with the downiest of mattresses, pillows, and plush counterpane, was so tall that we despaired of ever reaching the top. Even my wooden steps, which I had carried with me since childhood, were not high enough. With great embarrassment, I had to summon a hotel chambermaid to assist us in attaining our goal. Once ensconced, naturally we were required to put off any thoughts of nighttime ablutions, unless we wanted to sleep the rest of the night on the floor.

The newspapers, naturally, did not recount this particular detail of our visit. This is but one example of why I have decided to write down my own recollections of my life thus far, and I vow I will do my best to keep them free of humbug.

Humbug. I can still hear my mother's gentle voice admonishing me all those years ago. "Oh, Vinnie, my little chick," she said with a worried shake of her head. "If you go with this Barnum you will be just another one of his humbugs. You will be caught up in that man's snare, and however will you escape without losing your soul?"

Looking back, I'm forced to admit that my mother was right; I did lose my soul, and so much more. But I'm not sure that I didn't give it away freely. My mother did not know Mr. Barnum as I did; she did not understand him, nor did the world at large. My intimacy with him is a prize, one that I am not willing to share with anyone. Not even with my own husband, who knew him first.

Not even with Minnie, although she would never have asked this of me; she never asked anything at all of me, except to keep her safe. And in that, I let her down.

This is but one more reason why I am eager to share my life's experiences: because I will finally be able to provide a full account of my beloved sister's all-too-brief time on this earth. My name may be on this volume's cover, as it was on all the handbills, headlines, and invitations, but for once I will not allow Minnie to remain in my shadow, although she was happiest there. I consider it my duty and privilege—even more, my penance—to tell her story, too. She deserves to be remembered; her courage needs to be known—as does the identity of the person, or persons, who killed her.

I have spent the last ten years trying to decide who was most responsible for her death, Mr. Barnum or me. Perhaps by the time I'm finished with this story, I will have figured it out.

Perhaps I won't, for I'm not sure I want to know.

Listen to me! I am putting the exclamation point before the salutation, as Mr. Barnum used to say; I had best dim the lights and commence my story before the audience grows restless. And there is no better way to begin this tale than by revealing, once and for all, my real name.

It is not, in fact—despite the manner in which I have been

introduced to Queens, Presidents, and even Mormons—Mrs. Tom Thumb. It is not even Lavinia Warren, which is how I was first introduced to the public.

No, God saw fit to bestow upon me the lamentable name of Mercy Lavinia Warren *Bump*.

And of the many obstacles He handed me at birth, Reader, I have always believed this to be the biggest.

OVERTURE

From the *Republican Compiler,*
Gettysburg, Pennsylvania, December 13, 1842

RIDING ON AIR

Our readers (says the *New York Express*) may not be generally aware that Railroad Cars are now being constructed to rest on air springs, or in other words, on iron pistons, moving in air-tight cylinders. The effect is wonderful. The cars ride smoothly and comfortably, and one may read or write in them very easily. But this is not all. It has been found a great waste to carry flour in barrels on railroads, in consequence of the jar. This invention is a complete remedy, and flour may now be transported on railways as well as canals.

From the *Brooklyn Daily Eagle,* June 18, 1842

NATURAL CURIOSITY

Can be seen at Shaw's (museum) Hotel, a double pig, having one head, eight legs, four ears, and two bodies.

[illegible]

From the *Republican Compiler*, Gettysburg, Pennsylvania, December 15, 1862

Riding on Air

Our readers (says the *Newark Express*) may not be generally aware that Railroad Cars are now being constructed to rest on air springs, or in other words, on iron pistons, moving in air-tight cylinders. The effect is wonderful. The cars ride smoothly and comfortably, and one may read or write in them very easily. But this is not all. It has been found a great waste to carry liquor in barrels on railroads, in consequence of the jar. This invention is a complete remedy, and liquor may now be transported on railways as well as canals.

From the *Brooklyn Daily Eagle*, June 18, 1849

Natural Curiosity

Can be seen at Shaw's Commercial Hotel, a double pig, having one head, eight legs, four ears, and two bodies.

[ONE]

My Childhood, or the Early Life of a Tiny

I WILL BEGIN MY STORY IN THE CONVENTIONAL WAY, WITH my ancestry.

About the unfortunately named Bumps, I have little to say other than they were hardworking people of French descent who somehow felt that shortening "Bonpasse" to "Bump" was an improvement.

With some pride, however, I can trace my pedigree on my mother's side back through Richard Warren of the Mayflower Company, to William, Earl of Warren, who married Gundreda, daughter of William the Conqueror. This is as far back as I have followed my lineage, but I trust it will suffice. Certainly Mr. Barnum, when he first heard it, was quite astonished, and never failed to mention it to the Press!

I was born on 31 October, 1841, on the family farm in Middleborough, Massachusetts, to James and Huldah Bump. Most people cannot contain their surprise when I tell them that I was, in fact, the usual size and weight. Indeed, when the ceremonial weighing of the newborn was completed, I tipped the scales at precisely six pounds!

My entrance into the family was preceded by three siblings, two male and one female, and was followed by another three, two male and one female. All were of ordinary stature except my younger sister, Minnie, born in 1849.

I am told that I grew normally during the first year of my life, then suddenly stopped. My parents didn't notice it at first, but I cannot fault them for that. Who, when having been already blessed with three children, still has the time or interest to pay much attention to the fourth? My dear mother told me that it wasn't until I was nearly two years old that they realized I was still wearing the same clothes—clothes that should already have been outgrown, cleaned and pressed, and laid in the trunk for the next baby. It was only then that my parents grew somewhat alarmed; studying me carefully, they saw that I was maturing in the way of most children—standing, talking, displaying an increased interest in my surroundings. The only thing I was not doing was *growing*.

They took me to a physician, who appraised me, measured me, poked me. "I cannot offer any physical explanation for this," he informed my worried parents. "The child seems to be perfectly normal, except for her size. Keep an eye on her, and come back in a year's time. But be prepared for the possibility that she might be just one example of God's unexplainable whims, or fancies. She may be the only one I've seen, but I've certainly heard of others like her. In fact, there's one over in Rochester I've been meaning to go see. Heard he can play the violin, even. Astounding."

My parents did not share his enthusiasm for the violin-playing, unexplainable Divine whim. They carried me to another physician in the next town over, who, being a less pious man than the previous expert, explained that I represented "an excellent example of Nature's Occasional Mistakes." He assured my increasingly distressed parents that this was not a bad thing, for it made the world a much more interesting place, just as the occasional two-headed toad and one-eyed kitten did.

In despair, my parents whisked me back home, where they prayed and prayed over my tiny body. Yet no plea to the Almighty would induce me to grow; by my tenth birthday I reached only twenty-four inches and weighed twenty pounds. By this time my parents had welcomed my sister Minnie into the world, when she displayed the same reluctance to grow as I had, they did not take her to any physicians. They simply loved her, as they had always loved me.

"Vinnie," my mother was fond of telling me (Lavinia being the name by which I was called, shortened within the family to Vinnie), "it's not that you're too small, my little chick, but rather that the world is too big."

My poor, tenderhearted mother! She thought that she was reassuring me. She was a lovely, pious creature, tall and thin, a clean, starched apron constantly about her waist. She had shining brown hair that I inherited, slightly worried brown eyes, and an ever-patient smile upon her lips. She only wanted me to be happy, to be safe; she wanted to keep me home, where she was certain less harm could come to me. She was trying, in her simple way, to reconcile me to that future, the only future that she—or anyone else—could envision for one my size.

What she didn't understand was that she was only inciting my curiosity about that big world. *Everything* was bigger than me; if the world was so much larger that she had to constantly warn me of it, what wonders did it contain? What marvels? I could not understand why anyone would not want to see them.

My father never tried to fool me in this way. He was not a demonstrative man, but around me, and then around Minnie, who was even smaller, he was extremely reticent. I believe he was terrified he might crush us with his big, work-worn hands, so he did not touch us at all, not a pat or a hug. He never seemed able to understand why God had made Minnie and me so small, and I believe he was slightly ashamed of us. Whenever we were out together as a family, he always kept his head bent; this way, he did not have to look anyone in the eye. I'm not sure he completely understood why he did this, or what he was afraid to encounter in the gaze of his fellow man; perhaps he simply didn't want to see pity for us there—or for himself.

Yet he loved us. And in the way of most men, he reacted by trying to *solve* us, as if we were the one wagon wheel that stubbornly refused to match up with the others, causing the whole contraption to wobble. This took the form of practicality, which, in the end, was much more useful than Mama's clucking and soothing. My first memory was of my father presenting me with a set of wooden steps, lovingly made by his own hands, which were too clumsy for caresses. They had crafted a beautiful set of steps, however, sanded to a honeyed glow so that not a single splinter might puncture a tender, tiny foot. They were lightweight, a miracle of engineering, so that I could easily carry them with me wherever I went.

Later, after the fire, Mr. Barnum gave me a gorgeous set of steps covered in crushed red velvet with my initials embroidered upon them. But they have never been able to take the place of my father's simple gift.

My brothers and sister swooped and ran and carried on like all children, happily including Minnie and me in their play, not worrying very much about whether or not we could keep up. And we could—or rather, I could. Unlike me, Minnie was content with her small corner of the world; she knew she could not easily keep up with the others, so she didn't even try. She found happiness, instead, in what was easily within her reach; no stair steps for her! She spent hours playing with her dolls, sitting on her little stool by the hearth, sewing handkerchiefs or helping Mama prepare meals. She was very shy around others and felt their stares keenly, even though she was as beautiful as a china figurine. Minnie was blessed with impish dark eyes that were such a contrast to her bashful demeanor, black curls, and a smile that revealed one perfect dimple in her left cheek. Only with me, closest to her in size but still larger, able to protect her, did she ever sometimes show curiosity or boldness; once she surprised me by suggesting we creep outside in the middle of the night, to see if there really were fairies living beneath the flowers.

Amused, I took her outside, where we tiptoed, hand in hand, peeking under the forget-me-nots and ferns. While she lifted leaves and petals with dogged optimism, stifling an occasional squeal whenever she happened upon a frog or a startled rabbit, I found my gaze pulled upward. The moon was low and luminous in the night sky; cocking my head, I was just about to make out the face of the man in the moon when Minnie excitedly exclaimed, "Oh, look, Sister! I found one, with green wings!"

She tugged at my sleeve, and I bent down. "It's just a dragonfly," I told her.

"No, it's a fairy, don't you see?"

"I just see a sleepy dragonfly."

"You're not looking at it right, Vinnie. It's as beautiful as a fairy, all green and shimmery. Can't you see it?"

I looked at my sister, her eyes shining brighter than the moon above. Who would have the heart to contradict her?

Growing up, Minnie listened, much more closely than I, to Mama's worries about our safety. Horses were Mama's chief foes;

she feared, as long as she lived, that Minnie or I would be trampled or kicked by a stray hoof.

On our behalf, she also feared wells, rain barrels, unsteady tables, large dogs, poison left out for the rats (even after I had long passed the age where I could reasonably be expected not to eat it), doors that latched, broken window sashes, snowdrifts, and falling fireplace logs.

I never understood her terrors. Safe, to me, was exactly where I was; low to the ground, where I became more acquainted with the bottoms of things than the tops. For example, I grew very adept at judging a woman's character or station in life by the hem of her skirt. Tiny, too-perfect stitches or ornate ruffles of course denoted a woman of high class, although not necessarily one of good character. Sloppy, loose, or haphazard stitches didn't always mean that a woman was slovenly in appearance; more often than not, it simply meant that she had so many children and cares she could not spare the time to attend to her own clothing. Those whose skirts sported tiny handprints or burnt patches resulting from too much time in front of the kitchen fire were always the most kindhearted.

Skirts were not the only things with which I was acquainted. Naturally I was more familiar with flowers and weeds than the tops of trees; furniture legs and the unfinished undersides of tables than framed pictures or mirrors. And that is why I never was fearful, why I could not understand my mother's worries; the things with which I was most familiar were the sturdier, more substantial things in life. The legs of the table, the widest part of the tree trunk, the foundation of the house, the things upon which everything else was dependent, upon which everything else was built. These were my world.

What my mother feared most—even more than tables toppling over on either Minnie or myself—was other *children*.

While she dutifully brought us to church each Sunday, our Christian education ever in her thoughts, my mother was most reluctant to send me to school with my brothers and sister. Fearing merciless teasing, rough play with children who were not accustomed to one my size, she thought it would be best to educate me at home, herself.

I, however, did not share this belief. I'd heard my siblings talk of the wonders of school, of slates and lunch buckets and schoolyard games and the glories of being asked to stay after to wash the blackboard. They came home taunting me with their knowledge, singing multiplication tables and spelling enormous words and pointing to the odd shapes on the globe in the parlor, proudly telling me the names of the continents and oceans.

So when I heard my mother tell my father she thought it best that I stay home with her and the younger children, I stamped my foot with as much authority as a seven-year-old can muster.

"No, Mama, you must allow me to go to school! Aren't I as smart as my brothers and sister? Why shouldn't I go with them, now that I'm old enough? They will look out for me, if that's what you fear."

Mama started to protest, but to my surprise, my father interrupted her.

"Huldah, I am surprised to admit it, but I agree with our Vinnie. She's a sharp little thing, with an intelligence that must be fueled. You could not give her all she needs here. Let her satisfy her curiosity at school, for a life of books is likely all the life she will ever have. It's best we give her that now. She'll have the rest of her days, I'm afraid, to stay home with you."

I was too young to fully understand my father's meaning. I heard only that he wanted me to go to school, and that was all I needed; I threw my arms about him even though I knew he did not appreciate such demonstrations.

"Oh, Papa, I am so very happy! Thank you! I promise I will never make you regret your decision!"

It would be a pretty story, indeed, if I could say that I never did! Yet I have to admit that I was so eager to be allowed my first foray into that large world that I became rather mischievous.

Full of high spirits, so delighted to be where I was, at first I could not be induced to remain in my seat. At the time, you might recall, country school desks were one long table affixed to the perimeter of the room, three-quarters of the way around.

On a dare, I discovered that I was small enough to fit neatly underneath the desk without having to duck my head; basking in the approval of my schoolmates, I took it a step further. Whenever the schoolteacher's back was to us, I would slide off my perch—several large books piled on top of one another—and duck beneath the desk. Then I would run along, barely stifling my giggles as I pinched and poked at my schoolmates' legs: the little girls' sensible woolen pantalets, the boys' worn and patched knees. I was so nimble that they could not catch me; I could run around the entire room and reach the end of the desk almost before the first child had reacted to my lively tugs with a squeak or a squeal.

"Mercy Lavinia Warren Bump," Mr. Dunbar, our teacher, would sputter. "Sit back down immediately!" He would try to catch me, but being the imp that I was, I could elude his grasp easily; he was inclined to heaviness (from the many tarts and pies that the older female students showered upon him), and would flail about, breathing laboriously. By the time he straightened himself up, his face red, his oily hair hanging down upon his forehead, I would be sitting primly in my seat, seemingly oblivious to my classmates' giggles.

"What am I to do with you?" he asked one day; standing over me, he shook his finger angrily in my face, pushed finally beyond his limit. "Shut you up in my overshoe? It's just about the right size for a mite like you; how would you like me to sit you in it?"

To my astonishment, my schoolmates burst into laughter at this. I looked around, scarcely believing what I saw: My friends, who had so admired me just a moment before, were giggling at the notion of me sitting in the teacher's overshoe. They were *laughing* at me; they were laughing at my *size.*

Only my brother Benjamin—just two years older than I—was not laughing; he was hanging his head, unable to look my way. He was, I realized with a sick, hollow feeling in my stomach, ashamed of me. He was ashamed to be my brother. I had never before experienced such guilt and rejection, both.

This, I suddenly understood, was what Mama had so feared: that were I to venture out from the safety of home, I would not be the only one hurt. This realization hit me hard, knocking the very breath from my being; I hung my throbbing head and bit my trembling lip. Up to this point in my life, I had rarely given my size any thought other than for the many inconveniences it caused me—the constant strain at the back of my neck from looking up, even just to talk to my siblings; the extra effort required to do the simplest of tasks, since I had to haul my steps with me everywhere I went; the fear and worry I knew I caused my dear mother, which hurt me only because it hurt her.

Now, however, my size was no longer merely an inconvenience—it was an embarrassment and a weapon. One Mr. Dunbar had seized upon, first thing, in order to shame me into behaving.

Blinking furiously, staring at my slate—for it was the only object I dared look at—I took some comfort in the realization that my sums were just as neat as anyone else's. They, at least, were not remarkable for any reason other than their accuracy. And so, with a great effort, I managed not to cry, for I did not want my tears to wash away this precious evidence.

That day after school, my brother Benjamin walked ahead of me for the very first time. Even though he waited for me to catch up with him after the rest of the children had fallen away, and picked me up and hoisted me upon his back without my asking, knowing that I was tired, for the first time there was a strangeness between us. He had been my closest sibling up until now, the one who would patiently carry me about, hold me up so that I might see the world the way he did. Now, unexpectedly, I didn't know how to breach this frightening new gap between us and I realized, even at such a tender age, that I never would—and that the gap would only widen with time. It grieved me to think that I had shamed him so; I did not stop to think that he might bear some responsibility for his feelings, as well.

From that day on, I devoted myself to study in the classroom, leaving play for the schoolyard or on the long walk home. I realized that one my size could ill afford to play the imp; I resolved to be dignified, always. And indeed, when I first became known to the Public at Large, this was what people remembered most about me; my gentility and deportment were always remarked upon with no little admiration.

Evidently I also impressed Middleborough's elders with my studious, dignified ways. For when I was sixteen, it was decided to divide the school into a primary and a secondary room; soon after, the school committee showed up at my parents' door, asking to speak with me.

"We would like to offer Miss Lavinia the position of schoolteacher of the primary room," the chairman told my parents once we were all seated in the parlor. Mama was justifiably proud of this pretty room, full of her finest china lamps, snowy lace scarves covering the polished wood surfaces. She always kept it neat and scrubbed and ready for unexpected guests.

My parents' surprise, I must say, could not have been greater. Mama gasped. Tears filled her eyes, and Papa colored and ducked his head the way he always did when he was pleased.

"Oh, how wonderful! How kind, how very kind! Vinnie, what do you think?" Mama turned to me with shining eyes, a wondrous smile illuminating her gentle face.

Seated upon my own rocking chair—one of the few pieces of furniture in the house that was made to my scale; Papa had fashioned it himself—I studied my hands, gracefully folded upon my lap. My heart fluttered with excitement, but I waited until it calmed down before finally looking up and fixing the chairman with a steady gaze.

"I accept, naturally, although I do wish to inquire about my pay. How much remuneration per school term are you offering?"

For some reason this amused everyone; the entire party broke into helpless guffaws, the chairman—a large man whose waist could not be contained by his waistcoat—slapping his fleshy knee with such gusto he very nearly toppled one of Mama's prized lamps. Sitting there, my face burning so hotly I thought my cheeks must be very scarlet indeed, at first I failed to understand their laughter. What was so amusing about wishing to know what I would be earning?

Yet I did understand it. For by now I was well aware that some people found it very odd to hear perfectly sensible, rational notions coming from me. This was because of who I was—or, rather, *what* I was.

And what I was, of course, was both small—and *female*.

As a female, not to mention a female with no other prospects, I was supposed simply to accept their kind offer for what, even then, I suspected was likely an act of charity. Yet a *male* teacher would have been expected to inquire about his wages; if he hadn't, he would have been dismissed as a fool and not engaged.

I endured their laughter with flaming cheeks, allowed it to die, yet repeated my question without hesitation; I saw my father open his mouth to say something but then catch my gaze and hastily shut it.

"Miss Bump, I find it unusual, to say the least, that you would so boldly inquire about wages," the committee chairman said after he finally composed himself. "Naturally, I will speak to your father about what we will pay."

"But my father isn't the one teaching, is he?"

"No, but it is customary, of course—"

"As it is customary to engage a schoolteacher who will not be smaller than her pupils. Yet you have chosen to ignore this custom; let us dispense with the other. My wages?"

Perhaps it was because I remained—with great effort, struggling against my anger at the man's obtuseness—so composed that he finally managed to mutter the agreed-upon sum. I nodded in acceptance, to his obvious relief, and the matter was settled. When the committee rose to leave, I made it my business to quickly approach the chairman to shake hands, instead of leaving him to perform this customary ceremony with my father.

"Miss Bump, I declare, I'm mighty glad that I'm not going to be a pupil in your school. I suspect you won't put up with any mischief at all," he remarked as he bent down toward me, a twinkle in his eye.

"No, I assure you right now that I won't," I answered earnestly, for I would not allow him to make this—or me—into a joke. "There will not be a better run classroom in all of Massachusetts; just you see."

And I have to say, without false modesty, that there was not.

On the first day of class I induced Benjamin to drive me to school early, which he did despite his misgivings over this whole enterprise.

"Vinnie, don't you see they're making fun of you? Making you an experiment? How can you let them?"

"If that is true," I replied as we hit a deep rut in the road, causing me to bounce upon the wagon seat as my feet naturally could not reach the floorboards, "I intend to turn the tables upon them. Then we'll see who gets the last laugh."

"I don't understand you, Vinnie. It'd be so much easier for you not to be out as much in public."

"Easier for whom? For I can think of no fate drearier than sitting at home by the hearth for the rest of my life, watching all of you go off one by one."

Benjamin didn't reply, but once we arrived at the schoolhouse, he worked diligently to help me make sure the room was ready. He and I (aided by my indispensable stair steps) soon had the blackboards shining, the chairs smartly lined up, the *McGuffey's Readers* laid out upon the desks. Mama had made me a special cushion for my desk chair, so that I could keep a watchful eye upon my pupils.

I asked Benjamin then to go ring the school bell so that when the first of my students arrived, I was standing calmly in the middle of the room. I did not attempt to hide my size by staying behind my desk or perching upon any kind of platform. I simply stood there, as dignified, as tall, as I could possibly make myself appear.

Mama had made me a new dress, the skirt long and full so that it finally reached the ground, hiding my child's shoes, which were an unfortunate necessity. But I was wearing my first corset; Mama had ordered the smallest one that was carried at the general store, and altered it as best she could. She cut it down, removed several stays, stitched it all back up again, but still it gapped in odd places. Yet I *felt* somehow more correct, more upright, even so. My chestnut hair was secure in a simple, becoming twist; my head felt heavy on top, while my neck felt bare. It was the first time I had not worn my hair in long braids down my back.

Thus, appropriately attired and groomed, I absorbed the unbelieving stares, the nudges and whispers, as the children filed into the room. Many of the pupils, naturally, knew who I was; some did not. Yet even those who knew me seemed taken aback to see the teacher's pointer in my hand.

My heart beat fast, despite my best effort to calm my breathing. I was not afraid, exactly; it was more as if I was standing upon the edge of a table, ready to jump—believing, somehow, that I would fly instead of fall. I felt as if this was the first important moment of my life.

After the singing of the morning hymn, I addressed my young charges in a firm, clear voice; I had practiced my speech the night before.

(Little did I know this would be the first of many, many performances to come!)

"My dear children, I can see you have a number of questions. Let me begin by introducing myself as your teacher, Miss Bump. Some of you I know already; the rest I am eager to get to know. The school committee selected me to run the primary school based on my excellent academic record; only a year ago I was a pupil, just like all of you!"

I smiled at the unbelieving gasps and whispers.

"I say this only to remind you of what is possible if hard work and diligence are applied to your schoolwork. Now, there is the matter of my size."

More gasps, some giggles; holding myself perfectly still, I waited for them to fade away.

"Yes, my size. As you can well see for yourselves, I am of less-than-average height. In fact, I daresay the smallest of you is larger than me. Shall we see? Who is the smallest in the class?" I smiled at the astonished look of merriment that soon appeared on every young face; I knew, then, that this was the best way to approach the subject. The resolve that had first formed in my mind all those years ago, when Mr. Dunbar threatened to shut me up in his overshoe, now fully took shape: Never would I allow my size to define me. Instead, I would define *it*. My size may have been the first thing people noticed about me but never, I vowed at that moment, would it be the last.

I would repeat this vow so many times in the years to come. I repeat it even to this day. And to this day, I still don't know if I was successful in keeping it.

One small lad was selected by his classmates to stand next to me—Jimmy Morgan, I believe his name was, although my memory cannot be trusted—and he shyly approached, tugging nervously at his red suspenders.

"Come, come, don't dawdle; there's nothing to fear," I said briskly, holding my hand out to him. "See here, my head only comes up to your chin, doesn't it?" I tilted my face up to emphasize the disparity; Jimmy's blue eyes stared down at me, wide and astonished.

He nodded, his cheeks scarlet, as his classmates roared with delight. I motioned for Jimmy to go back to his seat; then I waited for the laughter to fade away.

"Now, you've had your fun, as I've had mine. We will forget about it from this moment forward; I am not your friend, not your doll, not your playmate. I am your teacher and will expect every consideration, every show of respect, that my position demands. You will see that my size has nothing to do with my mind or even my will; I am not afraid to use the whip or the ruler if the situation arises. Now open your readers to the first page, and let us begin."

Without a murmur, every child obeyed my command. And for the rest of the term, I had no trouble at all managing my classroom. The school committee chairman was most impressed, and soon became fond of bringing in other school committees, from neighboring townships, to observe my orderly pupils, their respectful harmony. If this was his idea of sport, I did not give him any satisfaction; I found myself growing more dignified by the minute when under the gaze of astonished onlookers, as if to make up in deportment what I so lacked in height.

Yet to my surprise—for I was still very sensitive, in those days, to remarks about my size—I enjoyed being watched; I basked in the attention, not minding what had prompted it so much as I minded that those who watched left admiring me. And I began to look forward to those days when I had an audience, planning special games and songs for my pupils. The rest of the time seemed dull and ordinary by comparison.

I do admit to having fun with my charges, though; I was still young, of course, and my high spirits could not be contained by my ill-fitting corset. While I refrained from joining them during recess, I did not always walk sedately home at the end of the day. On more than one occasion, stiff from sitting so long at my desk, I joined in footraces and sometimes allowed the biggest children to carry me on their shoulders, which was a privilege much sought after. And when the first snow fell, I was very touched when a contingent of boys appeared at my door with a sled; after I was tucked in with a bearskin, they pulled me merrily to school, sleigh bells jingling around their necks.

At the end of the fall term, when I handed out marks with the knowledge that not one of my pupils had failed, I felt the satisfaction of a job well done. I was seventeen now, an established schoolmarm. My future seemed secure, and it was a future with which my mother, at least, was very content—a decent wage that I could put away for the time when my parents were no longer able to provide for me; useful work to occupy my days and tire me so that my nights were not sleepless with longing; respect within our little community so that I was no longer an oddity but a beloved, vital member, protected and cared for.

Yet there was still a sadness that clung to my mother, despite all this. It was unspoken, but no one ever expected me to marry. No hope chest was begun for me as had been done for my older sister at the same age, no bridal lace set aside.

One day I rounded a corner only to hear my mother whispering to my sister Delia; stifling a giggle, I quickly hid inside a cupboard, rejoicing over the advantage my size gave me in eavesdropping. They were talking about the birds and the bees; I listened eagerly, until I was startled to hear my own name.

"Could Vinnie ever—" Dee began in a strangled voice.

"Oh, it would be dreadful, impossible," Mama replied, muffling a sob. "Don't you remember the little cow on Uncle's farm who . . ." And her voice trailed off.

I did not remember any little cow, but its fate was evident in my sister's sudden horrified exclamation. *That* I never forgot; it made my blood run cold, my heart seize in a nameless fear. I lived on a farm, after all; I knew cows—and horses and goats and sheep. I knew *life*—and how wrenching its beginning could be, even among creatures built far more sturdily than I. Shaking, I stole away from my hiding place wishing I had not been so clever. And for the first time, I looked at myself as Papa did; I felt that there might be something broken within me, after all.

That night I could hear my tenderhearted mother weeping for me, even through the thick plaster walls of the second-floor bedrooms. It was not the first night she had done so.

Did I share in her sorrow? In many ways, I was still too young to be given over to such dire, unhappy thoughts. No one would ever have predicted I would be a schoolteacher, and yet—wasn't that what I had become?

I did have a longing inside me, however, that I could not entirely ignore. I loved my family, loved the farm, loved my work. But contemplating a future only within these confines made me increasingly restless. There was something missing; I could define it only by its absence, but I yearned for it those nights when I heard my mother crying over my lonely, loveless fate.

It was around this time that I went for a walk in the near cow pasture; it was early spring but warm for the season, the weeds already high. They made my progress more difficult, but I didn't mind; pushing through them, I imagined myself in a mysterious forest, like the ones in so many of the fairy tales I read to my young pupils.

Soon, however, I came upon a familiar tree: a tall maple tree with an unusually wide trunk. Upon this trunk, my brothers and sister and I had once scratched our names and ages, according to our height. Craning my neck upward, I could make out *Benjamin, George, Sylvanus,* then *James,* and finally *Delia,* their names plainly visible, high up the tree—

But where was I? Where was my name? I remembered standing against the tree one summer while James took out a pocketknife and carved a line right above my head; he had then scratched my name to the side of it—I could still see his tongue sticking out with the effort as he complained that our names were so devilishly long. . . .

Brushing aside the weeds, I finally located my name; it had been covered up by the tall grasses and the climbing, glossy green tendrils of creeping myrtle, its starlike blue flowers not yet in bloom. I was only an inch or so taller than that line, even though

I was years older. My brothers and sister, however—grown up now, as well—were all much taller than their childish measurements.

I had the queerest feeling; it was as if a shadow had fallen over just me, while the rest of the world remained illuminated by bright sunlight. At that moment I felt hidden from all eyes; looking at my name, covered over by weeds, I saw how easily it could disappear forever. I saw how easily *I* could be forgotten, compared to my brothers and sister, compared to everyone else, everyone who was taller, more noticeable, more visible to the rest of the world.

I did not want to be forgotten. More than that, I wanted, desperately—I fell to my knees and began to tear out the weeds, the vines, by their very roots—to be *remembered.* I wanted my name to be known, beyond this tree, this hill, this pasture, this town.

The weeds were in a pile at the base of the tree; my hands were stained green, my nostrils filled with the pungent, mossy scent of new grass, and my skirt was damp where I had kneeled on it. But my name was now plainly visible; I smiled in satisfaction, brushed my hands off on my skirt, and continued my walk. My fierce desire soon faded away into the twilight; the air grew chilly, and I saw the warm, beckoning lights of home twinkle on, one by one, as Mama began to light the lamps, which shone, at that moment, more brightly than the faint stars on the horizon.

And then I heard Minnie calling, in her surprisingly strong, clear voice, "Vinnie! Where are you? I want to show you the most beautiful four-leaf clover I found!"

I smiled, for I knew she would be standing in the doorway looking for me, clutching that clover in her tiny fist until I came back, no matter how long I might take. So I was content to turn around and return home, content with what I knew was waiting for me there.

So it was that when we broke for vacation that spring of 1858—remember that at the time, country schools were open only during winter and summer, as the children were expected to help with farmwork—I truly had no plans other than to enjoy my time off, sleep in later than usual, and make some new dresses for the upcoming term.

An unexpected knock on our door one afternoon soon revealed that God—not to mention P. T. Barnum—had other plans for me, instead.

INTERMISSION

From *The New York Times,* January 25, 1853

Of domestic news, we have fewer shipwrecks, murders, defalcations and deaths to record than usual.

From *The New York Times,* March 2, 1853

The construction of a Magnetic Telegraph line to the Pacific Ocean is only second in importance to the project of a railroad across the continent to its western shore. The subject is before Congress; and even at this eleventh hour, a united, determined effort of its friends, and a few minutes of the time now so valuable, will be sufficient to secure the immediate initiative and early consummation of the work.

[TWO]

Leaving Home, or an Interlude of Heart-Tugging Music and Recitation

I'VE GOT YOU IN HERE WITH MISS HARDY. SHE'S A TROUPER; she'll show you the ropes," Colonel Wood said as he led me through a narrow, damp passageway. On either side were closed doors to various staterooms. Beneath us was the great engine of the boat, silent for now, as we were still docked. The green carpet in the passageway was dirty and smelled of mildew; the paint on the walls was chipped and dotted with mold. I was perspiring so in the humid, dank air that I could well imagine mold beginning to grow on *me;* my skin felt plastered to my underclothes and uncomfortable corset that still did not fit properly.

"Oh."

"She's simple enough, so don't let her appearance scare you any."

"Oh."

"Now, I know I promised your folks I'd see to you myself, but

I run a mighty big outfit here; I'm a very important man, you'll soon see. So don't come runnin' to me with every little thing. You'll have to stand on your own two feet, as tiny as they are." The Colonel chortled at this.

"Oh."

This one word was all that I had uttered for days; weeks, even, it seemed to me. Ever since I bade my family a tearful farewell just as the fields were ready for plowing. It was late April now, and here in Cincinnati the air was already as balmy as summer, and the wide, muddy Ohio River did not look as if it could ever freeze completely over.

"Here you go shove on in now, your trunk'll get delivered later." Without even knocking, Colonel Wood opened the door to a stateroom; he held it open for me in one of the few gentlemanly gestures I had observed from him during our brief acquaintance. I arranged my face into a pleasant, welcoming smile, then stepped with assurance across the threshold to meet my new traveling companion, my hand already thrust out in greeting.

"Hello, my name is Miss Lavini—Oh!" I couldn't help myself; I stopped dead in my tracks, all sensible notions drained from my being. My hands, my knees, began to quake, and I would have turned around and run back outside, had Colonel Wood not been immediately behind me, barring any escape.

For slowly rising from a bed—no, two beds, pushed together end to end—was a giantess. An actual giantess, such as I had read about in many a fairy tale, the kind of creature that ate little children who got into mischief or otherwise misbehaved.

The giantess continued to unwind herself, rising slowly—oh, so slowly!—until she had reached her full height, which seemed, from my perspective, to be twenty feet, at the very least! She had to stoop so that her head did not brush the sloping stateroom ceiling.

"Hello, Miss Lavini-o," she said in a basso profundo voice. With a smile, she extended her hand; a hand so massive, so bony, that I fought with every fiber of my being not to recoil from it. As it came near me—again, so excruciatingly slowly—I glanced quickly at the giantess's feet; they were the size of canoes, and I could easily imagine them squishing me into oblivion. I remembered Mama's silly terrors about horses' hooves; how quaint a fear that seemed now!

"M-m-my name is Lavini*a,*" I corrected the giantess as I placed my hand, my tiny, delicate hand, in her enormous one. I winced in anticipation, but to my relief she did not crush me. In fact, she seemed to be as hesitant to touch me as I was to touch her; her hand did not even close completely about mine, and she withdrew it with as much haste as she could muster.

I must confess, right here and now, to making a dreadful assumption. And that assumption was that a person this tall, who moved this slowly, must be very slow of mind and wit as well. All my life, I must admit, I have always associated quickness of mind with smaller people, quicker people, people like me. Large, clumsy creatures, freaks of nature to me—my initial assumption was always that they possessed inferior minds.

So I corrected the giantess, thinking she was not very bright, forgetting that I myself had mispronounced my own name in my initial consternation.

"And my name is Sylvia. Miss Sylvia Hardy, from Maine."

"For the love of Pete, just look at the two of you!"

I spun around, startled to find Colonel Wood still standing behind me; I had forgotten all about him. He stood gaping at the tableau before him, his head swiveling up and down as he took the pair of us in; there was an eager gleam in his eye as he appraised the situation.

"Oh, this is going to be rich! The two of you side by side—

by God, I'm a genius! Barnum who, I ask you? Eh? Colonel John Wood will be the name on everybody's lips, I wager!"

I was too speechless to respond. The giantess, however, was not; she dismissed him with a firmness I could not help but admire as she said, "Goodbye, Colonel Wood. Leave us to get better acquainted, for I imagine Lavinia is tired from her journey."

And despite the rumbling low pitch of her voice—it tickled my eardrums—and the slowness of her speech, I turned to her with gratitude, blinking back sudden tears. I *was* weary; the journey *was* exhausting. The excitement of my very first train trip had long since abandoned me. The exhilarating sense of discovery I had felt as I stared out soot-covered windows while unfamiliar scenery passed so swiftly by; the novelty of eating sandwiches wrapped in paper, bought from enterprising farm boys at various stops; the thrill of rattling over high bridges while far below, unfamiliar rivers ran—all was gone now.

I remembered only the dirt, the barnyard odors of being in such close company with strangers who did not wash regularly, the stiffness of my back from sitting up for so long even in sleep, the impossibility of making myself feel fresh with the dirty water in the lavatory basin. That is, even if I could *reach* the basin; I couldn't, unless I dragged my stair steps with me, but there usually wasn't enough room in those miserable little closets. And often there were no closets at all, just primitive dark corners with buckets full of human waste slopping out with every rattle over a railroad tie.

We changed trains so many times I lost count, always a chaotic affair. I had to submit to countless strangers lifting me up and down, for there was no way to manage the great difference between train and platform myself, and Colonel Wood was always gone somewhere, wrestling with our luggage or arguing with the ticket agent that I should cost him only half a fare because I took up only half a seat.

These dispiriting experiences were all I remembered now; they had left my clothes filthy and stained, my skin covered in a gritty film of dirt, my toes pinched and blistered. My first pair of adult shoes, custom-ordered to fit, had proven to be very uncomfortable for feet used to the soft soles of children's slippers.

I also remembered, suddenly and overwhelmingly, how sad my parents and Minnie had looked when they said goodbye. I had waved at them for as long as I could as I drove away with Colonel Wood in his wagon, all my clothes and mementos and my beloved stair steps packed in a trunk borrowed from my married sister, Delia, as there had been no time to purchase one of my own. I remembered Mama's tears, Minnie's wails, Papa's stoic face, his emotion betrayed only by the working of his Adam's apple.

The memories overwhelmed me, and I could not help it; as soon as the Colonel shut the door and I was left alone with the giantess, my tears could no longer be contained. I sat down on the floor, not caring about my dress, and I put my head in my hands and began to cry. Why, oh why, had I ever decided to leave home? My heart—too large for me all of a sudden, too full of pain and longing for family—felt as if it would break into pieces, so lost, so lonely, so dirty, and yes, so very *small,* did I feel.

Mama had been right all along. The world was too big for me. I would get lost in it, swallowed up or trampled by this giantess—

Who, without a word, without a sound, scooped me up in her arms and carried me to her bed. There she held me on her lap, rocking me as if I were a child, as I turned my head toward her vast, comforting bosom and sobbed my heart out.

A MONTH EARLIER, COLONEL JOHN WOOD HAD SHOWED UP AT our door. It was in March of 1858, during my first vacation from teaching. With a knock, a bow, a presentation of a card, he was ushered inside, where he brought with him the bracing air of a different world. He was dressed not in military clothing, as one might expect (I never did understand how he came by his title), but his costume was no less exciting. He wore a jacket made of red wool; I'd never seen such a thing on a man before! All the men in my life wore sober black, gray, or brown. Complementing his red jacket was an emerald-green vest, which was hung with a bright gold watch fob. His black hat, over graying curls, was shiny and tall, and he carried a polished ebony walking stick. He had a habit, I soon discovered, of pressing two fingers against his mustache—suspiciously black, considering how gray his curls were—whenever he desired to appear thoughtful.

In short, he looked to be quite a man of the world to us Bumps, so insulated in our rural community. I would come to know many men of the world and recognize that the Colonel was not quite the dandy he thought himself to be, but at the time he certainly impressed Mama and me; Papa, however, merely sat and regarded him with a skeptical eye, puffing on his pipe distrustfully.

"Sit down, sit down, and let us figure out our relation," Mama exclaimed as she ushered Colonel Wood into our parlor; he had introduced himself as a cousin, which was all the calling card one needed in Middleborough, Massachusetts.

"Don't mind if I do," Colonel Wood replied, taking the best chair before he was asked. While he addressed Mama, I felt his curious gaze still upon me, as it had been since his arrival. Minnie was off hiding in her room—she always vanished whenever we had visitors—and my three brothers who were still at home, while politely greeted, were given no further notice by our visitor. Colonel Wood seemed fascinated solely with me. His attention was different than what I usually encountered from the few strangers who happened through Middleborough; he did not look as if he was about to ask me if fairies had forgotten to give me my wings (one of the many fanciful sentiments that strangers were inspired to utter when first making my acquaintance).

Instead, I felt his gaze to be more calculated, more appraising, but for what purpose I could not begin to guess.

As Mama and he attempted to sort out their relation—I never did figure it out and later wondered if there really was such a connection—he still managed to throw glances my way, as if he was sizing me up. Whenever I ventured to speak, he listened carefully, and I could sense first his approval and then his excitement as I displayed my usual intelligence in my typical forthright way.

Finally, he admitted he had come here with a specific purpose in mind.

"Have you all ever heard of a fellow named Barnum?"

"Well, yes, Cousin, of course we read the newspaper. Do you think we're so ill informed, just because we're farmers?" Mama answered softly, chidingly; despite our humble abode and plain living, she was very conscious of her heritage as a descendent of one of the Mayflower Compact signers.

"Of course not, of course not," Colonel Wood replied hastily. "Forgive me, I've been so long in the West that I sometimes forget how civilized we are here in New England."

"What does that Barnum have to do with us?" my brother Benjamin asked, regarding Colonel Wood with barely concealed hostility.

"Well, he's had a great deal of success, you know. First with that Tom Thumb fellow, the one that visited England and had tea with the Queen and all. Then with Miss Jenny Lind, the Swedish Nightingale."

At the mention of Tom Thumb, Mama and Papa exchanged glances, careful not to look my way.

"Can't say as I approve of that man," Papa grumbled. "It seems wrong, somehow."

"Wrong? Why, both Jenny Lind and the little man are famous! Millionaires, they say! Living it up, meeting royalty—what's wrong with that? Sounds like a mighty fine life to me!" Colonel Wood was unable to keep up his careful nonchalance; he was now leaning forward, his dark eyes snapping.

"I'd wager it's that Barnum who's getting rich," Papa retorted. "Showing people about like they're *things*, not humans. Humbugging the public, like he did with that Joice Heth, claiming she was a hundred and sixty-one years old! George Washington's nurse, he said she was! George Washington's nurse, my eye. Anyone could tell she was just some old slave woman."

"Oh, but Papa—Miss Jenny Lind is not a thing! She's an artist! And what was the humbug there?" I couldn't help myself; I did not like to contradict my father, but on the subject of Jenny Lind, I could not keep quiet.

I was just a child when Jenny Lind came to America, back in 1850. I never heard her sing; she never came anywhere near Middleborough. But I followed her every move in the newspaper, drinking in every detail of the Swedish Nightingale—what she wore, how she did her hair, what her favorite foods were. And, of course, how she sang: like an angel, the newspapers said. With a voice of such incomparable beauty it made grown men weep, particularly when she ended her concerts with her signature song, "Home Sweet Home." There were Jenny Lind waltzes performed in her honor, Jenny Lind polkas, ballads, clothes, dolls, figurines. I had a china likeness of her that Papa and Mama had given me on my tenth birthday; I kept it on the windowsill in my bedroom.

Mr. P. T. Barnum, the famous promoter, brought her here from Europe; he arranged her concerts and made her a household name, although they parted ways in 1852 and she had since returned to Europe. He told of all this in his recent autobiography, which had caused an uproar, for in it he admitted to several humbugs he had perpetrated upon the public, including the one involving Joice Heth, as well as the one involving General Tom Thumb. Born Charles S. Stratton, the latter had been a lad of only five when Mr. Barnum had first presented him, back in 1843, as "General Tom Thumb, a marvel of miniature perfection, eleven years of age!"

Since then, the tiny general had traveled to Europe and met with Queen Victoria herself. I admit to my curiosity being aroused by the few newspaper illustrations I had seen of him, now a young man, three years my senior. So far in my life, the only other little person I knew was my sister Minnie. The evidence that there were others incited my curiosity and made me feel slightly less alone. Knowing that General Tom Thumb had sung and danced for huge crowds and become celebrated the world over gave me a peculiar sense of pride, I must confess. Also, he was a handsome fellow in the illustrations; boasting large, mischievous eyes and a winning smile, he looked very smart in his various miniature uniforms.

He was no Miss Jenny Lind, of course, but reading about either of them was like reading about royalty, or Presidents; their lives were special, remarkable, not at all like my own or my family's.

"Oh, Papa, you know how I longed to hear Jenny Lind sing! She's the reason I practice so very much on my own music," I reminded my father, who looked at me with a suddenly clenched jaw and narrowing eyes, as if he was trying silently to warn me not to speak further. But I did not heed his warning. "Do you know Mr. Barnum?" I asked Colonel Wood, unable to contain my excitement.

"Why, sure, sure," he answered smoothly, addressing me for the first time. "Naturally! We showmen all know each other."

"Really?" I couldn't help but be impressed. "Did you ever see Miss Jenny Lind?"

"Certainly! Many a time did she sing for me privately, when I was in New York working for Mr. Barnum himself. I take it you sing, Miss Lavinia?"

"Oh, I'm a schoolteacher, but I do love to sing." I returned Mama's fond smile; my songs were much loved not only within the family circle but also in the schoolroom. From an early age, I had enjoyed soothing my classmates with ballads. Mr. Dunbar used to pick me up and place me atop his desk, so that all could hear.

"A schoolteacher?" Colonel Wood seemed momentarily stunned; his face, which had been as smooth as his talk, suddenly creased in thought. "Hmmm. I didn't know that. I thought that you were just—well, just . . . at home. But I guess it don't really matter, at that."

"What doesn't matter?" Mama asked anxiously. Papa remained silent, but I could feel his whole body tense, even though I wasn't seated near him. He appeared as if he was steeling himself for bad news.

"My boat. My floating palace of entertainment. We sail up and down the rivers out west, bringing amusement to the poor, hard-working folks who have no other kind. I have minstrels, jugglers, dancers, and some curiosities—a man who can swallow nails, a tattooed man, a giantess. But what I don't have is a—I mean, as soon as I heard of Miss Lavinia here—and, of course, our cousinly connection—and now that I know she's a true artist, as well—I thought she might be interested in joining me. Singing, of course—just like a certain Miss Jenny Lind? A certain General Tom Thumb?" Colonel Wood winked at me.

You could have heard the proverbial pin drop in that parlor: Nobody moved; everyone looked stunned. Mama could not shut her mouth; had I not been as astonished as she, I would have teased her about catching flies. My three brothers likewise did not say a word. Papa's face turned a dangerous red.

My own heart beat fast. No, no, I couldn't possibly do what the Colonel suggested. An entertainer? On the stage—like Miss Jenny Lind? It was shocking, it was unheard of, it was—

Enticing.

Never before had I imagined leaving home, but that wasn't because of lack of desire, only lack of possibility. All those nights of yearning, of hearing my mother weep for my lonely fate! For a woman in a small town in Massachusetts, naturally, marriage was the only possible way out of anything. It was the only possible way *to* anything, as well; it was the only possibility, period. And I would never marry any of the men here in Middleborough; how could I? The idea seemed grotesque to me, for reasons I could not quite explain. I remembered my mother's and sister's horror that day I had eavesdropped, the lack of a hope chest, the relief my parents had felt when I had been offered the primary classes. This was my fate—to be a spinster schoolteacher. I knew I was supposed to be grateful for it.

Suddenly, however, another possibility had just been revealed; a way out presented itself to me. I could *leave;* I could see the world, that great big world Mama had unknowingly tempted me with for so long. I could see the Mississippi, that Queen of Rivers! I might even see bad men and women, and I admit to an unladylike thrill as I contemplated this, for there were no bad men and women in Middleborough, except for the peddler who sometimes stole chicken eggs. My yearning, seeking heart began to swell; it was as if a hidden dam of pent-up frustration had burst inside it, flooding me with desire and action. Oh, what else might I find, that I had not even known had been missing? What else might I see, that I had never before suspected was hidden from me?

I looked around at my family; they were beginning to regain

their senses. Not one of them glanced my way; they seemed acutely embarrassed by me at that moment. Embarrassed that I had brought such a man into their home and submitted them to such dreadful talk, talk that was not fit for descendents of one of the Mayflower signers. Benjamin was already shaking his head, ready to answer for me.

"I want to do it!" The words flew out of my mouth before I had even decided on them.

"You most certainly do not!" my father thundered, rising in anger, his face so dark the veins on his forehead pulsed. He had never before spoken one harsh word to me; now, he seemed perilously close to an apoplectic attack.

"Pa's right," Benjamin cried. "If Vinnie goes with this man, I'll leave this house forever! I won't be able to bear the shame!"

"What shame?" Colonel Wood asked the company at large, his demeanor suddenly calm in the face of our collected agitation. "What shame is there in bringing joy to people? Becoming rich and famous?"

"The shame of the theater! Of being around actors and dancers and who knows what else! The shame of being displayed before the public like a—it's bad enough with the school, you know, the way people talk, but if she goes out like that, like that Tom Thumb *freak* who—" Benjamin suddenly realized what he had said and sat back down, rumpling his hair until it stood on end. "Sorry, Vinnie! I didn't mean that, not really. But if you parade yourself about on the stage—I just don't see how you can even think about it, the way you are. That's all."

My face was burning, my breast heaving at being the center of such an uproar. I'd never seen my family in such a state; Mama was rocking back and forth in her chair, her arms crossed tight against her chest, making keening sounds as if someone had just died.

"It's my life, it's my future—you needn't be embarrassed by it any longer, Benjamin! You all may be content to stay here on the farm, that's all well and good because you're just like everyone else, but I'm *not*! I'm different, and you all know it, so why not allow me to consider a different fate? And I'm *not* content—I don't think I ever have been!"

"What do you mean?" Mama had stopped rocking; she was staring at me, her gentle brown eyes full of tears and pain. "What do you mean you never have been? Why, Vinnie, my little chick—aren't you happy with us? Don't we take good care of you?"

"Oh, Mama, I didn't mean that, but—we can't continue this way forever! Someday you'll—someday you and Papa won't be able to look out for me. And what will happen then? What will happen to Minnie and me, stuck here on the farm?"

"You'll always have a home with one of us, Vinnie," my brother James, who had been quiet until now, said. "We'll always take care of you, you know that. We don't mind."

"But that's just it!" I leaped off my chair, carried away by my passion. Colonel Wood discreetly rose and left the room; the front door creaked open, and he took a seat on the porch. He had the decency to understand this was a family matter. "That's just it, don't you see? I don't want to be taken care of! I don't want to be hidden away, a burden! I want to make my own way! To have a greater purpose!"

"But you do, you have your school," Benjamin pointed out. Of all of them, even Papa, he was the most distressed, and I was reminded of that day when I was seven, and the teacher had threatened to shut me up in his overshoe. How ashamed Benjamin had been of me then; I knew, now, that he had never really gotten over it.

"That's not what I mean," I said; I ran to him, clasped his big, rough hands in mine, and tried to get him to meet my gaze, but he would not. "Even with the school, I'll always be one of the little Bump girls, the spinster teacher who lives at home, who can expect nothing more than to be invited to the occasional Sunday dinner by those who pity her. If I stay here, don't you see—there's no escaping that fate. But if I leave—why, just think! I'll see things we can only imagine here! I'll experience not just books but life! I'll be *remembered*."

"Why, whatever do you mean, Vinnie?" Mama exclaimed, her face so open and honest and agonized; I hated the pain I was causing her—but hadn't I always caused her distress, just by *being*? She had always worried and agonized over me. "What do you mean you'll be remembered? How could we ever forget you?"

I shook my head. "I mean something *more,* Mama. I can't explain it, but I've felt, for a while now, that if I stay here, I'll just be forgotten somehow. Or worse—never even known in the first place. If I go with Colonel Wood, I'll meet so many people. Why, maybe I'll even meet Miss Jenny Lind! And General Tom Thumb! Wouldn't that be nice, meeting someone like me? Someone else, that is." For I could not forget Minnie, even in my excitement.

And during the lengthy emotional discussion that ensued, my father and my brothers trying desperately to change my mind, which grew more determined with every plea, while my mother wept piteously, I did not forget my sister. Minnie's face was before me always, even as I argued passionately to be allowed to go with Colonel Wood, who remained outside, calmly puffing away on his pipe.

Finally, Papa held his hand up, silencing us all; with a resigned shake of his head, he said, "I've never known what to do with you, Vinnie. I've never understood why God made you the way He did. I can't pretend to know what to do with you now. I'm just a simple man, but you're anything but. So if you're truly set on doing this, I don't see as how I can stop you. For all I know, it might be the very best thing for you. Just don't bring shame to us, daughter. You have the best head on your shoulders of us all—use it."

Benjamin stormed out of the room. Mama burst into a renewed torrent of tears as she ran after him. But all I wanted to do was hurry upstairs and find Minnie.

She was in the room that we shared; sitting on the low bed, made for us by Papa, she cradled her favorite doll in her lap, looking very much like a doll herself. She was so delicate, so winsome; she came up only to my shoulder. Her big dark eyes grew even bigger when she saw me; with a breathless little gasp she asked, "Is that dreadful man gone, Vinnie?"

"No, he's not." I sat down upon the bed next to her; the two of us together hardly made a dent in the feather tick.

"I wish he would go. I don't like him."

"You don't even know him."

"I don't care. I don't like him."

"You don't like anyone." I had to smile, remembering the other day when she had declared the man who bought Mama's eggs and butter "Simply dreadful!"

"No, I don't like anyone but you. And Mama and Papa. And James and Benjamin and everyone." Minnie looked up at me—she was the only person in my life who looked up at me—and smiled, that one dimple showing. She was so trusting, my sister. She smiled innocently at me as if she expected me to tell her a pretty story, a wonderful surprise. She always looked at me like that; my heart, which had been so light at the prospect of my adventure, began to flutter and flail about in my breast, and I had to turn away.

Even though she was now nine, Minnie was still as timid as she had always been; she had not followed the path I had tried to blaze for her. She had no eagerness to go to school; she trembled and clutched at Mama's skirts the first time I broached the subject, even after I assured her that I would be her teacher. So she remained at home, and I had to admit that Mama's limited education was more than enough to school our Minnie. She did not have the curiosity of mind and spirit that I possessed.

School was the only place she would not follow me, however; even when I performed my chores around the farm, she clung to me, holding my skirt or my hand. I reached under the chickens for the eggs; she carried the eggs in a basket. I snipped the lavender from Mama's garden; she tied it up in fragrant little bundles.

Nearly eight years separated us, so that at times it almost felt as if she was my child, not my little sister, so trusting, so dependent she was upon me. When I left the farm in the morning to go to school, she took her seat on a little stool by the kitchen hearth; when I returned in the evening, she was always where I had left her. I had the oddest sensation that her very breath was suspended until I came home.

And at night we slept in the same bed, her little arms encircled about my waist, her head resting upon my shoulder. "Rock me, Sister," she always implored, her curls already tangled around her neck, her eyes already drooping. I would rock her gently, singing some sweet song, often one I made up; before I could finish, Minnie would be fast asleep, a contented smile on her pretty face.

Now, as I began to wonder how she would sleep once I was gone, I realized my heart was not strong enough to withstand such questioning, and so I made myself think of something else.

"Guess what?" I asked my sister.

"What?"

"I'm going to ride on a train!"

"A train? How dreadful! Aren't you scared? I'd be scared, even if you were with me, Vinnie!" Minnie's eyes shone anxiously, reflecting stars that were not there.

"No, I'm not a bit scared. And anyway, Colonel Wood will be with me."

"He will? But why? He's so dreadful! Where will you go—to town? And you'll be home by dinner?"

"No, not to town." I stifled a smile; in Minnie's experience, there was nowhere else to go but to town. That big world that beckoned so brightly to me did not even exist for my sister.

"Then where?"

"To a boat, an enormous boat. On a very famous river. I'm going to take a holiday of sorts, and see some sights, and I promise I'll write to you every day and tell you all about them!" I tried to make it sound like a lark, but my voice did catch in my throat.

"You mean, away? From here—from home?"

"Yes."

"But you'll be back by dinner?" She frowned, struggling to understand; one of her curls escaped its pins and hung down upon her forehead in a perfect question mark, as if to underscore her confusion. In Minnie's entire life, never had I not been home by dinner.

"No, Pumpkin, not by dinner. I will be gone for a long time—I don't exactly know how long, but many months. It's a difficult journey, and I won't be able to come home very often."

"I don't understand, Vinnie! Why do you want to go away?" Tears filled her eyes as she flung her arms about me. The bodice of my dress was soon wet with my sister's tears, and I had a moment of regret and panic; what on earth was I doing? How could I leave her? How selfish was I?

But then I looked around our room, with its gentle, sloping ceiling, and I realized that *everything* here was gentle, everything here was peaceful and safe and designed to protect me and Minnie from—what, exactly? From life; that's what I believed at that moment. My family wanted to protect me from *life*. But it was life that I wanted to experience: a rich, full life, one I could call my own. And there was no possibility I would ever find it on the farm or in Middleborough, with its handful of streets, two general stores, and the occasional wayward peddler.

Maybe the world was too big for me; I expected that I would soon find out. But I also knew with certainty that if I remained in Middleborough, I would grow even smaller than I already was . . . until one day, like my name overgrown with weeds, I would cease to exist altogether.

"Minnie, darling, shhh. Look," I whispered to my little sister, still sobbing on my breast. With a gentle nudge, I pushed her away so that I could cross the room to retrieve something from the windowsill—my beloved figurine of Jenny Lind in a pink dress, with her hands crossed upon her breast, her mouth open in glorious song. I returned to the bed and presented the precious object to Minnie, who had often admired it.

"Here. You keep this for me—you know how much it means to me, don't you?"

Tears still streaming down her face, Minnie took it and nodded anxiously.

"You keep it for me, Pumpkin, until I come back. Because I promise I will—and then I'll take you with me, so you can see the things that I do. I won't leave you all alone here forever. I promise."

"You do?" Sniffling, she turned her wet little heart-shaped face up to me. "You promise, Vinnie?"

"I promise!" And I vowed at that very moment to keep my promise; to do so was the only way I could tell Minnie goodbye. I would not be there to rock her to sleep, but she could, at least, comfort herself at night with the warmth of her sister's promise.

"Then I will take very good care of Miss Jenny Lind until you come back. You can count on me, Vinnie!"

She looked so earnest, her eyes suddenly dry even though her eyelashes were still dewy, her previously trembling mouth set in a firm little line. This was the first thing I had ever asked of her, and she startled me with her eagerness, her readiness to comply. I hugged her to me once more, and smiled as she tried to conceal one last sniff with a very forced hiccup.

That evening passed in a frenzy of packing and organizing; Papa had to sell a milk cow to a neighbor in order to provide me with traveling money. At dawn the next morning, after I had eagerly signed a contract stipulating my employment with Colonel Wood and his exclusive right to exhibit me for three years in exchange for providing me with twenty dollars a week—a fortune!—my family gathered around his wagon. Benjamin was not there; he was too furious to say goodbye. My other brothers heaved my borrowed trunk into the back, and I embraced Mama, who looked suddenly older to me; her forehead was checkered with lines that must have appeared overnight, and her hair was more gray than brown. How long had it been this way? I felt a pang of guilt for not having noticed before, and for the first time I realized she was not the young woman I assumed her to always be.

"Vinnie, my little chick, don't forget us all!" Mama knelt down to my level, her skirt sopping up mud, but she did not notice. "Pray every night and trust in God, and don't talk to bad people if you can help it. Colonel Wood has promised to care for you with a cousinly concern and affection, but, oh! This is still hard!" With a sob, she covered her face with a handkerchief.

Minnie was already crying, her surprising resolve of the night before chased away by the sight of my trunk in the back of the wagon. She was holding on to my hand so tightly I could feel her nails through my gloves. "Vinnie, Vinnie, oh, why must you leave? Why?"

She was nine, but with her tear-stained face and her uncomprehending eyes, I thought she more closely resembled a child of five. My sister, my poor little sister! But I had to go; by now I had convinced myself that the only way I could make a good life for her was by making one first for myself. Then, I could come back and shower her with riches and show her the world, release her from her lonely cell, hidden away by well-meaning family.

This was what I told myself as finally I pried her small hand from mine and let Papa lift me up on the seat next to Colonel Wood. The Colonel was obviously impatient to start; we were traveling to his parents' home in Weedsport, New York—he had a note of welcome from his mother, which he showed Mama and Papa when I signed the contract, helping to ease their minds significantly. There, we would outfit me with an appropriate wardrobe before journeying on to Cincinnati, where his boat had wintered.

Papa settled me in, tucking a bearskin all about me even though it was not cold. But I let him fuss, knowing this was his way of saying goodbye, and that he would sorely miss me.

"Got your money hidden away?" he asked, suddenly very concerned with one corner of the skin that would not stay put.

"Yes, Papa."

"Keep it in case of an emergency. You never know what might come up."

"Yes, Papa."

"Don't let strangers pay for anything, you understand? That's the way to ruin; you pay your own way, if Colonel Wood can't."

"Yes, Papa."

"And don't forget to write. Your mother will surely look forward to a letter now and then."

"I won't forget, Papa, oh, I won't!" And I could not help but throw my arms around his rough and weathered neck; I heard him sniff just once, then he patted my arm and gently pushed me away, muttering something about checking the back wheel of the wagon, as it didn't look "put on right."

Of course it was put on right; Colonel Wood abruptly slapped the reins, and the horses started forward. I twisted around and waved at my family, memorizing their faces, until we rounded the bend in the road and I could see them no longer.

"Not going to cry, are you?" Colonel Wood asked just as I reached for my handkerchief. "I can't stand sniveling females."

"No, not a bit!" I replied, blinking furiously.

"Good. Now, let me tell you about my boat." And he began to spin a yarn of assorted colors and shapes, of minstrel singers and gamblers and cotton bales stacked up at southern docks by slaves dark as night; about the high bluffs of Minnesota, where eagles soared above the river, card games got up after midnight shows, the huge calliope that sang out merry tunes at every port of call; even a man who could spin two dozen plates at once without dropping a one!

And my heart, which had felt as heavy as a roof smothered in January snow, began to thaw, began to soar like the sun that was just beginning to peek through the trees. I felt as big as the sun; no, as big as the sky! The sky was a vast, endless sea in which the sun was just a small orb, the size of a coin. I held my thumb up to it; I blocked it neatly out.

So it was true; the sun was no larger than the tip of my thumb. The notion tickled me, tickled my rib cage until I had to laugh out loud.

I, Mercy Lavinia Warren Bump, was bigger than the sun.

INTERMISSION

"Riding on a Rail" (1853)

Sung with Unbounded Applause by Ossian's Bards.
(Words—anonymous.) Music by Charlie Crozat Converse.

CHORUS *(sung after each verse)*
Singing thro' the mountain,
Buzzing o'er the vale,
Bless me, this is pleasant,
A riding on a rail.
Singing thro' the mountain,
Buzzing o'er the vale,
Bless me, this is pleasant,
A riding on a rail.

VERSE
Men of different stations,
In the eye of fame,
Here are very quickly
Coming to the same;
High and lowly people,
Birds of every feather,
On a common level,
A travelling together.

From the Abbeville, South Carolina, *Banner,* November 23, 1854

Ranaway from the owner James SMITH, in Anderson District, a negro boy Bob, about 30 years of age, about 5 feet 10 inches high, black complexion, medium size, weight about 160 pounds. The said negro left on Sunday evening the 14th inst. The owner is now on his way to Texas. Any information concerning said boy will be communicated to Robert SMITH residing near Cokesbury in Abbeville district who will pay charges and take him into custody.

[THREE]

Life on the Mississippi, or My Education Truly Begins

"You look as pretty as a china doll," Sylvia pronounced with an approving smile; it broke slowly as usual across her rough, bony face with its cheekbones the size of large apples, deep hollows, the crooked nose that looked as if it had once been broken. Her smile brought her no beauty, but it did soften her face considerably.

"Do I?" I pretended not to know, but deep down I did; I *was* pretty. As pretty as a china doll.

The gown that Mrs. Wood had made for me was of the shiniest material we could find: a gossamer blue satin that reflected every light in every direction. While I was assured it would look brilliant behind the footlights, it was also of the highest fashion for the present year, 1858; Mrs. Wood had fastened hoops for me that allowed my skirts to sway and swing so that they did not touch my legs at all. She had not been able to send away for a custom corset, however, so she had done what Mama had done: cut down the smallest one she could find. It still gapped uncomfortably at my bosom, and did not cinch my waist as tightly as I naturally desired.

Still, admiring the lace and silk flower festoons that adorned my hem, my pretty new white satin slippers, the silk flowers in my glistening hair, I was happy with my appearance. My brown eyes sparkled almost as vibrantly as Minnie's, and for once I did not fret about my high, wide forehead; Sylvia had arranged my hair in a way that detracted from it.

"Now remember," Sylvia intoned in her considered, deep voice. "Whatever happens, I'll be right there."

" 'Whatever happens'?" I smoothed the bodice of my dress anxiously. "What do you mean? What usually happens?"

"You never know. It's a rough crowd, so you just never know. But you'll be fine, Vinnie; no one would ever want to harm you, as tiny as you are."

"Harm?" I recalled all I had read about Miss Jenny Lind; no newspaper had ever mentioned any kind of harm coming to her, except the threat of being crushed by adoring fans.

"I'm sure it'll be fine," Sylvia repeated as hastily as she possibly could. Rising from two chairs put together, for she could not fit comfortably on one, she had to duck her head in order to clear the ceiling of the private stateroom set aside for performers.

I had been surprised to learn that there were two boats that made up my new home. The one I first boarded, and where my room with Sylvia was located, was a tugboat that towed the larger, flat-bottomed boat when necessary. Both were powered by steam belowdecks, from a great hissing, churning apparatus that gleamed hellishly red at night, and which frightened me more than I was willing to admit. All the living quarters—staterooms, kitchen, and dining room—were on the smaller boat, while the theater, taking up almost the entire length, was on the larger boat. But there were private staterooms for the performers on the large boat, which was where Sylvia and I were, primping for our appearances. Or rather—I primped. Sylvia could hardly be induced to run a comb through her dull hair, and her gown, consisting of so many yards of rough, plain fabric, was not held up by hoops; if it had been, there would have been no space in the stateroom for me.

"Why won't you at least put a flower in your hair?" I asked her.

"Why? They'd never notice it."

"How do you know that? People notice performers' costumes; it's why they go to the theater!"

" 'Theater'?" Sylvia chuckled, so low and throaty that the vibration tickled my ears. "Where do you think we are? Who do you think comes aboard? Why do you think—" But she broke off, and complimented me on my dress again.

After two weeks, I was growing used to the vagaries of life upon a river. While there was something quite soothing about going to bed at night rocked to sleep by the movement of the water, the days were a frenzy of chaos and activity, of men casting off ropes, ramps pulled and lowered, scenery hammered, wood thrown into the boiler. All this activity was very exciting to me, so used to the stultifying sameness of life in Middleborough. While I was in constant peril of being stepped upon or swept overboard by deckhands and performers who had never before encountered anyone my size, I soon learned to shout out my presence whenever I turned a corner or entered a room. There was little privacy and even less decorum, but I enjoyed the easy camaraderie among the company, the way people moved in and out of one another's rooms without knocking, the impromptu "hen parties" that the ladies held late at night while we pinned up our hair and stitched up our stockings, paying no heed to the clinking of glasses just down the hall in one of the gentlemen's rooms. Some of the men even drank spirits on *Sunday*! I found this awfully thrilling, although I did not mention that particular detail in my letters home.

Thrilling as it was, my new life was perhaps not as glamorous as I had imagined. Colonel Wood did not consider things like clean linens and regularly scrubbed chamber pots necessities but rather luxuries, and, as he was fond of reminding me, he was not contractually obligated to provide me with any of *those.* And the dampness that I had first noticed soon revealed itself to be all-pervasive, as my clothes never felt completely dry and my hair developed a frizz it had never before exhibited.

Some wayward curls had escaped, I saw, as I took one last glimpse of myself in the cracked hand mirror Sylvia held up for me (a full-length mirror proving to be one of those luxuries Colonel Wood did not feel obligated to provide). But there was nothing to do but pat my curls, as Colonel Wood stuck his head inside the door and bellowed, "The ramp is down, the crowd's a comin'; get your asses down to the stage, for I think we can get in three shows today, at least!"

Sylvia rolled her eyes at him but did not take offense at his language, as I very much did.

"I cannot believe how differently he acts now, compared to when he visited me at home! If he had ever dared talk like that in front of my parents—why, I can't imagine!"

"We've all been wondering why someone like you agreed to come along with the likes of him," Sylvia said with a shake of her head. "That explains it some."

"He was very proper at home." I tried to ignore the growing gnawing feeling in the pit of my stomach that had presented itself ever since we'd arrived on the *Banjo.* Once he'd crossed the gangplank, Colonel Wood had shown a different—coarser—side to his personality. It was almost as if he were two different people on and off the water.

"Now, Vinnie, don't be nervous," Sylvia reminded me once more as we left the stateroom, which opened to the exterior of the boat. Even as slowly as she walked along the slippery deck, I had to hurry to catch up with her, taking at least five steps to her every one. My head barely reached past her knees, and her skirt was so massive that I was in constant fear of being swept off my feet by it. By now, however, everyone was quite used to the sight of the two of us. As we passed by members of the company—most of whom were either hanging over the railing spitting into the river (the chief occupation of many of the men on the boat) or practicing their acts—none remarked upon the disparity in our heights the way that Colonel Wood still did. "Here come the elephant and the mouse," he often said, snickering, whenever we approached.

"Knock 'em dead, Vinnie," Solomon Taylor, the plate spinner, said with a gallant bow, a stack of plates balanced precariously on one hand.

"Yeah, knock 'em dead," echoed one of the specialty dancers, a thin woman with legs so long they reached past the top of her head when she kicked them. Her smile was desperately gay, but it only deepened the spiderweb of lines around her eyes; she was obviously trying to look younger than her years. Her hair was dyed a vivid yellow not found in nature, and her cheeks were painted bright red. Oh, if Mama could only see her! I had to giggle at the notion. My poor mother would have fainted dead away.

Of course, I had not painted my face, although I did allow Mrs. Billy Birch, the wife of one of the minstrels, to rub a soft chamois cloth over my face "to take the shine off." Despite my excitement and my eagerness to begin my new career, I admit to a few opening-night (or rather, day, as it was only two o'clock in the afternoon) nerves. Singing in front of my schoolmates was one thing; performing in front of a mob of strangers on a floating stage docked in Madison, Indiana, was quite another. Would my voice even carry the length of the boat? Placing my hand upon my diaphragm, I took several deep breaths and reminded myself not to strain on the higher notes.

When we reached the cluttered area in the back of the stage, Billy Birch and his minstrels were in the midst of performing a lively number. I couldn't see them, as they were in front of the curtain, but I heard the banjos strumming gaily, felt the whole stage shudder beneath the stomping of their feet.

Oh! I just come afore you,
To sing a little song;
I plays it on de Banjo,
And dey calls it Lucy Long.

"You ready, Sylvia?" Mr. Lawson, the stage manager, asked my friend. Sylvia nodded, and as soon as the minstrels were done—I heard some scattered applause, a few shouts from the audience, and something hit the stage with a loud thump—Sylvia turned to me.

"Vinnie, I think I should lift you up somewhere. It's awfully dark back here, and you might get hurt."

I looked around; it was quite dark, the only light wafting through rips in the red-velvet stage curtain or spilling in when someone opened the door to the outside. Scattered about were tangled nests of ropes, musical instruments, and heavy pieces of scenery stacked, not very solidly, on top of one another. Stagehands and performers moved frantically to and fro while the entire floor undulated ever so slightly upon the water. Mama had never seen the backstage of a floating theater, but if she had, she would certainly have added it to her list of things to fear on my behalf.

"I suppose so. How about that trunk?"

Sylvia nodded and carefully picked me up and placed me on top of the trunk. Then she bent down—I still was no higher than her waist—to speak to me. "Now, stay here, and I'll come back for you when I'm done, just like we practiced."

"Sylvia!" I had a sudden panicked thought.

"What?"

"Do you think I should sing the ballad first, instead of 'The Soldier's Wedding'? Which do you think would go over best? I do want to make a good first impression."

"Vinnie, it doesn't matter what you— Whatever you think, dear. Whatever one you like the best."

"I suppose the ballad, then." I smiled up at her, but she only peered at me quizzically, an expression I could not interpret in her sad blue eyes. Then she straightened up, sighed, and moved slowly toward the curtain, as if she were on her way to her own execution. I couldn't understand her reluctance. Why, we were in the show business!

Billy Birch, his face covered in burnt cork (although the back of his neck and his ears remained defiantly pink), winked at me as he made his way offstage, he and his fellow minstrels resplendent in green-and-yellow checked waistcoats and orange pants. "You ain't afraid, are you, Vinnie?"

"No!" I was weary of people asking me this. "Why should I be?"

"No need," piped up the tenor minstrel, his voice high and reedy. "And if anything does happen, we'll all be here watching, so don't worry. We'll get you out in a jiffy."

"What might happen?" My heart was beginning to pound, but Billy only grinned. Frowning, I turned my attention back to Sylvia as she moved through the red-velvet curtain, allowing a sudden sliver of light to pierce the backstage gloom. Without a musical flourish or any introduction, she simply grabbed the curtain and stepped forward. I found this odd, but then again, Sylvia seemed perversely devoted to shattering every notion I'd ever had about life upon the stage. Earlier, when I'd asked to see her notices, she'd stared at me and shrugged, remarking that she'd never thought to keep them.

There was a startled, collective gasp from the audience the moment she pushed her way through the curtain. The gasp was quickly followed by silence, which was soon replaced by whispers that grew louder and louder. I held my breath, waiting for something to happen; the silence onstage seemed ominous.

Finally someone spoke, but it wasn't Sylvia; it was a voice from what I had to assume was the audience. "How tall is she?"

"Seven feet, I wager," someone else replied. And then suddenly Colonel Wood, in his role as master of ceremonies, began to speak in a smooth, practiced patter—yet another side of his personality I'd never before witnessed.

"Gentlemen, gentlemen, come this way! Come stand next to Miss Sylvia Hardy, the Maine Giantess, eight feet tall if she's an inch! Why, Miss Sylvia here used to be the finest nursemaid in all of Wilton, Maine—she could carry an infant quite easily in the palm of her hand!"

I heard gasps; I couldn't contain my curiosity, so I jumped nimbly off the trunk and hurried around to the side of the stage, pushing my way through boxes and crates and furniture. When I got to the edge of the curtain, I peeked around it, safely hidden; onstage, Sylvia was extending her large, meaty hand toward the audience. There was no doubt that a baby could fit within it.

"But what does she do?" I whispered to Billy, who was suddenly kneeling by my side. "What's her act?"

" 'Do'?"

"Yes—what does she *do*? Doesn't she sing? Recite?"

"Sylvia doesn't have to *do* anything. All she has to do is stand. She's not a performer, Vinnie."

"Not like us, you mean?" I didn't look at him; my eyes were still trained on Sylvia, who was now standing with her arms extended horizontally; beneath them, two men stood, with room to spare.

"Well—that is—no." Billy patted me on the shoulder gingerly; most of the members of the company still seemed afraid to touch me, as if I were made of glass. Sylvia, ironically, was the only one who did not display this tendency. "No, not like us. You sure do take the cake, Vinnie, I'll tell you that!"

"So why does she do it, then, if she doesn't want to perform? She looks miserable." And indeed, Sylvia's face reminded me of an illustration of Joan of Arc that I'd once seen in a schoolbook: stoic, unflinching, with upturned eyes that were overflowing with the pain the rest of her homely face could not express.

"Somehow that Barnum fellow found her up in Maine; she didn't have any family living. She's been alone most of her life, they say. I guess that Barnum can persuade a mouse to go after a cat, so he somehow persuaded Sylvia, of all people, to appear at his American Museum. Don't think it went over too well, though. Doesn't seem to have lasted very long, and anyway, she wouldn't be here if it had, would she?"

"Barnum? Sylvia was at the American Museum? Does Colonel Wood know that? I imagine he does, being they're such good friends."

"Wood and Barnum? Friends? Whoever told you that?"

"Why, Colonel Wood did, of course." I turned around and frowned up at Billy; he had an amused look in his light blue eyes, pale against the streaky black of the burnt cork smeared on his face.

"Barnum never heard of our dear Colonel, I'd bet my a—, er, hat on it."

"No, that's not what he told me; he said he'd worked with him in New York!"

"Maybe he swept the street behind the Museum." Billy grunted. "But Wood never worked with Barnum. He must have told you that to make sure you'd sign."

My heart sank; I turned and looked at the stage. Suddenly I saw that the red-velvet curtain, which had looked so glamorous, was patched, the scalloped shades of the footlights were cracked, and the floorboards on the stage itself were warped. Colonel Wood was standing to the side in a bright green jacket with a checkered vest, his curls now as blackened as his mustache, but under the glare of the chipped gaslights, both were beginning to run, inky black streaks appearing on his forehead and around his mouth.

What a fool I was! I'd heard only what I'd wanted to hear and ignored everything else. Why, I knew now he'd never even heard Miss Jenny Lind sing, let alone been given a private performance. At that moment, I had no idea what on earth I, Mercy Lavinia Warren Bump of the Massachusetts Warrens, was doing on this shabby boat, in this shabby dress that had seemed so glamorous, but now I saw that the fabric was as thin and gaudy as cheap wrapping paper.

I had no idea what Sylvia was doing here, either, if it was true she'd once performed at the American Museum. The American Museum! Even in two short weeks on the river, I'd learned that everyone on this boat aspired to appear at the American Museum someday. How odd that Sylvia had never once mentioned she already had!

I tried to look at my friend through different eyes, she who had been nothing but kindness itself. She had comforted me that first awful night, had listened to my weepy recitation of my family's wonderful qualities, had suffered much to make room for me in our cramped stateroom, her giant body perpetually folded up like a retracted telescope. Every morning she helped lace up my corset, which was not easy with her thick, fumbling fingers. And I spent half an hour each evening brushing out her long brown hair, which seemed to soothe her, for she was always in pain; her joints and bones constantly ached, and her feet suffered excruciatingly from carrying about her mammoth weight. All this contributed to her perpetual air of discomfort and sadness.

I loved my new friend dearly. But try as I might, I could not imagine her passive, lugubrious form on the same stage that dainty Miss Jenny Lind and nimble General Tom Thumb had graced.

Sylvia's shoulders slumped as if she was endeavoring to disappear within that ungainly body. She was now concealing an entire newspaper behind her gigantic hands, to *ooh*s and *aah*s from the crowd. Colonel Wood was standing onstage, pointing to her and reciting her particulars—height, weight, the color of her eyes—as if she were a slave to be auctioned off.

"Why on earth doesn't she *do* something, so that he doesn't have to resort to such a display?" I whispered to Billy as irritation stirred in my veins, irritation at both myself and Sylvia. Myself for believing Colonel Wood; Sylvia for letting him poke and prod her with his walking stick while she merely stood, obviously humiliated.

A brisk slap of applause startled me; Sylvia was now lurching offstage, pushing through the shabby curtain. My stomach fluttered as I rushed to meet her.

"Are you ready, Vinnie?" A fond smile pushed away the anguish on Sylvia's face.

"Of course." I nodded calmly, as if I wasn't suddenly unable to hear over the roaring in my ears. Then we were walking through the curtain together, and Colonel Wood was introducing me as *"a new sensation, a miniature chanteuse, a living doll—Miss Lavinia Warren Bump!"*

He was only a lime green blur in the corner of my eye; the footlights in front and the gaslights along the sides of the stage were so brilliant and hot that they blinded me. I relied on Sylvia to nudge me with her knee toward what must be the piano, and then she was lifting me up, up, up, until I felt the solid walnut vibrating beneath my feet as the pianist continued to play a flourish.

Blinking, safely above the glare of the flickering footlights, I tried to make out the scene before me. The upper seats, which I'd been told were for the Negroes, I could not distinguish; all was a dusky blur. But I could discern a few faces in the audience, seated on long, hard benches on the main floor. It was mostly made up of men, I realized: a few women, some children, but mostly men, dressed in rough farm clothes. The women at least had hats on, and Sunday cloaks, but the men did not appear to have donned special clothing for the occasion.

This, alone, caused my heart to slow down, the roaring in my ears to fade; I had no fear of these kinds of people, for they were just like my own folks. Even rougher and less schooled, I imagined from the dirt and the faded quality of some of the clothing, the stained spittoons at the end of every row.

Now I could hear the gasps and whispers, the creaking of the benches as people shifted and stood to get a better look at me. Colonel Wood had stopped speaking and was twirling his walking stick as he gestured to me. With a small nod, I turned to the accompanist, Mr. James, and whispered, "I'll start with the ballad."

He smiled and started playing the introduction. I cleared my throat, and the first tremulous notes pushed themselves out of my mouth. *"I dream of Jeannie with the light brown hair,"* I warbled, and knew that my pitch was off, my tone wobbly. But the audience didn't seem to mind; I could hear sounds of *"Shh, shhh,"* and one *"Gol' darn it, shut the hell up!"* as I sensed the individuals lean forward as one, one great, giant ocean wave rushing toward me.

I didn't recoil from it. Instead, I held my hand up, silencing everyone, including Mr. James.

"Excuse me, I'd like to start again," I said. And nodded, as Mr. James played the introduction over.

"I dream of Jeannie with the light brown hair." The words were clearer now, my tone steady, and I felt my throat relax so that every note wasn't pinched. With assurance, I lifted my head so that my voice could carry farther, even as Mr. James softened his accompaniment.

"I see her tripping where the bright streams play." The audience seemed transfixed by my voice; the creaking had stopped now, as no one moved a muscle. In the first row, there was more than one gentleman whose mouth was hanging open, perfectly enraptured.

"Many were the wild notes her merry voice would pour." This was the most difficult part of the song, and I strained a bit to hit the high notes; Mr. Jones, who wore a pained expression as we began that section, relaxed and smiled at me when it was over.

"Oh! I dream of Jeannie with the light brown hair, floating, like a vapor, on the soft summer air." I slowed the last notes, caressing them so they would linger. As the last note trailed off, I took a big breath and bowed my head.

There was a long silence, long enough that I almost looked up to see what was the matter—and then rapturous, thunderous applause! It fell over me like a warm embrace, tingling my skin; it was with some difficulty that I restrained myself from jumping up and down and clapping myself. I was a hit! An immediate success!

Just as Miss Jenny Lind had been when Mr. Barnum first brought her to America. Perhaps, after all, I hadn't been mistaken about Colonel Wood.

Then I started to hear the murmurs—

"She can't be real!"

"She's a doll! A windup toy!"

"I never saw such a thing in my life!"

"Hey, mister, how'd you teach a little *baby* to sing?"

A few people were standing now, making their way toward the stage. Naturally, I recoiled but realized that I was well and truly stuck up on the piano; it was only then that I remembered Billy Birch and Sylvia were backstage, ready in case "something happened." Now I understood what that "something" was.

"It's a doll, one of them puppets, ain't it?" A decidedly rough-looking young man, with a crimson face and boils on his neck, was now at the very foot of the stage, his hands upon it, ready to haul himself up. "Open your mouth, doll baby, and sing me another purty song!"

I was frozen with fear and disgust. I could not move or utter a word. But it didn't matter, as Colonel Wood now swung into his patter and began to talk for me—just as he had done for Sylvia.

"I assure you, Miss Lavinia Warren Bump is not a doll! She's a perfectly formed woman! A marvel of Lilliputian splendor!"

There was a gasp, then someone shouted, "My Myrtle's taller than that, and she's four years old! Go on up! Put her down on the floor so my Myrtle can stand next to her!"

"Yeah—put her down on the floor!"

"Make her walk! Make her sing!"

"Make her talk!"

To my horror, Colonel Wood was walking toward me with outstretched arms; he was about to pick me up and lift me down off the piano, as if I were indeed a doll. I realized, with a sickening twist of my stomach, that he was not going to ask my leave; his eyes simply swept over me as if he was trying to calculate how heavy I was. My fear and disgust melted away to anger as he placed his unwelcome, violating hands about my waist and I slapped him, hard, across the cheek.

"You may not touch me!" I cried, which had the instant effect of silencing the crowd just as Colonel Wood stepped back in surprise.

"Excuse me?" He rubbed his cheek, eyes darkening.

"I said you may not touch me! How dare you, picking me up as if I was a child! I am a lady, and I will not allow such behavior!"

As Colonel Wood's color deepened to a dangerous red, the audience tittered; someone called out, "Hey, Colonel, guess you'd better play nice with your dolly!"

"She ain't a doll!"

"Sure she is!"

"If you ever slap me again, I'll throw you across the stage," Colonel Wood hissed out the corner of his mouth as he faced the voluble audience with a broad smile, raising his hands to calm them. "Don't just stand there, say something to 'em! I could have found me another dwarf who'd be dumb as a rock, just like that dumb giant, but as soon as you said you were a schoolteacher I thought maybe I had something special. Thought maybe I'd found me a meal ticket just like that Tom Thumb. Thought maybe you were one of them special dwarfs."

Stunned, I could only stand there as hurt tears filled my eyes and my stomach churned with disgust. *Dwarf?* I had never before been called that word, not by any misbehaving schoolchild or exasperated teacher; certainly not by my own loving family, whom I missed more than I thought I could bear. *Dwarf?* I had read of dwarfs, ancient accounts of comical pets of royalty or grotesque creatures from fairy tales, like Rumpelstiltskin. The word was repulsive and had nothing to do with who I was.

Was that how he had seen me all along? I resolved to take the next train home, back to my family, who had only tried to protect me from people like him. Contract or no contract, I would—

Don't shame us, my father had said; the full weight of his words fell upon my shoulders like a cross to be born.

My body felt icy, separate from my brain. Colonel Wood was openly sneering as he moved again toward me. There were only two things I could do. I could stand there like Sylvia, a thing—a *dwarf*—and let him lift me off the piano—I could almost feel his huge, grasping hands about my waist, my legs dangling helplessly in the air. Or I could take control of the situation and not shame my family.

I will not let my size define me, I had told myself back in my school days. *I will define it.*

"Stop!" I held up my hand, surprising all, including myself. "Stop!" I had to repeat this several times, but after a moment the audience quieted down, although those standing did not return to their seats, and the ugly young man remained ominously close to the stage.

My training as a teacher now came to my rescue. I felt myself expand, perched atop that grand piano; my spine stiffened, my chin tilted, and I willed every molecule, every bit of muscle and flesh and bone and even the hair on my head, to exude *dignity*. I imagined it exploding from the very core of my being; I closed my eyes, picturing myself showering sparks and stars and diamonds of dignity. Then I opened my eyes to survey the audience as an eerie calm fell upon me.

I began to speak, and I was careful to overenunciate my words, as I had often found myself doing when trying to help a confused pupil. The audience was that pupil. So was Colonel Wood. They needed to be educated; they needed to be taught—about me, Mercy Lavinia Warren Bump, descendent of William the Conqueror and Richard Warren of the Mayflower Company.

"I assure you, I am neither a doll nor a windup toy. As Colonel Wood said, my name is Miss Bump, and I hope you enjoyed my song. Now, if you'll permit me, I'd—"

"How tall are you?" the sweaty young man at the footlights interrupted, quite rudely. I had a good mind to ignore him, except that he was echoed by several others repeating the same question.

"Miss Bump is—" Colonel Wood began, but I cut him off with a glare; he returned it but did back away from the piano.

"My height is two feet, eight inches; thank you for inquiring."

"How old are you? Why, you can't be more'n four or five!" another voice rang out.

"While I do not believe it is polite to ask a lady her age, I am not yet eighteen." To my surprise, this was received with a hoot of laughter.

"Almost eighteen, you say? Why, you must have a little fairy beau, then!" someone else exclaimed.

"Unfortunately, Miss Bump has yet to find anyone who measures up," Colonel Wood replied quickly; the audience roared with laughter, while I could do nothing but stand there, the butt of their joke.

"Are those doll clothes you're wearing?" This was from a female voice.

"No, I had them made, just as you do," I replied before Colonel Wood could say something boorish. "Now, I would like to sing another song. Would you allow me?" For I was suddenly weary, unsteady on my feet, although I would not allow myself to show it; my body felt as battered as if I'd been run through a butter churn. I don't know how long I'd been onstage, but it felt like a lifetime.

"You bet, little lady!" someone shouted, and there was a general stirring and creaking as people took their seats. It was a sound I would grow to recognize, the contented sound of an audience settling in, ready to be entertained. But at that moment, I noted it with only exquisite relief, for soon my humiliation would be over.

I nodded at Mr. James, who began the lively military introduction for "The Soldier's Wedding." With clenched fists, I held on to my skirts in an effort to keep myself from toppling over.

"Give me your hand, my own Jeanette . . ." I sang with determined force, and soon the audience was clapping along. Somehow I got through the song, I know not how, although Mr. James told me later that I had smiled the entire time. As soon as I was finished, I smoothed my skirts, took a deep breath, and stepped onto the keyboard, then the piano bench, then finally the floor; I couldn't wait to leave that stage.

The roar started; from the back of the audience it came, a deafening sound that made me clasp my hands over my ears. It was applause, my first ovation, and it was a sound I would never forget. Utterly astounded, I somehow found the presence of mind to curtsy, my hand over my heart, as if I was, indeed, Miss Jenny Lind.

A little smile tickled my lips as I turned around to go back through the curtains, passing Colonel Wood. But that dastardly man actually kicked at me as I walked by, laughing to see me jump in fright.

"That's not the last you've heard from me about that slap, little missy. I won't be made a fool of on my own stage, especially not by a dwarf," he hissed, before turning back around to quiet the still roaring audience.

I didn't think I would make it through the curtains; my stomach suddenly seized, and I knew I had to find a chamber pot so I could purge myself of all the humiliation and disgust inside me. I ran, as fast as I could, backstage, past Sylvia and Billy Birch and the Tattooed Man who was preparing to go on, out the door to the deck, where I scooted under the leg of the dancing girl as she practiced her high kicks. I ran and ran, stumbling on the slick boards, but I didn't make it; I turned suddenly and would have hung my head over the side of the boat, but, of course, I couldn't reach the rail.

I fell to my knees in a miserable heap instead, and was sick right there, on the dirty, damp deck littered with tobacco stains and muddy footprints, while behind me people continued to make their way to and from the stage area. It was as if I was invisible to them; it was as if I was too small for anyone to notice.

And at that moment I knew, with another sick heave to my stomach, I was.

NOW THAT MY EYES WERE OPEN, MY EDUCATION TRULY BEGAN. For it was made clear to me—as it must have always been to my family, who had pleaded with me so not to leave—that my value lay only in my unusual size. I could have had a pumpkin head stuck on my tiny body, could have spoken in unintelligible sentences and drooled upon myself—it wouldn't have mattered. People came to see me for my size alone, and naturally this caused me great humiliation and distress, feelings that seemed only to increase with every day. For it transpired that part of my contract—oh, that cursed contract! How stupid I had been not to read it more closely!—stipulated that Colonel Wood could exhibit me in any way he saw fit. And he saw fit to do it in the manner of a gross, disgusting boor with not a shred of consideration for a gentlewoman's propriety.

Now I understood Sylvia's constant pained expression. I also understood that I was not, despite my naïve belief, a performer just like Billy Birch, the minstrels, and the dancing girl.

No, I found myself labeled by Colonel Wood as one of his "oddities," like the Tattooed Man, the knife swallower; like Sylvia. Even though onstage I sang and danced (courtesy of some hasty lessons between shows) as enthusiastically as any of the minstrels, before and after each performance I found, to my disgust, that I was expected to be *displayed*. Like an unusual seashell, or a rock resembling a toad; like the two-headed kitten that long-forgotten doctor had likened me to. It pained me to realize how prescient he had been.

I had to stand upon a table in the galley on the opposite end of the boat from the stage. I had to allow total strangers to gape at me, whisper about me, even attempt to touch and fondle me despite my protestations, my constant reminders that I was not a doll, not a child, but a young lady with all the sense and sensibilities that entailed.

It was the men who persisted in doing this. Children whispered, giggled, but merely stared; women might reach out to finger the fabric of my skirt as women are wont to do. But men wanted to pick me up, put their hands about my waist, even attempt to kiss me without my leave. I could not tell if they thought me a child, despite my desperate attempts at genteel conversation, my blushes, my thoroughly ladylike demeanor—or if they wanted to ascertain that I was, indeed, of a womanly form, only miniaturized.

All I knew is that I had to insist, over and over, that I did not grant permission to be touched; I had to refuse, always, requests for "fairy kisses" upon rough, unshaven cheeks or, worse, lips. I know Colonel Wood did not like it when I was so bold and outspoken to those who paid admission for the privilege of doing so; he loomed over me, glaring, threatening, cursing. But he could not force me, not in front of customers, and also not in front of the rest of the company. After that horrible first performance, they had banded together to protect me; Mrs. Billy Birch had helped me to clean myself up, make myself presentable for the next show. Billy and the minstrels had assisted me in coming up with some rejoinders for the audience, so that Colonel Wood had nothing to say. Sylvia had seen Colonel Wood kick at me and had since attached herself to my side, particularly whenever he was around.

I greatly appreciated their support. For Colonel Wood had done what my mother's fears and worries had failed to do; he had made me understand, for the first time, how physically helpless my size truly made me. Back home on the farm, I'd never felt this way; animals I understood and trusted, both in their actions and in my ability to stay clear of them.

Human beings, I was learning, were much more dangerous and unpredictable.

"What did you expect?" Sylvia asked me in honest surprise one day as we departed the boat to walk about the town of Davenport, Iowa.

This was yet another humiliating lesson I had to learn. It was usual for showboats of this time to parade about some of their performers—especially the *oddities*—to drum up business for the shows. Colonel Wood found it amusing to pair Sylvia and me up for this purpose—"the elephant and the mouse"; obviously we drew attention because of the disparity in our heights. Every time we docked in a town, Sylvia and I were sent out to stroll for about an hour, accompanied by the Tattooed Man (a very stringy individual with ink of fabulous hues covering every inch of his skin, including inside his ears; I cannot recall his name, as I believe he gave a different one each time he was asked), and the sword swallower. Mr. Deacon was his given name, but he advertised himself as "Signor Silvestri, the Great Sword Swallower." He had an oddly short neck, which struck me as rather a liability in his chosen profession. But he was a very gentle man, the only member of the troupe who said grace before every meal.

Naturally, our "casual" strolls incited curiosity among the townspeople, curiosity that could be satisfied only by the purchase of a five-cent ticket to Colonel Wood's Floating Palace of Curiosities and Entertainment, or so said the flyers that the Tattooed Man passed out to the crowd that inevitably trailed behind us like a cumbersome dress train.

"I have to say, I don't understand why you left your home at all," Sylvia continued as we walked along. Poor Sylvia; she felt, even more keenly, perhaps, than did I, the stares and whispers we inevitably encountered, and so kept up a constant conversation as a way to drown them out. This was the only time she was so talkative; on the boat, she reverted to her usual taciturn habits. "Your family sounds so sweet; you had a respectable situation. With me, it was different. I didn't have anyone left; I felt like a freak of nature regardless, so I thought it wouldn't matter where I went. But you—I don't understand why you're here, Vinnie."

"I don't either." I sighed, avoiding the stares of a group of dockworkers who stopped unloading barrels to gape at us. "I didn't think that—well, I thought I was interesting to the Colonel for other reasons—my singing, for example. I thought I'd be able to sing like Miss Jenny Lind, and be treated with the same respect and dignity. Oh, yes, perhaps I knew, deep down, the Colonel was mainly interested in me because of my size, because of how popular Tom Thumb is, but I thought—I thought I was somehow *more*." Because I'd always believed I was, I thought but did not say aloud. The notion seemed ridiculous now, as I trudged along a dock accompanied by a giantess, a tattooed man, and a sword swallower. How was it I had ever been a schoolteacher? Despite all that I had taught, I had learned nothing about the world.

"But how could you leave your home and your family?" Sylvia persisted.

I clutched my cloak, which had been made by Mama long ago to wear as I walked to and from school. It felt like the warmth and tenderness of my entire family wrapped about my body, and I nuzzled my cheek against my shoulder and sniffed; it still smelled like home, like the dried lavender Mama always laid in every drawer, the lemon oil she used to polish the good furniture, the warm, yeasty smell of the endless loaves of bread that she baked.

How could I leave home? I tried to remember, for both Sylvia and myself.

"I wanted to see the world," I replied ruefully, then stopped to laugh at myself. We were at the end of the dock; the muddy street before us was utterly disgusting, stacked high with dirty crates and smelly barrels of fish, pungent bundles of animal skins ready to be shipped off to places unknown. The air was filled with the cursing and shouts of dockworkers and bursts of steam from boats about to push out. Very few women were in sight, and of those who were, even fewer could be called ladies. "I wanted to meet new people, see new things," I continued as we crossed the muddy street—I held my skirts up, sinking almost to my knees—and continued uphill, away from the river. "I didn't want to end up a spinster teacher, living only on the kindness and pity of her family. I didn't want to remain in Middleborough all my life."

"I would have loved to remain in Wilton," Sylvia said with a heavy sigh. "But there wasn't anyone left. And then Mr. Barnum came."

"Why did you leave him? What brought you—here?" I gestured about the shabby street, the heads poking out of windows to stare as we continued our progress. Oh, how bitterly I recalled strolling the quiet streets of Middleborough, where everyone knew me and no one thought to exclaim about my size or my fairy voice, where people conversed with me, not *above* me, as if my ears were too small to hear their ridiculous comments.

"Ma, lookit that!" a boy yelled out a window, right above our heads. "That tiny little person—reckon it can talk?"

"Yes, *it* can," I retorted loudly; away from Colonel Wood, I felt free to indulge myself and be rude to those who were rude to me. "And *it* knows better than to say 'reckon.' What year are you at school?"

The boy turned white and ducked his head back inside his house.

"Vinnie, you do beat all!" Sylvia chuckled in admiration. "How you talk! I can never think of anything to say."

"I just get so angry, I can't help myself. So back to Mr. Barnum—why ever did you leave his employ?"

"I didn't want to, but he sold my contract," she replied, slowing so I could catch up. She was patience itself, for shortening her stride was not easy on joints that ached with every movement.

"He sold it? To Colonel Wood? Then the Colonel does know Barnum?"

"No, Mr. Barnum sold it to a Mr. Peabody, who sold it to Colonel Wood."

"They can do that? Buy and sell us? Like slaves?"

"If you sign a long contract like I did, they can."

"Why—why did Mr. Barnum sell your contract?" I asked hesitantly, for I did not wish to cause Sylvia distress.

"He said I bored the audience. He said that's the kiss of death—boredom—and while he wished me every kindness, he had to sell my contract because he found another giantess, one who recited Shakespeare."

"Really? Shakespeare?" I was astonished. Imagine—a giantess reciting Shakespeare! I would pay to see that, myself! "Was he—was he nice to you? Nicer than Colonel Wood?"

"Oh, yes!" Sylvia stopped, and her heavily lidded eyes shone with fondness. "Mr. Barnum was the nicest man I ever met! He treated me like a lady, and nobody had ever done that before. After Mother died, it was like I was invisible, or worse. Mother was the last person to hug me, even touch me, until Mr. Barnum came up to visit. Why, Vinnie, he treated me just as if I was the daintiest little lady—just as dainty as you! He held chairs out for me, he opened doors, he brought me flowers! He's a good man. It's not his fault I'm not cut out for this life."

"No, you're not. I'm not, either. This wasn't the life I thought I'd be living now."

"Oh, yes, you are! Maybe not here on the boat, but Vinnie, the way you talk to people! The way you never forget you're a lady! And the way you light up when you're onstage! You're wonderful. I don't know how you do it. I just know Mr. Barnum will find you someday." My friend's admiration was honest and heartfelt, and I must admit I needed to hear it. I placed my tiny hand in her great one, and we walked along in silence for a bit, studiously ignoring all others. Davenport was a typical river town, something I could now identify with confidence, and I supposed that was one useful thing I'd learned since leaving home. River towns on the Mississippi were all somewhat the same; all had streets leading uphill from the riverfront, churches and schools dotting the ends of the streets highest above the river.

In this town, there were the usual newspaper office, dry goods stores, offices that took care of boating business and trading commodities, and one apothecary shop. Across the street was a candy store; Sylvia tugged at my hand and pointed, and I nodded. The Tattooed Man and Mr. Deacon had already peeled off into a tavern, as was their habit. Unescorted—but not alone, as a sizable contingent was now following us, speculating about us as if we could not hear them; one even speculated I must be Sylvia's child, which made us both smile—we crossed the muddy street. As the crowd followed, Sylvia ducked her head and slumped her shoulders terribly, poor thing, as if she truly believed she could *wish* herself smaller. But she did allow herself a smile; she had a powerful sweet tooth, although I knew that later tonight she would be moaning in her bed with a toothache.

After buying some chocolate drops from an astonished shopkeeper who shouted to his wife to "Come look at these show folks, this giantess and her little friend," we resumed our stroll until we came upon the gleaming storefront hung with a sign proclaiming *Mr. Greene, Fine Practitioner of the Art of Photography, Card Printing & Phrenology.*

The window was papered with photographs—some sepia-toned, others hand-tinted with traces of color—of famous personages. General Tom Thumb was chief among them. The photographs were for sale, twenty-five cents each.

"Did you ever?" I asked Sylvia, astonished.

"Did I ever what?" my dear, literal-minded companion answered.

"Did you ever see such a thing? Paying for someone's photograph! I've never even had my photograph taken, have you?"

"Oh, no! No, how dreadful!"

I had to laugh; despite her deep voice, she sounded just like Minnie. "I don't think it would be dreadful; I think it would be fun," I replied, still looking at the photographs, the one of General Tom Thumb in particular. The caption read *General Tom Thumb in Highland Dress,* and indeed, he was in a traditional Scottish kilt, with a feathered hat, his features rounder, more mature, than I recalled from the few newspaper illustrations I'd seen.

"Do you really think people pay for his photograph? Let's go inside and ask!" I tugged Sylvia's hand, and she reluctantly pushed the door open for me. Inside the hot little room, there was another glass case that contained a few more of these fascinating portraits; I had to stand on tiptoe and lean my forehead against the cool glass, but I could see them. I recognized President Buchanan, and his golden-haired niece, Harriet, who was his pretty hostess in the White House. There were photographs of Queen Victoria; one of the famous actor Edwin Booth, dressed as Hamlet; and another of General Tom Thumb costumed as Napoléon.

There was also one photograph of him standing on a tall table, leaning his hand upon the shoulder of another man, who stood next to him.

"That's Mr. Barnum," Sylvia said, groaning as she knelt down so she could see the images. "The man standing. That's Mr. Barnum."

"Really?" I was surprised and, I confess, a little disappointed; the man in the photograph looked so very . . . *ordinary*. Curly hair parted on the side, a wide forehead, a somewhat bulbous nose, an unremarkable smile. He resembled any man I might have passed in the street; he certainly did not resemble a world-famous impresario. Colonel Wood, I had to admit, looked much more the part than did this man.

"Good God Almighty!"

Sylvia and I both looked up, she rising as hastily as she could, leaning heavily upon the glass case, which shuddered alarmingly beneath her weight. A very surprised young man, with thick spectacles and a pale complexion, stood behind the case. Wiping his hands on a long white apron, he didn't look like a photographer; he looked like a butcher. Except instead of blood on the apron, there were inky black stains.

"Hello," I said with a smile, since he appeared unable to do anything but gape at the two of us. "I was hoping you could help me. What are these?" And I pointed to the photographs behind the case.

"The—the—they're *cartes de visites,*" he finally stammered, pronouncing it *car-tays-vizeetz*. "I got 'em from a supplier in Paris. Folks here are crazy about 'em, but I'm almost plum out. Say, ladies, I'd take your photographs right here on the spot, free of charge, if you'd let me sell them. Whaddya say?"

Sylvia began to tremble, but I answered firmly, "I'm afraid we couldn't do that, not now. But perhaps later. Do you have a card?"

"Would you like to buy one of the little General's? He's our top seller." The man gave me a conspiratorial smile as he handed over his card. "I bet you're sweet on him, ain't you?"

"Why on earth would you think such a thing?" I asked, insulted by his impertinence, and not inclined to hide it.

"Why, because—well, because. He's a mighty handsome little man."

"And I suppose I'm a mighty pretty little lady?"

"Sure! Why, sure you are!"

"And because he's handsome and I'm pretty, we must make a match?"

"No, because you're little and he's little!"

"Really," I said to Sylvia, who was watching me with her usual admiring, openmouthed smile. "The nerve!"

"Well, anyway," the young man said with a shrug. "Take it for free. And come back if you change your mind about being photographed."

"No, really, I couldn't—"

"I'll take it." Sylvia held out her massive gloved hand. "That one." She pointed to the photograph of General Tom Thumb in Highland dress. The young man placed the *carte de visite* into her hand with trembling fingers.

"Gosh" was all he could say as we left the store; a crowd of children, who had been pressed, nose first, against the store window while we were inside, scattered like frightened mice before us.

"I never saw anyone so rude," I muttered as we began to walk back toward the river, the busy hum of activity drawing us like bees to a hive.

"Do you want the picture?" Sylvia asked. I looked up at my friend, in whose shadow I could easily walk; despite the parasols we both carried—each painted with the words *Follow Me to the Show!*—she shielded me from the peculiarly pale sun I had already learned to associate with the West.

"No, you keep it. But thank you." I had no interest in General Tom Thumb beyond his association with Mr. Barnum.

As the *Banjo,* docked in all its desperate jauntiness, came into sight, however, I reconsidered. There it was, the long, flat boat trimmed in peeling shades of red, white, and blue—with a new sign hanging over the ticket office proclaiming, in huge letters, *The One, the Only, Floating Palace of Curiosities Including the Only Dwarf Woman This Side of the Alleghenies*. There I was, my name not of any value, nor my face, nor my talent—only my size and, of much less importance, my gender.

And here was General Tom Thumb, his photograph being sold for twenty-five cents beside those of Queens and Presidents.

How had this happened? I had not left my family to become the only dwarf woman this side of the Alleghenies, stuck on this miserable boat. I was educated; I was descended from the first Americans; I was gifted with a fine voice, face, and form, not to mention manners and intellect.

As far as I could tell, Charles S. Stratton, General Tom Thumb himself, was not blessed with any of these advantages.

Suddenly I felt a fire burning in my very soul; perhaps it had been tamped down these last few weeks, but it was a fire that had always been there. It had begun as that ember that kept me warm at night while my mother wept for my lonely fate, the same spark that had inflamed me to excel in my job as schoolteacher, even as

I knew it was offered out of pity. It was the fire of ambition, and I knew it was the only thing that would save me from spending the rest of my life a sad curiosity—like Sylvia—or from going back to the farm and hiding from the world, like my beloved Minnie. At that moment, I wasn't sure which of the two fates was the least desirable; I only knew I didn't want either one.

"I'll take that after all," I said to Sylvia, who handed me the photograph of the General. I tucked it carefully into my reticule, then drew up the strings tightly, to keep out the dust.

It may have been only a photograph, but it was necessary fuel to that fire I was determined to nurture or else I would be lost, or else I would be forgotten, just a nameless memory in the minds of some rough folk who lived along a river. "Remember, Ma, remember, Pa," I could imagine them saying to each other years from now. "Remember that dwarf woman we saw? Wasn't she something?"

"She sure was," it would be agreed. And that would be all.

No, I couldn't allow that to happen. And this photograph of General Tom Thumb in an outlandish costume—perhaps it could be my ticket out of here, away from such a sad, anonymous fate.

It could also be my ticket *to* somewhere: to New York, and the Great Barnum himself, who was fast becoming, in my mind, the only person who could repair my dignity and give me the career I so desired. Perhaps he could be persuaded to buy my contract from Colonel Wood.

But first, of course, he would have to know about me. A photograph would be the perfect introduction. And I imagined that I would take a very nice photograph, indeed.

INTERMISSION

From the *Brooklyn Daily Eagle,* September 14, 1855

The Syracuse *Standard* says a healthy lady with four babies, all born at once, passed through that city and took dinner at the St. Charles Hotel yesterday. The children are three boys and one girl, and were born in Tompkins County. They are a trifle over seven weeks old, and are represented to be very hearty and handsome children, and so much alike that it is impossible to tell "t'other from which." They were bound for the Boston Baby Show. Physically, the lady may be healthy, but morally and mentally she cannot be, for no sane or modest lady would make a "show" of herself. To sit in a public place, courting the notoriety of having produced an unusual number of children is neither ennobling nor modest.

From *The New York Times,* November 30, 1859

The North and South

We are in the receipt of numerous communications concerning the Harpers Ferry affair, and the various topics connected with it. They are from all quarters, and on all sides,—some defending the North, assailing Slavery, urging the policy of not hanging John Brown, etc., and others presenting the gloomiest pictures of the state of public feeling at the South, and insisting on the necessity of some immediate step to avert the disastrous political crisis which seems to be impending.

We must decline to publish them all,—simply because we see no possible good which they could accomplish.

[FOUR]

In Which Our Heroine Nearly Comes to Ruin

INTO EACH LIFE SOME RAIN MUST FALL," MR. LONGFELLOW wrote, and thus far, I fear I have done an excellent job recounting the rain that fell upon my life on the river. It is time to remember something another great man once said.

"Every crowd has a silver lining," Mr. Barnum told me once as I recounted to him some woe or another. I laughed, as he intended, but have never forgotten it. Now I shall attempt to recount the silver linings among the clouds—as well as the crowds.

Life on the Mississippi: How romantic it sounds, still, especially to those familiar with the novels of Mr. Twain! Long before anyone had ever heard of their adventures, I passed by Cairo, Illinois, where Huck and Jim were bound; I saw the sleepy streets of Hannibal, Missouri, where Tom Sawyer whitewashed his fence; I passed scores of mysterious islands, any one of which could have been Injun Joe's hideout.

The scenery truly was thrilling, especially to one reared in the snug, protective hills of New England. The wild islands appearing, as if conjured, in the middle of the widest parts of the river. The high, rocky bluffs in Minnesota, just as Colonel Wood had described, where I saw my first bald eagle, that soaring symbol of our Grand Republic! The bustling docks of St. Louis, rows of boats and barges lined up, like floating dominoes, with exotic names such as *La Belle du Jour* and *El Caballo del Mar*. I was introduced to my first Negro there, a man with skin so dark his eyes popped blinding white; he was as fascinated by me as I was by him, so we shook hands cordially and parted as friends. Then New Orleans, where accents flew as thick and flavorful as the gumbo I tasted for the first time, a mixture of sharp, staccato French and lazy, drawling southern accents, combined with the occasional nasal twang of a Yankee tradesman.

I was presented with a slave once, in New Orleans! A beautiful girl, so graceful and delicate. When I first saw her, accompanying one of her young charges to the show, I was unable to take my eyes off her. Her owner—a smooth southern gentleman, well fed, obviously satisfied with his status as master—noticed and then sent her back aboard the *Banjo* that night as a gift to me. Naturally I could not accept this "gift," but it took me several days to convince the girl to go back to her master.

I had felt morally obligated to refuse her, as no human being should ever be given as chattel! It was the great debate of our time, this decision as to whether or not new states should be allowed in as free or slave-holding, and of course, as a New Englander, I was firmly on the side of the abolitionists like Mr. Garrison and Mrs. Stowe. Yet after the girl left, reluctantly, I felt a surprising wrench; it only then occurred to me that the moral thing would have been to accept her and take her back north, where I could set her free. Even as I realized this, however, I remembered that I was almost as indentured as she; Colonel Wood would not have allowed it. She would have been one more mouth to feed, for obviously a slave could not perform and earn her keep, as the rest of us did.

I dreamed about the girl many nights after; she appeared, silent and reproachful, staring at me before vanishing into a soupy southern mist.

The dangers we faced as our little company cruised up and down the capricious Mississippi were more numerous than any plot from a dime novel! There was the ever-present terror of the boiler exploding, a fate that met many a steamship in those days, causing hundreds of gruesome deaths. We used to read about them in newspapers, exclaiming over the gory details of flesh melting away from bone, of decapitations caused by flying shards of steel. No mere schoolmarm ever faced such thrilling peril!

There were also dangers from the river itself; one never knew if, just around a bend, there might be submerged trees or even wreckage from other boats. Pirates, too, were rumored to be lurking in every hidden cove (although I'm sad to report that we never encountered any). Western storms were a constant threat; the weather in this part of the country was wilder, more electric, than I'd ever experienced back east. Once we came upon a town that had been nearly leveled by a tornado, and we could see the tempest's path from the broken and uprooted trees on either side of the river. It was as if a heavenly foot had stomped through on its ruthless way to somewhere else.

The incessant mosquitoes and flies brought fever, aided by the dank, humid air, so that at one time or another, everyone in our company was felled by the ague. Despite my strong constitution, even I was laid low by it, tended to, with great care, by Sylvia. Soon enough, however, I was up and about, although I cannot say my recovery was aided by the food we were served. Oh, how the thought of one of Mama's layer cakes or delicate pies could bring tears to my eyes, a rumble to my ever-empty stomach! Our cook did not deserve her apron; well-cooked meat was a foreign concept to the woman, and she insisted upon boiling, rather than frying, the fish. A dense, chewy bread was our staple, as apparently she had never learned to put up vegetables or fruit!

Even when we left the boat and ventured onto shore—often in search of a boardinghouse that would serve a decent meal—there were many dangers awaiting our valiant little troupe.

Late at night, after the last show, was a particularly hazardous time. It was not unusual for the male members of the company to want to explore the streets, generally closest to the docks, which were lit up with gaslights, music, and sin. There were often brawls and disturbances; minstrel singers and plate spinners did not blend in well with farmers and fishermen. On more than one occasion we had to beat a hasty retreat late at night, the hands jumping down to the steam engine, many with their nightcaps on, to throw wood in the boilers as Captain Tucker ordered full steam, bullets screeching our way from the docks.

Naturally, I was never part of this kind of mischief. But when bullets were fired toward the boat, they were not particular about their target; I clasped my hands about my ears and ducked, but I heard my share of bullets whistling by my head, anyway. Fortunately, none of us ever came to peril, although once Colonel Wood found a bullet hole squarely in the middle of his silk top hat.

The safest place for any of us was onstage, in front of an eager crowd; that silver lining that Mr. Barnum would one day talk about. To see the joy on plain, work-worn faces as I sang, to hear the delighted laughter when I told a funny story—that was where I felt truly at home, loved, *safe*.

Although my fellow performers did not always feel quite so loved! Western audiences were swift to show boredom or displeasure with an act that did not measure up. Tomatoes, apples, masticated wads of tobacco—all were thrown freely at the stage at one time or another. None, however, were thrown at me.

Why I was never so threatened, I can only ascribe to the peculiar effect I had upon most people, even those who could not refrain from remarking upon my size. Far from wanting to cause me harm, the audience seemed, as one, to desire to shelter me from it. This behavior was so marked, so pronounced, that some of the other acts tried to convince me to appear with them.

"C'mon, Vinnie," the plate spinner, in particular, would beg. "I been hit with so many tomatoes lately I'm turning red! Just step out onstage with me, please? I'll pay you, say, a dollar a week?"

I smiled but declined. I couldn't appear in every act!

There was one person, however, who did not desire to shelter me from harm—one person, in fact, who seemed to go out of his way to cause me grief. And that was Colonel Wood.

"Move your tiny ass, Vinnie—if I catch you being late for an entrance again, I'll boot you from here to kingdom come," he would snarl, kicking at me with his dirty shoe. This was something he became very fond of doing, just as I became very fond of jumping nimbly aside to avoid him.

Or—"I'm sick of your uppity airs, Miss Uptight Yankee. Why don't I just throw you in the boiler; you're so little, I bet nobody would even notice you were missing," he would growl, taking a swig of his jugful of whiskey. "Slap me on my own boat, in front of my own people, the hell you did." That, of course, had been my fatal mistake; on his boat, he claimed his title of "Colonel," placed it on his head like the gaudy hats he wore, and never let anyone forget it. Woe to anyone who challenged him—especially in front of an audience.

"Never thought I'd live to see the day when a dwarf would be the biggest draw on my boat. God Almighty, what idiots these rubes are," he would slobber after he was well and truly in his cups. Once drunk, he had a tendency to fall asleep in the oddest places; you never knew, in the morning, when you might stumble upon his drooling, snoring form sprawled all over a staircase or curled up among a coil of ropes on the deck—or even, more than once, leaning against the door to my stateroom.

The first time I discovered him there, bile rose in my throat until I feared I might contribute to the puddle of vomit in the hallway at his feet. I uttered a swift prayer of thanks for the presence of Sylvia in my room, and couldn't fall asleep that night until she had moved my trunk against the door.

But the fact remained that I made the man money; knowing this, I could not completely believe that he would ever actually harm me. As the months went by, and 1858 passed into 1859 and then 1860, as the *Banjo* drifted up and down the river, its company so oddly detached from the ever-escalating political situation on both shores, my fame grew beyond what the Colonel could have predicted.

After showing him the *carte de visite* of General Tom Thumb, eventually I had persuaded Colonel Wood to have my photograph taken (by stressing the lucrative nature of such an enterprise; he sold the *cartes de visites* for twenty-five cents each, and kept all the profit himself). And over time, these postcards reached people who might otherwise have never visited a floating palace; they reached good people, respectable people. People who clamored only to see me—not anyone else.

The postcards had not, thus far, reached Mr. Barnum, as I had hoped; my fame may have been growing, but only along the Mississippi.

"Get in here, Vinnie," Colonel Wood grumbled to me one morning as I was making my way to the dining room. As usual,

Sylvia was with me; she stopped, gazing down at me with a questioning look. I nodded for her to go ahead, watching as she lumbered down the hall, her shoulders rounded so that her head did not hit the ceiling, and then followed the Colonel into his office. He shut the door; it latched with a terrifying thud, and I realized, a sharp razor of panic cutting itself through my still-sleepy consciousness, that I could not reach the handle myself. I was as good as trapped.

But no, I told myself sternly. It was broad daylight, he appeared sober, and outside I could hear deckhands and members of the troupe bustling about, engaged in their usual morning activity.

"Sit," Colonel Wood barked.

With some effort, I struggled into the only chair available to me, while he took his seat behind his cluttered desk. He did not offer to place a cushion upon my seat, so that I might be on his level; on the contrary, he grinned down at me with ill-concealed delight, while I sat so low I could barely see over the stacks of paper on his desk.

I hid my anger, as I was teaching myself to do, behind an excess of manners. "Yes, Colonel Wood? I'm eager to hear what you wish to discuss."

"Always so damn polite," he muttered. "That tiny mouth always pursed so prim and proper. Think you're above us all out here—you know the rest of the company talks about your airs, don't you?"

This was not the first time he had tried to insinuate himself between my friends and me; I knew enough not to rise to the bait. "Thank you for complimenting me on my manners," I responded with a polite smile. "It is much appreciated."

"Hmmph. Well, keep talking like that, Miss Dainty Dwarf. Because you're going to start doing extra duty. I've had some requests for private audiences for you, from some pretty important folks, and they're willing to pay double the regular price."

"Private audience? What do you mean?"

"Some hoity-toity types, who claim they're above stepping foot on my boat, want to meet you. Privately, they say. Not onstage."

"But where?" I couldn't conceive of such an idea. I was finally accustomed to being on display in the galley before and after performances; I could not say I looked forward to it, but I had learned how to put the onlookers—and myself—at ease. I could not completely avoid being scooped up as if I were a mere child; there were those who would persist in doing so, no matter how much I protested. I had discovered, though, that if I spoke first, about the most normal of topics—the weather, the political situation, the latest fashions—fewer people were inclined to do so.

But always I was surrounded by others—Sylvia, the Tattooed Man, the Bearded Lady who had recently joined our troupe, Billy Birch and his men. The notion of being entirely alone with strangers was vaguely troubling to me.

"I'm going to have to secure some sort of private parlor in hotels, I guess. Most of these towns have one, and I'm sure some arrangement can be made so I won't have to pay—free advertising, something. Up in Galena, there's a Mr. Grant who would like to meet you, so that'll be the first one."

"Alone? This Mr. Grant—he'll be alone?" Uneasiness filled my breast; I shifted in my chair, which was much too big for me. It served only to sharpen my acute awareness—it was almost an electric sensation, my skin tingling and burning—of my physical helplessness.

"How the hell do I know? If he's alone, he's alone. You'll meet Grant, and you'll do whatever he asks you to—none of this holier-than-thou behavior, Missy. You understand? He wants a kiss, you get off your high horse and give him a goddamned kiss." With a leer, Colonel Wood leaned across his desk toward me. His liver-colored lips, beneath his awful mustache still bearing traces of the blackening he used onstage, smacked at me, making disgusting kissing sounds. "You know, you ain't half bad looking in that photograph of yours. Not so bad in person, either. Is *all* of you so pretty and tiny? Might have to check that out someday, what the hell, cousin or not." And he started to laugh again, making those awful kissing sounds.

It was as if a slimy snake had slithered down my spine; I shivered, even though the air was close and hot about me, threatening to cut off my breath. I slid off the chair and ran to the door but could not open it; I could not reach the latch no matter how high I jumped—and jump I did, panic closing in around my throat like a vise, cutting off my breath, my thoughts.

Finally, with a great leap, I did reach the latch, but my hand was so small it was difficult to grasp and pull; my panic did not help matters. My grip kept slipping and slipping until suddenly the door gave way, opened from the outside; I nearly fell into the hallway. The thin dancing girl, Carlotta, was staring down at me in surprise.

"Why, Vinnie, are you all right?"

I nodded. Glancing over my shoulder, I saw that Colonel Wood had not moved a muscle. He remained seated at his desk; he was even going through some papers as if I wasn't there. And I had to wonder if he had actually said the things that I thought he had.

All at once my mind shifted, as if it were a mechanical thing and completely out of my control, toward Minnie, my dear sister. I thought of how small she was, so much smaller than me. How sweet, how innocent. Thank goodness she was still home; had I ever thought to go back for her, to show her that the world was not to be feared? "That dreadful man," she had declared Colonel Wood before she had even seen him. I thought her so simple then; I had laughed at her. Now I wondered how she'd known.

But, of course, she didn't. She was only afraid of the unknown in a way that I was not, at least not until this moment. I took a deep breath and told myself I would not begin to embrace such ideas. Mr. Grant was most likely a perfectly respectable man with a family; why else would he not wish to step foot upon the boat?

As for Colonel Wood—why, I would simply not allow myself to be alone with him again. It was an easy enough thing to accomplish; the boat was always full of people. There was no reason why I ever had to be alone with that man. And I knew I had only to ask and Sylvia would not leave my side.

Calm again, I walked with Carlotta toward the dining room, where I could hear my traveling companions talking, joshing, breaking into bits of song over the clash of silver and china. My heart lightened, for I knew they would be happy to see me. And indeed they were; as soon as I entered the dining room, there were cries of "Vinnie, Vinnie, come sit by me!"

I took a seat next to Mrs. Billy Birch and listened to all the good-natured gossip. Apparently Carlotta, seated by my side and suddenly all blushes and modest glances, was engaged to one of the regulars—the unattached young men who followed our boat up and down the river on their own pathetic rafts or canoes, looking for occasional work or trying to make a living fishing or peddling. Mrs. Billy asked me if I'd like to help make her a decent trousseau.

I nodded, happy for Carlotta. She had no future as a performer, poor dear. Getting married was the wisest thing she could do.

I joined in the congratulations without the slightest twinge of jealousy, and promised to contribute a cotton nightgown.

* * *

GALENA WAS A PRETTY LITTLE RIVER TOWN, LIKE ALL THE others—hilly, with a main thoroughfare lined with shops. I followed Colonel Wood through the bustling street to a handsome building called the DeSoto House; I had never stepped foot in a hotel before and was excited at the prospect. I had no inkling that in the years to come, I would stay in the finest of them all, with the most luxurious accommodations. I would even return to this hotel, occupying the largest suite!

But at the time, I managed not to betray my astonishment at the elegance of this establishment; indeed, I sailed through the door, clad in my most respectable gown, not one I would ever wear onstage but rather one of my church dresses, with matching bonnet, from home. It was a modest blue satin, with a high collar and black-velvet scallops along the hem and sleeves. With my head held high, I managed to give the appearance that I was quite at home in the ornate lobby, wallpapered and carpeted to a fault. Colonel Wood, however, could not maintain his composure. He stopped and gaped, forgetting to remove his hat. He looked cheap and gaudy, totally out of place, and I stared at him through new eyes, secure in my matchless deportment and bearing. Away from the boat, in such genteel surroundings, the unease he stirred in me melted away. He looked exactly what he was—a posturing, insignificant little man. And I felt exactly what I was—an elegant gentlewoman with superior breeding and appearance. A much larger personality, in every way.

Yet as soon as we were led to a little side parlor, where the Colonel left me with an admonition to "Remember, no hoity-toity airs—I'm not paying you to disappoint the customers," that unease crept back. Nervously I paced around, trying to admire the ornately carved woodwork and plush carpeting. The furniture was all large and overstuffed, and I remembered, with a pang of despair, that my stair steps were back on the boat. Locating a footstool, I dragged it over to a chair so that I might be able to climb onto it with some dignity.

Anxious and unsettled, my composure having deserted me, I could not help but recall what Mrs. Billy Birch and Carlotta each had said to me before I left the boat.

Mrs. Billy had tucked a large stone in my hand. "Put this in your reticule," she whispered, as Colonel Wood was hovering nearby. "Don't be afraid to swing it at that Mr. Grant's head if you need to!" I had accepted the unusual gift with gratitude, and tucked it into my reticule, thankful for its sudden heft.

Carlotta had summoned me to her room earlier. I did not usually visit her here; when we females gathered for our nightly gossip, it was generally in Mrs. Billy Birch's room, which was neat and homey, with a spirit lamp for making tea.

Carlotta's room, by contrast, was slovenly, her stockings and petticoats draped over every surface, all in need of repair or washing. I tried not to notice them; obviously she wasn't bothered by the chaos, as she had no blush or apology as she handed me a small envelope. Opening it, I saw that it contained a grayish powdery substance.

"Prevention powders," she said matter-of-factly. "You're so little, Vinnie, I don't know what to tell you to do so that it don't hurt. But you oughtn't to be havin' babies, so use these. Mix 'em with water and then douse yourself with them down there." And she pointed to her—I still blush to recall—womanly parts.

" 'It'? What do you mean 'it'? What might hurt?"

"It. Screwin'. I don't know what the Colonel thinks these men are going to want to do to you in private, and God knows I hope it ain't what I'm thinkin', but just in case. You don't want to have a baby, do you?"

"I—I—I have no earthly idea what to say!" And I didn't; I sat down upon the floor, my legs suddenly giving out, and I stared up at the girl who, I saw, thought she was only being kind.

"I know your ma probably never told you these things. My own ma didn't. But you're such a little thing, and I feel like someone ought. You do know what screwin' is, don't you?" She frowned in concern, her crow's-feet crinkling up; against her sallow skin, bare of the cheap paint she used onstage, her yellow hair appeared even more artificial.

"I, well, yes, I believe so. Copulating, you mean?"

"Listen to you, Vinnie!" She grinned, her pale blue eyes round with admiration. "Always coming up with such fancy words—I plum forget you were a schoolmarm sometimes, and then you go and remind me. *Copulating*—I swear!" And she repeated it again, as if learning a new word in a new language.

"But why would you give me this?" I held out the envelope, away from my person, as if it might taint me by proximity. I struggled to understand what she was implying.

"So you don't have a baby." She repeated herself patiently, as if I were a child. "Don't you understand? Screwin' is how babies get made."

"I understand that, Carlotta, but what I don't quite see is why I would have need for this kind of—of *prevention*?"

"Oh, Vinnie! You're such a smart little thing that I forget you don't know much of the world! Why do you think men want to meet you alone? There's only one reason for that, although I have to say it's not right, not for someone your size, but Lord, I've learned it takes all kinds in this world. You have no idea some of the things these river men want—animals, sisters, even other men—"

"Stop!" I was sickened, horrified, by her meaning. Scrambling up from the floor, I felt my face burn, and I couldn't look her in the eyes. "Stop—I don't want to hear this! I have no intention of engaging in—in—what it was you just said. Even Colonel Wood would not—these are respectable people, he said! There is no need for this!" And I thrust the envelope into her hands.

"But, Vinnie, I'm just looking out for you—you have to be prepared!"

"No, I thank you, but—no. There is no need, no need at all!" I hurried out of Carlotta's room, still unable to look her in the face. How did she know of these things? I felt sorry for her, for her life; I felt even sorrier for her fiancé, who must not have any idea of her past. I knew she was only trying to be kind, but I could not help but feel sickened and insulted, all the same.

I refused even to consider the scenario she had so easily conjured up; still, I felt grateful, as I waited nervously in the parlor for Mr. Grant, that Mrs. Billy Birch's rock was securely in my reticule, which was attached to my wrist.

There was a knock on the parlor door; my stomach plummeted to my feet, and I clasped my reticule to my breast. "C-come in," I barely managed to say, through cold, trembling lips.

"Miss Bump?" A short, stocky man with a beard opened the door, hat in hand. His gaze swept the room at his own height; it took him a moment to remember to look down. Finally, he saw me; his eyes widened, and his face creased into a slow grin. "Oh, goodness! Just a moment—" He ducked his head back outside the door, and I heard him say, "Julia! Children! She's in here!"

At the mention of a female name, my entire body, which I had been holding stiff as a corpse, perhaps in anticipation of my imminent doom, relaxed. I reached up to place my reticule upon an end table and turned to receive my visitors.

Mr. Grant ushered in his family: his wife and four children, the youngest a little boy still in skirts, carried by Mrs. Grant. The children shyly hung back while their parents approached me, somewhat timidly, as if I might suddenly attack *them*. They were, I was astonished to realize, almost as frightened of me as I had been of them! This realization made me relax even further; I stepped forward and held my hand out to Mr. Grant, hoping to put him at ease.

"Allow me to introduce myself. I am Miss Bump."

"Thank you for meeting with us, Miss Bump. I am Mr. Grant. This is my wife, Mrs. Grant, and our children. Freddie, Buck, Nellie, and little Jesse."

Mr. Grant bowed stiffly, while Mrs. Grant, a plain woman with small, crossed eyes, shook my hand very timidly and shifted the child in her arms.

"Please, let us sit," I said, and holding my skirts, I stepped upon the stool and climbed, as gracefully as possible, upon the chair I had chosen.

The children could not prevent themselves from giggling at my exertions; I pretended not to notice, and arranged myself and my skirts in my chair, my legs dangling above the stool.

"I thank you much for agreeing to meet us here," Mr. Grant said pleasantly. "But the children did so want to see you, after we saw your photograph in the paper, and I couldn't take them on a boat, you see—you understand."

"Indeed," I said coolly, as if there were no reason to take offense. Then I fell silent, as I could not begin to think what to say. I did not know them, after all. And I was not onstage, I could not break out into song. I had never been bashful in my life, but then nothing had ever prepared me for this; I had a wild impulse to shout that they were all "simply dreadful" and run out of the room. Only the thought of Colonel Wood, who must be hovering outside the door, prevented me from doing so.

"How tall is she, Papa?" one of the boys asked, and while his parents exchanged anxious looks, I was happy to hear his question. At least I could answer that.

"Thirty-two inches, which is how many feet, young man?" I could not help it; my teacher's training came to the fore, and I looked at him sternly—although I had to smile when I saw his face pale and his eyes bulge.

"I—I—I don't know?" He looked desperately at his father, who had an amused glint in his dark eyes.

"Two feet, eight inches," I replied briskly. "You look old enough to know your mathematics!"

"For sure, for sure, son Frederick is lax with his schoolwork," Mr. Grant chortled, slapping his knee. "Well done, Miss Bump! That you should know such a thing yourself!"

I swallowed my anger, continuing to smile politely. "Naturally I know such a thing, as I was a schoolteacher before coming west."

"A schoolteacher!" Mrs. Grant almost dropped her child from her knee. "How can that be?"

"I was an excellent scholar and was asked to take over a classroom."

"Extraordinary! Can you imagine your teacher being smaller than you, Nellie?" Mr. Grant addressed his daughter, for whom he obviously had a great fondness; he had sat with his arm about her shoulders from the moment they took their seats. She was a pretty thing, with long blond curls.

"No, Papa! I can't! You're really old enough to be a schoolteacher? How old are you?"

"Nellie, that's not polite," her mother scolded, and I exchanged a knowing look with her.

"Tell us more about yourself, Miss Bump, for that is why we wanted to meet you, after all." Mr. Grant leaned back and removed a cigar from his pocket; I wrinkled my nose, for I found the smell of cigars distasteful—at home, Papa had smoked a pipe, which I much preferred—but I did not say anything. Instead, I gave a quick recitation of my life thus far; soon we were discussing the weather, the town of Galena, which was as new to the Grants as it was to me. They had recently moved there from St. Louis, I discovered, so that Mr. Grant could take over management of his father's store.

Politics, naturally, were discussed. The presidential election of 1860 was only a few months away.

"I don't really think too much of politics," Mr. Grant admitted, his cigar spattering ash upon his trousers, which he did not notice, although Mrs. Grant did. "But I suppose I have to vote Republican. I can't abide slavery, and I guess that Lincoln's the best man to put an end to it, although at what cost, I don't know."

"Do you think there will be war?" I asked, just to be polite; the increasingly fierce tensions between the North and South did not trouble me and seemed not to affect our troupe as, of course, we moved freely up and down the Mississippi, crossing the Mason-Dixon Line without thought. Even so, I had noticed that more and more, lately, Billy Birch and his minstrels discussed the situation at mealtimes; they were, after all, men.

"If there is war, will you go, like you did before, Papa?" the oldest son said, scratching his nose.

"We won't talk of this now," his mother said hastily, before Mr. Grant could answer.

"Were you in the military?" I asked him.

"Yes, but that was long ago," he replied evasively, stroking his beard. "Don't know that anyone would want me back, anyway. Well, if this fellow Lincoln is elected, there very well may be a war. I don't think the South will stand for him."

"Well, then I hope he won't win!" And with this mutually happy thought, we continued to converse pleasantly. The boys fidgeted and poked at each other but with obvious good nature; Mrs. Grant kept the babe upon her knee the entire time, jostling him gently, while Mr. Grant sat with his arm about his daughter's shoulders. In short, I felt it was a most pleasant afternoon spent with a family similar to my own. My earlier fears and unease were forgotten.

Finally conversation lagged, and we all rose and walked toward the door, the children giggling and asking if they could stand next to me and measure my height, which I agreed to without hesitation. Mrs. Grant once again expressed her surprise that I had ever been a schoolmarm. I imagined my youthful appearance made it very difficult for her to fully comprehend it.

"It's been such a pleasure meeting you all," I said, extending my hand graciously and feeling it clasped with warmth and affection. "I hope we see one another again soon."

"As do we," Mr. Grant said with a smile that crinkled his eyes. And as the Grants left the room, I heard Mrs. Grant remark to her husband, "What a dear little lady! Her manners could not have been nicer."

I smiled, refreshed from this interlude away from the boat, and collected my cloak and reticule. As I walked toward the lobby, where Colonel Wood was saying goodbye to the Grants, they all looked my way, waving; I waved back. They really were very lovely people, such a pleasant family, obviously of good breeding; I did hope we would meet again soon, perhaps for a picnic, or dinner, or—

Mr. Grant reached into his breast pocket and took out a fistful of bills; he handed them to Colonel Wood, who bowed and pocketed the money quickly. The Grants left, and Colonel Wood turned toward me, grinning in almost a friendly way.

"Five dollars! Five dollars, for an hour! What suckers they are! C'mon, we have a show to get back to. But whatever you did in there to charm those folks, Miss Hoity-Toity, remember to do it again. I'm going to put the word out far and wide. Imagine, five dollars! I bet I can charge twice that in a place like St. Louis or New Orleans!"

Colonel Wood held the door open for me, for only the second time in our acquaintance. We found ourselves on the bustling sidewalk of Galena; I saw the Grant family turn into one of the shops, Mr. Grant already reaching into his breast pocket, ready to purchase some new distraction for his family.

As he had just done, back in the DeSoto House.

WAR. DESPITE MY STUDIED INDIFFERENCE TO ITS CAUSES, IT appeared it was coming anyway. Abraham Lincoln was elected President in November of 1860, and immediately secession meetings popped up all over the Deep South—which was where we happened to be, as we were every winter.

"Colonel, I think we ought to think about heading north," Billy Birch announced early one December morning at breakfast. The bright southern light, reflected from the water, shone through one of the narrow windows and illuminated Billy's head, bald as a polished billiard ball (save for the permanent black stain of burnt cork behind his ears). He wore a hat while performing, but other than that was completely unashamed of his naked pate.

"North? During the winter? You know we can't do that—the river might ice over, and besides, what the hell for?" Colonel Wood was hunched over his plate, his graying curls, clumped with traces of blackening, dangling over his greasy eggs. The sight of him eating in the morning was one more reason why I found it difficult to consume the first meal of the day. (The limp toast and runny eggs, fried not in butter but in rancid bacon grease, were another.)

"Haven't you been reading the papers? Here—look at the headline this morning." Billy thrust a copy of the Vicksburg, Mississippi, *Daily Citizen* across the table. **"Secession Meeting TONIGHT! Cowardly Unionists Urged to Leave Town, Declares Mayor. ALL HAIL THE GLORIOUS CAUSE!!!"**

"What's that got to do with us? The box office could be better, I admit, but it'll pick up this evening; not everyone's going to those goddamned Secessionist meetings, you know. It's just a few rabble-rousers." Colonel Wood reached for his coffee cup and drank greedily, his mustache dipping into the cup.

"Colonel, I think you're wrong," Mr. Deacon, the sword swallower, piped up. He was such a mild man; it was unusual for him to speak at the table. "Ever since the election, things have felt different down here. I been performing for years, and I ain't never seen anything like it. These folks are angry, as angry as a hen going after a fox. I don't think they're in the mood for any entertainment."

"And none of us is a southerner," Mrs. Billy Birch said. "What if there is war and we're stuck down here? What will happen to us?"

"I'm not going to be a slave!" Carlotta whimpered. She and her fiancé were still engaged; he was trying to put away some money before their wedding and, to that end, had decided to stay in St. Louis, working at the docks.

"You silly ass, you're not going to be any slave! You have yellow hair, I think—at least it used to be, probably all gray by now underneath that dye." Colonel Wood laughed rudely.

"My great-gran was a Creole girl, they say. Which means I have some nigger blood in me, and I'm not going to be no slave!" Carlotta started to cry.

"Oh, for Christ's sake, shut up. Let a man have his breakfast in peace." Colonel Wood threw a piece of toast at the sobbing girl.

"Colonel, please! She's frightened, poor thing." I couldn't help it; I scolded him in front of everyone even though I knew he detested it. But lately he had let pass a number of my spirited remarks, remarks that he would have mocked me for a year previous.

I slid off my chair and went to comfort Carlotta; ever since she had tried to "help" me with her preventative powders, I had felt a kinship with her. I sensed she needed a good Christian influence; I think she sensed I needed a woman of the world to watch out for me. We probably were both correct.

Colonel Wood glared at me but did not reply; abruptly he rose and shoved his chair back toward the table. "We're not running away from rumors about something that's not going to happen. We have engagements—I have fifty dollars' worth of private audiences for Vinnie in the next week alone, including one tonight, so obviously not everyone is going to the Secesh meeting. And then the boat needs some repairs in New Orleans, where we're heading next. You all have contracts, you just remember that. I don't want to see anyone sneaking out on me—you think Secessionists are angry? Just you see me trying to collect on a broken contract!" And with one last swig of his coffee, he was gone.

We all stared at one another. Billy and the other minstrels, who were our de facto leaders—the performers with the most legitimate experience—scratched their chins and consulted over the newspaper. Mrs. Billy shook her head and poured Carlotta another cup of coffee, her mothering instincts, never far from the surface, coming out in full force.

Sylvia didn't say a word. She seemed sadder than ever, these days. She claimed she had dreams of her dead mother, dreams in which she was told to leave the boat and go back home. So she increasingly longed for Maine yet seemed unable to do anything to get there. It was as if she was paralyzed by her longing; her already agonizing lethargy of movement increased. At times, I thought she was almost asleep onstage, her eyes barely open, as she swayed upon her feet.

The only time she ever seemed motivated to action was if she thought Colonel Wood was being particularly harsh to me. But Colonel Wood lately seemed mollified by the money I was bringing in, the numerous private engagements that continued to line up. He had stopped threatening to kick me, although he did still act strangely toward me, particularly late at night when he had already emptied half a whiskey bottle. The strangeness was in his gaze, more and more; I felt its hot glare burn over my skin as he looked me up and down, as if he was attempting to see me in a different way—a predatory way. At times, I felt almost naked in his presence. It was in the manner with which he studied every inch of my form, as if he was trying to uncover a great secret with only his eyes.

This was when I was most afraid. But Sylvia was my ever-present bodyguard, although she wasn't allowed to accompany me to my private audiences. Those were in hotels, however, that were always filled with people—genteel people, people who could afford luxuries. With only a few exceptions, these audiences were reminiscent of my meeting with the Grants. They consisted mainly of curious families of good breeding who simply didn't want to step foot on a showboat. More and more, my photograph, alone, appeared in the newspaper ahead of our engagements; I saved these notices whenever possible, amassing an impressive collection. I had an idea of what I would do with these once my contract was up.

There had been a few times, however, more recently, when I met with lone gentlemen. I made sure to keep the door open then, my reticule—with that heavy stone in it—clutched in my hand. These meetings had been uncomfortable, for conversation was difficult. These men—great men, some of them men I would hear about later, such as Stephen Douglas of Illinois, Jefferson Davis of Mississippi—were somehow rendered mute by my presence, content to simply stare—or touch. As always, it seemed impossible to persuade these men that I was not a child in women's clothing, eager to be lifted and carried and petted. Usually the gentleman would turn beet-red at my admonishment and apologize profusely—*after* he had kissed me, his beard and mustache rough against my cheek, so overly fragrant with toilet water that my eyes burned. On such occasions, I was embarrassed for us both.

Once or twice, however, I had noticed a different attitude accompanied by a different look—a look very like the one Colonel Wood sometimes gave me. That voracious, curious look that I had to shut my eyes against, even as I took comfort in the hefty weight of Mrs. Billy Birch's rock in my reticule.

"Vinnie, we think you ought to talk to the Colonel," Billy Birch declared, folding the newspaper and interrupting my reverie. Carlotta was still sobbing some nonsense about being forced to work in a cotton field; I had been patting her arm absently. The other minstrels, backing Billy up as they did onstage, nodded in unison.

"What? Me? Talk to the Colonel?" I went back to my seat, for it was there, upon my special cushion, that I was nearer the height of my companions. And I felt, keenly, the need to be on equal footing at this moment.

"Yes, you. Face it—you're the biggest star on this boat. You're the one who brings in the most money. And that's the only thing the Colonel respects."

"The Colonel does not respect me, I assure you. He tolerates me. But he wouldn't listen to me, Billy, no more than he'll listen to anything but the clink of coins in his pocket."

"Fair enough, but still. You're the best chance we have. We're in danger here, all of us. We're a northern troupe on a northern boat. Why, any moment now someone's going to commandeer this thing if they're thinking about war at all, and where will we be left? Stuck down here, and even the trains are having a hard time getting out."

"They are?" I felt a paralyzing chill in my chest, as if I'd swallowed a block of ice. Why had I no idea the situation was so bad? While once I would have been abreast of the latest political news, more and more, I had to admit, I had been focused only on my career. I scanned the papers not for mentions of the political situation but for mentions of my own name. Just when had I become so self-absorbed? It was a form of self-preservation, I realized now; I had resolved that I could survive Colonel Wood's cruelty if my heart, my mind, had shrunk to a size designed to absorb my own troubles only.

"Yes, they are. Very hard. If any of us tries to leave the boat on our own, that old devil will be after us with bloodhounds, worse than any overseer. We have to make him understand and get us out himself. That's the only way; we have to stay together—and you're the only one he might listen to."

I was silent, thinking. My contract was up in April. I hadn't been home in all this time, and I could scarcely wait until then to see Mama and Papa, and especially Minnie. Her letters arrived as regularly as letters could on the river; they were tear-stained, hardly legible, usually one long, punctuation-free plea: *"Please come home, Sister, Sister, come home I miss you what do you look like now are you still as small as me please come home."* I did not want to be stuck here in the South if war did come. I so longed to see my family, to tell them of my adventures, to assure us all that it had been worthwhile to leave.

I also did not want to be away from the reach of Mr. Barnum, who was most definitely in New York, still running his American Museum.

"All right," I agreed, sipping my cold, weak coffee. "I'll try to talk to him, although I warn you I don't know how much influence I'll have. But I'll do my best to convince him."

"Hurray for Vinnie!" Billy Birch cried out, throwing his knife into the air. Mr. Deacon caught it with an expert flourish and swallowed it neatly, his hand disappearing into his mouth. His throat moved, as if he were truly swallowing it, then he showed us both hands, which were empty. He gulped and dabbed at his mouth with his napkin, then made as if to go; with a sly grin, he turned back to us and produced the knife, which he had neatly hidden up his sleeve.

We all applauded, everyone happy, everyone united. Despite the threat of war, at that moment it felt as if we would remain untouched, in a protective bubble, just a happy little band of performers.

Little did we know that this was the last time we would laugh together like this.

"C'MON, VINNIE, MOVE YOUR ASS. AT LEAST THIS ONE DIDN'T cancel."

I hurriedly grabbed my cloak, leaving Sylvia in our room to read by the sputtering oil lamp. Then I followed Colonel Wood down the hall, in such a hurry that it wasn't until we were off the boat that I remembered I had quite forgotten my reticule.

"Oh, wait!" I called after him, turning to go back and get it.

"Move your ass, I said—we're late!" Without breaking his stride, Colonel Wood grabbed my arm; he practically dragged me through the raucous crowd, much louder, much angrier, than any I had ever seen.

"But I forgot my reticule!"

"Such a goddamned *lady*. 'I forgot my reticule!'" He mimicked me cruelly, while still dragging me so that my slippers skimmed the ground; my arm felt wrenched from its socket. "We're late, and I'm not going to lose a penny of this because you forgot your damn reticule. This has been one hell of a day."

For it turned out Billy Birch was correct: Nobody cared a whit about coming aboard our boat this day. The box office was scarce; the few people in the audience hardly paid any attention to the stage at all, so we did only one show. The rest of the day we stood along the deck, me on my steps so that I could see over the railing, watching the excitement on the shore. People running to and fro, pamphlets being handed out, guns firing up in the air, high-pitched yells that would later become the famous Rebel cry of the Confederacy. Strange flags, flags I'd never seen before, were flying everywhere; they were blue, with a white star in the middle. "Secesh flags," said Billy Birch miserably. "They're going to secede, they're all going to secede, just you wait."

"How?" I didn't completely understand. "How can they do that?"

"They just can. States' rights and all. But Lincoln won't let 'em, he vowed to preserve the Union, and so there'll be bloody hell to pay."

"'Hell to pay'! Imagine, fighting right here in our own country! How horrid!" Yet my pulse raced at all the history I was witnessing. If the South was going to secede and take that first step toward war, how thrilling it was to be there when it happened! I couldn't wait to tell my family all about it when I got home.

But first I had to get there, and the effect of all this excitement and war talk on our situation seemed increasingly ominous. I couldn't help but notice several men pointing to the boat and gesturing excitedly; more than once my ears caught the phrase "bunch of Yankee freaks" as it was hurled toward me and my compatriots. Rumors were flying from boat to boat, all lined up like sitting ducks at the docks, that soon all ships would be commandeered to move war munitions about the South. Not only ships but trains, as well, were rumored to be closed to paying passengers—particularly those with northern accents.

I had dutifully apprised Colonel Wood of the situation, bolstered by Billy Birch. The Colonel cursed and swore but still insisted that we would keep to our schedule and travel downriver; getting to New Orleans by December 12 was of utmost importance to him. "Vinnie has an important engagement then, and I need to get the boat fixed" was all he would say when we asked why. Then he cursed the poor box-office receipt from the morning, and the names of the two of my three private audiences that had sent word they would not be coming.

Hence his agitation as he dragged me through the crowded streets of Vicksburg, which, although there were no gaslights, were amply illuminated this night by torches and burning effigies of Abraham Lincoln, complete with tall stovepipe hat. Although I could barely see them; I was pulled so forcibly through the crowd, concentrating intently upon not tripping or stumbling, that I had little opportunity to look up. I was aware, mainly, only of trouser legs, some creased, some not, and the occasional hoopskirt, hem mud-splattered from the recent rains. It was a measure of how worked up the crowd was that few people stopped to gape down at me as Colonel Wood tugged me along.

Finally, we reached the hotel. Colonel Wood stomped up to the desk and was directed to a parlor off the lobby, which was crowded with men smoking, drinking, and arguing; I followed him, and after being told to "Keep him here as long as possible; maybe I can charge extra," practically shoved inside. There I tried to collect myself. My skirt was not torn, although the soles of my slippers were shredded. I looked about for a mirror, but of course there were none at my level. The only one was stationed above a fireplace, and there was nothing for me to climb upon that I might reach it. So I straightened my bonnet, patted my hair, trying to tuck stray strands back into my chignon, dragged a stool over to a velvet chair, took my seat, and waited.

The room was eerily still and dark; only one oil lamp was lit, so that the corners were hidden and long shadows smudged the carpet. But I could hear the agitation in the streets outside continue to build; shouts of "If South Carolina goes, we go!" and "Damn the Abolitionist Ape going to the White House!" reached my ears through the tightly drawn velvet curtains. These threats were punctuated by the tinkling of shattering glass and muffled thumps. With every sound I jumped, wanting to run to the window and look out at what must have been a tremendous scene. But I made myself stay perfectly still, collecting my composure before my visitor arrived. And as I sat there, so isolated yet also exposed, a curious conviction filled my breast. I felt that whatever happened this night, both in this room and outside on the streets, would be something I would never forget.

I sat for a very long time; I heard the determined tick of a mantel clock piling up whole minutes, and I knew that my audience would not be showing up. I slid off the chair and gathered up my cloak; I was about to go out into the hall and find the Colonel when I felt the building shudder, then heard a thunderous crash, a cascade of breaking glass. My heart was in my throat, my skin prickling with fear and excitement, and I ran toward the window to see what had happened. I was just about to climb, in a very unladylike fashion, atop a small table and pull back the heavy velvet portieres when I heard the *click* of a door handle; whirling around, my heart once again threatening to burst through my bodice, I saw, through the gloom of the parlor, that it was only Colonel Wood.

"Oh! You startled me! What was that sound?"

"Someone threw a log through the lobby window. Turns out the hotel owner is a Yankee, a New Englander. Just like us."

"Heavens!" Now I began to wonder how we'd get back to the boat through the angry crowd.

"Your appointment canceled. These damn Rebels—I don't know how I'm going to get through to New Orleans by the twelfth. I guess I don't think I can now." The Colonel trudged over to the settee, which was illuminated by that one flickering oil lamp. I could see his face more clearly; in the shadows his eyes appeared hollow, his cheekbones sharp and threatening. He plopped down, removed his hat, and wiped his brow with his sleeve.

"Surely we can get out?" Hesitantly, I stepped toward him. For the first time ever, Colonel Wood appeared truly out of options. Beaten. He seemed too stunned to move, staring into the darkness, his bushy brows drawn together over his sharp nose.

"I don't know. We'll have to make it to Kentucky somehow; that's still neutral territory. Then I'll figure out what to do to salvage the rest of the season. Goddamn it, I wish I could get to New Orleans!"

"But the boat will make a trip upriver, won't it? Whatever repairs you were going to get in New Orleans, they can wait?"

"'Repairs'?" He turned to me, a quizzical expression in his eyes. He blinked twice, as if just now registering my presence. "Repairs? Oh—yes. It ain't the repairs I'm talking about. It's that appointment of yours."

"It can't matter, I'm sure whoever it is doesn't care about me at all, not with all this war talk." I tried to soothe him, for some odd reason; I felt responsible for his agitation, as it was my appointment he was worried about. I found myself placing my hand upon his sleeve before I could even think what I was doing.

He looked at my hand, my small, manicured hand, my nails pink and shiny, my fingers small and delicate. He studied it, and then all of a sudden his face split into a terrifying, wolfish grin; I could see all his back teeth, even in the dim light.

"You don't think he *cares*? You know how much I was going to *charge* for that one? Five hundred dollars, that's what!"

"Five hundred dollars?" I was stunned—too stunned to remove my hand. "Whatever for? Who would want to pay five hundred dollars—it wasn't Mr. Barnum, was it?" My heart quickened, and I looked eagerly into Colonel Wood's amused eyes. They widened, then narrowed; their gaze swept me up and down again, lingering upon my bosom.

"Barnum? Ha! No, it ain't no Barnum. I don't know his damn name—an intermediary contacted me. But he wanted to pay to have you, my tiny cousin. Five hundred dollars, to be the first one to touch those sweet little breasts of yours, to take that sweet little c—"

"Don't!" I shrieked, the word tearing itself from my throat. "Don't say that! Don't!" I put my hands over my ears, the searing, animalistic nature of my fear surprising me. Yet I knew it had always been there, always that quivering, fearful understanding of the true nature of man—and my utter helplessness in the face of it. I had buried it under layers of manners and deportment and denial, but I had carried it deep within me, from the first moment I had stepped foot on his riverboat.

"Listen to her shout! My, my, the famously composed Miss Mercy Lavinia Warren Bump, yelling like a whore!" Colonel Wood laughed, amused by my revulsion. "You know, I didn't understand, at first, these men. Oh, I received many such requests, my dear, you can be sure of it. Men who wanted to touch you, feel you, have you. I thought they were queer, at first, figured they were sick. And maybe they are. But I held out for the highest bidder, and over time I started to understand their—curiosity, shall we call it? I mean, look at you." With a leer, Colonel Wood leaned over me; before I could say a word he had picked me up, my legs dangling helplessly, and flung me down upon the sofa.

I lay there, frozen for a moment, unable to register anything but his hot, hungry breath in my face. Then terror claimed me, but I welcomed it. It surged through me like lightning, giving me strength, propelling my legs to kick out at him and my fists to strike him.

But he easily—oh, God, how easily!—trapped my legs with one knee, gathered both my wrists in one hand and held them over my head. His hot, whiskey-soured breath curdled my skin, moving lower and lower until I felt his mustache tickle my neck. The back of my spine began to quiver, turning to liquid; I felt as if I was going to be sick.

"You're perfect, you know. Tiny, but perfectly formed—why, just look at the way you fill out that dress. I've always wanted to touch 'em, feel 'em, see what they looked like." His breath came in rapid pants, like a dog's, as he placed his huge, grasping hand against the curve of my bodice. He spread his fingers out; his little finger reached the top of my waist, the rest of his hand caressed, so delicately I thought I was imagining it, the swell of my breast. His breath grew ragged then, and I shut my eyes, my ears, and willed my mind to take me somewhere else. Desperately, I tried to summon up images from home, of sweetly babbling brooks and the comforting creak of Mama's rocking chair and Papa's workbench in the barn, where he loved to make things for me and Minnie, little toys and chairs and my stair steps. And then

I saw Minnie, her sweet, angelic face with the black curls drooping over her forehead, her innocent, deep blue eyes, and I began to sob and laugh, both. For I was suddenly glad, glad that it was I who had to endure this, instead of her. If this was the price I had to pay to protect her from men like Colonel Wood, from men like that nameless, faceless ogre in New Orleans who wanted to force themselves upon women like me, like Minnie—I began to imagine the size of him, what it would do to me, it would probably split me in two, and then I wasn't glad. I was terrified, and I began to sob even harder as I felt the fragile cloth of my bodice tear beneath his ugly hands, the soft ripping sound it made a scolding, hushed betrayal.

And then I heard a moan. A soft moan, a bleat, like a little lamb. "Oh," Wood said in quiet surprise, and he fell off me, his eyes first open, then closing with a flutter as weak as the cry he had just uttered.

I looked up. Sylvia was standing before me, my reticule in her hand, an expression of utter amazement on her suddenly beautiful face as she gazed down at Colonel Wood, who was grasping his head, eyes still closed. Then she looked at me.

"You forgot this," she said in that deep rumble of hers that always tickled my eardrums. "You forgot your reticule, and I brought it to you. Also, they're taking the boat. Some men."

"Oh." It was all I could say. I felt for my bodice, fingered the torn cloth, and sought to cover it up; my cheeks were hot and sticky with tears, and in that moment I felt as helpless as a baby. Sylvia reached down to scoop me up, and it would have been bliss to allow her to do so, to carry me back to the boat in her arms, and tuck me into my bed, and sing me songs.

But something inside my soul would not allow it; I struggled to hold on to that feeling, that hot little burst of feeling deep within a place that no Colonel Wood could ever touch. I coaxed it, and finally it propelled me out of my stupor. I stepped over Colonel Wood, who still lay upon the carpet, clutching his head, beginning to curse so that I knew he would recover. I tidied myself up, buttoned my cloak, and patted my hair. Then I turned to Sylvia.

"They're taking the boat?"

"Yes, they say we have to leave, we only have an hour to get our things. How will we get home, Vinnie?"

"Don't worry, I'll think of something. Grab him and drag him back with us." I didn't even glance at Colonel Wood, but I did register Sylvia's deep smile of satisfaction as she reached down and hauled him up by his arm, ignoring his curses and moans. It was the happiest I had seen her in a very long time; we looked at each other and almost burst into laughter before mutually deciding against it.

Then I led us out of the parlor, through the crowded hotel lobby, where, despite the excitement of the evening, people stopped to gape at the sight of the dwarf leading the giant, who was dragging a limp man as if he were made of straw. Then we pushed our way through the frenzied, war-crazed streets of Vicksburg, back toward the *Banjo,* where already members of the troupe were carrying trunks and bags and costumes and piling them up on the dock; Mr. Deacon's swords, wrapped in velvet cloth, were piled next to a wooden crate full of the plate spinner's china.

"Vinnie! Colonel Wood! What happened?" The troupe was upon us as we joined them on the dock; strange men with pistols were standing on the upper deck of the boat, staring at Sylvia and me with open mouths.

"Someone should look after him," I said with a dismissive kick at Colonel Wood, who lay crumpled at my feet where Sylvia had deposited him. "What's going on here?" I shouted at Billy over the sizzle of firecrackers popping in the streets, the far-off boom of what sounded like a canon, and that spectral, high-pitched Rebel yell that even bounced off the water, so that it sounded as if we were surrounded on all sides by banshees. Although, from the strutting, military posturing of the men on the boat and in the streets—they all had red scarves tied around their hats and those who had rifles carried them stiff against their shoulders—I knew what was happening.

"They're commandeering the boat," Billy Birch said. "Taking it over to move troops and munitions. We have to find another way back home. There's a steamer coming here any minute that's going north, but they say it's already full."

"Where's the ticket office?" I looked around; gaslights from the boat illuminated the dock, torches flickered a brilliant orange, as if we were at the very gates of Hell—but just past the boat, the Mississippi loomed blacker than the sky above us.

"Up around the corner, but I already been. That's how I learned it was full. But, Vinnie, I bet you can persuade the agent to let us on. As good as you talk, as little as you are—if anyone can do it, you can."

"All right, I'll go. Come with me, Sylvia." And I turned on my heel and began to walk back up the dock, toward the wild streets, where men were drinking openly, singing a new song, one I'd never heard before but it began, *"Oh, I wish I was in the land of cotton . . ."* It was very catchy, I decided, humming a bit of it.

I was without fear at that moment. I had been saved from Colonel Wood; I had been given a second chance. I detested how physically helpless I had been in his presence; the memory of how I had simply closed my eyes and surrendered myself to fate made my mouth taste sour. I would not be so helpless again, I vowed, not even on this unprecedented night. People needed me. I had a duty to them—and to myself.

But I did pause to tug at Sylvia's skirt. "Thank you," I said as she looked down at me. She nodded, unable to speak. And that's all I ever said to her, and she to me, about what had happened that night. Remarkably, soon it faded into just another thread of the tapestry of my life upon the river, just another story remembered. But this one, I told to only one person. And he never repeated it.

It will come as no surprise to the Reader—as it came as no surprise to me—that I succeeded in getting all of us out of Vicksburg. Once at the ticket office, I climbed upon a chair and spoke to the agent face-to-face; I told him of our dilemma, of our desire to get back to our homes, to our families who had been parted from us for so long. I informed him of the many dignitaries—including Jefferson Davis, at that time only a senator from Mississippi—whom I had met in my personal appearances. And just for good measure, I invited him to plant a kiss upon my cheek, the one and only time I ever did so to a strange man, until I met President Lincoln.

But that was to come much, much later, when my life was changed so that had I not still had my beloved stair steps, made by my father's own hand, the tread worn smooth in the middle, I never would have recognized it. For the present I was still the one, the only Dwarf Girl This Side of the Alleghenies, pleading for passage home.

Finally the ticket agent relented, and, with tickets in hand, Sylvia and I went back to the dock, where we spent the night beneath the stars and burning torches, the gunshots and firecrackers only diminishing once the sun came up. The steamer arrived early the next morning, and soon we all—including Colonel Wood, whom I could not simply leave behind, no matter how tempting the thought—were on our way to Louisville. There we disbanded with tearful goodbyes.

Except for Colonel Wood; he slunk off in the confusion of

sorting out our baggage, crying out, "You all still have contracts with me! This ain't no act of God—it's an act of war, and I'm tacking that time onto your contracts!"

"Let 'im try," Billy Birch muttered. "Let 'im try to find me. I'm enlisting first chance I get—do you think that bastard will?" We all laughed at the notion.

Sylvia and I journeyed together as far as Boston. From there, she took one train north, and I another south. When we disembarked from the train, snow was beginning to fall; big, gentle flakes, welcoming me back home.

Sylvia bent to hug me tearfully; she actually fell upon her knees, even though I knew how much that must have hurt her. I asked her what she was going to do.

"I don't know," she said as tears fell, slowly as ever, upon her mammoth cheeks. For once she did not notice the strange looks and whispers we attracted. Her sorrow and uncertainty were too apparent, even though I knew she was relieved to be headed home. "I thought my mother might tell me in a dream, but I haven't slept well these last few nights."

"Who has?" I smiled, patting her on the back. Then a thought occurred to me; I didn't know why I hadn't figured it out sooner. "Sylvia!" I exclaimed, so excitedly that she nearly knocked me over in her surprise. "That's it—I know what you can do and still stay at home in Wilton! You talk so often of seeing your mother in dreams. Why don't you become a spiritualist? You're so sympathetic, I know you'll help any number of people who have lost dear ones."

"A spiritualist? I don't know, Vinnie. . . ."

"Sylvia, you're lonely. This would be good for you, and you'd never have to leave home again. Why, people will come to see you from everywhere! And I promise I'll help, in any way I can. I'll write to all my friends and tell everyone I meet." Little did either of us realize how many, many people I would meet in the coming years—and how happy I would be to learn that Sylvia was able to make a decent living because of them, because of me.

The stationmaster called out that the train to Maine was about to leave.

"Vinnie, you've helped me so much already. You're the only friend I've ever had. Write me, won't you?"

"Of course." Sylvia got up, tears still rolling down those granite cheekbones, but before she walked away, I called out to her.

"Wait! Sylvia, will you do—will you do one thing for me?"

"Anything, Vinnie. Anything you want."

"Will you—will you pick me up and hold me high? I always wanted to see the world the way you see it. I want to see how different your view is from mine."

Sylvia smiled, then picked me up carefully, holding me in her arms so that my feet did not dangle. She lifted me up so that my face was level with hers. And then we turned to look at the world.

I could see roads leading away from the station, snow-blanketed, peaceful ribbons of roads, leading to places unknown. I could see the tops of buildings, the rooflines, the chimneys. I could see over people's heads, so that I was looking down upon them; how insignificant they all looked, how ordinary! The tops of hats were flat and round; the tops of bonnets were thin and worn, catching snowflakes in the creases.

I could see all the way to the end of the train platforms, my view unobstructed by legs and skirts and trunks and poles. From here, the distance between train and platform appeared small and manageable—not the wide, terrifying chasm that I experienced, fearful of missing the platform altogether and rolling onto the track, where I could be crushed.

Yet for all I could see, nothing was as grand as how I'd imagined it. Nothing was as big as my dreams.

"You can put me down now," I told Sylvia, whose blue eyes were full of tears, huge tears—tears as big as her heart. She did, and then she grabbed her two valises, which looked like toys in her hands. I waved as she lumbered along the narrow wooden platform. I knew I would never forget her.

Turning, I made my way to my own platform, after paying a porter to carry my trunk and stand by to lift me onto the train. I was back home by the next morning—dreaming my big dreams in the comfort of my own dear feather bed, my sister's happy, contented face nestled into my shoulder, her arms tight around me, binding me to her. She whispered that I was never to leave her again.

But I knew, even before I drifted off to sleep, the grime of travel still upon me like a second skin, that I would.

INTERMISSION

From *Godey's Lady's Book,* September 1860—Sara J. Hale

This year the **last Thursday in November** falls on the 29th. If all the States and Territories hold their Thanksgiving on that day, there will be a complete moral and social reunion of the **people** of America in 1860. Would not this be a good omen for the perpetual political union of the States? May God grant us not only the omen, but the fulfillment is our dearest wish!

From *Harper's Weekly,* January 19, 1861

Secession of Mississippi, Florida, and Alabama

The Mississippi State Convention on 8th adopted an ordinance providing for immediate secession from the Union. Reports from Jackson, the capital of Mississippi, confirm this news. On 10th, Florida seceded by 62 to 7. On 11th, Alabama seceded by 61 to 39.

[FIVE]

Another Brief Interlude of Music and Tender Reunion

VINNIE, WHAT ARE YOU DOING?"

"Nothing!" I whisked the paper off my desk and tucked it inside my apron pocket, placing the pen in the ink bottle so forcibly the ink splattered. Then I massaged my hand; no pen was small or light enough for me to use easily, and my fingers and palm often ached when I wrote long letters. Turning to greet my sister, I smiled broadly. "Just writing to an old friend! What do you want, Pumpkin?"

"Mama said to come down for dinner," Minnie said with a scolding frown; I couldn't help but smile at her. How serious she had grown in my absence! She was now twelve, almost a young woman, although her body had not filled out as much as mine; she still looked quite childish, even in long skirts, and she came up to only my chin. This impression was not helped by the fact that she continued to play with dolls. But her manner was much more serious, even as her deep brown eyes retained their incongruous twinkle. Her thick black brows were often drawn over her nose in a suspicious frown. Papa joked that Minnie was the family inquisitor, judge and jury all wrapped up into one—although her distrust reminded me more of a child's resistance to change.

"Are you sure that was what you were doing?" she asked, folding her arms suspiciously across her flat chest; I decided I ought to introduce her to ruffled corset covers. Carlotta had taught me that trick.

"Absolutely—just writing an old friend!" I slid off the cushions of the chair, pushed it back toward the writing desk, and followed Minnie out of our room.

"Then I don't know why you'd try to hide the letter, Vinnie. Why would you?"

"Why, I didn't! Would you like to read it, if you don't trust me?" I tucked my hand inside my apron, as if to show it to her.

"No, no, I didn't mean that!" Her eyes grew big with remorse as her face paled. "Forgive me, Vinnie! I'm sorry! I do trust you, more than anyone in the world!" And her little rosebud lips trembled as she fought back tears.

I put my arm about her as we made our way down the narrow back stairs—more shallowly spaced than the front stairs, and so the ones that Minnie and I used the most—and into the kitchen. My dear, simple little sister! Every mood so fleeting yet so obvious; there was no mystery to Minnie, none at all. She loved whom she knew, distrusted everyone else, and shared her emotions, her thoughts, as freely as they occurred to her. I remembered how I had promised myself I would come for her and take her with me on my adventures; I knew, now, what a selfish notion that had been. Minnie must not leave home and experience the things I had; this was where she belonged, safe and loved and hidden from people like Colonel Wood. I could not reclaim my own innocence. And so she must keep hers, remaining unspoiled for the both of us.

"What are you sorry about, my chick?" Mama was placing platters of stewed meat, covered in bubbling gravy and topped with airy dumplings, upon the linen tablecloth; my stomach growled in anticipation. I had been home for nearly a year, yet I had not tired of Mama's delicious cooking.

It was December of 1861, and the War that had started so vividly and personally for me was being fought in bloody earnest all across the South. I had spent so much time there, seeing it only as a place where simple people were eager to be entertained, just like their brethren up north, that I had a difficult time thinking of them as the enemy.

But two of my brothers were now in Yankee blue, so I could not be neutral. Benjamin had been the first to enlist, joining up with the Massachusetts Volunteer Militia even before I came home. I missed his presence keenly; I still felt pain at the way we had parted. I needed to know that he was not ashamed of me.

Both he and James, who joined up as soon as the first bullets were fired on Fort Sumter in April, were now in Virginia, so very far away to Mama and Papa—a foreign country, almost! But not to me. I could mentally calculate how quickly I could get there; I knew by heart the train timetables, where you had to get off and take a ferry across the Chesapeake, then get back on the train again. I had spent a good amount of time at the station in Middleborough, poring over the schedules and maps of trains leaving for all destinations. I couldn't help myself. I was drawn to the train station like a fly to a cow patty. I became obsessed in my need to study every method of travel available, to follow the debate in the newspaper about the possibility of building a train clear across our great nation, from Atlantic to Pacific. I had no plans to leave home again, as of yet; I simply hungered to know how easily I could do so. This knowledge gave me peace, where my parents' clucking and soothing did not.

"I'm sorry that I almost made Vinnie show me the letter she was writing," Minnie said with a shy, apologetic smile as she took her seat, piled high with cushions, one more than mine. "Now, Papa, take the best piece for yourself, as you work the hardest!" And Minnie tucked her napkin into her collar and waited patiently to be served.

"Thank you, Miss, I certainly will," Papa said with a serious nod, although his eyes twinkled. "Do you want me to post that letter for you, Vinnie?" he asked as he began to pass around the plates. "I have to go into town tomorrow."

"No—I, that is, thank you. But I thought I might get some exercise and walk into town myself. I can post it then." I took my own seat, across from Minnie.

"I would never walk to town by myself!" She shook her head decidedly. "Think of all those houses and buildings you have to walk past—how dreadful! And people do talk so. You're so brave, Vinnie!"

I wanted to laugh, given what I had endured upon the river. But my sister's admiration was pure and heartfelt, and I never wished to hurt her feelings.

"Minnie's right, it is a long walk for you, Vinnie, and you know how those wagon ruts can trip you up," Mama began, automatically. But when she caught my eye, she stopped.

"You sure you want to go all that way by yourself?" Papa asked, but he did not meet my gaze. Unlike Mama, he asked out of courtesy alone; he knew too well I would make my own mind up and do as I pleased. He did not enjoy knowing this, he did not approve of it, but he allowed it. As he had ever since I returned home.

"Yes, Papa, I do want to go alone. Anyway, I can use the exercise, for Mama's cooking is making my dresses too tight! Soon enough I will look like Mrs. Lincoln, just as people say I do!" I laughed at the joke, happy to deflect interest from my letter. Since the Lincolns had gone to the White House, many people had commented on my likeness to the President's wife.

"Oh, no, Vinnie! You're much more beautiful than that plain Mrs. Lincoln. She has the most awful way of doing her hair, not fashionable at all." Minnie spoke with such disdain that the rest of us couldn't help but laugh. Since when did Minnie concern herself with fashionable coiffures? I tried to imagine my little sister poring over *Godey's Lady's Book,* and failed.

We continued our meal without further inquiries into my letter-writing habits. Although twice I caught Papa looking my way with his eyes scrunched up, as if he was trying to get a good read on me.

He was still trying to figure me out.

THE NEXT MORNING I BUNDLED UP IN A CLOAK AND MITTENS and stout boots. It had been a mild December for Massachusetts; the lanes were not piled high with snow. The sun was shining, and I soon warmed up as I walked the short distance toward town. I enjoyed being alone; ever since I had returned home, I had found myself craving such solitude.

Everything had changed since my return. My family treated me differently, gingerly, as if I might break, or worse—as if I might leave them again. At first they had peppered me with questions, but soon they realized they didn't really know what to ask; they had no comprehension of the details of my life those three eventful years. They knew only that it was very different from theirs. I produced my clippings and told of meeting people like the Grants. I spoke lovingly of Sylvia, and the rest of the troupe. (Carlotta I decided not to mention.)

I did not speak of Colonel Wood. At first they asked all about him, but soon they picked up on my reluctance to mention his name and ceased their questioning.

My family loved me, welcomed me, yet frequently I felt like a guest in my own home. I caught Papa looking at me at times with something close to shyness, as if he did not quite recognize me. And I felt the strangeness myself; the farm was so quiet, my family so loving and good, it all seemed dreamlike, almost. As if I would wake up and find myself back on the river, the hard, pulsing *life* of the river; that felt, now, like the most real time of my life. The bad things that had happened soon receded from memory. I remembered only the excitement, the ever-changing scenery, the cheerful camaraderie of my fellow performers, the elegance of the hotels contrasted with the wildness of the audience—oh, to think of it all made me want to throw my clothes in a valise, grab my cloak, and run out of the house! It made me long to cast off all possessions so that I might always be ready to leave at a moment's notice.

Recalling that life also made me pick up my pen and compose the letter I was determined to post today. The letter was bulky; I had included a number of my press clippings and, of course, my *carte de visite,* which I had inscribed. The address on the outside, which I had copied so carefully from a newspaper article, read as follows:

MR. PHINEAS TAYLOR BARNUM
The American Museum, corner of Ann Street and Broadway
New York, New York

The letter was sealed with a dollop of wax, hard and cold as a button against my thumb. Despite my eagerness to post it, I took my time on this walk; I was in no hurry to get back home, where nothing ever changed. I had no purpose, no task, but to rise early with the family; help Mama with sewing, cleaning, cooking; keep Minnie company and try to improve her mind with reading and conversation; rock her to sleep at night before rolling over to my side of our little bed, where I tried, unsuccessfully, to sleep. But these days sleep did not come easily to me. Try as I might to tire myself with long walks and endless turns at the spinning wheel, I was never as physically exhausted—every joint throbbing, the arches of my feet aching, even my tongue worn out from constant conversation—as I had been after two or three performances a day, not including private audiences.

I couldn't even go back to teaching if I wanted to; the school committee had engaged someone else in my absence.

The trees were bare, the limbs like splayed fingers against the vivid blue sky. It was so quiet, just a few birds rustling in evergreens, a far-off echo of an ax chopping wood. How loud my life on the Mississippi had been! Never was there complete quiet on the steamboat; there was always someone singing a song, laughing at a joke, telling a story. The steady hum of the engines, the constant swish of the river's currents—all had filled my ears for so long that I found the quiet of home jarring. My nerves thrummed in anticipation for some unexpected, unpredictable noise or diversion.

I wandered along the lane, which was crisscrossed with the occasional cow path leading off toward other farms, watching out for the deep wagon ruts, so much trouble for one my size. Too soon did I reach town, where the streets were sparsely populated by people who no longer knew how to think about me.

Since coming home, I had realized that when the school committee appointed me as a schoolteacher years earlier, it wasn't entirely for my welfare. Giving me a title, a job, gave the town a way to look at me that was easy; it meant that they did not have to think about my size, first thing, each time they encountered me. Miss Bump, the teacher, was a much easier thing to consider than Miss Bump, that poor little woman. But I had angered them by rejecting their neat package and leaving to go out west. I had shocked them by performing on a boat. Now I was gazed at, whispered about, more pointedly than I ever had been out west, even when I had paraded around with Sylvia.

Mrs. Putnam, the minister's wife, stopped to observe me as she exited the dry goods store.

"Good morning," I called out pleasantly.

"Oh!" She looked around to see if there was anyone observing us; there was, but she was trapped. "Well, good morning, Miss Bump." She sniffed and looked down her long nose at me. "What a surprise to see you out and about this early."

"A surprise? Why is that?" I smiled up at her; her bonnet was as plain and red as her face. The people of Middleborough looked so *ordinary* to me now. *She could use some of Carlotta's paint,* I thought wickedly, stifling a giggle.

"Why, I'm sure I don't know, I just supposed that you were used to sleeping late back on that showboat of yours. It's a mercy to see you up at a good Christian hour."

"But I saw many a sunrise out west," I protested with a sweet, pious smile.

"You did?"

"Of course! Many a sunrise I saw as I came home after a late night of carousing and unseemly behavior!"

"Why, Lavinia Bump! I never—the wickedness! The shame!" The old woman sputtered and hissed like a cat in heat as she hurried off to be swallowed up by a small band of other churchwomen, all of whom muttered and looked over their shoulders at me.

I tilted my chin and met their collective gaze evenly; they

looked away, still buzzing with disapproval. I didn't care. I was even a bit tickled by my impertinence, although I did hope it wouldn't cause Papa or Mama any grief later. But my spirits were lightened, as well as my step, and soon I was at the post office. It was located at the main intersection of the town, called the Four Corners; the streets that comprised this area housed most of the commerce of the village—dry goods stores, a millinery, lawyer and physician offices, the building where workers toiled at the large shoe manufacturer. Middleborough wasn't a small town, not by New England standards. Yet after the dirty, humid, colorful excitement that was New Orleans or St. Louis, it was so staid and sleepy to me, all the same. Everything here was so stolid; nothing ever changed. Certainly we had no streets dedicated solely to vice!

I knocked politely on the post office door; the handle was too high and heavy for me to reach. Mr. Jones, the clerk, opened the door, peered out over my head for a moment, then looked down. He smiled in recognition. I couldn't help but notice his pants were worn thin at the knees, like those of the good working New England man he was; he would get a new pair for Christmas, just coming up.

"Well, hello, Miss Lavinia. Come on in."

"Thank you," I replied, following him inside; I waited for him to raise the hinged section that allowed him to go behind the counter, although I had to reflect how easily I could have passed beneath it! Then I reached up and handed him my letter, along with thirty cents for postage.

"All the way to New York?" Mr. Jones looked at the address. "Phineas Taylor Barnum? Who's he—not that humbug feller, I hope?"

I sighed. I should have realized that of course Mr. Jones would make it his business to see where my letter was going; of course he would end up telling my parents or my brothers or my married sister or whichever member of my annoyingly large family he might encounter. Which he was sure to do.

"No, of course not," I said with a sniff, as if to indicate I was insulted he might suggest such a thing. "This is about some unfinished business of mine, from out west."

"Oh." Mr. Jones pulled on his chin, lengthening his already sorrowfully long New England face—sharp nose, suspicious eyes, permanently ruddy complexion. "Yes, that business out west of yours. Well, we're glad to have you back here safe and sound. I reckon you're glad to be back, too. Don't like to think of a little lady like you out there consorting with those types of people."

I simply smiled and watched as he took my letter and placed it in the leather mail pouch. Then I asked after his children (who had been students of mine), thanked him, and asked him to open the door for me.

I began my walk back to the farm, after first stopping to purchase a stick of peppermint candy for Minnie, who would be anxious for my return. So would Papa and Mama. They would welcome me home with loving eyes, kind hearts, open—yet stifling—arms.

My thoughts returned to the letter I had just posted. I wished that I could give it wings.

INTERMISSION

From *Harper's Weekly,* March 22,1862

The crisis which the war has reached imparts fresh interest to the war-pictures which are appearing in every number of *Harper's Weekly.* We have now regular Artist Correspondents, to wit:

Mr. A. R. WAUD, with the army of the Potomac; MR. ALEXANDER SIMPLOT, with Gen. Grant's Army; MR. HENRY MOSLER, with Gen. Buell's army; MR. THEO. R. DAVIS, with Gen. Sherman's army; MR. ANGELO WISER, with Gen. Burnside's army; besides a large number of occasional and volunteer correspondents in the Army and Navy at various points. These gentlemen will furnish us faithful sketches of every battle which takes place, and every other event of interest, which will be reproduced in our pages in the best style. People who do not see *Harper's Weekly* will have but a limited comprehension of the momentous events which are occurring.

From *The Defiance Democrat,* Defiance County, Ohio, May 31, 1862

The New Mormon Complication

Brigham Young has been inaugurated as the Governor of the New State of Desert, and Mr. Ashley's bill for the punishment of polygamy has passed the House of Representatives. Here is a conflict at our doors at once. The Mormons have organized their state government with polygamy as "the corner-stone" just as slavery is the corner-stone of the Confederates. . . . Brigham's wants, like his wives, are many.

[SIX]

At Last I Meet the Great Man Himself

"OH, GOODNESS!" MAMA EXCLAIMED AS SHE OPENED HER reticule and removed a clean yellow handkerchief, which seemed to turn to a sooty gray before our eyes. "The dirt! Vinnie, my chick, however did you manage on those trains out west with all this dirt?"

"I didn't," I admitted, bouncing about on the uncomfortable wooden seat, barely able to see out the window to my right, but it didn't matter; it was smeared with the same sooty gray as Mama's handkerchief. "I was filthy when I got to the boat."

"These contraptions are no place for a lady," Mama muttered, pressing the handkerchief to the inner corner of her eye, trying to remove some minuscule piece of dirt, although it wouldn't make a difference; her cheeks had smudges on them, as well.

Papa sat next to me with his eyes squeezed shut; the moment the train had pulled out of the station in Middleborough, he had paled. Upon my suggestion that he look at the scenery, beginning to pass by ever faster, he turned decidedly green. From that moment on, he had refused to open his eyes or move his head; he sat as straight and stiff as a corpse against the hard back of his seat. I patted his hand in sympathy; his occasional squeeze was the sole indication I had that he had not passed on to the Great Beyond.

I was sorry for him, but even that could not dampen my excitement, excitement that had been building ever since that fateful afternoon a month ago when a Mr. Fuller had sent word—by telegram! We had never seen such a thing!—that, acting on behalf of Mr. Phineas Taylor Barnum, he, Mr. Fuller, would very much like to meet me.

Oh, the stir this simple message caused! Mama began cleaning right away, even as she and Papa argued with me about the obvious intent of the coming visit. Did I have any idea what I might be getting myself into? Why couldn't I just stay home like the rest of their children? (Although when I pointed out that two of their sons were soldiers, they pretended not to hear.) Did I have no heart in me? Had I so enjoyed being surrounded by morally depraved show people that I was eager to escape the bosom of a Christian home to take up with them again? And that Barnum? That master of humbug! What might he do, in my name, in the good name of this good family, to dupe the public once more?

And most frequently asked of all the questions my parents hurtled at me, when they weren't tidying and scrubbing and consoling Minnie, who flew into tears at the thought of another stranger coming to take me away—

How? How on earth had he heard of me? It had been almost two years since I had made my escape from the clutches of Colonel Wood (they made it sound so dramatic, I wondered if they pictured me running barefoot through a swamp just like Eliza in *Uncle Tom's Cabin,* pursued by alligators, show folk, and Rebel soldiers) and come back, safe and sound, so they didn't have to worry about me any longer. How had that Barnum (for this was how they began to refer to him, "*that Barnum,*" as if he had no other Christian name) heard of me in that time?

Naturally, I declined to join in this last speculation. For of course I knew: I was the one who had told him. That letter I mailed back in December—that had been my ticket out into the world, I dearly hoped.

And so it would seem to have proved. Mr. Fuller duly arrived; we chatted in the parlor (where I tried very hard to push away the memory of Colonel Wood's fateful visit). I showed him my press clippings, the letters written to me by many a fine citizen of the West. I saved the most distinguished letter for last; in this late summer of 1862, any mention of Mr. Grant, with whom I had passed such a charming hour in Galena, was extremely impressive, indeed. After the Battle of Fort Donelson, when he had demanded "unconditional and immediate surrender" of the Rebel troops, Major General Ulysses S. Grant had become a household name. I could see that Mr. Fuller was very taken by my account of that visit and the letter of thanks, in Mrs. Grant's hand, that had reached me on the boat.

Mr. Fuller departed with no indication of what he felt about me and my clippings, which worried me, even as it enabled Mama and Papa to cease their fretting. But Mr. Fuller must have made a favorable report to Mr. Barnum, for the former was soon back again, armed this time with a contract. At this point Mama and Papa began to protest even more forcibly. In the most polite language—and while simultaneously serving Mr. Fuller some of her most delicate shortbread cookies and tea—Mama made it known that she did not trust Mr. Barnum's reputation for telling lies to the public, as she saw it.

"Perhaps we should meet Mr. Barnum himself," I finally suggested, in desperation. "For I believe only he can put my parents' minds at ease."

Mr. Fuller grumbled and departed again, contract unsigned but still in my possession; days later we received an invitation from Mr. Barnum to visit him in his home in Bridgeport, Connecticut. Thus it was that we three were on the train going west.

There was one more obstacle in the way, one more potentially dire than my parents' objections, and one that I kept to myself: I was still technically under contract to Colonel Wood. After he had crept away in Louisville, I tried to assure myself that I would see him no more. Yet I couldn't trust him, even though, for all I knew, the Colonel might be in the army, or a prisoner of war, or even dead, as thousands were, more and more every day. Although I disliked imagining that evil man clad in the glory of Yankee blue, just like my brothers.

"Do you think that Barnum will meet us at the station?" Mama fretted, patting her graying bun that peeked out of the back of her bonnet, so tightly wound and secured that no amount of train travel could disturb it.

"Mama, please, I beg of you, try to refrain from calling him 'that Barnum.'"

"Mercy Lavinia Warren Bump, you know that I will address him in the most polite manner! Who do you think I am? Is this why you're so eager to leave home again? Are you so ashamed of us?" Mama's eyes began to water and tears rolled down her cheeks, leaving an oily trail of grime.

I sighed and handed her my unspoiled handkerchief. "No, Mama, of course not. I'm sorry—I'm just a trifle nervous, you see. I do so want to make a good impression."

"You have no need to be nervous about that," Mama replied with a sniff. "*He's* the one who should be worried about making a good impression on *us*. He's just a showman. You're a descendent of one of the Mayflower Company!"

"Yes, Mama." I had to smile; my mother's righteous anger at the idea of a man such as *that Barnum* having to impress the Bump family was so powerful that it dried her tears and caused her to sit up so straight, her spine was a good six inches away from the back of the seat.

We passed the rest of the journey mostly in silence, after changing trains in Providence. It was late afternoon before we pulled into the Bridgeport station.

As we disembarked—Papa, his color returning to his usual ruddy hue, gently lifting me off the train onto the platform—a liveried coachman approached. He was clad in a dusky red driving jacket and a tall silk hat; when he reached us, he bowed smartly.

"Miss Bump?" He looked down at me, yet his face betrayed no surprise or amusement at my size.

"Yes?"

"With Mr. Barnum's regards, Miss, I'm to take you and your family to Lindencroft in the carriage. Please come this way." And he turned; we followed him through the crowded station to a waiting open carriage. It was black, polished to a gleam so high that we could see our reflections in it, with brass handles and hinges, a fine pair of chestnut horses, their harnesses also polished and gleaming in the sun. Papa handed me up into the carriage and we all settled in. The coachman climbed atop his perch and coaxed the horses into motion.

"What do you think so far, Mama?" I couldn't help myself, but Mama had been so quiet ever since the coachman had greeted us. I knew she was impressed.

"I think Mr. Barnum affords a lovely carriage" was all she would allow.

Papa nodded, passing his hand over the seat next to him. "Real leather," he said in tones usually reserved for church. "And them horses—a matched pair!"

I smiled and turned my attention to the streets of Bridgeport. We quickly passed through the business section and soon found ourselves on wide streets lined with gracious homes, bigger than any we had back in Middleborough. These were newer, in the more modern architectural style featuring ornately scrolled embellishments, cupolas, wide porches, two and even three stories high, all set back from the street on enormous, beautifully tended lawns. I glimpsed large carriage houses—some larger than our farmhouse!—set far back from the street. Occasionally we passed land set aside as parks, with well-tended gardens, gazebos, and benches.

As we passed so many houses, each one seemingly grander than the one before, I sensed that the coachman was taking us down the most picturesque streets. Mama's constant exclamations of "Oh, my," and Papa's involuntary utterances of "Will you look at that?" were growing wearisome to me; as impressed as I was by the beautiful homes and streets of Bridgeport, they were not the reason I had come.

"That house there, to the right, is the home of Mr. Charles Stratton himself. Or as you may know him, Tom Thumb," the coachman called over his shoulder, slowing the horses down to a stately walk. As this was the one time he had pointed out a home's ownership, I was suddenly very sure that he had driven this way deliberately.

Papa and Mama both twisted in their seats to get a better look. I remained where I was for a moment, impatience to reach our destination rooting me to my seat. But finally I, too, turned to look.

It was a fine home. That was all I would say for it at the moment. It was three stories with a cupola, a wide lawn, an inviting porch. It was very grand, very big, and if I was meant to be impressed by it and by the implication that if I signed with Mr. Barnum I, too, might one day live on such an estate, I suppose I was.

But I was also annoyed by this transparent sales technique. I felt it in poor taste. Turning back around, I instructed the driver, curtly, to please continue to Mr. Barnum's home.

"Yes, Miss," he said apologetically. Then he flicked the reins and we trotted off again. Ten minutes later we pulled into a gated circular drive, the coachman saying, with unmistakable pride in his tone, "Welcome to Lindencroft."

We had driven up to a set of granite stepping-stones so tall, I could exit the carriage without assistance. Once I alighted, I shook my skirts out—dust flying everywhere, fine grains captured in the sunlight—and surveyed my surroundings. The lawn was manicured, with a circular pool embellished with a statue of Poseidon in the middle. The house itself was grand but not ostentatious; I'd certainly seen larger, more elaborate homes on the drive over.

It was built of buff-colored stone, three stories high, with ornately carved cornices. A deep porch was framed by columns, and wide marble steps led up to the imposing front door.

Mama and Papa didn't say a word; none of us had ever been to a house this fine before, but somehow I felt they looked to me to take the lead. Both hung back just a little; I felt their country shyness acutely, and resolved to ease their minds.

"This way," I said with determination. And I walked up the porch steps—rather steep for me, but I would not falter—and motioned for Papa to tug the velvet rope hanging to the right of the door; when he did, a deep gong sounded.

"Well, I never!" He stepped back in alarm, dropping the rope as if it had scorched his hands.

"It's only a bell to summon the maid," I told my father, although I did not know how I knew that. I simply did.

Sure enough, an aproned and capped young woman opened the door; I gave her our names, and she ushered us inside to the cool interior. We blinked at the sudden change in light; inside the house, all was dark: darkly paneled walls, polished wooden floors, shutters and drapes keeping out the summer heat.

"I'll show you to a room where you can freshen up," the maid whispered to Mama and me; Mama clutched my arm gratefully, for I knew she was worried about her disheveled appearance. After showing Papa into one of the rooms opening up to the main hall, the maid led us up a grand staircase, kindly slowing her steps to accommodate mine; she ushered us into a bedroom where pitchers of water, basins, and the finest of linen towels and cloths were waiting on a shining dressing table arrayed with pins, hairbrushes, and a clothes brush. She withdrew, and Mama and I fell upon the water as if we'd just been rescued from the desert, washing our faces, our hands, tidying up our hair, brushing each other's dresses off. Mama pointed to a stool that had been placed strategically in front of the dressing table so that I could reach everything myself.

"How thoughtful!" she whispered, as if afraid someone might overhear. I tried not to smile at her nervousness, which had the effect of making my own disappear. "Should we tidy the room up?" she asked when we had finished our toilettes. She glanced nervously at the towels, which were no longer snowy white; the water in the basin was now a soupy gray.

"No," I said; once again, I did not know how I knew that. But I did. Ever since we'd stepped foot in that magnificent carriage, I had instinctively known how to behave among such riches. My parents, however, did not; never had I seen them so unsure of themselves. I could not imagine either of them happily living in a mansion; Mama would wear herself out scrubbing all those marble floors, for she would never trust anyone else to clean them!

That did not mean, however, that I could not imagine living in a mansion myself. As we left the room, refreshed and presentable, the maid led us back down the wide carpeted staircase. With each step I felt my spine straighten, my head lift itself upon my neck until my chin was almost pointed straight up to the ceiling. I imagined myself in a Parisian ball gown—in a properly fitting corset!—descending a staircase like this to greet my guests. Despite the huge proportions of this house—the ceilings enormously tall, the woodwork deep, the windowpanes more expansive than any I'd ever seen—I did not feel overwhelmed. Rather, I felt every inch a great lady, expanding to match the generosity of her surroundings.

We were ushered into a library, where Papa was already seated next to a fireplace flanked by bookshelves; the polished grate was empty save for an enormous Oriental fan. He had a cigar in his hand, which he handled as gingerly as if it might suddenly turn into a snake and bite him. As soon as he saw Mama and me, he dropped it—fortunately, it was not lit—and shot from his chair.

"Vinnie!" he cried out in obvious relief; he said my name as if he had given up hope of ever saying it again.

"So this is the famously contrary Miss Bump, who would not sign her contract until she met me herself." Another voice rang out; it was a wry, humorous voice. I heard laughter lurking behind it, kept just barely at bay.

From the depths of a high-backed wing chair, a man rose. He was a tall man; taller than Papa, who was not short. He had large hands, a fleshy nose, high forehead with luxurious graying curls, and bushy eyebrows. His lips were rather thin, held together in a crooked line that gave him a very whimsical look. His eyes, beneath those eyebrows, were piercing gray and alert, the most watchful eyes I'd ever seen. They were kindly, however: observant, wary, yet kindly. I sensed a light behind them, a twinkle that—like the laughter in his voice—was never far from the surface yet held firmly in check.

"I am Miss Bump," I said, crossing toward this man and extending my hand without hesitation. "And am I to believe you are the equally famous Mr. Barnum?"

"That I am, that I am, indeed." He took my hand solemnly, shook it, then suddenly bent down to peer directly into my face. His eyes were level with mine, so close that I could see myself reflected in them, and I had the startling, dizzy impression of a carnival, of colors and sounds and mirrors of every shape and size; of music, joyous, merry music tooted from horns and plucked by fiddles. How one man's gaze could engage so many senses, I had no idea; I only knew his did. It nearly knocked the breath out of me; my heart did a riotous somersault as the back of my neck tickled with excitement, and I fought an undignified urge to giggle.

However, I managed to keep my composure. I looked back at him, meeting him halfway; for a long moment our gazes held. I do not know what he saw in mine, but it appeared to satisfy him; with a businesslike nod, he straightened up, shook hands with my mother, then motioned for us to take a seat. One chair had a footstool placed strategically in front of it; I knew it had been placed there for me.

Once we were all seated, Mr. Barnum rang a silver bell; another maid appeared, and he asked for lemonade and cookies to be served. I felt Mama approved of this, as she smiled in genuine pleasure and relaxed a fraction, just enough so that I did not fear she might break into brittle little pieces if she moved too quickly.

"Did you have a pleasant journey?" Mr. Barnum asked my father.

"Well, I guess. Nothing bad happened, anyway. But I'm not

looking forward to the return home." Papa picked up the dropped cigar and held it, once again, at arm's length. I knew he did not approve of cigars, only pipes.

"This was my parents' first train journey," I explained to Mr. Barnum, who nodded in sympathy.

"Oh, I remember my first trip! Like to have scared the daylights out of me, all the noise and steam and speed. Nothing beats the old horse and buggy, does it, Mr. Bump?"

"No, sirree, not by a long shot!" My father smiled for the first time since we left Middleborough; relaxing, he dropped the cigar in a cut-glass ashtray and left it there.

"But now, why—can't get along without it! I couldn't keep up with my business if I didn't take the train into New York every day!"

"Every day? You take the train every day?" Papa looked at him in horror.

"Can't deny it! Every weekday morning, just about, ol' William—that's the coachman—takes me to the station, and I take the train into New York, then I walk to my museum. I take the train home at night, and William drives me back here. Very efficient—and I don't have to live in the city anymore. I can't imagine living anyplace but Bridgeport now—my wife's health, you know, requires rest and sea air."

"I'm so sorry," Mama murmured automatically, but Mr. Barnum merely waved his hand.

"'Tis nothing new to me; Charity has long been prone to sickness. I tire her out, that's the thing; it takes a lot out of a woman to keep up with me!" And Mr. Barnum laughed, as if it were truly nothing, but behind his eyes that little light wavered a bit.

The maid brought in a tray with tall frosty glasses of lemonade and plates of delicate sugar cookies; she served them all around, then left the tray and silently retired.

"Now, let's get to the point of this. I understand you don't think very highly of me." Mr. Barnum spoke to my father, although I felt as if he was really addressing my mother. He turned to Papa, but his eyes looked at her.

"Oh, my, well, I never intended to be rude!" Mama was very flustered—but she was the one who answered, as Papa chose that moment to conveniently stuff a cookie into his mouth.

"Not rude, just prudent," Mr. Barnum replied cheerfully, with an understanding nod. He sat back in his chair and folded his arms across his chest—an attitude I would soon grow to know very well. It was an attitude of waiting—waiting for someone to give him the answer that he sought. Rarely was he left waiting for long.

"Yes, prudent, of course!" Mama nodded vigorously. "You see, Vinnie—Lavinia—is our eldest daughter left at home, and naturally we worry about her. We are quite an old family, you know—the Warrens from Massachusetts; five of my ancestors came over on the *Mayflower*." Mama smiled in that prim way she had whenever she spoke of her ancestry.

"You don't say?" Mr. Barnum's eyebrows raised and his eyes narrowed intently. He appeared to be filing this information away, for what purpose my mother of course could not suspect—but I did, and I smiled to myself, nibbling daintily at a cookie.

"So naturally we have concerns about her future," Mama continued. "We want only what is proper and dignified for Lavinia and for our family."

"Naturally." Mr. Barnum sat for a second, apparently deep in thought. The room was silent, save for the sound of my father nervously clearing his throat. "Yet you had no qualms about letting her travel about the Mississippi on a rowboat?"

Mama gasped, and Papa, who had been uneasily silent until now, said, "See here!"

Mr. Barnum merely smiled, turning to me for the first time

in this conversation. And then he sat back, his arms still folded across his chest, and waited.

"It was not a rowboat," I replied, struggling not to smile, for I knew he was but toying with us. "It was a floating palace of curiosities, and a very popular one at that."

"Run by a cousin of yours, I understand?"

"Yes, Colonel Wood, a cousin of mine. That was the only reason we let Lavinia go with him," Mama interjected, her forehead wrinkling in concern and puzzlement.

"Cousin." Mr. Barnum snorted dismissively. "Be that as it may, I assure you that what I am offering Miss Bump is much more than a lazy ride up the Mississippi in some rickety boat. But, of course, I'm no cousin. Just a humble farmer's son from Connecticut—no descendent of the *Mayflower*."

"Well, now, I'm a farmer myself." Papa stirred uncomfortably. "I can't fault a man for being that!"

"No, of course not, that's not at all what I meant." Mama, more flustered than I'd ever seen her, frowned down at her hands.

"My poor father died when I was but a lad, and I had to care for my mother and sisters, so I was not able to have the kind of education I'm sure the Warrens of Massachusetts were able to provide for their sons," Mr. Barnum continued, his face so serious but his eyes so close to merry. I was the only one who saw them, however; my parents were too ashamed to meet his gaze.

"Well, it's not as if we were able to send our boys to Harvard, either," Papa said agreeably. "They're farmers, too, the ones who aren't off fighting."

"Fighting for our grand Union?" Mr. Barnum's voice now filled with musical emotion—fifes and drums and "Yankee Doodle." Sitting up straight, he placed his hand over his heart—and I had to look away, biting the inside of my cheek so as not to burst into laughter. He rose and laid his other hand gently upon Mama's arm. "Madam, I cannot begin to convey my gratitude to you, a mother of such brave boys. Your noble sacrifice will never be forgotten."

Mama, her face covered in mortification, simply nodded, still unable to look Mr. Barnum in the eye. He returned to his seat with a loud, dramatic sniff—then turned to give me a brazen wink, which made me gasp out loud.

Mama and Papa looked at me, but I simply shook my head and dabbed my eye, as if contemplating my brothers' courage.

"I do understand your concerns," Mr. Barnum said, his voice still choked with emotion. "I have nothing but the utmost respect for you and your noble family. I'm a father myself, you know—I have three lovely daughters living, and one angel taken from us far too soon."

"Oh, no!" Mama exclaimed.

"So you see, I have no desire to do anything but keep Miss Bump virtuous and safe from harm, while naturally allowing her the opportunity to see a bit of the world in the manner deserving of such a fine lady, from such a fine family. I know I'm merely a farmer's son, a patriot, a father of daughters—but I vow, with all my heart, to protect your daughter. I'd die myself before I would bring shame upon your good name."

During this speech, Mr. Barnum had leaned forward toward my parents in a beseeching attitude, his hands outstretched, his face open and earnest. Mama and Papa listened intently, transfixed.

I leaned forward as well; I did so want my parents' blessing. I could not imagine continuing to live in Middleborough, where I would never fit in, not only because of my size but now because of my reputation. I could imagine no future for me there that did not consist of staying at home with Mama and Papa and Minnie, growing smaller and older with each tick of the kitchen mantel clock, which Mama faithfully wound every day—until I disappeared completely.

I had known Mr. Barnum only a quarter of an hour, but already I felt my wits quicken with every word he spoke, every move he made, as if he were the sharpening stone and I the edge of the knife. It was as if I had at last found someone with a personality, with dreams, as big as my own.

"What I can't understand is how you heard of Lavinia in the first place." Mama shook her head. "She's been back home for almost two years now. I thought that she'd gotten this whole thing out of her system."

"Why, I—" Mr. Barnum happened to turn my way; he caught me shaking my head and he clamped his mouth shut—after first giving me a small, admiring nod. "That is, your daughter's reputation reached my ears from other performers who spoke highly of her; her beauty and grace are known far beyond the Mississippi."

"They are?" Papa looked at me, then scratched his head, as if trying to see these attributes and failing. I smiled fondly; I knew I was just his daughter, just his Vinnie, and I loved him for that. Even though he had never known precisely what to do with me, he had always loved me for no special reason at all, which satisfied my heart more than I could ever tell him.

"Yes, they are. This is quite a daughter you have here." And they all three beamed upon me as if I were an unopened Christmas present.

"We just don't want any deception perpetuated in her name," Mama announced, in an almost apologetic tone. "I'm sure you understand."

"Madam, I assure you. Anything I say in public will be only with Miss Bump's knowledge and approval." Mr. Barnum turned to me, and once again I saw that sparkle flickering behind his gaze.

"Now, Mama, Papa, I would very much like to talk to Mr. Barnum alone," I said decisively. This was my future, after all, and I had sat by, discussed to no end, for long enough. I wanted to talk to the man plainly; I had no desire to bind myself to anyone like Colonel Wood ever again. Even though he was the Great Barnum, I was determined not to let my vanity cloud my judgment this time.

"Really? Do you think that's wise?" Mama asked Papa, as if I wasn't there.

"Yes, I do," I answered for him. Papa looked at me in that odd way again. I nodded gently at him and then waited as he and Mama withdrew outside, at Mr. Barnum's suggestion, to stroll about the grounds and see the stables.

"Now," he said, pulling his chair over to mine and slouching so that we sat, knee to knee, eye to eye. "Let's have it. I perceive you are a most remarkable woman, Miss Bump."

"Why is that, Mr. Barnum?"

"You sent me that letter, didn't you? The one with all your clippings—but you didn't tell your parents?"

"No, I did not."

"And why is that? I have to say, it's very unusual for me to hear from a performer directly in this way; I was surprised to find you weren't already under contract with someone."

I hesitated for only a moment before replying, "Well, I'm not. And I desire only the best for my career, which prompted me to write to you."

"And about that career." Mr. Barnum leaned back a little and lit a cigar, puffing it for a few moments before continuing. "Tell me about it. I know those showboats. I know the West. I know it's a wild and woolly place. How did you survive it?"

Again, I hesitated for only a fraction of a second. "I got out just in time, because the War came. I won't deceive you; it was not easy. I was not pleased with the vulgar manner in which—in which my cousin decided to exhibit me. For that matter, I would like to know your plans before I agree to anything. I think you should know, right off, I have no intention of being a female Tom Thumb."

"You don't?" He raised a bushy eyebrow, and I had a sense of the steely flint that gave that merry light its spark.

"No, I don't, sir. I will not be paraded around in costumes and uniforms; I will not do imitations; I will not be your performing puppet. I think it's not fitting for a woman, and it's certainly not fitting for me."

"You think Charlie Stratton's my puppet? Why, you know nothing of it," Mr. Barnum growled, reminding me of a grumpy bulldog with his round face, round nose, crooked mouth. "He's my good friend, and he bailed me out of a real jam recently, agreeing to go on tour again because I needed the money. He was just a child when he dressed up in those costumes; it worked for him then. Now he's a man—as you're obviously a woman."

"That's precisely my point. I am a woman, not a puppet. I desire respectability in all things. And protection, too, from—from—well, protection that any lady would require from those who would take advantage of her—vulnerability." My voice did falter, as I could not prevent myself from thinking of Colonel Wood's plans for me in New Orleans.

Mr. Barnum fixed me with a bright, hard gaze, searching for the truth I was so obviously unwilling to speak. He found it; I'm sure he did, as he suddenly paled, then growled, the tip of his nose and his ears turning a dangerous red. He squashed his cigar down in the ashtray beside him with a violence I did not expect, then muttered something under his breath.

I hung my head, my face suffused with warmth; at that moment I could not meet his gaze. Yet when he finally spoke, it was with a voice so gentle, so careful, it reminded me of a child cradling a kitten. "Miss Bump, I'm sorry. I appreciate your delicacy in conveying this to me. When I spoke of the showboats being wild, I assure you—I had no idea of something of this nature, particularly happening to one so fine, so ladylike, as you. You have my word that nothing like that will ever happen, as long as you're employed by me. You asked me how I intend to exhibit you—would you like to hear my plans?"

I nodded, still unable to look at him.

"As a lady. As a model lady, a lady of deportment, a lady deserving of every consideration, every finery. Do you remember Miss Jenny Lind?"

"Oh, yes!" I raised my face eagerly. "I do!"

"She was a model of womanhood." He gestured to a painting I hadn't noticed before; it hung on the opposite wall of the fireplace, and it was illuminated by a discreetly placed gaslight. It was of the Swedish Nightingale herself; a glorious portrait of a woman with softly waving brown hair, luminous eyes, in a virginal white dress. Mr. Barnum followed my gaze; I thought I saw a softer light in his eyes as they fell upon this portrait. I wondered at their relationship, and was surprised to feel a small prick of jealousy. I wanted, suddenly, someday, for someone to look at me in that reverent, adoring way.

"Miss Lind was—is—a model of womanhood, and that is how I displayed her—her voice, of course, was without parallel. That was always understood. But there are other fine singers, most of whom you've never heard, Miss Bump. Why is that? Because I decided to play up her modesty, her gentility, her virtue. No singer had ever been promoted in that way. I have something of the same in mind for you. That your size makes you different is not in question; why call attention to it only? But your manner, your intelligence, your family heritage—that makes you just as socially acceptable as Mrs. Astor or Mrs. Belmont. That is how I intend to present you to the public—as a perfect little lady, a gentlewoman, a Society woman. This is what people will remember about you."

Tears stung my eyes as I listened to him; he had put into words what I myself had desired for so long. Yes, my height would be the first thing people noticed about me, but it would not be the last. Colonel Wood had never understood this very fine point; he had been such a rough, despicable man. I hoped never to have to utter his name again.

"Then I agree to work with you," I told Mr. Barnum, holding my hand out to seal the bargain. He leaned forward and shook my hand heartily—not timidly, as most men did—and began to laugh.

"Of course," I interrupted him coolly. "I will require a salary commensurate to a lady of my fine breeding. And a percentage of all souvenirs and *cartes de visites* sold."

Mr. Barnum stopped laughing. He squinted at me with that bright, hard gaze. Then he laughed again, but not joyfully; just one short, rueful bark.

"Five percent is all I'll give."

"Ten."

"Seven."

"Eight, and I want to go to Europe first, to see the Queen, before I perform here. First-class passage, naturally."

"Eight. And I'll consider Europe. It worked for Charlie, back in the day. Our good patriotic citizens never fail to be impressed by a Royal stamp of approval, for some reason."

"Deal," I said, extending my hand once more.

"Deal." Once more, he shook it. Then he leaned even closer to me, suddenly deadly serious. "But there's something we need to settle right away, Miss Bump."

"What is that?" My thoughts raced wildly; did he suspect about Colonel Wood's contract?

"It's the one thing that could doom this whole enterprise." He gazed at me, not blinking; I gazed right back, holding my breath. I waited for him to speak, for a terrifyingly long time; I heard every creak and movement in the house, a muffled door slam, a silvery tinkle of china, so many clocks ticking out of sync. Still, he stared at me, until I was about to blurt out Colonel Wood's name—then, finally, he grinned.

"Now, what are we going to do about your last name? *Bump* will never do."

I drew in my breath sharply, then exhaled. And I began to laugh, out of pure relief and delight. He joined in, and suddenly I felt as if I'd known him all my life. He was no longer the great, revered P. T. Barnum, nor "that Barnum," nor even the Prince of Humbug.

He was my mentor and friend. Mr. Barnum. And that was what he would remain.

Or so we both believed at the time.

INTERMISSION

From the *Brooklyn Daily Eagle,* February 6, 1863

A Surprise

Doctor Colton is preparing a surprise for Ladies and Pupils of Schools at the Athenaeum tomorrow afternoon. In addition to the Laughing Gas exhibition, he proposes to condense into half an hour a great variety of experiments, illustrating the properties of the air, with simple explanations—among other things a Balloon, holding thirty gallons of hydrogen gas, is to be sent up with a car full of "little folks." Such a lecture must prove highly instructive, and as the admission is only five cents for children, we trust they will be allowed to attend.

From *Harper's Weekly,* February 14, 1863

The Inevitable Question

The question that every body has seen from the beginning of the war must be answered has at last been asked. Shall there be colored soldiers? It is a question upon which there need be no loss of temper. If a man says that he is willing to see the Government lost rather than maintained by such allies, he must answer the question whether, then, he cares enough for the Government to fight for it.

[SEVEN]

I Prepare to Make My Grand Entrance

How swiftly things happened after that meeting! Mama and Papa and I returned home, where I spent the next few weeks washing and mending my wardrobe. Minnie helped, even as she valiantly sniffed away her tears, to no avail; every five minutes she dropped something and threw her arms about my waist to cry, "Oh, how can you leave again, Sister? Why don't you like it here with us? I wish I could make you love it here like I do!"

"Oh, Minnie, I do! Of course I do, but you and I are so very—I promise you, things will be different this time. I fully intend to come home often. And maybe even you'll visit me in New York; Mama and Papa might bring you on the train!" I smiled as I said this, but inwardly, my stomach tightened. Mr. Barnum had asked, jokingly, if I had a sister just like me at home—"The more

Bumps, the merrier!" I hastily replied that I did not; perhaps too hastily, as his eyes narrowed suspiciously.

I had no desire ever to inform him of Minnie's existence. Even as I eagerly looked forward to my next adventure, I needed to know that Minnie would remain where she always was—back on the farm, protected by Mama and Papa, waiting for me to return. It was almost as if she were my conscience, my anchor, the one thing tethering me to home, reeling me back in occasionally so that I wouldn't completely lose my way.

"I might want to take the train," she admitted with a reluctant, shy smile. "Mama said it wasn't as dreadful as all that. But now that I think about it, it must be, because it keeps taking you away! What a terrible, nasty old thing it is, carrying people away from their homes so easily. No, I don't want to take it, at that." And she shook her head so vigorously she almost lost her balance.

"Minnie, darling, you don't understand, even though you're thirteen now—imagine! Trains are wonderful things—you'll see, someday. But you have to know that this time, it's going to be so different—I'm going to be so grand!"

"As grand as Jenny Lind?" Minnie looked over at the figurine, back in its place on my bureau; almost the very minute I returned home, she had handed it over to me solemnly, with the assurance that she had dusted it every single day.

"Even grander!" I promised. "And I will bring home beautiful presents for you—dolls and gowns and necklaces, and we'll put them on and have balls right here at home, right in the parlor, just the two of us!" I dropped the frock I was folding and began to waltz my little sister around the floor; she giggled and followed my lead surprisingly well, her tangle of black curls tumbling down over her face.

But when that fateful day arrived and my family drove me to

the station, she sobbed as uncontrollably as she had the first time I left. I, however, had no tears. I bowed regally to some of my fellow townspeople who just *happened* to be at the station that day; to Mrs. Putnam, the minister's wife, I gave a special farewell. I extended my hand to her and said that I hoped that God would be with her and that I wouldn't stop praying for her, not even all the way in New York City, and then Europe. Why, I might even enlist the Queen in my efforts!

She sputtered in horror, but Papa was already lifting me up on the train before she could think of something to retort. Then I was waving to my family, but only for a moment; soon enough I turned around and looked ahead, at the familiar, peaceful buildings and houses and farms that soon fell away as I sped west, toward New York.

The scenery changed, from farmland to coastland; we passed cranberry bogs and fishing villages, and then we found ourselves back in rolling farmland again. Eventually the houses and buildings grew closer and closer together as we went south. Even with the train windows shut tightly, I soon detected a noise, a pulse, I'd never heard before, and I knew we were in New York City. Automatically I clutched my reticule to my bosom, my mother's last-minute warnings still in my ear, but I also couldn't refrain from kneeling up on the seat to see more easily. The train was chugging past what seemed to be a maze of buildings, all perilously close to the track, right on the same level; there were so many people on the sidewalks that I was quite fearful someone would step right into the path of the onrushing train and be killed.

To my great relief, no one did. We continued to chug, slowing down by increments, until we reached a yard full of tracks branching out in every direction. The train stopped, and I waited for everyone else to disembark before I finally ventured forth, looking for a porter to lift me down.

"Where is the station house?" I inquired, after finding myself on the ground, in the middle of all those tracks.

"Are you lost, little girl?" He squinted down at me.

I sighed but decided not to correct him. "No, I'm not lost, I simply want to get to the station, where I'm being met."

"Over there." The porter pointed, across several tracks, to a large wooden building.

"How do I get there?"

"You walk. Across the tracks. Can you do that? I must say, you're a mite of a thing, traveling all alone."

"I'm not—that is—would you mind carrying me?" For despite my eagerness to correct his impression, I heard trains approaching from other directions and I had a momentary fear of being caught on one of the tracks, unable to scramble out of the way in time.

"Sure thing, little lady." And so I found myself being carried across the tracks, much like a sack of potatoes, and deposited unceremoniously upon the station platform. Hastily, I brushed off my skirt and smoothed my shawl. Perhaps it was not the most dignified way to make my entrance into this great metropolis, but it was certainly the safest.

"You must be Miss Warren?" A tall man with a drooping gray mustache and beard approached me.

"No, I'm—Oh, yes! That is, yes, I'm Miss Warren." So flustered was I, I had quite forgotten my new name. Mr. Barnum and I had disposed, once and for all, of the ugly "Bump," and settled on Mama's family name.

"I'm Mr. Bleeker. Mr. Barnum sent me to greet you and get you out of here right away. I'm to take you straight to his daughter's house—do you have any luggage?"

"Yes, a trunk and some wooden steps."

"Give me the ticket, and I'll fetch them. Come—I hate to ask you after your long trip, but do you mind hurrying up a bit? We don't want to cause a stir." Indeed, people were beginning to gather and point at me; I was so accustomed to this that I scarcely noticed it. But this tall man did, and it appeared to cause him great concern; he put his hand upon my head and gave me a little push, even as he apologized for doing so.

It was his kind concern that made me trust him immediately. He was so very solicitous, even as he was obviously anxious to get me to the carriage. So I followed this stranger, so gaunt that his clothes practically hung off him, as if I trusted him with my life. Little did I know that one day, he would repay this trust, abundantly, many times over. But he was no saint, no mythological creature. For in the end, there was one life he would not be able to spare: the life dearest to him, above all others.

At that moment, of course, I could not suspect any of this; I only followed Mr. Bleeker because I had no alternative, and because I trusted Mr. Barnum implicitly. Soon I found myself in a carriage—not as fine as the one back in Bridgeport; this one was coated in dirt, which I immediately discovered was one thing everyone in New York, no matter the class, gender, or heritage, had in common. Dirt. It was the great equalizer.

Dirt covered everything; my white satin slippers were soon coated in it, even before I stepped into the carriage. Dirt covered the buildings, so tall I couldn't see the tops of some of them—four and five stories tall, imagine! Dirt covered the cobblestoned streets, which were also filled with animal filth, garbage, rats, and humans—who were also covered in dirt. Newsboys, lugging great armfuls of papers, their faces streaked with grime and newsprint; men in black coats and top hats, carrying walking sticks, their white gloves sooty gray; women wrapped in shawls and long aprons, pulling along sickly-looking children spattered with mud; vendors pushing carts filled with things I'd never seen before, fruits and vegetables of unknown names, pickles, fish in jars, trinkets—all coated in dirt.

I'd never seen such a kaleidoscope of people, of things, all of so many different colors yet muted with the same grimy gray.

And high above the buildings, in patches, I could glimpse blue sky. And the occasional oasis of green, pastures for horses and even cows and sheep, so oddly out of place in the shadows of the tall buildings.

I was speechless, content to keep looking out the window, again up on my knees, although I knew it was not dignified. Mr. Bleeker simply grinned, saying, "It sure is good to see this place through someone else's eyes."

"I don't see how you could ever get used to it! It looks as if it's always changing!" Just then, a man with long black curls on either side of his head, wearing a funny hat and coat, emerged from a building. He carried an impressive-looking scroll under one arm, a huge fish wrapped in newspaper under the other. I was enthralled.

Mr. Bleeker didn't reply; he seemed to be a man content with silence, much like my father. I liked him already. Although he did say, after I hung my head out the carriage window to get a better look at a man roasting chestnuts in a tin bucket over coals and selling them in paper cones, "Miss Warren, I do wish you'd shut the window, for Mr. Barnum will have my hide if anyone sees you."

I shut the window, not unwillingly; one other aspect of New York—the stinking, rotting smell of human and animal refuse ripening in the sun and stagnant water—had immediately made my eyes water. I sat back down and turned to Mr. Bleeker.

"Why is that? Why does he want no one to see me?"

"Because that's the way he works. He needs to build you up himself, present you in the proper way. And if some newspaper writes about a little lady wandering about town, he won't be able to control the Press. You'll see—Mr. Barnum is a genius." Mr. Bleeker's long face, which had a tendency to look immensely sad when he wasn't talking, lit up considerably as he spoke about his employer.

"Do you like Mr. Barnum very much?"

"Yes, yes, I do."

"How long have you worked for him?"

"Oh, years and years now. Got my start working at the Museum, and now I do pretty much what Mr. Barnum tells me to. I manage some of the acts, did a tour with the General last time he went to Europe—that kind of thing." This lengthy speech appeared to surprise Mr. Bleeker, for he slumped back against his seat and swiped his forehead with a handkerchief.

I left him to his silence and continued to stare out the window, up at the tops of the passing buildings, the only things I could see while seated. At one point we drove by a very long expanse of trees, which Mr. Bleeker kindly pointed out as "the new Central Park; they're always working on it, but it's just as nice as Hyde Park or Versailles."

"Oh." I was very impressed, not only by the park but by the offhand way Mr. Bleeker said "Hyde Park" and "Versailles," as if he was very familiar with them. And I supposed he must be, if he had accompanied General Tom Thumb to Europe. I smiled and shivered in delicious anticipation; soon *I* would be visiting Europe's grand capitals! First Europe, then the American Museum, just as Mr. Barnum had promised. I could hardly wait.

Finally the carriage rumbled to a halt; it had been a rough ride over the cobblestones. Mr. Bleeker unspooled himself from the carriage—he was a very tall man indeed, although not nearly as tall as Sylvia!—and swung me down. Then he helped me up some imposing marble stairs to the front door of a narrow home, which was part of a row of similar homes, all joined together, constructed of a muddy-colored brown stone. I'd never seen so many houses so close together, no grass or trees between them.

"Miss Warren!" A robust-looking young woman greeted us as a maid let us inside. She was obviously Mr. Barnum's daughter, for she shared his same round nose and chin, and curly black hair. "I'm Mrs. Thompson, Mr. Barnum's daughter, but please, call me Caroline. Come, let me show you to your room, for you must be exhausted."

I followed her gratefully up a narrow set of stairs, which were not as shallow as the ones at home, so it took me some effort and time. This was one of the inconveniences I had to put up with as I aged; when I was a child, I had simply scampered up stairs using my hands to propel me. Now, as a proper young lady in a corset, I could not do that. And there were so *many* stairs in this house! We went up two flights until finally Caroline opened a door and showed me to my room; I gathered this was to be my home for the next few weeks.

I thanked Caroline, who discreetly left me alone to freshen up. The bed was tall but not taller than my wooden steps, which were soon deposited in my room along with my trunk. A very pretty Irish maid unpacked that with alarming efficiency, pausing only now and then to exclaim over the diminutive nature of my clothing.

When she was done, I pulled my steps over to the window and looked out; my view was of another row of houses exactly like this one, all in that same dull stone. The street was very narrow, but I saw a procession of nurses with infants in tow strolling along the sidewalks, and the only carriages that turned down it were beautifully maintained. Mr. Barnum's daughter obviously lived in Society.

Beyond the houses, I could not see. But out there was the

great city of New York! I itched to explore every nook of it, the rich parts and the poor parts, both. I wanted to see the immigrants in the Five Points; I wanted to attend a musical performance at the famous Academy of Music, where all the Society people gathered.

Even through the windows, I could hear the rhythm of New York; it was in the constant, staccato punctuation of steel carriage wheels upon cobblestone, a sound that I would soon discover never abated, no matter the time of day or night. Already it was ringing in my ears—I knew I would sleep well tonight; none of that awful, nerve-jangling *quiet* of home!

Most of all, I was eager to see the American Museum, where Miss Jenny Lind had sung, where Charles Stratton, as General Tom Thumb, had performed. Soon, Miss Lavinia Warren would grace the very same stage. Oh! I could scarcely believe it; I had to hug myself, pinch myself, to know it was all real. I was here! It was truly happening! I was going to be famous; my photograph would be sold along with those of Queens and Kings.

For the first time, I really and truly allowed myself to believe that I would not be forgotten after all. No weeds would cover my name; it would be known in every household in the land.

And with this reassuring thought to sing me to sleep, I prepared for bed. I did so want to be refreshed and ready for Mr. Barnum, on the morrow.

The weeks between my arrival and my debut passed in a frenzy of fittings and finery; I was Cinderella, and Mr. Barnum was a most unusual fairy godmother. I would not have been surprised to find out that he could turn a pumpkin into a coach!

Standing patiently, hour after hour, while being fitted for a custom-designed wardrobe was hard work, I soon discovered. Naturally, my proportions gave the designer some difficulty;

Madame Demorest did not have a dressmaker's dummy in anything near the right size, so everything had to be pinned directly upon my person!

In addition to the fittings for my wardrobe, I had numerous appointments with Mr. Charles Tiffany and Messrs. Ball and Black for my jewels; there were endless trips to A. T. Stewart's store for gloves and accessories, most of which had to be custom-ordered. All conducted, per Mr. Barnum's orders, in the utmost secrecy, under cover of night. I did not enter a single building through the front door during the first three weeks I was in New York; I felt rather like a Confederate spy!

During those weeks, I came to know Mr. Barnum's daughters very well: sturdy, reliable Caroline, my hostess; the slightly bad-tempered Helen, also married, whose mouth was always pursed in disapproval of some perceived slight; and the charming Pauline, the only unmarried daughter, obviously her father's favorite. These three fussed over me as if I were a pet or a doll, Pauline pronouncing every single item of my accumulating finery more cunning than the last.

I must pause here to admit to my feeling of utter bliss upon being laced, by Pauline Barnum herself, into my very first custom-made corset. She giggled at my delight; Pauline was always bubbling over with giggles, being only sixteen at the time. But, oh, how that corset felt against the silk undergarment, smooth and cool as a flower petal against my skin! It fit exquisitely, not a gap, not a wrinkle. When I was laced into it, I stood for almost a quarter of an hour before a looking glass, just gazing at myself, at my womanly figure, how my breasts were pushed up perfectly, my waist fashionably narrow, my hips rounded and utterly feminine. The corset itself, in a fine buff silk, the whalebones delicate yet sturdy, was so beautiful I truly hated to cover it up.

Not once during all the time I stayed at her daughter's home did I meet Mrs. Barnum. She remained, indisposed, in Connecticut. Apparently this was not new, as her daughters merely sighed and rolled their eyes at the mention of "Mother's maladies." And I cannot say I mourned her absence, as it enabled my friendship with her husband to blossom in these dazzling weeks with the intensity of a hothouse flower.

For I found, to my great delight, that Mr. Barnum often stayed in New York with Caroline, instead of taking the late train back to Bridgeport. Every evening I would descend the stairs eagerly, looking for his gold-tipped walking stick indicating he was back from the Museum. The two of us often dined alone, as Caroline and her husband usually had a social function to attend. Naturally, we discussed my upcoming debut, all the myriad details of which Mr. Barnum oversaw with the sensitive attention of an artist. No detail was too tiny for his interest; he discussed the placement of a rosette on one of my slippers until even I was weary of the subject!

I began to notice that whenever we were together, he made a point of sitting down. This may appear to be an insignificant detail, but it was one that I greatly appreciated. This was in such contrast with Colonel Wood, who had taken every opportunity to loom over me—he had rarely sat in my presence, never offered me cushions, was fond of standing as close to me as possible so that he could literally look down upon me.

Mr. Barnum did not do this. In fact, he and I soon fell into the habit of sitting knee-to-knee, as we had done that first day, whenever we had something important to discuss. Thus situated in front of a crackling fire, a plate of cookies or walnuts, glasses of lemonade or sometimes fine Madeira, on a table within reach, we would talk for hours and hours. Not only about my plans but about the War, the political situation, his receipts from the Museum; he was soon asking my opinion about other acts and exhibits, and I felt he always weighed my answers very carefully.

Looking back, I believe this was the most satisfying time of my life. I would soon meet public figures, millionaires and monarchs, beyond anything I could have imagined. But it was this time, this sweet, anticipatory time, that I remember most fondly.

I told him all about my life on the river, not varnishing the roughness but, under his eager, hungry gaze that was always on the lookout for an anecdote or unusual story, finding the humor in my memories, as well. I came to believe he was fueled, almost alone, by words and imagination; by a hunger for knowledge and experience that paralleled my own. Never before had I felt such a kinship with anyone, not even Sylvia. It was a meeting of the minds, first and foremost.

The night before my debut, as Mr. Barnum and I sat together in Caroline's snug parlor, I felt a trifle melancholy. My new trunks—made of the finest leather monogrammed with my initials—were packed up in the dear little bedroom that had been my first New York home. On the morrow, I would be moving into the St. Nicholas Hotel, where I would remain while I held my series of grand receptions—invitation-only, highly sought-after, Mr. Barnum reported with glee. Already I missed the warm hospitality of Caroline's home; already I missed these quiet, conspiratorial evenings with my new friend.

"Are you all right, Vinnie?" Mr. Barnum asked as he handed me a glass of wine.

"Yes, I am. Although I admit, I'm a little nervous about tomorrow. You'll make sure no man picks me up or kisses me without my permission, won't you?" This old fear of mine would not leave me. Despite my elegant new wardrobe, I worried that I would be touched and picked up and squeezed as if I were a child. Or worse.

"Mr. Bleeker will be vigilant, I assure you. He's to be considered your bodyguard. You must trust him as you trust me." Mr.

Barnum, a red silk dressing gown covering his shirt and trousers, nodded smartly. His cigar, ever-present, glowed mysteriously in the cozy darkness. Only the light from the fire illuminated us; he did not like to have the gaslights lit at night, for he enjoyed the shadows. He said it reminded him of his childhood, when he would walk long miles back to his home late at night from his grandfather's store, where he first learned to sell things to people who did not know they wanted them.

"Then I am satisfied." I tried to push those worries out of my mind, but others swiftly took their place. "And I'm to meet all the gentlemen of the Press, at once?"

"Yes, but don't think of it that way. People will be introduced to you, one by one, just like any reception. You'll simply stand and shake hands and chat—that's all we need to do at first. And I trust that your charming powers of speech will not desert you." Mr. Barnum winked at me, but behind his smile I detected a stern rejoinder: a reminder that I must not fail him. And I would not, I vowed silently. I would not let him down; the responsibility of this did not fall lightly upon me, but it did not completely bend me, either. I felt myself rising up to shoulder it without complaint.

"Might I not sing a little song?" I asked after a moment, as I tried to imagine what the morrow would be like. "That went over very well on the river."

"I suppose."

"I could sing 'Home Sweet Home,'" I offered. "So everyone will know when to leave."

"No." He shook his head in a very decided way.

"Why not?"

"That was Jenny's song. You must find another."

I bit my lip, my stomach tightening in a curious way. I did not like the way he said "Jenny," as if he had a right. I did not like the gleam that turned his eyes from gray to almost blue when he did so. I did not care for the way he stared into the fire and sighed, as if entangled in a memory.

Most of all, in some soft, womanly part of my heart—a part that I had not, until now, taken the time to explore with any frequency—I did not like the fact that no one had ever said *my* name in that way, that softly proprietary way.

"Fine," I said grudgingly. "Then I'll sing 'Annie of the Vale.' I'm told I sing it exceedingly well."

Mr. Barnum smiled at me, nodding approvingly. "Good girl. I knew you'd come up with something right away. You've got a head on your shoulders, Vinnie. I've not met many your equal."

I smiled back, basking in the glow of his approval, content to be admired for my mind.

For now.

INTERMISSION

From the *New York Tribune,* December 23, 1862

Yesterday we saw a very pretty and intelligent little lady at the St. Nicholas Hotel, in this city. This woman in miniature is twenty-one years of age, weighs twenty-nine pounds, thirty-two inches in height. She moves about the drawing-room with the grace and dignity of a queen, and yet she is entirely devoid of affectation, is modest and ladylike in her deportment. Her voice is soft and sweet, and she sings excellently well.

From *The New York Times,* December 23, 1862

We attended Miss Warren's reception yesterday at the St. Nicholas. It was a festive gathering. All were paying court to a very beautiful, an exceedingly symmetrical, a remarkably well-developed, and an absolutely choice specimen of feminine humanity, whose silken tresses beautified and adorned a head, the top of which was not quite thirty-two inches from the floor. In other words, we saw a miniature woman—aye, and the queen of them.

[EIGHT]

Or, A Star Is Born

AND SO IT ALL CULMINATED IN ONE GRAND, GLORIOUS reception, successful beyond anything we could have imagined. Standing upon a small velvet-draped platform in the lovely parlor of the St. Nicholas Hotel, I softly cleared my throat, nodded to the pianist Mr. Barnum had secured for me, and began to sing.

I had shaken many hands, engaged in much conversation, discussed the myriad details of my wardrobe (at least, the details that a lady could discuss in public). I had posed for illustrators eager to sketch my likeness, I had answered questions about my family and ancestors (these, I surmised, were discreetly planted by Mr. Barnum, who was circling the edge of the crowd like a proud parent, careful not to take any attention away from me). All in all, I was an astonishing success. I knew it by the hum of approval in the room, the admiring glances; I knew it by Mr. Barnum's unapologetic smile of pure, boyish glee. There was only one thing left to do, and that was to sing my song.

Fixing my gaze at some spot across the room—in the sudden yellow, flickering glare of the gaslights, which seemed to have been turned up to a blaze, I could not make out anything specific. Then I began to sing. Very softly at first, for it had been a long while since I had sung in public, and my voice was a little rusty and uncertain.

"*The young stars are glowing . . . their clear light bestowing . . . their radiance fills the calm clear Summer night . . .*"

All I could see were smiles around me; smiles from these men, serious professionals, but my singing, I could tell, brought them much pleasure and delight. So I sang even louder, my eyes adjusting to the light now.

"*Come . . . come . . . come love, come . . . come 'ere the night torches pale . . .*"

My vision cleared so that I could make out that spot on the far wall; to my surprise, it was Mr. Barnum to whom I had chosen to sing. It was Mr. Barnum whose face I now saw, a smile upon it as broad as any I had seen. Did I also detect a tear in his eye? I was too far away, but I decided that yes, I did.

"*Oh, come in thy beauty, thou marvel of duty . . . Dear Annie, dear Annie of the vale.*"

I bowed my head after the last note and accepted the applause of the room; it was different from the applause I had heard on the river. This was respectful, from men who were cultured, men who had heard Miss Jenny Lind sing.

But there was only one man whose applause fell sweetly upon my ear, all the way from across the room. It was the one man who heard the Nightingale sing, still, in his memory.

His was the admiration I truly sought. And in that moment, when I knew that I possessed it, I allowed myself to wonder, for the very first time, how it would feel to be known simply as a woman—

And not a woman in miniature.

INTERMISSION

From *The New York Times,* February 26, 1863

A Case of Furious Driving

Mrs. E. GREEN, residing at No. 22 Watts-street, while crossing Fifth-avenue, near Tenth-street, was knocked down and run over by a horse and sleigh, which was being driven at a furious rate, by LEVI L. HUFF, the colored coachman of Mr. CHARLES GOODHUE, of Madison-avenue. Mrs. GREEN, who was severely injured, was taken to her residence by a policeman. HUFF was arrested and taken before Justice KELLY, who committed him, in default of $300 bail.

From *Harper's Weekly,* March 21, 1863

Foreign News—England—Revulsion of Public Sentiment

There was a great demonstration at the amphitheatre in Liverpool on the 19th ult., in support of President Lincoln's Emancipation Proclamation. The *Liverpool Post* says that a more unanimous meeting was never witnessed on any question on which public opinion has been divided. Resolutions applauding the course of Mr. Lincoln on the slavery question, and an address to be provided to him through Mr. Adams were adopted. Some uproar and confusion occurred toward the conclusion of the meeting; but with this exception everything passed off very happily.

[NINE]

Or, Another Player Makes His Long-Anticipated Entrance

MY SUCCESS WAS COMPLETE—TOO COMPLETE, PERHAPS. For Mr. Barnum decided I was so popular, it would be prudent to postpone the expensive European tour. We argued, but finally he showed me the projections for the income we could expect if I appeared at his Museum right away.

I had no reply to that—other than to show him that he could add an extra two hundred dollars a week to my salary, as compensation for my understandable disappointment. He swore mildly but in the end did not appear to mind too much as he signed the check.

Indeed, I think he admired me even more.

P. T. Barnum's American Museum! How sad to note how little it is remembered these days! Children of this time have no memory of it. They don't even realize how very much they have missed by not growing up while it was still standing.

I first entered it, accompanied by Mr. Barnum, through a private door that the majority of the public did not even know was there. But later, I insisted upon entering it through the front, just like any member of the public that paid, without grumbling, twenty-five cents each. For nowhere else on earth had there ever been such an assemblage of novelties, animals, music, culture, science, and entertainment all in one place.

You first approached the Museum from the corner of Broadway and Ann Street in Lower Manhattan; it was surrounded by many thriving businesses, including Mr. Mathew Brady's daguerreotype studio, which I would come to know quite well. The street at this intersection was wide enough to accommodate the throngs of people always milling about in case one of the living exhibits might appear for a stroll or a brief, tempting display of his talent. The building itself was five stories of white stone, with the name "Barnum" prominently featured in red letters above the third-floor windows. Panels depicting the various animals and exhibits, including Tom Thumb, were painted gaudily on the face of the stone. Flags flew in a line atop the roof, and the second and third stories each had a wrought-iron fenced balcony stretching their lengths. On one of these balconies, a band in brightly festooned uniforms played; they were singular for their absolutely awful musicianship. Indeed, Mr. Barnum confessed to me that he had hired them expressly for their lack of talent! He wanted the people *inside* the Museum, and if they had to endure a cacophony of out-of-tune instruments, he reasoned, they would not remain long *outside*.

After paying admission, families, immigrants, Society people, farmers in their finest, and a constant parade of newspapermen from all over the world mingled together as they took in the wonders to be seen. And such wonders! On the first floor, there were halls lined with display cases brimming with the most unusual artifacts, exotic animal bones and skins, minerals, the world's largest baby tooth, horrifying medical instruments all gleaming with steel and sharp edges, a part of an asteroid that had once killed a farmer's cow, a thread of the blanket that the Baby Jesus was swaddled in, a real live flea circus, dioramas of all sorts of scenes, even miniature naval battles on real water. There were cases and cages full of preserved animals and skeletons. In one room was the famous "Happy Family," where, in the same cage, a lion, a tiger, a lamb, and assorted birds all lived together in apparent harmony. (Although Mr. Barnum confessed that the exhibit could continue only as long as he had a fresh supply of lambs and birds!)

On the second floor was the waxworks, where mannequins of famous personalities stood milling about companionably, as if at a silent tea party. There was George Washington, Queen Victoria, the Apostles, Napoléon, Joice Heth (the original humbug herself, the old Negro slave whom Mr. Barnum had tried to pass off as George Washington's one-hundred-and-sixty-year-old nursemaid, until she died and was discovered to be only eighty), and Jenny Lind. Naturally, Charles Stratton was represented in this hall as well. In one corner stood a tree trunk upon which Jesus Himself had once sat—or so read the inscription. On this floor too was a picture gallery of astoundingly realistic portraits, some that even appeared to pop out of their frames, so breathtakingly lifelike were they. The famous Feejee mermaid was still on display—the crudely stitched-together torso of a monkey and a fish tail that had been the second great example of Mr. Barnum's ability to whip a gullible public up into a frenzy. This phenomenon was safely behind glass, thank heavens, for I could well imagine how it must smell by now!

And in the middle of the second floor rose the enormous saltwater tank in which a real beluga whale lolled about, alive, but barely. I felt sorry for the poor thing, so confined, so miserable. But it was an extremely popular attraction, indeed. Rare was the person who had ever seen a whale up close, save for Captain Ahab himself!

Strategically placed at intervals were signs that promised *This Way to the Egress!* I bit my lip when I saw people eagerly going in the direction they pointed, and chided Mr. Barnum about it later. "That is an awful trick to play upon people," I scolded him.

"I'm not saying anything deceitful at all. It's not my fault if the educational system in this country is so appalling, no one knows that 'egress' is Latin for 'exit.'"

"And so you sit here and take another twenty-five cents each from these poor people who find themselves locked outside, forced to enter again through the ticket booth!"

"Yes, I do. And I need every extra twenty-five cents I can get so that I can pay your heartlessly negotiated contract, cruel woman! So if there's anyone to blame, it is yourself."

I had to smile at him. I always smiled at him in those days.

Of course, the noise in the place was horrendous; animals and people all chattering, heavy boots and spurs being dragged across wooden floors, the constant importunate cries of the ticket sellers and the men hired to keep the crowds moving. The smell, too, could be overwhelming: so many humans and animals in close quarters, despite the fact that there were fans everywhere, ventilation holes hidden along the walls. Every part of the Museum was illuminated by the new limelight, which was different than gaslight; it shone much brighter, not nearly so yellow, and lit up the stage of the Lecture Hall brilliantly.

The enormous, elegantly appointed Lecture Hall took up almost the entire third floor of the building, its velvet-curtained balconies extending up to the fourth and fifth floors. I know that in these more modern times, it is difficult to conceive of the necessity of calling what was really a theater a "lecture hall." But in those Civil War days, the word "theater" was shocking—not just shocking but amoral. It was considered a sin of the highest consequence to step foot into a "theater."

However, a "lecture hall" was another thing entirely; why, it was a place of learning, of enlightenment! Lectures were given here: scientific lectures, magic lantern shows of foreign lands. That it was also, occasionally, a place where plays were performed, operas sung, and ballets danced was merely convenient, as well as palatable, to the good, upright citizens of this Grand Republic of ours.

January 2, 1863: this was the date I made my debut in the Lecture Hall. On that enormous stage where Miss Jenny Lind had sung and bewitched her listeners, I felt as if I had completed a very long journey. I had finally arrived where I belonged, surely.

I'm certain I went dutifully through my rehearsed program that night. I sang my songs, told more stories, enacted a graceful little dance, answered planted questions from my audience. I was a professional; my body could go through its paces, even if my mind was not fully engaged. And I don't believe it was that night. I remember only the most serene feeling, almost one of complete detachment from this elegantly attired woman standing in the middle of this famous stage, moving about so competently, watched by hundreds of avid eyes. And even as I danced and chatted and sang, I knew, somehow, that I would long remember the details of my humiliation on Colonel Wood's boat much more intensely than I would the details of this evening's triumph.

I wondered why that was. I wondered if this was how it always felt when all your dreams came true. Perhaps, after living with them for so long, did you simply toss them away—and begin to dream about something else?

One of the first evenings I appeared at the Museum, I was

resting in my sitting room—everything in it made to my size, down to the exquisite silver hairbrushes and mirrors on my dressing table—between levees. I had already grown to love this oasis, for I now could not stir one foot in this city without causing a sensation. I had tried to take a stroll through the footpaths of Central Park, but soon found well-meaning citizens too eager to lift me over the snow banks. The first time I entered the grand establishment of A. T. Stewart's through the front door, simply because I wanted to look at the new bonnets, I was immediately surrounded by a crush of people who blocked my progress, some of whom earnestly tried to show me where the children's clothing could be ordered!

And my hand, my delicate, manicured hand, throbbed so at night after shaking so many much larger hands, that I had to soak it in lavender water!

So I was enjoying my respite, intending to finally begin *Lady Audley's Secret,* which I'd heard so much about, when there was a knock on my door.

"Yes?" I called out.

"Miss Warren, it's me. Barnum."

I leaped off the sofa, my book sliding to the floor; opening the door, I smiled and said, teasingly, "What is this 'Miss Warren' business? You're not still angry with me about that extra two hundred a week?"

But Mr. Barnum did not answer; he was not alone. "Miss Warren, it is such a pleasure to meet you," said a little boy, hat in hand, standing in front of Mr. Barnum.

But no. He was no boy. I stared at him in puzzlement, trying to place him, for he looked very familiar. Then the dawn broke upon me, as I remembered the *carte de visite* that I still possessed, somewhere, possibly in an old valise back at the farm, the photograph of an impish young man with light brown hair, merry eyes, clad in a Scottish kilt.

He was bigger now, fleshier, boasting a decided double chin and a mustache, which looked absurd, almost as if it were pasted on. I could not now picture him in a kilt; the idea almost made me giggle. He was immaculately attired, however: a perfectly tailored navy blue suit with snowy white cuffs, gold cuff links. He looked prosperous, well fed, and surprisingly, as I continued to stare, somewhat rudely, at him, extremely nervous.

This was Charles Stratton. Or as he was known to the rest of the world, General Tom Thumb.

"I hope you don't mind, but we thought we'd see if you'd like some company," Mr. Barnum said, following Mr. Stratton into my room. I still hadn't uttered a word; I could only continue gaping, for the two of them aped each other's movements with odd perfection, as if they had spent a lifetime polishing this act. I wasn't sure, at first, who was imitating whom. But as they sat down—Mr. Barnum upon one of the two regular-size chairs I kept for visitors; Mr. Stratton settling happily upon one of my small armchairs—they crossed their legs at the same time, loosened their vests, checked their pocket watches—exactly in unison, as if choreographed.

I very nearly laughed, but there was something in the earnestly dignified expression upon Mr. Stratton's face that stopped me.

"Of course I do not mind. And it is a pleasure for me, as well, Mr. Stratton."

"My friend came up from Connecticut today expressly to see your performance," Mr. Barnum told me with an odd little laugh; I noticed he was twisting his hat about in his hands as if he didn't know what he was doing. If I hadn't known him better, I would have thought he was nervous! But no, the Great Barnum was never nervous.

"Oh? I hope I did not disappoint you, then."

"Oh, no! It was grand! You dance right smart, and sing like an angel!" Mr. Stratton could not contain his enthusiasm; forgetting his practiced dignity, he bounced around in his seat like a jack-in-the-box. "I can't believe you've never performed before! Can you, Phineas?"

Mr. Barnum and I exchanged a quick look; he had taken great pains to present me as his latest discovery, great pains indeed not to mention my previous performing history. I did not mind this omission in the least; in fact, I welcomed it. I suppose it was our very first humbug. But it was a mild one, and it had the added value of somehow convincing me that this might prevent Colonel Wood from making any claim toward my services.

"Thank you, that is very kind, Mr. Stratton. Especially coming from one as experienced in this business as yourself."

Mr. Stratton puffed and preened but looked to Mr. Barnum as if seeking permission to do so. Mr. Barnum, however, did not respond; indeed, his mouth was clamped shut, his eyes bright: He was observing us, keenly, and I did not like it. I managed to hide my uneasiness and continued to listen politely to Mr. Stratton, who could hardly contain himself; conversation poured out of him as if from a bubbling coffeepot.

"I was just saying to Phineas here that I have some business that will keep me in New York for a few days. Gosh, I do want to tell you all about it! I have so many business dealings these days—real estate, insurance, horses, investments. Do you know what investments are, Miss Warren?"

"I do," I replied but immediately regretted it, for his plump face fell; obviously, he had wanted to inform me himself.

"Oh. I'm just learning all about this, for Phineas says I need to di-di—what was the word, old chap?"

"Diversify," Mr. Barnum supplied.

"Diversify! You see, it's best not to limit myself to performing interests. You don't want to put all your eggs in one basket, especially these days!"

I had to smile at Mr. Stratton's enthusiasm, but I could not shake the feeling that he was simply reciting a speech that someone—Mr. Barnum—had taught him.

"How very smart of you," I said warmly.

"Thank you!"

"You know, Charlie here bailed me out of a jam recently, Miss Warren. He really is a true friend," Mr. Barnum interjected as the conversation lulled; apparently, Mr. Stratton had run out of rehearsed topics of discussion.

Again, I found his speech a trifle off. "Miss Warren" sounded odd, given how familiar he and I were by now. I wondered why he was acting so strangely; there was no hint of the intimacy that had grown between us.

"True friends are the best friends," I replied automatically. But Charles Stratton mistook this little aphorism as a compliment; he blushed and shook his head violently.

"No, I was just doing what anyone would do in the same situation. I owe Mr. Barnum everything, and I will never forget it."

For the first time, I decided, Charles Stratton sounded sincere and unrehearsed. I peered at him, attempting to see beyond the obviously calculated appearance—he tried too hard to resemble a gentleman of the world, with his careful grooming (his odd little mustache glistened as if it had been oiled), the cuff links polished to a gleam. Yet despite his earnestly grown-up manner, his brown eyes were appealingly boyish, almost bashful; I found myself wondering what it had been like to live in the public spotlight since the age of five. It must not have been easy for him; it was little wonder he had learned to cloak himself in practiced attitudes and rehearsed speeches!

Suddenly I felt a tickle along the back of my neck; glancing up, I observed Mr. Barnum observing me. He was not smiling; he looked grave, almost concerned.

There was another knock at my door; before I could rise to open it, I heard a childishly treble voice call out, "May I dare enter the domain of the lovely and popular Miss Warren?"

I immediately frowned, as did Mr. Barnum and Mr. Stratton. What was *he* doing there?

He was Commodore Nutt, or as he was better known, "the Thirty Thousand Dollar Nutt," Mr. Barnum's discovery prior to me. He was a little taller than me, thirty-six inches, from New Hampshire; Mr. Barnum had hoped to present him as something of a copy of General Tom Thumb. So he'd outfitted him, given him a military title—so popular in those war days—and taught him to sing and dance a little.

(I will remind the reader that Mr. Barnum had no need to train me; I came to him with a full complement of talents.)

Commodore Nutt was younger than me by about seven years; he was closer to Minnie's age. But he acted much older, putting on airs, smoking endless cigars, consuming whiskey with an efficiency that was alarming. Upon being introduced to me, on my very first day at the Museum, he pronounced me "the lovely and popular Miss Warren." He had thus addressed me, ever since. It was obvious he was enraptured by me, puffed up beyond his years by an inflated sense of self-importance.

"Ah, the lovely and popular Miss Warren," he said now, as I opened the door, stifling a sigh; he placed his hand upon his heart and bowed deeply. I suppressed an urge to pat him on his head and tell him to run off to play. He was such a *boy,* not unpleasant to look at, with shiny brown hair and eyes, a mischievous, almost elfin little smile. His voice was not as high-pitched as Charles Stratton's, yet I could not think of him as anything but a very nice lad—and one who was not earning nearly as much money as I was.

"Pray sit down, Mr. Nutt." I refused to call him by his military title; his real name was George Washington Morrison Nutt. I felt the tribute to the Father of our Country rather misplaced; there was nothing grand or imposing about this fellow. He capered about the stage like a child on leave from school; for some reason, the audiences enjoyed seeing him cut up so. I could not help but notice, moreover, that his audiences were not quite as big as mine—and he sold far fewer *cartes de visites*. "Of course, you know Mr. Barnum and Mr. Stratton."

"Whatever the lovely and popular Miss Warren desires," he replied, eyeing my other visitors disapprovingly. But then he flashed an expansive smile as he shook hands all around. "Mr. Barnum, as always. And Mr. Stratton, what a pleasure and honor. What brings you out of retirement, old fellow?"

Mr. Stratton did not appear to perceive the insult from the younger man; indeed, he grinned sunnily and exclaimed, "Miss Warren, of course!"

"Indeed!" Mr. Nutt's nostrils flared, and his chest puffed out like a bantam rooster's. "What a tragedy for you. For naturally she and I are in each other's company every day, while you are stuck at home in Connecticut."

"No, I'm not, for I'm to be in New York often, now that I'm in Business!" Mr. Stratton nodded eagerly.

"Oh, really. How fascinating. Ah, beauty, cruel, cruel beauty!" Mr. Nutt whirled and reached for my hand, raising it to his lips, kissing it. "You know not how many hearts you break!"

"Now, see here!" Charles Stratton rose, a faint, puzzled frown almost creasing his face. "I was here first, old chap."

"All's fair in love and war, as the poet says," Nutt retorted, with a grin.

"Ridiculous!" I yanked my hand away, then pointed to an empty chair. "You—sit over there. And you"—I gestured at Mr. Stratton—"just—sit. And you!" I whirled around and glared at Mr. Barnum.

He was watching the three of us pensively, as if we were performers upon a stage, a stage of his own design. His eyebrows drew together, his crooked mouth pursed, and I saw that piercing, all-seeing light in his eyes escape from behind its gray curtain.

If I hadn't known any better, I would have sworn I heard a cash register jingle in his brain. Actually, I did know better. And I knew that I had.

I was disgusted, I was insulted.

I was also, in spite of myself, intrigued.

INTERMISSION

From *The Scientific American*, April 4, 1863

PRESENT CONDITION OF THE "ROANOAKE"

The iron-clad steam battery, *ROANOAKE*, is rapidly approaching completion and it is thought that steam will be applied by 1st of April. The turrets are nearly finished and the pilot-houses are completed. . . . Her armament will be one 15-inch gun and one rifled 200-pound Parrot gun in the forward turret; one 11-inch gun and one 15-inch gun in the midship turret, one 11-inch gun and one rifled 200-pound Parrot gun in the after tower.

From the *Brooklyn Daily Eagle*, May 23, 1863

POLITICS IN PETTICOATS

The people of Brooklyn in turning out largely last evening to hear a young lady talk politics, and in very warmly applauding the incoherent nonsense which she uttered, gave a marked proof—not of their good sense—but of their chivalric feeling for the sex. Miss Dickinson labored for an hour last evening (the thermometer was at eighty-seven), to show a sweltering crowd the way in which Providence is teaching the nation.

Miss Dickinson came to an abrupt conclusion, and left her audience about as wise as she found it. As the ways of Providence are interpreted by Miss Dickinson, our salvation depends solely upon the darkey. She is not very clear on this or any other point, but as nearly as we can guess at it, this is what she means.

[TEN]

Two Rivals for One Hand

CHARLES STRATTON WAS BORN IN 1838 NEAR BRIDGEPORT, Connecticut, where Mr. Barnum had not yet made his home but soon would. It was there, in 1842 while visiting his brother, that Mr. Barnum heard of this remarkable child who was barely two feet tall, even though the lad was nearly four years old.

Phineas Taylor Barnum was still in the early stages of his career as a showman; he had already come to some fame by exhibiting Joice Heth and the Feejee mermaid. But he was looking for something even more remarkable, and the moment he discovered this tiny child, he realized he had found it.

Convincing the child's parents—whom I never did like, finding them coarse and vulgar and, worse, stupid—to entrust little Charlie into his care, Mr. Barnum began to teach him how to sing, to dance, and to do popular impressions of the day. ("Yankee Doodle" became his best known.) He clothed him in miniature uniforms, increased his age from five to eleven (in order to play up his diminutive form), and began to exhibit him, to mild acclaim, in the United States as Tom Thumb. However, he soon decided to take little Charlie overseas, where he was an instant sensation and received the best publicity possible by being asked to perform for Queen Victoria. It was the young Queen who gave Charles his title of "General," as well as a miniature blue carriage, matching miniature Shetland ponies, and the right to call himself a Royal favorite.

Mr. Barnum brought his Royal protégée back home, and from that point on General Tom Thumb, as he was now universally called, was a household name, the top performer at the Museum (until Miss Jenny Lind came along), and a true friend of Mr. Barnum's. He was also a miniature adult who had never been a little boy, and that was the part of him that always managed to touch me. The lost, sad part of Charlie, the part that caused him to say, so wistfully, whenever he saw a child absorbed in a toy, "Vinnie, I like to watch them play. You know I never had any childhood, any boy-life."

This poor soul had been taught to take wine at dinner when only five, to smoke at seven, to chew tobacco at nine. Little wonder, then, that by the age of twenty-five, when we met, he was already showing signs of an overly indulgent lifestyle; he was growing portly, short of breath, and was much too fond of wine.

Charles Stratton told me all this about himself, and more; he was soon escorting me out to the lobby after my levees in the Lecture Hall, where he waited patiently and proudly for me to sign my photographs. The public saw this, saw his attention to me, and soon there were whispers and rumors of a romance. Whispers and rumors that Mr. Barnum did not appear to mind in the least. In fact, I suspect he planted more than one anonymous letter to a diminutive Cupid in the newspapers himself.

Commodore Nutt also saw this; he grumbled and tried to

shoo Charles away, as if he were simply a pesky insect, and once the two even came to blows over who would escort me to my dressing room. Commodore Nutt continued to give me pathetic looks, spouting flowery paeans to Love. The public also became aware of this budding rivalry, and I didn't have to wonder who was responsible for informing them.

"I blame you for all this mess," I told Mr. Barnum curtly one evening after Nutt tried to read me a love poem, and Charles threatened to thrash him.

Mr. Barnum had offered to drive me back to my hotel himself, so for once neither of the two "rivals for the exquisitely manicured hand of the Queen of Lilliput," as a newspaper article had tittered, was present. I felt a great relief, as if I had suddenly been released from a stifling, airless room; it was such bliss to speak my mind freely, to sit without fear of being clutched at or mooned over or scrutinized for my every gesture, look, or sigh.

"What mess?"

"Between Nutt and Stratton. Although Nutt is the worst. That boy is so maddening with his looks and sighs."

"So you've made your mind up?"

"What do you mean?"

"Between the two. You've settled on Charles?"

"I've done no such thing!" I turned my head and, perched upon two velvet cushions as if I was an expensive bauble, gazed out the carriage window. We were rumbling over the cobblestones of Fifth Avenue, whose tall, imposing buildings were all dark and looming, while the round streetlights shone bright pools of light upon the clean sidewalks (relatively clean, that is, compared to the sidewalks in less desirable parts of town). The streets were quieter this time of night, but of course they were never completely free of carriages and wagons and carts; the rumbling of wheels upon cobblestones never ceased.

"Ah, Vinnie, what are you waiting for?" Mr. Barnum removed his spectacles and massaged the red indentation on the bridge of his nose; he looked weary, especially in the grainy shadows of the carriage. Weary and older, somehow; he was only in his early fifties, but he had lived more than one lifetime. Successes, bankruptcies, more successes: He had built palaces only to see them burnt to the ground. In the 1850s, he even temporarily lost ownership of his American Museum. It was then that Charles Stratton had volunteered to go out on tour again, bringing in enough money that Mr. Barnum was able to buy it back.

I often forgot this part of his life, this rocky, unsettled business of buying and selling and betting on the taste of the public. He put on such a good face, even to me. But sometimes he dropped that mask to reveal his uncertainty and weariness; those were the moments I most cherished.

I frowned; he did not look at all well. "Are you eating properly? Getting exercise?"

"Yes, m'dear, I am."

"I don't believe you. Is Charity taking care of you? How is she these days?" I still had not met his wife.

"She is as usual. You realize I have three daughters to fuss and fidget over me; I don't need a fourth, Vinnie." He said it kindly, but there was a hint of frost in his voice, in his gaze; it was a warning.

"I assure you, I have no desire to be thought of as one of your daughters," I replied with my own chilly attitude.

There was an uncomfortable pause, which he broke first; he always did. Mr. Barnum could not long stand silence.

"All right, then. Now, about your future—"

"What about it? You're not thinking of kicking me out of the Museum already, are you?"

"Heavens, no—the very idea! Tell me, Vinnie, how old are you? Twenty-one?" Now he sounded very much like a father, and

I did not like it. But I nodded, my cheeks burning, as any lady's would at the mention of her age.

"I know things seem as if they've just begun for you, and of course you want to enjoy them, but you cannot ignore the fact that you have two highly eligible suitors vying for your hand. It's cruel to allow them to go on in this way."

I shook my head, closed my eyes, and sank against the plush cushioned seat; how romantic, how sweet—how very *ordinary*—it sounded when put that way! How unlike my life, the life with which I was so acquainted, the life that Mama had wept over, late at night, as I lay sleeping with my sister.

"They are simply two ridiculous, spoiled boys playing a game, and I happen to be the prize. Yet no one has asked what I want." I opened my eyes, considering Mr. Barnum. He was my confidante, my mentor; he was the person I thought of when I went to bed, and the person I looked forward to seeing when I opened my eyes, eager to begin the day. How quickly he had assumed that place in my life!

"What do you want, Vinnie?" He smiled down at me; in the carriage, we could not sit knee to knee.

"I—I want—" What did I want? Oh, so many things; what *didn't* I want? What didn't I desire? It was because I wanted that I had left home in the first place, shunning the simple life my family so happily led.

Yet there was one thing—one simple, *ordinary* thing—that I did desire; I hadn't known it until recently.

I wanted, to my great astonishment, to be loved. I wanted to be cared for, desired, not desiring; I wanted to be cherished not for my size, not for anything other than for my heart, my mind—just like any woman.

But I wanted these things not from any man; I wanted them from a great man, a man worthy of me. And this was the one thing

I knew that I could never have—a great love. I must settle for something else—*someone* less, in every way. I must settle for a love in miniature. I did not quite know how to do that—settle; it was not a lesson I had ever bothered to learn.

"You've orchestrated this whole thing!" I burst out, tears suddenly in my eyes, my anger at what I could not have lashing out at the one thing I wanted. "*You* brought Charles Stratton to New York, filling his head with that business nonsense! *You* egged on poor Nutt. You've thrown me in the company of these two time and again, encouraged them both, planted items in the paper—oh, don't try to pretend that you haven't! And you've played with us, as if we were your own personal set of marionettes. You know," I said, struggling to sort through my various emotions, all jumbled up like a ball of twine, "I was once nearly sold to a man. In New Orleans. Colonel Wood was offered five hundred dollars to give me to him. So he could do whatever he pleased with me. *Whatever!* It did not matter to him; *I* did not matter! Only the money that he could receive for it mattered to him."

"Vinnie, that's—that's—"

But I would not listen to his protests. "That's what? Appalling? Immoral? Illegal? Yet what you are proposing isn't that very far off, is it? *Is it?*" I wrapped my arms about my shoulders, rocking myself, suddenly desperate for an answer, and not just any answer. The *correct* answer. I needed to know he was not like Colonel Wood, after all.

"Vinnie, excuse me for speaking plainly, but I sometimes forget that you have a heart. Now, don't take offense!" Mr. Barnum raised his hand, anticipating my horrified protest. "I mean that as a compliment. Your mind is so sharp, you're so terrifyingly intelligent and driven—well, you're a lot like me, I like to think, which is why we get along so well. So please accept my apology, for I have no wish to cause you distress or pain; I'm not like that cousin of yours, who ought to be taken out and shot for the scoundrel that he is. We'll not discuss the matter further. I truly believed you were enjoying the situation, the attention."

Sniffing—trying to dab the cursed tears from my eyes, for, perversely, I had an intense desire for him *not* to see me as just another woman—I turned and stared out the window. He did the same thing, and we rode along in silence for a few minutes.

"I've seen it, too, you know," I said at last, my voice thick with swallowed tears—and pride.

"Seen what?"

"I've seen the way people look at me when I'm with those two. I've seen the glances, heard the whispers, the ridiculous romantic sighs. Individually, we will all do well. But matched up, there is the possibility of something beyond what any of us have ever imagined. I'm not wrong, am I?" Finally I turned to face him, once again feeling composed, rational—*just like him*.

Mr. Barnum regarded me levelly. "No, Vinnie, you are not wrong. I'm very glad you understand this. I don't believe either of the other two does, however, and that's not a bad thing. They are both truly smitten with you; please don't forget that—please don't forget that you have a great deal of feminine charm. I may be good at selling, but I have yet to find a way to sell the heart on something it truly doesn't want. I wish to goodness I had," he grumbled, a sudden sadness in his voice. And I knew he was thinking of someone else; I knew, too, whom that someone was. I'd only ever seen him look so appealingly sad at one other person—

Jenny Lind, whose portrait he kept in his library, whose photograph he kept on his desk at the Museum. I turned away, sickened by my insight; oh, what good was a brain like mine if it didn't allow me to have any illusions? For I knew he would never, ever look at me in this way. Yet—

Charles Stratton did.

"Charles and Nutt are smitten with me because neither has ever seen an attractive woman his own size before," I muttered sourly.

"Again, Vinnie, don't disparage yourself. Could it possibly be that they both simply enjoy being with you—as do I?" Mr. Barnum smiled at me, but there was no trace of longing or regret in it, and I decided, right then, never to look for that trace again. I was a busy woman; I had no time to keep looking for something I would never find.

"Very few people marry whom they truly want, do they?" I looked at him levelly. He did not contradict me.

Instead, he asked, "And so you do wish to marry?"

"I can see the benefits of a marriage like this, for a life such as I have chosen. It is a difficult life for a woman alone, even under your management." I thought of how it had felt to have someone beside me as I signed my photographs and met notable strangers; I had felt a measure of safety that I had never experienced before. Also a measure of respectability: I would never again have to fear the likes of the anonymous man in New Orleans, if I were a married woman. "I think I could make it work," I continued boldly, but couldn't bring myself to look at him. "We all have to settle for something—less, eventually. Don't we?"

There was a silence. A long, ponderous silence that told me all I needed to hear.

"So." I cleared my throat and nodded decisively. "We compensate with other things. I will expect the biggest wedding New York has ever seen. And I choose Charles Stratton, for your information. Nutt is a posturing little boy, but that is all."

Mr. Barnum had laughed when I mentioned my ambitions for the wedding, but he turned very serious when he heard my choice. "Vinnie, I feel I must ask if you are at least fond of him. For

Charlie is my friend. I'll not have you hurting him by being cruel or indifferent."

"Have you asked him the same thing about me?"

"No. But Charlie isn't like us; he's all heart, and he needs genuine affection. As smitten as he is with you, I give you my word—I'll not condone this thing if I think, for one moment, that you'll be cruel to him." Mr. Barnum spoke so quietly, so plainly, that I was startled; I hadn't realized how devoted he was to Charles. It touched me; it touched my heart, which was in danger of icing over, so much was I determined to neglect it for other, more practical matters.

"I needed to hear that," I admitted, returning the compliment of honesty. "I needed to be reminded of that. You have my word, I'll be kindness itself. I cannot promise to love him. But I can promise to care for him. I do have that capacity, although I'm not entirely sure you believe me."

"Vinnie, Vinnie, my dear girl. I believe anything you tell me; I believe in *you*. More than I can adequately express."

We smiled at each other, and then he leaned forward and for a moment—oh, such a brief, precious moment—he placed his hand upon my face, gentle as a sigh. It was the first time he had touched me like this; indeed, it was the first time any man had touched me so reverently, tenderly. I shut my eyes, hoping to memorize his touch; I knew it would have to last me a long time. A lifetime.

Then I looked up at him with a bright, capable smile upon my face; continuing to discuss the matter, we both swore we would never repeat our conversation to anyone. We both knew the value of romance as a marketing tool; we also knew we did not want to hurt Charles.

Should you care to read further about the details of my

engagement to Charles Stratton, or General Tom Thumb, Mr. Barnum's autobiography provides a very interesting, entertaining account. It was the story that the world—and Charles himself—came to believe. It was the story that both Mr. Barnum and I told him, individually and together, through our actions and our words; you would be hard-pressed to find better actors than Phineas Taylor Barnum and Lavinia Warren, working together.

It was a story of a bashful maiden reluctant, at first, to all overtures on the part of the dashing, beloved hero, a story of a benevolent friend who slyly arranged to help the hero overcome all obstacles and win the fair maiden's hand.

It was a romantic story, a true fairy tale; Charles always did enjoy those. He never lost his little boy's eagerness for happily-ever-after endings. Neither did Presidents, Queens, newspaper magnates, shopgirls, Vanderbilts, and Astors.

Neither did a world sickened and weary of war, we were all soon to discover.

INTERMISSION

An advertisement in *The New York Times,* January 18, 1863—

BARNUM'S AMERICAN MUSEUM

Now or Never! The wedding is positively fixed for TUESDAY, Feb. 10th, on which the world-renowned Chas. S. Stratton, known as TOM THUMB, will be married to little MISS LAVINIA WARREN THE QUEEN OF BEAUTY, who has been visited and admired by over TWO HUNDRED THOUSAND PEOPLE, every one of whom pronounced her THE MOST BEAUTIFUL MODEL OF A WOMAN . . . see her NOW OR NEVER as her engagement ends with her NUPTIAL CEREMONY . . .

[ELEVEN]

In Which Our Heroine Finds True Love at Last

My dear friend did not hesitate a moment before capitalizing on our engagement; as soon as Charles placed the ring upon my finger, the unbelieving grin upon his face thawing my increasingly icy heart a fraction, he was appearing with me at the Museum. Between my levees, we both appeared in the Great Hall, selling our individual *cartes de visites*—and reminding everyone that, soon, there would be photographs of us together to purchase. The crowds were endless, the excitement palpable; never had I experienced anything like it. Policemen had to be called in to keep the crowds at bay as we entered the hall, and to keep the lines for our photographs orderly.

There were moments when I paused and looked around, trying to absorb the scene, the frenzy, trying to make sense of it all. How was it that just a month ago, I was excitedly preparing for my little reception at the St. Nicholas Hotel?

Now everywhere I looked I saw faces, happy shining faces, smiling down at me, calling my name; even in my dreams I saw outstretched hands, all wanting to shake mine, clamoring for my signature, clutching my photograph. The noise, the chatter, was incessant, and at night, when I was blessedly alone in my hotel room, my ears still rang from it. My neck ached alarmingly, as there were simply so many more people to *see*. It was as if Charles and I were one pebble, tossed into a pond, staring up in astonishment at the ever-widening ripples caused by our presence.

I had always looked up, of course; that was my natural position, just as a flamingo stands on one leg or an otter swims on its back. But for the first time, I was so acutely aware of the strain it put on me—my muscles always knotted, both at the base of my skull and where my neck met my shoulders. And my hand, my tiny, delicate hand! I thought it had ached before! Now, so crushed it felt at the end of the day, I finally decided to carry a nosegay, so that my hands might be occupied and thus not available for shaking.

And through it all, through this outpouring of joy and heartfelt wishes for our future—even then, I knew that our union had struck a chord in a nation heartsick of casualty lists—a stranger was by my side. A man who tucked his arm in mine to escort me wherever we went; a man who sat beside me while we signed photos, our elbows often bumping, my skirts often draped over his knee; a man who, in the rare moments we were alone, sighed and whispered my name, brushed his lips against my cheek, held me in a clumsy embrace. Very tentatively, as if he were seeking permission, which he was.

And it was up to me to bestow it; it was up to me to put him at ease, to blushingly return his shy affection, his timid glances. I had to pretend to be thrilled by his trembling, fumbling caresses, so thrilled that I might desire to return them myself, one day. One far-off day, a day I could not yet bring myself to imagine. And because I could not, I concentrated solely on the now; telling myself that at least we had this astonishing experience to bond us together, and hoping that perhaps it would be enough of a foundation to build a believable marriage. Believable to him, to my family, to my public.

For myself, I did not hold out such hope.

Marriage. I truly could not comprehend it. Right now, it was just the curtain that would soon fall upon a very elaborate, precisely plotted play. What happened after the principals retired backstage, I simply could not imagine.

I don't believe Charles could, either, and this somehow gave me courage. He was such a creature of the public; he had grown up knowing no other life. I suspected he viewed everything as a performance, even the act of brushing his teeth or combing his hair. So that his idea of marriage was no more real than mine; we had that, at least, to unite us.

And so I continued my part in this elaborate play and, little by little, day by day, I began to enjoy myself; perhaps, like Charles, I even began to believe it was real. I started each morning hungrily scouring the newspapers for articles and illustrations about us, and I was never disappointed. The Civil War was still raging, but you would not know it by looking at the front pages of the New York newspapers; body counts and war maneuvers were displaced by articles about my upcoming nuptials. When I went to Madame Demorest to be fitted for my wedding gown, I was accompanied by two lady reporters who enthusiastically described my bridal finery. (Oh, it was beautiful; an exquisite concoction of white satin and lace with a flowing train, decorated with pearls and beads!) I also modestly released such details of the rest of my trousseau as Mr. Barnum felt necessary, as well as illustrations of my jewels. Mr. Barnum took care of releasing the details of everything else.

He, of course, oversaw the entire operation; it was his gift to us—and to himself.

"Vinnie, Charlie, now, who are you going to have as your wedding party?" Mr. Barnum asked us one evening, after the Museum had closed. We were in his office, both of us exhausted; Charles was too tired even to hold my hand, as he did, much like Minnie, whenever he was near me. In fact, I was beginning to think of him in much the same way as I did my beloved sister: someone just a little more delicate, just a little more innocent, than I was. Someone in need of my constant protection, perhaps more in need of protection than he was of my love.

Maybe it was because I was thinking of her that her name popped out of my mouth. "Minnie," I said, stifling a yawn. Then I realized what I had said and sat up straight.

"Minnie?" Mr. Barnum looked confused. "Who's Minnie?"

"Why, she's Vinnie's sister!" Charles piped up, even though I shook my head, warningly, at him. But he did not pay any attention. "And say, Phineas, she's just like us! Smaller than Vinnie, even. I met her when I asked Vinnie's parents for her hand. I'm awfully glad to have a sister I don't have to look up to."

"You have a sister?" Mr. Barnum looked at me; there was surprise and hurt, both, in his eyes. "You never mentioned that to me before."

"I never—I just didn't think it necessary, as Minnie's so shy. She's content to stay at home with Papa and Mama."

"What other secrets do you keep from me, Vinnie? I have to say, I'm quite hurt!"

I could not decide if he was joking or not; he had a teasing, crooked grin upon his face, but his eyes glittered, hard.

"None. It's not exactly as if Minnie is a secret, of course, it's just—"

"That you never felt like telling me, your friend, about her?"

"No, it's not that—you don't understand." I shook my head and attempted to undo the damage. "Actually, to get back to the subject, I think Pauline would make a wonderful bridesmaid, and I'd be honored if she would accept."

"And of course you'll be my best man, Phineas." Charles rubbed his eyes sleepily.

"I am much honored," Mr. Barnum replied seriously, patting Charles on the shoulder. "But I can just imagine what the newspapers would say to that—accusing me of hogging the spotlight or some such nonsense. No, I think it would be better if you found someone else. What about Nutt?"

"Old Nutt? Well, he's a jolly old fellow, but he's mad at me, you know. I guess he's still mad about Vinnie."

"I think that he might appreciate it if you ask him, Charles. I wouldn't be surprised if he'd put aside his wounded pride out of happiness for the two of you."

"Well, if you think it's best, Phineas—"

"I do, old fellow. Now, Vinnie, obviously you want your sister to stand up with you—why pretend otherwise?" Mr. Barnum turned to me, again with that hard glitter in his eyes; I could hear the gears in his brain turning now, as well, as he chewed his lip, drummed a pencil against his desk. "I have an idea. Listen to me. We haven't discussed what you'll do after your honeymoon tour—by the way, the Lincolns have definitely invited you two to a reception at the Executive Mansion, and that's a bit of publicity beyond anything I could dream up, bless their Republican souls—but now I'm coming up with a plan. Imagine this: a quartet of the most wonderful, intelligent, and perfectly formed ladies and gentlemen the world ever produced, presented for the first time ever before the public. You two, Nutt, and now—Miss Minnie Warren. What do you think of that?"

"No." I shook my head so vigorously that some of my hair

escaped its pins, falling down and tickling my nose. "No. Not Minnie. She is not cut out for this life, and I've promised that I will keep her safe. And safe, for her, is back home, on the farm, where she belongs."

"Vinnie, Vinnie, what's the danger in the life that you are living now? Surely you don't feel as if you're physically at risk in my beautiful Museum?"

"Of course not." I waved my hand impatiently; Mr. Barnum was being deliberately obtuse, and both he and I knew it. Charles, however, did not.

"Why, Phineas is right, you know, Vinnie. Look at how long I've been with him—the worst thing that ever happened to me was when Queen Victoria's dog almost bit me, remember, Phineas? We were at the palace, you know, and I had my little toy sword that I used onstage, and when that dog came yapping toward me, I waved my sword at it—how everyone laughed! Remember, Phineas?" Charles's eyes gleamed bright, as they always did when he was relating stories of his past successes. I tried to smile patiently; he had told me this story many times before.

"Charles." I placed a gentle hand upon his arm, something I knew soothed and pleased him. "You hardly know my sister. Minnie is the sweetest soul in the world, but simple. Trusting. The type of timid soul who can be wounded by so many things, not just physical ones but a glance, a word, an idea, even."

"No, you're the sweetest soul in the world," my erstwhile lover argued, right on cue. I turned back to Mr. Barnum with a sigh.

"I still say Pauline will be perfect. She was such a help to me when I first came to New York, and she is exquisite—think of how lovely she'll look, how the Press will remark upon the beauty of Mr. Barnum's daughter, such a compliment to you!"

"You can't fool a fooler, Vinnie." Mr. Barnum laughed. "It

won't work. I don't want Pauline, and that's that. I am her father, after all; I can forbid it."

"Is this my wedding or yours?" I retorted.

"That's a fair enough question, isn't it? Which, do you think?" He sounded amused.

"Don't you mean our wedding, Vinnie? Not just yours? It is *our* wedding, isn't it?" Charles looked at me so anxiously that Mr. Barnum and I both colored with shame.

"Yes, absolutely, dear, it's our wedding. Not Mr. Barnum's."

"Absolutely, old chap—I'm throwing you and your lovely bride the biggest shindig this city has ever seen, and actually I wanted to suggest something. We've been bringing in a lot of money, the three of us together, in all of this. We could easily keep it up for at least a month. Why not rethink the date, and I'll throw in fifteen thousand dollars as a nest egg?"

I had to laugh; the man was impossible! Like a child, really. A child obsessed with one toy and one toy alone, who always steered the conversation back around to that one thing, who took it to bed with him at night. Then I had to laugh again; I had an image of Mr. Barnum sleeping with the day's receipts tucked under his pillow. I would not be surprised!

But Charles did not laugh. He puffed out his chest, as he did whenever he felt the need to assert his manliness, and declared, "No! Not for fifty thousand dollars would I wait one more minute to marry Vinnie!"

"Not for one hundred thousand dollars!" I chimed in, just to see the look on Mr. Barnum's face. And I was not disappointed; his mouth dropped open so that his ever-present cigar fell to his lap, burning a hole in his trousers. Cursing mildly, he jumped up and brushed the ash off, hopping about in a very undignified manner.

"Well, if that isn't all—look at the monsters I've created, the heartless creatures! Putting the old man in the poorhouse, all in the name of love!"

"Oh, Phineas, no—I'm not heartless! I would never put you in the poorhouse!" Just as suddenly, Charles's manliness faded away; he was an anxious, repentant child once more.

"Charles, he's exaggerating, as usual." I patted his plump, warm hand. "Just wait—he'll extract something else equally dear, in exchange for the money."

"Commodore Nutt will be bitterly disappointed if he's not your best man." Mr. Barnum turned to Charles, beseechingly. And my heart began to sink.

"Oh, I couldn't do that to him," my tenderhearted fiancé said. "Very well. I'll ask the old chap to stand up for me."

"I think that's best, to keep peace, and help the poor soul get over his disappointment." Mr. Barnum turned to me with a coaxing smile, that barely suppressed glimmer in his eyes. "Come, Vinnie, think of it. The wedding party now consists of you three absolutely perfect, charming people—who do you think best completes such a tableau?"

"Oh, Vinnie, do ask your sister, do!" Charles turned to me as well, grasping my hand. "For your sister naturally will be dear to me as any of my own, and this would be the perfect way for us all to begin. And how convenient, as well—think of the photographs of the bridal party! Why, none of us would have to be seated or standing on a step; we'd all be the same. I've never before had my photograph taken with people all of my same size—imagine!"

Charles looked so eager, so happy; Mr. Barnum did, as well, although his eagerness was more likely caused by the dollar signs he saw at the mention of photographs.

I didn't know what to do. It wasn't just the wedding; it was what would happen after. *That* was what I feared.

"Just the wedding," I decided. "That's all. After that, Minnie goes back home."

"Of course," Mr. Barnum agreed with that admiring, approving look that blinded me so that I did not always see what else was behind it. "Just as you wish, Vinnie. You know I promised your parents I would never do a thing without your approval first."

"I know," I said reluctantly, ruefully. "And that's exactly what I'm afraid of."

"SISTER! SISTER! WE TOOK THE TRAIN AND IT WASN'T DREADFUL at all, although Papa looked awfully sick and kept his eyes closed the whole time even though I know he wasn't sleeping. And then I was hungry but Mama said we'd eat at the next stop but there wasn't any food there, only some dreadful boy selling black bananas. Mama says New York smells awful, doesn't it? And then we saw buildings that almost blocked out the sun, and I ate a piece of ice that was flavored like cherry, in a paper cup, and then we rode in the most beautiful carriage and Mr. Barnum kissed my hand, just like I was a lady, just like I was you! Oh, Sister, I'm *so* glad to see you!" And Minnie finally paused for breath only to fling her arms about me, nearly knocking me over; she squeezed so tightly I thought she might crack one of my stays. I held her close for a moment, laying my cheek against her tangled, glossy black curls, which Mama had tried to put up in a ladylike sweep. But it hadn't survived the trip; those curls had a mind of their own, and obviously they had decided the occasion was much too exciting to remain in so sedate a style.

"Minnie, Pumpkin, let me look at you!" I held her at arm's length, hungrily taking her in as if it had been years since I'd seen her, not just weeks. Even when I came home from the river, I hadn't been this happy to greet her; I think I'd been so numbed from the whole experience. But I wasn't numb now! Something new, something wonderful, seemed to happen every day, and I wanted to share each and every experience with my family.

Minnie smiled, that dimple, that impish sparkle in her eyes, warming my heart. She was wearing the new dress I had sent to her, in the newest fashion—hoops so wide they swayed like the Liberty Bell, tiny waist, brown velvet panels alternating with gold satin. She wore a fur-tipped cloak and gloves and a fur hat (also gifts from me); she looked adorably ladylike.

Mama, too, looked very fine, in a similar dress and cloak, carrying a muff. I had never seen her dressed so handsomely, and it suited her to a remarkable degree. No longer in her comforting apron and homespun dress, she looked every inch a Warren of Massachusetts. Papa, so bashful and cowed, his shoulders pinched, his head bent, did not look so nice in his new suit and coat. A farmer's clothes were all he would ever be comfortable in.

But I didn't mind; I was just happy that they had arrived for my wedding. Mr. Barnum had arranged for a nice suite in the Metropolitan Hotel, on the same floor as mine, where I was newly ensconced in preparation for the festivities. I hooked my arm through Minnie's and led them all down the plush carpeted hall, the ornate wallpaper illuminated by softly flickering gaslights.

"Now, Minnie, once you get settled we'll need to rush right over to the dressmaker's for a fitting. You, too, Mama; I picked out the loveliest gray watered silk for your gown. Now, Mama, you have to remember you're in a hotel. Everything is done for you—you don't have to lift a finger! You don't have to make your own bed or even scrub out the chamber pot; someone will come every morning and do that for you. Mrs. Astor has asked, expressly, to meet you, so she would like very much to throw a reception for us on Monday before the wedding. I still have to do a few levees at the Museum, and I can't wait for Minnie to see the sights! Mr. Barnum has arranged it so that you all can have a private hour or so seeing everything on Saturday. Oh, and Minnie, we're going to have our photograph taken! Can you imagine?"

"My photograph? I don't know—will it hurt very much?"

"No, darling, it doesn't hurt a bit. Mr. Brady is the nicest man, and while it's rather tedious and you have to stand absolutely still, it's over very quickly. Can you do that?"

"Of course, if you're there with me, Vinnie."

"I will be, I promise. I won't let you out of my sight. Here we are!" And I motioned for the porter, who had been following respectfully behind with the luggage, to open the door to their suite. I ran ahead so that I could see their faces as they took it all in; I was so happy, so thrilled, to show them this side of life. Oh, how they deserved the finer things!

"Oh, Vinnie," Mama breathed as she fingered the fine velvet portieres, draped ceiling to floor, covering the windows. "How on earth do they clean them? You can't wash velvet!"

"I don't know, Mama." I laughed, for it had never before occurred to me to wonder. "I'll have to ask someone."

"Vinnie, they don't leave these lights on all the time, do they?" Papa, who had been studying one of the hissing gaslights jutting out from the wall, turned to me with a frown. "Think of the expense! How much do they get for a room like this, anyway? I'm not sure I like that Barnum fellow paying my way, after all. I'd like to give him something for all this—do you think he needs a milk cow for his place in Connecticut?"

"I doubt it, Papa. But I'll ask, just for you."

"Well, I'd appreciate it." And my father went back to studying the gaslight, passing his hand over the top of the globe, checking to see how hot it was.

"Oh, Vinnie, look!" Minnie came running out of her bedroom clutching the beautiful gift that I had placed on her bed. It was a

Jumeau doll, from France, an exquisite creature with a china face, real black curls, and the most sumptuous dress of blue silk, with lace petticoats and pantalets, and even satin slippers. I had chosen it because I thought it looked like Minnie, with those curls; as my sister cradled the doll in her arm reverently, smoothing her ringlets, I was satisfied that I had been right.

"Do you like it, Pumpkin?"

"Oh, more than anything I've ever seen! Even more than my new kitten back home. Thank you so much, Vinnie!"

And the light in my sister's eyes as she sat carefully upon a small stool, cradling the new doll as if it were her own child, made me smile; it made my heart warm and expand so that I felt, in that moment, as full of love as any bride. For it was Charles who had bought the doll for Minnie; he had taken me shopping for it, insisting that he wanted to make her a present, and quite gravely asking my advice on the matter.

"Thank Charles, your new brother. He was the one who bought it. You can thank him tonight, at dinner. We're dining with Mr. Barnum at Delmonico's on East Fourteenth Street—ladies can only dine there in a private room—and oh, just wait until you all see it!" I was Father Christmas at that moment, showering my family with unknown delights. "It's all crystal and marble and the finest silver and china, and waiters who whisk away your plate as soon as you're finished and give you another, full of something else delicious! It's like nothing you've ever seen before—so many dishes! And the wedding reception will be just as grand, I assure you!"

Mama and Papa exchanged an odd glance. Then Mama turned to me, her gentle eyes filling with tears, and she said, "Vinnie, dear, we need to discuss something with you."

"What? What is it—are the boys all right? Benjamin? Nothing happened to them, did it?" Oh, how stupid of me—it was so easy to forget about the War, with all that was happening to me, especially here in New York. Despite it being the most prominent northern town, a great many citizens were very sympathetic to the Confederacy. So much of the commerce and manufacturing had depended upon the cotton from the South, and with the blockades, business was slowing down. And there were so many immigrants; were the slaves truly to be freed, the immigrants were fearful that their jobs would be taken away. And then, of course, there were rumors of an impending military draft, which did not sit well with the Copperheads, the name by which the Rebel sympathizers called themselves.

All that was but a faint, nagging buzzing, like an insect circling about my head, easily swatted away by the more immediate, personal demands upon my time and attention these days. But Mama and Papa, of course, did not have such pleasant distraction; they lived every day in fear for their soldier sons.

"The boys are all right, aren't they?" I repeated, anxiously, when they did not reply.

"Yes, dear, as far as we know, they're fine." Mama tried to reassure me, but the lines around her mouth deepened, as if from the effort of holding in her constant worry.

"Then what is it? Why do you look so strangely at me? Papa?" I turned to my father. He could not meet my gaze; he sidled back to the gaslight, to further inspect its construction.

"Vinnie, dear, it's just that—it's just that we don't feel entirely comfortable with all—this." Mama gestured around at the ornate room. But her suddenly furtive eyes betrayed her; I knew instantly that their accommodations were not what she was talking about.

"What do you mean, 'all this'?"

"I mean, dear, that Papa and I have decided not to stay for the wedding. We came up to bring Minnie, and entrust her to your care. But we have tickets for the train home tomorrow."

"Oh." I decided to examine the portiere nearest me; I pulled it to the side and, standing on tiptoe, surveyed the street below, concentrating on the smallest details—the way the Negro man in front of the hotel doorway stood with his heels pressed together, his feet splayed out in a *V,* like duck feet. I observed how a basket of some kind of fruit—apples, they must be—fell off a wagon as it rounded a corner, and was immediately set upon by a pack of feral children who appeared as if conjured up, for they had not been visible a moment ago. I studied how the filth that gathered between the cobblestones was covered in a filmy sheet of gray ice, and how this dressed it up, made it appear not as it was—a sludge of horse manure, sewage, rotting produce, and who knew what else—but rather like the icing on top of a cinnamon bun.

"You do understand, don't you, Vinnie?" My mother's voice was very gentle, as if she was afraid it might break.

"No," I said, baldly. "I'm afraid I don't."

"It's just that—it's not that we don't believe we won't grow to like Charles, and look at him as our own. It's not that we don't truly believe you know what is best for you, for you always have, and you've never let us down. But this is all so grand—my heavens, Astors and Vanderbilts, you say!—and we're so simple. We're not comfortable with all this, not the way you are, and, well—"

"It's not as if this is just a *performance,* Mama." Finally I turned away from the window, anger doing its best to smother the hurt. "It's not as if Mr. Barnum is selling tickets to my *wedding*." (I did not reveal that at one point, I was afraid that he was—and had to ask him, flat out, not to. He claimed that it never crossed his mind, but I was not so sure.) "We're getting married in a church, you know, Grace Church, and Reverend Putnam from home is even going to assist. *Mrs.* Putnam will be there, for heaven's sake!" I shuddered, remembering how rude that woman had been to me back home. Now she was swanning about Manhattan, telling all who would listen that she was "the wife of the minister who will be uniting those adorable little sweethearts in Holy Matrimony."

"I know, dearest, and we don't want to hurt you. That's the last thing we want to do."

"But you have, you have, and I don't know *why*!"

To my horror, I began to cry, and Minnie, alarmed, placed her doll carefully down on a chair and ran over to me to pat my hand; she soon had tears running down her own rosy cheeks, although she had no idea why I was crying.

"Vinnie." Papa was suddenly kneeling next to me, carefully pulling up his new trousers so as not to tear them. "Blame this all on me. I'm the one who's a country fool, not your mother. I'm the one who asked to go right back home. Don't blame her—blame me."

"Oh, Papa!" I looked into his sweet, simple brown eyes, those eyes that had never understood me, never known what to do with me—but had never gazed upon me with anything other than pure, unselfish love. And I knew that he was not telling the truth. I knew that it was my mother who had made this decision. A lifetime of worrying about me, about all her children, had made its mark upon her so that now her handsome face was falling, as if under the weight of it all—me, Minnie, my brothers off fighting in a war. She was dear, she was sweet—but she was also far more knowledgeable about the world than Papa was. She had never trusted Mr. Barnum, and now some of that distrust was throwing its shadow across me as well. I did not know what I had to do to win back her trust, and at that moment, frankly, I did not much care to learn. I was simply stunned, my heart pierced by the sting of her rejection.

"It's all right, Papa," I said, stroking his large, weathered hand; my small white one looking like a delicate glove against it. "I understand. I don't want you to be uncomfortable."

"Good," Mama said, clearly relieved that I appeared to believe him. "Now, Vinnie, after the honeymoon I want you and your Charles to come home for a nice long visit. I mean it. Delia and I are planning for it; you're going to get the boys' room, we'll spruce it up, we're already sewing some new curtains, and I'm going to have a lovely at-home to introduce you all to our neighbors. I'm sure that you have plans with Mr. Barnum, but he'll allow you that time with your family, won't he?" Mama looked anxious; I knew she was apologizing in the most meaningful way she knew how—by diving into a cooking and cleaning extravaganza. I had seen her attack a floor with a brush and a bucket of soap as if she were scrubbing the deviltry from Lucifer himself; I suspected she needed to scrub away some of her own demons right now.

"Of course, Mama." I wiped away my tears and smiled at her. "I can't wait. And I'm sure Charles will be pleased as well."

"I'm so glad." Mama nodded, reassuring us both. "Now, you'll take good care of Minnie, won't you? You know we'd never think of leaving her with anyone but you. You're the only one we trust—and you're the only one she trusts, as well!" Mama smoothed Minnie's curls and planted a kiss atop her head.

"Of course! I won't let her out of my sight for a moment! I have so much planned for the two of us, Charles will get very jealous, indeed!" I seized upon this request, fell upon it as a soldier might fall upon his own sword. This was how I could recapture Mama's trust: by caring for Minnie as if she was my daughter, too. Nothing bad would come to her, no harm, no disappointment, no pain or sorrow. Not as long as she was with me.

"And I'll take care of you, too, Vinnie," Minnie assured me solemnly. "So Mama won't have to worry at all!"

"We'll take care of each other," I agreed. "I'll begin by moving you into my suite right away. You can't stay down here by yourself." I rose, happy to begin my rehabilitation. "Come, Pumpkin, and help me! Be careful with your doll—she's made of china, not wax!"

"Vinnie, for goodness' sake! You forget how old I am now! I know how to carry a doll!" Minnie's little nose stuck up in the air as she sighed with disdain; I shared a smile with Mama and Papa. I could do this; I could keep my sister safe and innocent. I could preserve her childlike ways.

If only it had been that easy! For the one thing that I did not realize—and I don't believe my parents did, either—was that my sister was really no longer a child. She was a young woman, despite the fact that none of us was willing to see it. And young women have passions and yearnings that even the most vigilant sister cannot always anticipate or even acknowledge.

Particularly when she hasn't yet experienced them herself.

AND SO WE WERE MARRIED. THERE HAVE BEEN SO MANY ACCOUNTS of that day; I'll simply enclose the following report, which was printed in the Manitou, Wisconsin, *Daily Bugle*.

LILIPUTIAN WEDDING, A FAIRY'S DREAM

This Tuesday last, a ceremony like no other took place in Grace Church in New York City. It was there that that miniature gentleman, Charles Stratton or as he is more popularly known, GENERAL TOM THUMB, at last married his dainty bride-in-miniature, Lavinia Warren.

The bride wore an exquisite gown of white satin and lace, and her hair was arranged à la Empress Eugenie, with a bridal veil held in place by a coronet of orange blossoms. Her little white kid gloves measured from wrist to tip of the finger only four and one-half inches! The bridal bouquet consisted of roses and japonicas, and the jewels adorning the lovely bride were a gift from her dashing little groom, all of dazzling diamonds.

The bride and groom were attended by Commodore Nutt, whose broken heart was much evident, as he had competed for, and lost, the lily-white hand of the tiny Queen of Beauty. However, he was much consoled by the fact that, upon his arm was the tiny bridesmaid, Minnie Warren, younger sister of the bride and even more petite.

The four tiny principals took their places before the chancel, and the ceremony began. The responses of the bride and groom were given in clear, distinct tones, easily heard throughout the packed church where the likes of Vanderbilts, Astors, Generals, Governors and Ambassadors all sat in rapt attention, honored to have been invited to so solemn and heartfelt a ceremony.

After the ceremony, the fairy-like wedding party then entered their tiny carriages and were driven through cheering crowds to the Metropolitan Hotel, where a reception was held for ten thousand guests! The petite party had to be lifted upon a grand piano, from where they greeted their guests, to avoid being crushed by their loyal subjects, all eager to bestow their blessings upon their little King and Queen of Cupid's Arrow.

The hundreds of wedding gifts were displayed, only a few of which will be mentioned, as there is not enough newsprint to list them all:

A Miniature Silver Horse and Chariot, Eyes of the Horse Made of Garnets, the Chariot Decorated with Rubies, Given by Tiffany & Company

A Chinese Firescreen of Gold, Silver, and Pearl, A Gift of Mrs. Abraham Lincoln

A Set of Gold Charms, All of the Tiniest Size, To Be Worn by the Bride, a Gift of August Belmont

A Set of Perfectly Matched Pearls, Given by Mrs. Cornelius Vanderbilt

A Quaint Gift of Embroidered Slippers, Personally Worked and Given by Mr. Edwin Booth

A Cunning Bird Automaton, Bejeweled and Covered in Real Feathers, Given by Mr. P. T. Barnum

After the reception, the tiny pair retired to the Honeymoon suite; they were serenaded by the New York Excelsior Band, which prompted the newly minted bridal couple to appear on the balcony where the General addressed the crowd, beginning with the words, "I will make this speech, like myself, short."

The General and his new wife will leave on a bridal tour which will commence in Philadelphia, ending up in Washington where the President and Mrs. Lincoln will give a reception in their honor.

This account is accurate for what it relates. It is also glaring for what it does not.

It makes no mention, for example, of how slowly, almost reluctantly, I walked down the aisle toward my groom, who was very handsome and dignified in full black dress suit. Minnie, in the sweetest white silk, a crown of rosebuds in her hair, smiled so happily at me. I remember blinking at her in surprise; she was so poised, she had so eagerly participated in all the festivities, that I almost didn't recognize her.

The article also does not relate how mechanical, how tinny, my voice sounded to me, despite having rehearsed the responses until I no longer had to think of them, until they were like lines in a play.

It does not describe how proud Mr. Barnum was, like the grandest, most successful parent of them all—like Adam himself. The father of us all. He beamed, he shook hands, he poured champagne at the reception; he slapped Charles on the back and gave me a paternal kiss, the only time he had ever kissed me, and it felt wrong. Awkward, forced—unlike anything that had ever passed between the two of us.

The biggest omission of all, however, is what took place after the reporters left to file their stories, after Charles and I retired to our honeymoon suite. There, we encountered an enormous bed the size of a boat, sprinkled with rose petals. I almost laughed at the absurdity of it; did the Metropolitan not realize whose wedding reception it had hosted? Although a set of velvet steps had been thoughtfully placed beside it—a very nice touch, indeed.

A table had been laid for us, with two slices of our wedding cake, a bottle of champagne, and a lovely roast quail. But the bottle was simply too big and unwieldy for Charles; he tried to pop the cork, huffing and grunting; he suffered not a little loss of pride upon not being able to manage it, and I felt for him. Discreetly, I turned away from him during his exertions but finally summoned a porter to do this chore, reassuring my husband, "A groom should not do anything as ordinary as open a bottle of champagne on his wedding night."

I believe Charles was mollified, for he relaxed over dinner, and we managed to chat about the odd little details that stood out to us after this very long, endlessly ceremonial day—the comical things, such as when the minister called him "Charlie" instead of "Charles"; how Mrs. Astor, in all her diamond-encrusted finery, actually elbowed Mrs. Belmont out of the way in her excitement to greet us first.

As we began to talk, I realized we hadn't truly spoken to each other at all until that moment. How odd, on our wedding day!

Eventually we exhausted trivial conversation, and we both simply stared at each other. Mr. Barnum was not here to wink and cajole and suggest; it was up to us now—alone. Finally my mind—which had been clenched all day, as if holding a line of defense against some onslaught of memory or feeling—relaxed. And a memory did assault me, paralyzing me, leaving me to stare at my new husband in horror.

"Oh, it would be dreadful, impossible," I heard my mother's stricken voice, from long ago. *"Don't you remember the little cow on Uncle's farm who . . ."*

I felt my stomach lurch, my skin turn clammy, beads of moisture pop out along my forehead. The room started to sway, and I had to run to the lavatory, reaching a chamber pot just in time. Wedding cake, quail, it all came up—along with the fear that I had carried with me ever since that day I had eavesdropped upon Mama and Delia, talking about the birds and the bees and the perils of childbirth for little cows. And little women.

A fear that was now terrifyingly real, as was my life; no longer was I playacting. The curtain had fallen at last; the crowds, for the moment, dispersed. Suddenly, I had real decisions to make, decisions that would have consequences not just for me but for the person pounding on the door as I hovered over the pot, my stomach still heaving, asking me what was wrong. The person I must now, and forever more, call my husband.

Just as he was reasonably expecting to call me his wife.

INTERMISSION

From *Harper's Weekly,* July 25, 1863

The Taking of Vicksburg

We publish on page 465 a new portrait of Major-General Grant, the hero of Vicksburg. Most of the portraits in existence represent him as he was at the commencement of the war, with a flowing beard. He has since trimmed this hirsute appendage, and now looks as he is shown in our picture. For a life of the General we refer to page 365, No. 336, of *Harper's Weekly.* He has just been appointed by the President Major-General in the regular army.

The Draft

The attempt to enforce the draft in the city of New York has led to rioting. Men have been killed and houses burned; worst of all, an orphan asylum—a noble monument of charity for the reception of colored orphans—has been ruthlessly destroyed, and children and nurses have lost every thing they had in the world.

[TWELVE]

And So She Is Married

General and Mrs. Charles Stratton are cordially invited to . . .

The pleasure of the company of General and Mrs. Charles Stratton is requested . . .

With kind regards, would General and Mrs. Charles Stratton please accept . . .

So many invitations, so many kind, generous invitations! Mrs. Astor—dear, dear Caroline Astor!—never tired of throwing dinners in honor of we newlyweds, seating us at her enormous dining table so that all might see and converse with us. She even introduced me to her Parisienne dressmaker, and insisted that her hairdresser visit me daily to do my hair in the same fashion as hers.

And Mrs. Hamilton Fish! Sweet, pious Julia, who was so ill-at-ease in society, despite her husband's wealth—even she overcame her shyness to throw an elaborate reception for the General and me, where every guest left with a sterling silver replica of our famous blue carriage, which was such a fixture now, no social event was complete unless our elegant equipage, with its matched pair of Shetland ponies, was seen to be parked outside.

Then there was Mrs. Theodore Roosevelt—beautiful, gentle Mittie; she threw a grand ball in our honor. As we were ushered into her lovely brownstone on East Twentieth Street, I spied two little boys peeking around a corner. The youngest clung to the hand of the oldest and when Charles saw them, he beckoned mischievously, so that they had to come forward.

"Hello, young gentlemen! What are you up to this fine evening?"

"We were waiting for you," the eldest replied. He had spectacles, was painfully thin, and spoke in a wheezy, high-pitched voice. His younger brother had golden hair and the face of an angel. "We wanted to see if you really were as small as Mama said."

"Well, are we?" Charles asked, cocking his head quizzically.

"No! I thought you might be as small as a gopher. But you're not! You're not much smaller than me!"

"Charles." I gently nudged my husband and glanced upstairs, where we could hear the violins tuning up for the ball.

"Can't we stay here a little longer, Vinnie? I'd much rather play with these chaps than parade around a ballroom." Charles looked at me so eagerly—as did the two boys.

I shook my head, feeling every inch the schoolteacher. "No, of course not. Say goodbye to these nice young men."

"Well, goodbye, then—what were your names?" Charles shook hands solemnly with the eldest, but the youngest hung shyly back.

"I'm Theodore Roosevelt the second," the older boy replied with comical gravity. "And this is my brother, Elliott."

"That is a very big name for such a little boy." I smiled as I nudged Charles again. He waved, sadly, as we headed up the massive staircase; so many of these grand homes had very steep stairs!

I understood Charles's reluctance to leave them; the truth was, we were not fond of balls, although it was very kind of our friends to want to give them in our honor. But Charles and I had to dance almost exclusively with each other, all eyes upon us. I attempted to dance with other gentlemen, but it was difficult; they had to take such mincing steps, and my arms ached with the strain of reaching so high up. And for Charles it was impossible to dance with other women, what with the fashions the way they were; those huge, swaying hoops kept him from getting near enough to a woman to grasp her hands.

But, of course, we did not complain in public, as it would have been hurtful to our new friends. And so many of them did I make in those heady days in the late spring of 1863! The General and I were back in New York, back in the St. Nicholas Hotel, once more, after our whirlwind honeymoon tour, the culmination of which—for Mr. Barnum, at least—was our reception at the White House. You can be sure he trumpeted this in all the Press!

While this was, indeed, a once-in-a-lifetime experience (or so I imagined at the time; I've since been to the White House to meet every subsequent president), for me the highlight of our trip was the day after the reception. Mr. Lincoln himself bestowed upon the General and me a pass to drive over "The Long Bridge" that led from the capital out to Arlington Heights, an army camp where one hundred and fifty thousand soldiers were stationed. And among these thousands was my brother Benjamin, whose regiment had arrived from the front just the day before.

I was so nervous that day! Of all the dignitaries and Society people I had met in my new role as the General's wife, no one's approval mattered to me as much as my brother's. I had not seen him since that day five years earlier when I left home with Colonel Wood, that awful day when he had quit our house, as he had promised, simply because I desired something more for myself than he did. I had always keenly felt his embarrassment over my size, yet he was the sibling—other than Minnie—whom I missed the most.

We were given a military carriage and a military escort to drive us through the endless rows of white canvas tents stretching before us as far as the eye could see. We had the windows down despite the cold, and the General and I kneeled on our seats and leaned out, waving at the troops, drawing cheers and enthusiastic shouts as we drove along. It warmed my heart so to see the joy we brought to our brave soldier lads, so many of whom would never come home; it brings a tear to my eye to think of this, even now.

Finally we stopped, and our carriage was mobbed so that some tall soldier had to pick the General and me both up, and set us atop the conveyance. From there, we could better make out each individual face, some of them so young it made my heart constrict; they reminded me of my pupils, when I taught school. These boys should have been thinking of nothing more dangerous than what tree to climb, what hill to sled down. Yet they all carried guns with an ease that I found terrifying.

The General and I were chatting amiably with the crowd, sharing details of our wedding, which, naturally, they had all read about, when suddenly I heard my name. "Vinnie! Vinnie! *Over here!*" Looking out, I spied Benjamin pushing his way through the sea of tattered blue; had he not called my name, I would not have recognized him. For he was a man now, not a boy, a hardened, muscular man with a beard and mustache and a set to his jaw that reminded me so much of Papa's. I burst into tears at the sight of him—and at the joy in his eyes as they lit upon me. The last time we had seen each other, I had found only accusation and pain there.

"Benjamin! Oh, Benjamin!" So overjoyed was I to see him, I tried to stand up, forgetting that I was perched atop a somewhat unstable carriage! A nearby soldier, however, instantly understood the situation and picked me up, placing me neatly on the ground just as Benjamin approached. My brother scooped me up in his arms, twirling me around and around so that my legs flew out and I was afraid the soldiers might see my petticoats. I wrapped my arms around him as best I could—I could not reach all the way around—and I buried my face in his chest. The fabric of his uniform was rough; he smelled like tobacco juice and sweat and smoked meat and some kind of liquor. Then he set me down upon the ground; the soldiers nearest us had respectfully stepped back, so that we were alone inside a circle of dirty, tattered blue legs and muddy black boots.

Benjamin knelt and gripped my shoulders, gazing so piercingly into my face that I felt a moment of foreboding.

"Vinnie, Vinnie—let me have a look at you! Why, how pretty you are, what a fine lady! I can't believe it!"

"And you, Ben—you look fine! Such a soldier—are you well?"

"As well as ol' Bobby Lee lets me be; he keeps us on the run, but we have good generals now, and I think the tide might be turning."

"Oh, that's wonderful! I can't wait to tell Mama and Papa all about you!"

"Are they all fine? The cows—is Papa able to keep up with the cows and all?"

"Yes, yes—everyone's well."

"And Minnie? Is she—is she still at home?"

"She came up to New York for my wedding, but she went home after."

"So she's not traveling with you?"

"No."

He nodded, and I knew he was relieved to hear this. But then he swallowed and said softly, "Vinnie . . . about the way we left things . . . I don't know what to say, still. I never understood how you could go off and—"

"Is this my new brother-in-law?"

Suddenly Charles was next to us, clasping Benjamin's hand. Charles, ever sunny, ever simple, beamed up at Benjamin, completely unaware of any tension between us.

"It's a pleasure to meet you, Sir," Benjamin replied quietly. Then he colored, and seemed suddenly aware that he was kneeling on the ground. Hastily, he rose.

Just then a soldier shouted, "General, I seen you once when I was but a lad, up at that American Museum. It sure is a pleasure to see you again."

Another chimed in, "Me, too. Saw him when I was just a little mite. Never thought I'd see him out here in all this muck."

"We wish you much happiness, General!" another voice called out.

"You sure did make me laugh when I was little, with that tiny sword of yours! I'll never forget that day!"

Charles grinned and trotted over to talk to these soldiers, moving among them with ease, dancing, capering—bringing a smile to faces still filthy with the grime of battle. As he did, I looked up at Benjamin. He was gazing at my husband with an open mouth.

"What do you say to that?" I asked my brother, with a triumphant smile.

"Well, I guess he's pretty popular, that Tom Thumb, isn't he?

I didn't tell anyone in my regiment about you and him, but somebody found out, and you know what, Vinnie? They didn't tease me at all. Matter of fact, I'm supposed to get your autographs for some of the men." He scratched his head, unbelieving, still. "I guess you did all right for yourself after all, Vinnie."

"Do you really think so, Benjamin?"

"I do." He knelt back down and took my hand in his; I looked at his hand, so rough, the nails bitten off, bearing red scars from gunpowder, I assumed. I couldn't begin to imagine all he'd been through, but still I could think of him only as the brother who had carried me to and from school whenever my legs were too tired. "Vinnie, you're my sister and I love you, and I'm sorry I was ever ashamed of you. I was wrong in all that, 'cause look at you now! These fellows sure are happy you came out here. So'm I."

"Me, too!" I embraced my brother once more, my arms about his dirty neck. Then he joined the General and myself in our carriage as we continued to drive through the camp, the General, in particular, being greeted so warmly by those who had seen him perform. And it seemed to me practically every soldier in the Union army had done so; I was very proud of him at that moment.

How proud I was, as well, to be escorted through that army camp by my brother and my husband; how touched I was to see the joy my husband and I brought our boys in blue, fighting so valiantly to preserve our Union! It was a moment I would never forget, and I was eternally grateful to Charles for making it possible. For I knew I would never have experienced it on my own, as Lavinia Warren Bump.

And then we were back in New York, back in Society, the whirlwind of it all; every morning the silver tray next to our door was piled high with thick white envelopes of invitation. One morning, about two weeks after our return, I spied an envelope that was more ornate than the rest; opening it, I quickly read it, then laughed out loud.

The pleasure of the company of the esteemed General Charles Stratton and his very popular wife Lavinia Warren Stratton is requested by their friend Mr. Phineas Taylor Barnum, that is, should the Astors, Belmonts, Depews, and Roosevelts decide they can spare them for a few minutes this afternoon. While Mr. Barnum has nothing to recommend him but his friendship and kind regard (as well as a contract), nevertheless, he would greatly appreciate it if the General and his Lady would deign to come down to a little establishment called the American Museum (perhaps they have heard of it?) to discuss matters that might be mutually beneficial. The visit will not take long and soon enough, the esteemed couple will be back breathing the rarified air of Mt. Olympus—also known as the St. Nicholas Hotel—and cavorting with their fellow gods and goddesses on Fifth Avenue.

Sincerely, Citizen Barnum

"Charles!" I showed the letter to my husband, who was in his bedroom, being fitted for a new suit, as he simply did not have enough to keep up with our social engagements.

"Old Phineas!" Charles read the letter and laughed, which made the tailor—a thin Italian man with a scolding look and ever-flapping hands—drop his tape measure in disgust.

"I suppose we have been neglecting him. I'll send word that we'll be there this afternoon."

"Will we be back in time for dinner with the Vanderbilts?"

"Yes, dear," I said distractedly, as I mentally went through my wardrobe; the pink satin had a tear where someone had stepped upon my train (people were always stepping upon my train); the green silk was clean, but I'd worn it just last week. The gray flowered satin with the lace overskirt might do well. And had my new order of gloves arrived? I certainly hoped so, for I could not dine out without gloves, and I simply could not send my maid out to Stewart's to buy some; mine had to be custom-made.

"Make sure that you have a fresh shirt," I reminded my husband. "And don't forget that Mr. Vanderbilt likes Cuban cigars; you must bring him some tonight."

"Yes, dear," my husband said absentmindedly, as he began to fuss with the tailor over the fit of his jacket.

And I left him in his bedroom, while I went off to my own.

"I CAN'T BELIEVE IT, NOT EVEN WITH MY OWN EYES. THE FAMOUS General and Mrs. Tom Thumb—or is it Stratton only, these days?"

"Our friends call us General and Mrs. Stratton. So, too, may you, if you promise not to be vulgar." I nodded regally, bestowing permission.

Mr. Barnum stared at me; then he allowed that twinkle in his eyes to sneak out from behind its gray curtain, and we all laughed.

"What a life you two are living now! Why, Charles, what's this I hear about a yacht?"

"Mr. Belmont suggested I purchase one, and he invited us to race with him on the Sound this summer. I think it's a good business decision, don't you, Phineas?"

"I don't know about a business decision—those things depreciate terribly. But it sure will look good, and I can use it in some publicity. So go ahead, enjoy yourself—or rather, selves. For I take it you're not sitting at home while Charles is out smoking cigars in smoke-filled rooms, are you, Vinnie?"

"No, I've been so touched by how gracious Society has been to us, how eager they are to befriend us. Of course, being a Warren of Massachusetts does help, you know." I sat up straight, tilted my nose—and caught a glimpse of myself in the reflection from one of the glass-encased bookshelves along Mr. Barnum's office wall. Goodness, but I looked just like my mother! Stifling a cough, I turned away from my reflection.

"Society later, business first. No, actually—remember, I'm just a sentimental old father asking this—any notion of the pitter-patter of little feet? *Very* little feet, that is? You wouldn't believe the letters we get here at the Museum, asking—we've even had baby blankets and toys sent in. Your adoring fans are most eager to see the most popular couple in America become the most popular family."

Charles blushed, and I consulted my hands, folded primly in my lap. I was aware of the intense interest in our family plans. It insulted my sensibility, but I also had to allow it, since we had married in such a public way. Logically, it would follow that we would be expected to present an infant Thumb to the public sooner rather than later.

"Vinnie says—Vinnie says she is unable to—Vinnie says that we should count our blessings and enjoy life, just the two of us," poor Charles sputtered, his face reddening with each heartbeat.

I blushed as well; while I was not surprised that we were having this conversation with Mr. Barnum—nothing surprised me about him any longer—that did not mean I enjoyed it.

"I see. I'm sorry to hear that, Vinnie. You must be devastated," Mr. Barnum murmured.

I could not return his sympathetic gaze. I knew I could not deceive him, as I had managed to deceive my husband.

I had told Charles, that first night, that I would never be able to have children. He was disappointed; he so loved children, and at first I felt much guilt in my deception.

But I could not silence the memory of that horrified gasp of

Delia's as she contemplated the little cow that had died. I also remembered something, something that was such a part of our family lore that we all ceased to understand the ramifications of it. But I had been a normal-size baby, as had Minnie. We were not fairy creatures at birth; we were healthy-size infants whose growth was not slowed in the womb but long after we had emerged from it. That was the fact I could not forget; that was the realization that had chilled me on our wedding night. I would die in childbirth, I knew it as well as I knew the freckle on the back of my left hand. It was a fact of me, one that was present at my own birth, the one part of me that needed fixing, but how? I simply was not made to bear children without great danger to myself. And so I told my husband that I could not—not that I would not. In my mind, they were one and the same.

As far as the physical aspect of our arrangement, well—I'm afraid I did not ask him how he felt about *that*. I told him that most couples did not share a bed, as they were together so much during the day; I think he believed me. And the times when we did have to share a bed—such as our wedding night, and naturally during our honeymoon tour, when every hotel had ridiculously provided us with the most enormous bed possible—I managed to pat him away after a quick embrace and kiss.

Did he have needs? Again, I did not ask him. Did I? My longings were of a more profound nature than simply skin against skin; they were for intimate conversations, long into the night; lazy days spent reading together, debating topics small and large.

They were for a union, but not merely of flesh. A union I would never have, and that was by my own design. But then again, it was not a fate that I had ever thought would be mine in the first place. And so, as time went on, my longing faded. As I hoped any longings that Charles possessed would as well.

"Well, that's that, then." Mr. Barnum sounded disappointed,

as Charles and I exchanged uncomfortable glances. Then—deliberately avoiding my gaze—Mr. Barnum cleared his throat and said, "Charles, I promised Nutt you'd drop by and see how he's doing. Poor fellow has been rather down lately. If I didn't know better, I'd say that he was pining over Miss Minnie—I think he was quite smitten with her when she was up here. But why don't you go see him? Vinnie can stay here and keep me company; it wouldn't do to have her taunt the poor lad with her loveliness."

Charles nodded eagerly and trotted off to seek Commodore Nutt. I watched him go, nervously; then I took a breath, summoning up my courage. I pulled my chair over to Mr. Barnum's, and we sat knee to knee, eye to eye, just like old times.

"What is it? Why did you send Charles away? Is something wrong?"

"Not wrong, not exactly. But Vinnie, I have to say, I never thought I'd see the day when you would lie to me."

" 'Lie'?" I colored; I truly did not wish to have this conversation with him. "Mr. Barnum, please, you must not make me explain. I simply cannot have children, that's all, and I wish you would leave it at that."

"What? Oh, no—no, that's not what I was talking about, no." Mr. Barnum looked as mortified as I was; he even deliberately dropped his tobacco pouch to give himself a moment to collect his bearings. "Vinnie, I am sorry about your, er, situation. Forgive me for not having considered something of that nature before I blundered on. However—well, first things first. No, I'm talking about the fact that you were still under contract to someone else when you signed with me."

"Oh." I sank back into my chair and allowed my feet to dangle, something I generally tried very hard not to do. "Colonel Wood. He contacted you." It was not a question; I knew it was true. I had always known it would be true, someday.

"Yes, he did. Tell me, Vinnie, why didn't you mention it from the first? It would have been no problem at all—I would have paid the scoundrel off with a pittance, and no more would be heard. But now you're famous, you're Society—you're worth so much more. And this Wood, whatever he may be, is no fool."

"No, he's not, although he is an evil, evil man!" I spat the words bitterly, for they were bile in my mouth. All the humiliation, all the times he had kicked at me, threatened to pick me up, throw me across a room—and then the ultimate mortification of trying to *sell* me as if I were a slave—it all came back, washing over me so that I felt my very skin turn grimy and dirty with riverboat muck once more.

"Is he—he is the one who you told me about? Who tried to sell you?" Mr. Barnum's voice was very gentle; I longed to look into his face, knowing that I would see absolution there. But I could not bring myself to. I simply nodded.

"I see. Rest assured, next time I see him I will thrash him with my own cane. However, before I thrash him, I have to pay him off, and he is demanding quite a sum not to go to the papers and complain that the dastardly Barnum has cheated him out of a livelihood—not to mention, he made some ridiculous threat to tell stories about you that would make Mrs. Astor's hair stand up on end. Now I understand what he was alluding to—although no one would ever fault you, of course. Still, talk of it would be damaging. So you see, Vinnie—come, look at me, friend." Mr. Barnum hooked his finger beneath my chin and lifted my face so that I could not look away. His eyes were kindness and understanding, both; I searched and searched, but could not find one hint of accusation or disappointment in them. And so I was able to nod and bravely smile back, ready to follow him into battle.

"What do I have to do?"

"Well, this is going to cost us both, Vinnie, as both our reputations are at stake. Look, I'm willing to pay the man what he asks. But it's a very pretty sum, I don't mind telling you. It's going to take me a while to make it back. This is where you can help."

"How? I'll do anything—absolutely anything, I promise. I give you my word."

"I'm glad to hear that, very glad to hear that. For I want you to convince Minnie to sign with me."

"No." I shook my head violently. I repeated it just in case he didn't understand, as he wasn't used to being contradicted. "No."

"Vinnie, consider the facts. I believe Minnie had a very good time at your wedding, didn't she?"

I didn't reply. Yes, my shy little sister did have a good time at our wedding, much to my surprise. While she had clutched at my hand with every step, she had never been completely overwhelmed; indeed, she accepted it all with an equanimity that surprised me. And at night, she had even stayed up late to talk everything over; that was when her excitement truly could not be contained. During the day she was a model of bashful maidenhood; at night, she bubbled over as she tried to process all the lovely things she was experiencing. And as happy as she was to board the train back home, her letters since had betrayed a thirst for news they never had before. No more were they tear-stained pleas for me to come home; now she asked, in a clear hand, how Charles was, how her good friend Mr. Barnum was, did I have any new gowns made up yet, did I think she might be able to come visit again soon?

But I had promised myself—and more important, I had promised Mama, from whom I still felt somewhat estranged—that I would keep my sister safe. And that did not mean dragging her up onstage with me; indeed, the thought of Minnie onstage was so foreign that I could not comprehend it. What on earth would she do? Hold my hand and clutch her doll?

"No!" My tongue was almost tired of saying the word; would he not listen to me? "I told you before, this is not the life for her. If you want Nutt to join Charles and me, that's fine, as long as he behaves like a gentleman. But no, Minnie must not. She's much too young."

"She's no younger than Nutt; she's not much younger than you were when you first left home."

"That's entirely different. Minnie is not me. She's not as strong; she's not as—"

"What?" He cocked a bushy eyebrow. "She's not as bright as you? As capable of understanding the world? I don't know if that's true or not, but what you must acknowledge is that she'll have you with her the entire time. You're in a very different position now, and I'm no Colonel Wood. You'll never be in the kind of danger you were then, and you're a married woman, anyhow. You won't be attracting the kind of people who prey on maidens."

"Perhaps not, but—"

"And the four of you, together—now, you must know you will cause a sensation the likes of which this country has never seen. You will be the most famous quartet in America, I'll bet my hat on it. Think of the audience you will reach; think of how many people will see how proper, how intelligent you all are—what joy you will bring! And you miss your sister, I know it. Charles is a good soul, but—I can see that you are lonely, at times."

"Yes, maybe." I was reluctant to admit it, but I was. "But that's not the point. And anyway, I don't believe Mama and Papa would allow it." And I hoped that they wouldn't, but I knew, deep down in my sinking soul, that they would. They were both anxious to repair our breach, and entrusting me with Minnie's care would do that.

"You can talk them into it, I know."

"I can't refuse this, can I?" I was suddenly weary; I had a long evening ahead of me. The Vanderbilts' dinner would run well past midnight.

"I don't know why you would want to. Think of the possibilities for us all—and especially for Minnie. Think of the things she will see now! Think of how delighted she will be to join you!"

"I suppose so." She would be happy to be with me; that was the one bright hope I clung to, defeated and deflated as I was—also ashamed, for it was my own actions, after all, that had brought about this situation. "Is there anything else you require of me? Does this repay my debt to you?"

"Now, don't talk like that. There are no debts between friends, are there?"

"No, but between business partners, there often are."

He pursed those crooked lips and looked away; his bushy brows gathered threateningly over his eyes. "Very well. Consider your debt fifty percent repaid. We'll talk about the other fifty percent later."

"I warn you, I do not have any other siblings to offer up as collateral."

"I understand."

"Fine." I rose, and was about to leave when I felt compelled to turn around; I did not like leaving him this way. "I do apologize for not telling you about Colonel Wood. I simply wanted, so much, for you to like me and sign me. I was afraid to bring anything up that might prevent that."

"Vinnie, I liked you from the instant I saw you. I would have done anything to keep you from going off—I would do anything, still, to prevent that. Friends?"

He looked so kindly, so earnest—it always surprised me to see how open and honest his face was. One would expect the Great Barnum to have the best poker face in the world, but he did not. His genius lay not in concealing but in sharing—his enthusiasms, his opinions, his disappointments, even. That he did not always reveal all the facts of the matter was really a small quibble; the great thing about him was that he, himself, believed everything he ever said.

So he believed we were friends—and so did I. He believed he had extracted a reasonable price from me—and for a time, I did, as well. So we shook hands and parted cordially, peace restored.

I would remember that handshake later. And recognize it as the moment that I gave away my sister, as well as my soul.

INTERMISSION

From *Harper's Weekly*, December 24, 1864

SHERMAN

How often, as the alarm of Sherman's march has rung into some neighborhood in Georgia which had before only heard the war afar off, it must have bitterly recalled to mind of some thoughtful Georgian the prophecy of Alexander Stephens four years ago. He foretold ravage and destruction. . . . And now at last, after four years, the prophecy is fulfilled where it was uttered.

From *The American Woman's Home*,
by Catharine E. Beecher and Harriet Beecher Stowe

In the Divine Word it is written, "The wise woman buildeth her house." To be "wise" is to "choose the best means for accomplishing the best end." It has been shown that the best end for a woman to seek is the training of God's children for their eternal home, by guiding them to intelligence, virtue, and true happiness.

[THIRTEEN]

And Baby Makes Three

"DO YOU THINK WE'LL LIKE THE NEW BABY?" MINNIE ASKED anxiously as she sat upon a stool, watching the stewardess unpack her trunk. We were in our stateroom on the S.S. *City of Washington*; finally, I was on my way to see Europe!

It was October 1864, and we were now a corporation—officially known as the General Tom Thumb Company, in partnership with Mr. Barnum. Newly incorporated, we had toured New England and Canada starting in the fall of 1863, presenting a "marvelous, miniature quartet of the most perfectly formed men and women ever seen," just as Mr. Barnum had imagined. Charles performed his most famous impersonations (unfortunately, he could no longer fit into the body stocking required for him to imitate Hercules, so that was dropped), I sang songs, we both danced, Commodore Nutt performed some sketches, and Minnie recited a simple poem as Mr. Bleeker invited the smallest child in the audience to stand next to her, for effect.

Each performance ended with a reenactment of our wedding, all four of us wearing our original clothes—a touching tableau suggested by Mr. Barnum, who soon got wind of an odd phenomenon sweeping our nation: a phenomenon known as the "Tom Thumb wedding."

Newspaper reports began to appear, describing children being dressed up in wedding finery and arranged in pretend weddings, complete with cake and roses and infant minister. It was the nuptial ceremony in miniature, reenacted in our honor. There were hundreds of "Tom Thumb wedding" parties; "Tom Thumb wedding" fundraisers; "Tom Thumb wedding" pageants at schools.

Was I supposed to be touched by this, viewing it as a tribute to our love? Or was I supposed to be offended, seeing it as a mockery, a joke? I never could decide. After all, my own married life still seemed to be pretend. So much of it took place under the microscope of the public eye. At the end of a long day of performing—of waltzing together, singing together, presenting the perfect little married couple, capped by reciting the marriage vows themselves—Charles and I had nothing to talk about, and no house to keep. We took our meals at our hotel in silence and went to our separate bedrooms, exhausted.

I shared my bed with Minnie, just as we had when we were young; I rocked her to sleep every night. Charles did not seem to mind, for he was so very fond of her. In my sister, he'd found the playmate he had been looking for all his life, a partner in mischief and fun. I often came upon the two of them playing a game of marbles upon their knees, or whispering plans to tie Mr. Bleeker's shoelaces together while he and I sat discussing business.

Minnie, now fifteen and maturing into a very pretty young

woman, had settled in with the troupe remarkably well. Her serious nature was now lightened by flashes of humor, and while she was quite shy onstage, offstage she was invariably eager to explore her new surroundings—enjoying museums, taking strolls in hidden parks, and trying on bonnets in millinery stores. I promised Mama and Papa that I would see that she ate well, never walked alone without an escort, and went to church every Sunday. Above all, I promised myself that I would keep her sweet, innocent nature just the way it was. And to that end, I kept her close by me at all times. Much closer than I did my husband.

Our inaugural tour was so immensely successful that Mr. Bleeker felt compelled to write to Mr. Barnum proposing the postponement of our European tour for a year. "Leaving now," he cautioned, "would be throwing away the cream."

To no one's surprise, Mr. Barnum wrote back, "My dear Bleeker, Go on; save the cream. Your returns show it to be cream and not skim milk. Yours, P.T. Barnum." So we continued our travels in the United States, this time heading south. We even crossed enemy lines for one brief, confused moment when Mr. Bleeker couldn't read a map, although to my disappointment, the enemy did not appear to notice. We soon got our bearings and turned around, crossing back into the safety of Kentucky.

It was there, in Louisville, where I saw my old friend General Grant, who was on his way to take command of the Army of the Potomac. The tide of war was turning, ever so slightly; after New York was torn apart by the Draft Riots of 1863 (we were on the last train out, heading north to Canada, before rioters tore up the train tracks leading to and from the city!), the Union was amassing more and more victories. Chattanooga, Spotsylvania, Cold Harbor—these battles had drained the Confederacy of more men than it could afford to lose. And General Sherman was at that time planning his assault on Atlanta.

It was also in Louisville that I exchanged photographs with a handsome young actor staying in our hotel; he introduced himself by reminding us his brother had attended our wedding.

A year later, I tore that photograph up in horror; John Wilkes Booth had just shot the President.

And now, at last, we were turning our sights to Europe. Our company remained the same, including Mr. Bleeker as manager, and his dear wife, Julia, who mothered Minnie and me in the best possible way, proving to be a boon companion and loyal friend as well as an experienced seamstress. We also employed Mr. Kellogg as treasurer (the poor man developed a nervous tic; as there were so few banks in those days, he practically slept with our proceeds under his pillow at night, forever fearful of robbers!); Mr. Davis, who assisted Mr. Bleeker; Mr. Richardson, our pianist; Rodney Nutt, George's brother, who served as footman and groom for our small Shetland ponies; and Mr. Keeler, who did everything else that needed to be done.

There was one member, however, whom we had to leave behind, and whose replacement we would not meet until after we crossed the Atlantic. It was the very smallest person in a troupe of very small people, and it was the person whom Minnie was so eager to meet, as the *City of Washington* steamed its way down the Hudson toward open sea.

"Do you, Vinnie? Do you think we'll like the new baby?" Minnie asked again, as the stewardess left our stateroom with a curtsy and a wish, in a strong Irish brogue, that we "have safe travels, wee that ye are, mind that you don't get swept overboard!"

"I imagine we'll like it. We liked the other one well enough." I shrugged; I had not gotten too attached to the previous infant, regarding it as simply another prop I had to use onstage. However, both Charles and Minnie had become alarmingly attached, and I had warned Mr. Barnum that this would happen.

This, then, was the last thing I owed him, the last price—or so I thought at the time—that I had to pay for my carelessness regarding Colonel Wood: I had to agree to participate in one colossal humbug, the biggest one of them all.

I had to pretend that I was the mother of an infant daughter. I had to allow Mr. Barnum to fill the papers with the news that General Tom Thumb and his wife, Mrs. Stratton, were the proud parents of an infant daughter, as yet unnamed. I had to accept the mountains of cards and letters of congratulations, the acres of miniature blankets and nightgowns that would not cover a chipmunk, let alone an infant, but the public, naturally, assumed our child was of fairylike proportions. Mrs. Astor sent an exquisite miniature cradle; Mrs. Vanderbilt, a tiny christening gown.

We borrowed a baby. How callous that sounds now! But Mr. Barnum persuaded me to pose with a foundling—a very small one—that he had personally selected from a charity hospital. In Mr. Mathew Brady's studio, just across the street from the Museum, I sat holding that infant, who was beribboned and beruffled in borrowed baby finery (for the things given to us were much too small), smiling at Mr. Brady's camera.

The child, I must say, was well behaved, although rather heavy for me; by the time we were done, the crook of my arm ached.

In our last few appearances at the Museum, in preparation for our European tour, we had introduced our "child" to the public. "Miss General Tom Thumb," she was called, as I paraded her about the stage; no one thought to christen her with a first name. Although I suppose this made it easier to return her to the hospital, as if she were a pair of shoes that did not fit, on the eve of our sailing.

Easier for me, at any rate; not for Minnie, and not for Charles, either. They both grew quite fond of the child, who was cared for by a hired nurse when we weren't performing. Charles had so enjoyed playing with her; he dangled his watch chain above her until she gurgled and cooed; he tickled her; he sang her songs.

And Minnie, who loved all children, who still traveled with a doll although she no longer played with it, well—she had cried and cried when we had to give the baby back, kissing the infant until I was alarmed that she might smother her.

She had tears in her eyes now, as she thought of it. "She was such a little thing. I hope someone good takes care of her. It seems so sad to give her up like that."

"I know, but it's much easier to get a new child when we land. Traveling on a boat would not be fun for an infant—and besides, Mr. Barnum felt that that baby was getting too big. Babies will grow, of course."

"But Vinnie, don't you miss her? Don't you want a baby of your own? One you'll never have to give back?"

I stopped in the middle of arranging some flowers that had been sent to our room by General Winfield Scott, conveying his best wishes for a safe voyage. The boat was starting to rock a bit, as we must have been heading out through the Narrows. And although I was a very good sailor, my stomach lurched at that moment, as I contemplated the notion of ever having a baby. It was still the one thing that could make me have nightmares. Always, it was a dream of blood and pain and cries and finally—nothing.

I wanted to cry out, "No! No, I never want a child, and neither do you!" But I knew it would hurt Minnie, who loved children so; I didn't want her to think I was as coldhearted as I really was. So instead I answered, "Of course, Minnie. But wanting a baby isn't the same as actually having one. And you know—I've told you, darling, remember?—that I can't."

"But Charles wants a baby, I know he does. He told me. Oh, poor Charles!"

"Poor Charles will be just fine. And in the meantime, we can all play with the new baby, and care for it, and I imagine it will be a very nice one, at that. Perhaps, since we're getting it in France, it will even cry with an accent!" I smiled, coaxingly, at my sister. She looked so pretty in her new traveling dress, nearly identical to mine, which was black satin while hers was brown. We both had such lovely wardrobes for this trip, smart cloaks and fur caps and muffs, so many pairs of gloves I couldn't imagine ever running out, but of course knew that I would. I always ran out of gloves, at an appalling rate; I simply shook far too many hands. My husband might kiss every lady he met—and he did, much to my annoyance—but I shook the hands of them all, plus their husbands. And my supply of gloves could not keep up.

Minnie's dark eyes twinkled at the thought of a baby crying in French, even as tears still rolled down her cheeks. She laughed, just as I'd hoped she would, her little dimple showing. And I relaxed—for the moment, anyway—and proposed that we dress for dinner.

I have fond memories of that first journey across the ocean. The weather was fine much of the time, and, dragging my steps with me wherever I went, I was able to look over the railing, marveling at the whitecaps, the seagulls that followed us like a noisy white cloud, the occasional whale surfacing perilously close to the boat, so much more thrilling to see than the poor whale in his tub back at the Museum!

In particular, I enjoyed the brisk, salty slap of wind against my face. I timed it so that I would walk out, bareheaded, stairs in hand, toward the prow of the ship just when the winds were fiercest; the sailors at first were amused, but soon enough they ignored me. I would climb my stairs—well away from the rail—and face the wind with gritted teeth and shut eyes, welcoming that first harsh sting against my soft, protected skin that had never been without a hat, bonnet, or veil. Invariably, it brought tears to my eyes—welcome tears.

For I needed to be punished. I needed to atone for what I had done and for what I still must do, as Minnie continued her discussions of the new baby and even knitted a blanket for it. I deserved every slap in the face that the cold North Atlantic winds could give me. I deserved more, even. But I had to content myself with that.

Landing in Liverpool, we spent the night at Linn's Waterloo Hotel, thinking that we would make a very quiet journey on to London the next day. The next day, however, was Mayor's Day, and the city was thronged with sightseers eager to see the grand parade. So loud were the crowds that we ran to our balconies to see what was happening; in a flash, the crowd had turned toward us and was waving and shouting its welcome.

"Well, if it isn't Tom Thumb and his little bride!"

"Welcome back, General!"

"'Ope you 'ad a safe crossing!"

Soon the street in front of our balcony was thoroughly blocked—and so was the mayor's parade! We retired quickly inside our suite so that the parade could continue, although the cheering for us resounded unabated.

This was just a glimpse of the extraordinary adoration we found waiting for us all through the rest of our trip. I had dreamed and dreamed of this moment, and was not disappointed. To see, with my own eyes, the places I had read of in my history books was an experience I will always cherish.

From Liverpool we journeyed to London. There we were guests of the Prince and Princess of Wales at Marlborough

House. The Prince and Charles shared a touching reunion, as the Prince had been a boy the time Charles visited his mother the Queen in 1847, and remembered him well. He also remembered being sent up to bed much too soon; fancy, the future King of England being sent up to bed just like any boy!

The Princess of Wales, a stunning dark-haired, dark-eyed beauty with the tiniest waist I'd ever seen, did not say a great deal; I felt she was not very confident of her English, since she was of Dutch ancestry. However, she did not have to speak; her beauty was more than enough contribution to our pleasure, Charles's and mine. (Minnie and Commodore Nutt did not join us; they were not always invited where we were, and while Minnie never minded, I'm afraid Commodore Nutt did. His impish, elfin face could scrunch itself up into petulance so swiftly, as if it were made of rubber. Indeed, he threatened, many times, to go off by himself at night and find his own fun. This worried good Mr. Bleeker so that I'm quite sure he spent more than one night camped out before the Commodore's door as a precaution!)

While I truly felt bad for Minnie and the Commodore, my spirits could not be dampened, and at times I had to refrain from pinching myself. Was it possible that I, Mercy Lavinia Warren Bump Stratton, was having tea with the future King and Queen of England? "Mrs. General," they both called me, with all the deference I could wish for; I addressed them as "Your Royal Highness," and returned the favor, curtsying deeply whenever we met.

Oh, if only that sour-faced Mrs. Putnam could see!

After a brief stay in London, we prepared for the first real destination of our tour, Paris. In December of 1864 we took the famous ferry across the channel and landed at Calais, that cold, empty-looking city.

Calais happened to have a charity hospital, though, and upon landing, Mrs. Bleeker went directly there, as instructed by Mr.

Barnum. He had contributed enough money to ensure discretion in the matter. Mrs. Bleeker came back to our hotel with a cherubic infant girl, whom Minnie clasped to her childlike bosom immediately. But the stern English nursemaid we had engaged took the child away, saying grimly, "There's nothing worse for a child than to be coddled and cosseted! Mrs. Stratton, Ma'am, if you please, I think I know what's best."

"I'm sure you do," I replied with relief. After that, I saw the child only during performances, although once more, both Minnie and Charles snuck into the temporary nursery whenever the maid's back was turned.

It was in France that I came to rely upon Charles for the first time in our marriage. So far in our life together, I had felt it natural to assume some kind of position of direction, and indeed, Charles seemed relieved to rely upon my judgment and good sense. He was a seasoned performer, yes—far more seasoned than I. But regarding the ways of the world, I felt my life upon the river equipped me to deal with them in a far more practical way than he could. After all, he had been sheltered by Mr. Barnum from the time he was five until the time of our marriage.

Charles, however, was the only one of our party who spoke French. And so, faced with that slippery language that would not stay upon my tongue no matter how much I tried, I found myself turning, more and more, to him for direction. He made all our travel arrangements to Paris, with the assistance of Mr. Bleeker; he ordered for us all the few times we ventured out into restaurants. Every morning when we gathered for breakfast in Mr. and Mrs. Bleeker's hotel suite, Charles translated out loud all the newspaper accounts of our visit. Some mornings he had to read to us for what seemed like hours, so numerous were our notices! Accounts of my wardrobe, Charles's cigars, our every stroll and dinner—each detail was devoured by our French admirers.

The notices were even more numerous when we were summoned to appear at court, for this was before the Republic; the Emperor Napoléon III and his exquisite wife, the Empress Eugénie, were on the throne. And while I was delighted by the pageantry—the beautiful Worth gowns on every attending lady, the glittering jewels adorning the Empress's scandalously low-cut neckline—all I could do was smile and nod. I had to rely on Charles to speak for me, for the very first time.

I must admit that I was proud of him. The manners and courtliness that he had learned, even before his letters, as a child traveling on the Continent served him well; that mind that had absorbed everything that Mr. Barnum had taught him when only a child of five was on display. Reader, I'll not pretend that I ever felt Charles to be my intellectual equal. I'll even go so far as to admit to some feelings of frustration over my husband's immature ways—his habit of simply repeating what others said while conversing about politics or music or art, rather than forming his own opinion; his eagerness to introduce himself with a full recitation of the places he'd seen and the people he'd met; his gullibility, for my husband would believe every tall tale ever told to him, every pipe dream sold, every pot of gold promised.

But in Paris, I was finally able to find more things to appreciate about him. After our invitation to the palace, our success was assured in that gray city (for that was how I remembered it; we were there in winter, and every building, sidewalk, street, and even the sky all seemed the same gunmetal gray to me). I may not have been able to understand the language, but there was no mistaking the interest in the throngs and throngs that we encountered whenever we attempted to leave our hotel. It grew tiresome; it was much too difficult to navigate the narrow Paris streets hemmed in on every side, ears assaulted by the excitable Gallic language. I was quite accustomed to being stared at and pointed to, but hearing myself discussed in a language I could not understand began to wear on my nerves.

The crowds were so pressing that when we tried to go see Napoléon I's tomb, we had to turn around after just a few blocks and return to our hotel. So it was that Charles and I found ourselves spending long, lonely afternoons together. Minnie was usually with the infant, and Nutt was usually off with one of his conquests—one of his many conquests, if his boasts were to be believed—so it was just the two of us. One of my talents long being an aptitude for fine embroidery, I began to teach Charles. To my surprise, he took it up very quickly and soon proved himself even superior to me—and he did not mind Nutt's teasing about it, or even Mr. Bleeker's gentle jokes. Charles retorted that a man had to occupy himself somehow, and this way he'd have something useful to show for it. And indeed, he embroidered many seat covers and pillows and fireplace screens that I still use to this day.

It touched me to see him so intent upon choosing thread of the right hue or a perfect needle. His head bent over his work, his tongue sticking out between his teeth, he was the very picture of virtuous industry. He tugged at that reluctant heart of mine, almost as if he had embroidered himself to a very small, remote corner of it. I don't believe I ever liked my husband as much as I did during our time in Paris.

Yet most of our marriage was still spent upon the stage; whether or not they could understand us, the enthusiastic Paris audiences always applauded ecstatically. Our act was the same as it had been at home, except that we no longer reenacted our wedding. Our wedding clothes were on display before the performance, but now I ended the show by bringing out the child (whose name I still had not learned), doing my best to smile maternally, while in reality, I trembled with fear.

I may have been able to face down a crowd of Rebels to get passageway home from the South, but when called upon to care for an actual infant, I admit to some cowardice. It, or rather, *she,* proved to be very wiggly indeed; squirming, waving clenched fists in the air, so close to my face they almost hit my nose, blinking her eyes against the bright gaslights. Automatically I tightened my grasp about her; this wriggling, live *thing* in my arms reminding me of the time I had dressed up a baby pig in doll clothes, back when I was a girl. The pig had shot out of my arm like it was greased, landing with a sickening thump on the floor, where it lay for a moment, stunned, before it shook its head and ran squealing off, dragging its clothing behind. I was most afraid the same thing would happen now.

After what seemed an interminable amount of time walking the perimeter of the stage with this fussing child in my arms, holding it up, laying my cheek against it, while the audience *ooh*ed and *ahh*ed, I very gratefully handed it off to Minnie, who was standing in the wings with her arms greedily outstretched. Then Charles joined me onstage and together we danced around to the strains of "The Tom Thumb Polka," one of the many songs that had been written in honor of our marriage.

Finally, the curtain came down; we repeated this at least three times a day.

Our notices were rapturous; we were the *"crème de la crème."* Soon there were dolls, songs, greeting cards featuring "M. et Mme. Tom Pouce" all over the city.

Mr. Barnum sent us huge bouquets and cabled us his congratulations—ending with what almost seemed an afterthought. Queen Victoria had asked, once we returned to London, he wrote, if we would come to tea. The Queen was quite fond of babies, of course; would we mind bringing our precious daughter with us, so that Her Majesty could see her and give her a gift?

I stared at the telegram, paralyzed. When I had agreed to this humbug, it was onstage only—or posing for photographs. I had never imagined that I might have to play the part of mother up close, where others could see how ill equipped, how terrified, I was.

"Minnie! Oh, Minnie, you must help me!" I ran to find my sister; Charles said she was in the child's bedroom while the nursemaid was having her dinner. Then I had to ask him where the child's bedroom was; he pointed down the hall, and I burst into the room. "Minnie, I need your—oh!"

Minnie, who was kneeling on the floor next to the cradle, rocking it gently with a beautiful smile upon her face, looked up. "What is it, Vinnie? What's wrong?"

"I didn't know—why, it's so pretty in here! Who did all this?"

For this room, unlike the other stuffy rooms in our suite, was utterly lovely. Scattered around were dolls—several that I recognized as Minnie's—and watercolors of animals and cherubs. Pastel scarves were draped over the lamps, softening the light. Simple vases of posies graced the tables and mantel, and a stuffed white lamb perched on a rocking chair. The whole effect was one of peace and security—exactly how a nursery should feel. It had never once occurred to me to make sure that the infant had appropriate surroundings; it had never occurred to me to buy any toys for it, or to check to make sure the nurse wasn't harming it in some way.

"I did," replied Minnie. "I hope you don't mind, Vinnie, but Mrs. Bleeker took me shopping one afternoon when you were out, and I picked everything out for Cosette. That's what we named her—Cosette—because the poor thing didn't have a real name. And everyone deserves a name, don't you think?"

Minnie looked at me so anxiously, wanting to be right. And, of course, she was. Everyone deserves a name.

Even a foundling child who was beginning life as a stage prop.

"Yes, darling, of course. And Cosette is a beautiful name. Now, could you help me, please, dear? I need to—that is, I want to—learn how to hold her better, how to care for her, just a little, just enough to pretend—I think it would be good for me to learn, don't you?"

"Oh, yes, Vinnie! You do hold her awfully strangely. You never did play with dolls when you were little, did you?"

"No," I admitted ruefully, gathering up my hoopskirt and joining Minnie on the floor. The fire in the hearth, just behind us, crackled and popped. The room was scented with lavender and powder. The child in the cradle was sleeping peacefully, her little eyes scrunched up; she had long black eyelashes and black curling hair. She could have easily passed for Minnie's child, so identically sweet and untroubled were their countenances.

But that was absurd, of course. My baby sister could not have a baby. I suppressed a laugh at the very idea.

"Now, watch what I do," Minnie instructed me, and then I did have to smile. She had never instructed me in anything before; it was such an odd reversal of roles. I led, she followed; that was the way it had always been. Since when had she become such a serious little grown-up?

Minnie reached into the cradle, placing one tiny hand—much tinier than mine; Minnie was so petite and delicate, her hoopskirts often threatened to swallow her whole—beneath the child's head, the other beneath her back. Then she gently scooped it—her—*Cosette*—up from the cradle, and clasped her, reverently, to her chest. The motion was so fluid, so instinctive, that it looked like part of a dance. The child, small as she was, really was too big for Minnie, but my sister did not appear to notice; she simply rocked the child, easily, naturally, against her chest. As if the weight of the child in her arms had triggered some hidden switch,

Minnie began to sing softly, to murmur words and phrases that I could not completely understand, but they were soothing and melodious, like the echoing fragments of songs long after they were finished.

"How do you do that?" I whispered, truly in awe; it was almost as if I was in church, with a real life Madonna and child before me. Minnie's face, with her halo of tangled curls, was lit up from behind by the glow of the fire, so that the only thing you could see was her cameo profile as she bent her head toward Cosette's.

"I don't know, I just do. I don't even think about it. Oh, Vinnie, can't we keep her? Can't we?" Despite her passion, Minnie's voice never rose above a whisper as she continued to rock the infant.

"Minnie, I just don't see how. I would love to, truly, but arrangements are arrangements, and it's for the best. This is no life for a baby."

"It could be. I'd help, you know! I'd do everything; I wouldn't mind a bit. I don't need to be before the public like you. I'd much prefer to stay behind stage and take care of Cosette—you wouldn't even have to pay the nursemaid!"

"Oh, Minnie." It was not in my nature to deny my sister anything, and I struggled against it, trying to sort out the thorny details. The child had no papers, not with our name on them. But would an actual child of ours? I didn't even know. I supposed there would be a baptismal record at least; I knew that Mama kept all of ours in her family Bible. So that would have to be created, somehow. If we actually adopted it, would someone find that out? Or could Mr. Barnum cover it up? But what about later—when the child grew big? We couldn't use her in the act then, could we? I couldn't imagine how. But then, that wasn't the point; Minnie was talking about real life: raising a child, caring for her, kissing her scraped knees, soothing her cries at night, worrying about her schooling, her future—all the things my own parents had done so well.

I couldn't imagine it. Minnie couldn't do it all by herself; I would have to be involved somehow, and I did not wish to be. That was it, pure and simple; my life was onstage, next to my husband, either reenacting a pretend wedding ceremony or holding a pretend infant.

I had no room for big love, big decisions, big messes, big happiness; not in this miniature life, spent under the magnifying glare of so many eyes, that I had made for myself.

"See how sweetly she's sleeping, Vinnie?" Minnie whispered, bending closer to me; she leaned in to hand me the child, careful not to wake her up.

"No," I said, recoiling, as if the child was a hex or a bad omen—something I did not want to touch for fear of how it might affect my future. Hastily I scrambled up from the floor, hiding my trembling hands behind my skirts. "No, no, I'm sorry but we'll just have to take very good care of Cosette now." I avoided Minnie's surprised, hurt gaze. "And when the time comes, we must return her and trust that she will find a good family who will love her just as much."

Minnie didn't speak at first; she merely bent her head down to Cosette and kissed her on the tip of her snub nose. Then she looked up at me, so that I could not help but see the single tear rolling down her cheek; it continued to fall until it landed upon Cosette's smooth, untroubled brow. "I don't see how," Minnie whispered, careful not to wake the child. "I don't see how anyone can love her just as much as me. I don't see how I can ever love any other baby just as much as Cosette."

I turned away. I detested this whole charade. But I could see no way of ending it without exposing it—and Mr. Barnum, not to mention myself. I left the room with a bitter taste in my mouth and a bitterer stain on my soul, knowing that Minnie felt, in her sweet, susceptible heart, that what she had said was true; she could never love another baby as much as she loved Cosette.

I also knew that she would say the same thing again, in a few weeks, when we went to England. Only instead of Cosette, it would be Isabel. Or Alice, or Beatrice—or whatever she decided to name the next one. My sister's heart was endlessly elastic, but I had to wonder, even then, how long she could go on mourning baby after baby after baby.

I also had to wonder why I, the mother in this particular play written by Mr. P.T. Barnum, never did. I never shed one tear over any of those infants—not until much, much later in my life.

INTERMISSION

From *The New York Times,* December 26, 1865

GENERAL NEWS

The Commissioner of Agriculture has received from the American Legation at Jeddo, Japan, several hundred varieties of fruit and flower seeds indigenous to that country, many of which, the consul believes, may be cultivated to advantage in this country.

One thousand four hundred men are now employed on the Reno, Oil Creek and Pit Hole Railroad. In about two weeks the railroad will be open.

Quite a number of plantations near Augusta, Ga., have changed hands; lately the purchasers are mostly from the North.

Frederick Douglass has written a letter accepting the position of delegate in Washington of the colored men of New York.

From *The Blairsville Press,* Blairsville, Pennsylvania, April 19, 1869

General Sheridan received a few days since the following report from Maj. General Schofield, at Ft. Leavenworth: "General Custer reports from the headwaters of the Washita, March 21st, the successful termination of his expedition. He has rescued the captive white women, Mrs. Morgan and Miss White; made the Indians submit to the Government, and holds three Cheyenne chiefs as security for the fulfillment of his promise. The troops are in good health."

[FOURTEEN]

Thrills and Chills Guaranteed to Tingle the Spine!
(or, Trains, Indians, Runaway Wagons, and Mormons)

OUR DAUGHTER DIED IN SEPTEMBER 1866. MR. BARNUM put out the press release: **"The Infant Daughter of General and Mrs. Tom Thumb Dead of Brain Inflammation."** Even in death, she remained nameless.

I killed her; I demanded her death. But I did not mourn her; that was Minnie's duty, one that she begged to be allowed to perform.

"Let me reply to these letters, Sister. It will give me some pleasure."

"Oh, Minnie, no, darling. You don't have to do that—Mr. Barnum's secretaries will send out a card."

"No, let me, Vinnie. It's odd, but I feel as if I owe that to her—to all the babies entrusted to us these past few years. It will soothe me to do so—and the people are so nice to write like this." Minnie held up a letter for me to read.

Dear Mrs. General Tom Thumb, I am very sorry to here of the loss of your Fairy Angel who will surely be in Heaven now waiting for you. We lost a Daughter ourselves to the fever and I trust that they are both in a better place.

I returned the letter with a shaking hand and shakier conscience; I could not bear to keep reading. As relieved as I was to end this charade, I did not enjoy knowing that we had played so upon the emotions of those to whom we had previously given only joy. But I could not continue the practice of snatching babies and returning them as they grew too big; too big to complete the happy tableau that Mr. Barnum was determined to present of perfectly formed miniature father, mother, and child. So I demanded that we end it; we had made enough money on the European tour that Mr. Barnum had no choice but to agree with me.

Unfortunately, the only possible way to end the charade was to "kill" the child that had never really existed, except in the public's mind. And so I was a murderer now.

But the deed was done; the letters and cards would soon subside. We would never have to speak of babies again—or so I thought.

"All right, you answer them. But, Minnie, promise me, if it gets too hard for you, you must stop. I know you—I know your tender heart."

Minnie nodded, picked up her pen, and began to write; her sweet eyes were full of tears, but she answered every one in my name, writing as tenderly as if it had been her own child who died.

This was late September of 1866; we were back from Europe, resting up in Middleborough—enjoying a nation now at peace.

Mama and Papa were growing older, but they were content, now that all their children were back home. Safely returned from combat, Benjamin and James had begun families of their own; indeed, all of Mama and Papa's children were married, with the exception of Minnie. And of course no one ever expected her to wed; she was fully part of my household, as Charles was quite as devoted to her as I was. We made our own little family. Whatever fears I had in taking her away from home and exposing her to the bigger world were forgotten as I relied upon her, more and more, for companionship. With Minnie always with me, I never had to spend much time alone with Charles.

Mama and Papa, however, had come to view my marriage most favorably. Papa especially doted upon Charles. He made him a complete set of miniature hand tools, such as any industrious Middleborough man would need. They were beautiful, hand-carved, and he made an equally handsome miniature toolbox in which to store them.

As disturbed as Mama was by the baby business, she never blamed Charles for it. She took to referring to Mr. Barnum as "that Barnum" once more, and sent back every present he ever gave her until finally he got the message. It bothered him, for he respected my mother immensely, often saying she was of "good, reliable New England stock." But Mama could not forgive him—even if she could not help herself from loving me in spite of my own guilt, and trying, over and over, to find an excuse for my behavior.

"I suppose that man left you no choice," she said one day soon after we returned from Europe. We were in the kitchen, knitting companionably. I was wearing a simple country gown without hoops, and my hair was parted plainly and loosely in the middle, gathered in a knot at the base of my neck. My feet were clad in those flat child's slippers I used to find so tiresome but which now brought me sweet relief. It was such a blessing not to have to dress fashionably, mindful of hoops and trains; not to have my hair done up elaborately, anchored with heavy jeweled combs that caused my head to ache; not to have to converse nonstop with total strangers. Rocking with my mother in her cozy kitchen full of freshly preserved vegetables and fruits, jugs full of orange bittersweet branches with their red berries, the scent of apples in the brisk New England autumn air—it was utter bliss.

"I suppose he just put up handbills declaring it a fact, and you could do nothing but go along with him," my mother said with a sniff.

"Mama, it wasn't exactly that way."

"Do you know how many people here in Middleborough wanted to see your daughter after they read about her in the newspapers? Do you know how many times I have had to make excuses to my own neighbors? Vinnie, that Barnum simply doesn't consider other people in anything he does. I don't know why you admire him so."

"There are more sides to this story than you know" was all I could tell my dear mother. But I refused to continue this line of talk about Mr. Barnum; the man had sorrows of his own to bear. For he was still feeling, keenly, the loss of the American Museum in a horrific fire that occurred in 1865.

Oh, to think of that grand building and all that was in it, going up in flames! To imagine the horror, the spectacle, the heartbreaking screams of the animals panicking and running into the street only to be shot by police, fearful for the public's safety; the sickening stench of burning flesh and feathers; the heat of the conflagration as it spread greedily from floor to floor. Mr. Barnum was not present at the time, thank Providence! But many a brave employee endeavored to save what they could; miraculously, none lost his life.

Mr. Barnum soon opened another museum, farther uptown, but I never thought his heart was fully in it; so much of his own history—as well as mine—had gone up in flames on Ann Street.

"Mr. Barnum has suffered such terrible losses," I reminded my mother. "And his wife is no helpmeet for him."

"Have you ever met her?"

"Once, in Bridgeport, while we were visiting Charles's parents."

"What is she like?"

I laid my knitting down for a moment and frowned, remembering. "She was as I had pictured her—thin, sallow, with graying hair, sunken eyes. A sour set to her mouth. She carried smelling salts with her everywhere she went, and retired at least four times a day to her room to nap. Poor Mr. Barnum!"

"'Poor Mr. Barnum'?" Mama snorted. "It sounds as if he got the kind of woman he deserves. I'm sure he's dragged her to the devil and back many times, that man!"

"Oh, Mama, no. You don't know him, not like I do. You don't—" But I broke off.

Mama did not reply, but she did look at me with a sudden sharpness. I had seen her look at my brothers and sisters like this, as if she could see right through to their hearts—and all the secrets they thought they carried within them. But she had never before looked at me in this piercing, knowing way, as I had always confounded her so.

I attacked my knitting with such dedication, sparks must have flown from my needles; at least I assumed that was what made my face burn with such surprising heat. No more was spoken of Mr. Barnum that day.

Not long after that, however, I was ready to pack my trunk again. Left too long to my own devices, to muse and ponder and dream, left to be truly a wife to my husband in the dull, flickering glow of lantern light instead of footlights, I felt as if I was suffocating. Over and over, I returned to that tree trunk in Papa's cow pasture to pull up the weeds that continued to grow over my name.

What did I fear so, in the warm bosom of those who only loved me? I could not say, as at the time I did not recognize it for the fear it was. I simply felt driven to see, to experience—to give of myself to those whose approval should have meant less than my own husband's but instead meant so much more. I simply knew that I could relax and sleep only on a rocking train or a bobbing boat. I simply realized I needed the warmth of an audience like a plant needs sun.

And I simply understood that the most satisfying moments in my life were spent poring over maps and train routes, discovering new towns that were popping up all over this great country of ours. I could not bear to think that there was somewhere I had never been, someone who might not know my name.

So in late autumn of 1866—after remaining in Middleborough for a suitable period of mourning for our "child"—Mr. Barnum and I decided that the Tom Thumb Company should once again set out, this time to the Deep South, where we had not been able to go during the four bloody years of the War Between the States.

"It will be lonely without a baby," Minnie said softly as we settled into the train for our first leg of the trip. Eastern trains were becoming much more commodious for the traveler; some, like this one, even had upholstered seats if you paid extra to travel in what was called the "first class" section. There were also separate, private water closets for ladies and gentlemen! The modern world was astounding!

Commodore Nutt was once again with us, completing the perfect miniature foursome; across the aisle, he and Charles soon had a lively game of cards going with Mr. Bleeker and the other men of our troupe. While I did not approve of cards, at least the game kept Nutt out of more serious trouble. How a man could have such an appealing, impish presence onstage and be so completely unpleasant off, I could not fathom! Perhaps it was because of our earlier history, or perhaps it was because he sensed my disapproval now—either way, he kept as far away from me as possible. Although Charles, of course, held no grudge; Charles would not recognize a grudge if it came up and bit him on his pug little nose.

"It won't be lonely, dear—think of how many people we will meet!" I patted Minnie's arm excitedly; I had a pleasant, bubbly feeling in my stomach, as if I had swallowed a giggle. I always felt this way at the beginning of a journey.

"But we always have to say goodbye to them." My sister sighed, leaning her curly head against my shoulder. "And that's dreadful."

I smiled and kissed her forehead. "Remember how you used to call everyone 'dreadful'?"

"Did I?" She laughed, shaking her head so that her hair tickled my chin. "I don't remember."

"You did. You even thought Mr. Barnum was dreadful at first."

"How silly of me! I was so little then! I don't think anyone is dreadful now."

"You don't? Not anyone?" I couldn't help myself; I inclined my head toward Nutt, who was slapping down a card and laughing boisterously, causing all the other passengers in the car to look his way.

Minnie followed my gaze. "Oh! Well, yes, I suppose I do think *he* is rather dreadful, at that. I'm so bored by his everlasting sonnets!" Then she closed her eyes and yawned, nestling her body even closer to mine.

I was glad to hear her say this. For I had feared lately that that horrid man had become quite smitten with her. He followed her around and attempted to sit next to her at mealtimes, reciting Shakespeare's sonnets to her—which, kind as she was, she always applauded, complimenting him upon his memory. Several news articles had hinted at a romance or even assumed a marriage between these two—and Mr. Barnum, I knew, would not be displeased if there was.

But I would, for I wanted to keep Minnie to myself. She was the one person in my life whom I could love without guilt or shame or pretense. I was also selfish enough to think that I could fulfill that same role for her, and that she would be content with that. She always had been, after all; there was no reason to believe that we couldn't continue on in this way.

And so, as the train began its comforting sway, back and forth, back and forth, along the rickety railroad ties, I rocked my sister to sleep. Just as I always had, just as I always would. It was a comforting, pleasant thought with which to begin our latest journey together.

If eastern trains were becoming more comfortable, then southern trains were still mired in the past—if they existed at all. For it soon was evident that the only thing left of the South, now that the War was over, was poverty. The scenery that we passed was a smoky nightmare of burnt-out plantations, scorched cotton fields, wrecked locomotives piled up next to railroad tracks. Our travel through these states was disjointed and unpredictable, as so many of the train routes had been broken up by the Union: tracks pulled up, bridges destroyed so that the Rebels could not move their troops easily from one point to the next. And there simply wasn't enough money to rebuild them—so we often had to travel by stage or omnibus, hiring wagons to cart our miniature carriages, in which we always drove about town before our first show.

It was such a pleasure to see the joy on the faces of those poor, noble citizens of the Old South whenever they spied our polished little blue carriage, or Commodore Nutt's walnut-shaped one. Shouts of "Tom Thumb! Ol' Tom Thumb! Mrs. General! Minnie Warren!" would follow us to our hotel, where we would disembark and greet the crowd that had gathered to laugh and applaud. After the hardships they had endured, it was clear they needed entertainment, and we were happy to provide it as we continued the same program we had performed throughout England and France—without the baby, of course.

Charles and I barely glanced at each other while we danced "The Tom Thumb Polka"; watched by so many other eyes, we had no need to look into each other's. Our true intimacy was with the audience. Never did we talk so animatedly as we did with our visitors after the performance, in the little informal levees that we held, where we signed our *cartes de visites*. Charles happily bestowed his kiss upon every female who wanted one, and even those who didn't, and while I still could not approve of such indiscreet behavior, I enjoyed shaking hands with my many admirers. I often thought about how frightened, how ashamed, I had been in my early days upon the river; those dangerous times were like a dream to me. For I was Mrs. General Tom Thumb, beloved and admired, and no one would want to harm me now.

I always made it a point to wave to my new friends as they left clutching my photograph; I turned and greeted the next in line just as I heard the clink of coins rattling in the money box.

While none of our many admirers would ever have harmed us, we did face dangers on the road. We had, by necessity, to travel with great sums of money, Mr. Kellogg's constant nightmare. There was always the danger of being robbed, particularly as our travel arrangements were often detailed in the Press.

One night we stopped at a very desolate hotel in Opelika, Alabama; the stairs leading up from the "lobby"—really just one large, stained spittoon—were merely rough boards loosely nailed to the rail. Our rooms were on the second floor, which was a blessing, as the third floor was reachable only by ladder!

The few inhabitants we had seen on the first floor were of such rough, dissipated appearance that our entire company was happy to gather in one room for the night, especially as Commodore Nutt was feeling poorly, suffering from the quinsy. We passed an uneasy few minutes until we heard a sudden scratching at the door, followed by retreating footsteps.

"Look here," Charles suddenly said, as we all rushed to open the door; on it was freshly chalked the message *11:35*.

"Whatever can it mean?" I wondered, and Rodney Nutt piped up, "It must be a message from the Ku Klux! It must mean someone is going to die at precisely eleven-thirty-five tonight!"

At this, we all froze in fear. The Ku Klux had just started to make its terrible presence felt, swearing vengeance against former slaves and northerners, and the name alone could strike terror in even the stoutest heart. Just as we were absorbing this, we heard the unmistakable report of two pistols fired successively.

"Sylvester!" Mrs. Bleeker cried; Mr. Bleeker had remained outside to settle the horses. She wanted to run downstairs, but we enjoined her to stay; just at that moment, Mr. Bleeker burst into the room, his long face pale, his hair standing on end.

"Get your wraps, there's a 'bus for the station at the door; we need to be on it."

Half the company ran downstairs; the other half remained to bundle up Commodore Nutt, who was carried downstairs in Mr. Bleeker's arms. Just as our half reached the door, we saw the 'bus pull off with the rest of the party, to our dismay.

"It'll be back soon enough," the toothless hotel proprietor

told us as he spat on the floor. "And if it ain't, you can all stay here until the morning, when the train comes."

"No!" Mr. Bleeker said in a strange, strangled voice. "We must get to the station!"

I was surprised by his urgency, for Mr. Bleeker was such a patient, mild man. Minnie held tightly to my hand, and I felt her shivering. Charles, I noticed, was trying very hard to look as brave as Mr. Bleeker, but he could not help but tremble, too.

Finally the omnibus returned, and we all piled in, Mr. Bleeker urging the driver to hurry the horses on as he kept looking over his shoulder. But before we could reach the station, the driver pulled up with a cry.

"Get down!" Mr. Bleeker hissed, pushing Charles down to the floor of the wagon. I pulled Minnie down next to me, and we hid behind the seat in front of us. But I could still see; passing us on the narrow road was a line of horses, all covered in white fabric, with only holes cut out for their eyes and ears. Upon these horses were ghostly figures in white sheets and hoods; they passed us in silence as they rode in the direction of the hotel. Not a breath was exhaled, not a sound was made, from our party or theirs. Even the horses did not whinny. Minnie trembled and clutched at my hand, and Charles shut his eyes, like a child who wishes to believe himself invisible. But I did not blink as I watched those masked men ride by, erect in their saddles, ominous in their number.

Finally they passed, and we proceeded to the station at a breakneck speed; once we joined the rest of our party, Mr. Bleeker finally exhaled, a little color returning to his face.

"Those shots you heard back at the hotel," he began, pausing to take a gulp of whiskey from the Commodore's ever-present flask. "There were two men downstairs who tried to get me to take a drink with them. I said I had to get upstairs to my friends, but they kept insisting, getting meaner by the minute. Finally, I broke away, only to see them exchange a look and run outside. I was curious. So when I got upstairs, I went to take a look out on the landing. In the yard were two figures in white, like the men who just passed us, and they both pointed a pistol at me and fired. They nearly got my hat! I ducked inside, and that's when I found all of you in the room with that message on the door, and I said to myself, *Bleeker, get everybody the heck out of here!* I just know they were planning to rob us, and if we'd stayed there they surely would have, or worse! Why nothing happened when they passed us on the road, I'll never know—maybe they just didn't recognize us."

Mrs. Bleeker paled and nearly fainted upon her husband's shoulder. Charles, too, turned an awful green color, and Minnie laid her head upon my shoulder and shut her eyes.

I remained upright on that cold, hard station bench, unable to stop seeing that ghostly line of horses and riders, pale, almost luminous, against the black of the Alabama forest. I couldn't believe I'd actually seen the Ku Klux with my own eyes. How terrifying!

I couldn't wait to write Mr. Barnum all about it.

Our travels continued, no less adventurous—I saw my first alligator in Texas while crossing the Red River!—and in May of 1869, while staying in San Antonio, we received the following letter from Mr. Barnum:

> *My Dear Bleeker:*
>
> *An idea has occurred to me in which I can see a "Golden Gate" opening for the Gen. Tom Thumb Co. What do you think of a "Tour around the World," including a visit to Australia? The new Pacific Railroad will be finished in a few weeks; you will then be*

enabled to cross the American Continent to California, thence by steam to Japan, China, British India, etc. I declare, in anticipation, I already envy you the pleasures and opportunities which such a trip will afford.

For the next three days I shall study all the maps I can lay my hands upon and, in imagination, mark you crossing the briny deep to those far-off countries. And as for gold! Tell the General that in Australia alone (don't fail to go to Australia) he will be sure to make more money than a horse can draw.

Decide quickly. If you consent to undertake the journey, prepare to start next month. Love to all,

Truly yours,
P. T. Barnum

"Well, isn't this something," Mr. Bleeker said after he finished reading the letter out loud to us all.

"A world tour," his gentle wife exclaimed, and as usual, I could not detect her own wishes in it; our dear Mrs. Bleeker was a cipher, a genuinely loving, soothing presence who seemed to exist only for us. I could never imagine her in her own home, mending her own clothes, deciding on her own entertainment or enjoyment. She was expressly put upon this earth to live in the service of P. T. Barnum, the General Tom Thumb Company, and her husband—and possibly in that order.

"Australia?" Charles blinked, nervously lighting up a cigar, as Mr. Barnum would have done. "That wild place? Why, has any American ever been there?"

"Which is all the more reason that we should go," I said decidedly; my husband's nervous fears never ceased to challenge me, stirring up a recklessness I did not always know I possessed. "Imagine, to be among the first! And to travel the new Union

Pacific railroad, too—I imagine we'll see buffalo. And Indians, naturally!"

"Indians!" Charles puffed even more nervously, blowing a quick succession of smoke rings into the air.

"Oh, Sister—Indians?" Minnie, seated next to Mrs. Bleeker on a sofa, paled.

"From a distance, I'm sure," I said hastily, although inwardly I did hope to see one or two up close; I had always wondered if their skin was as red as the clay earth they roamed, as was said.

"It's a tremendous opportunity." Mr. Bleeker consulted the letter again, spreading it upon the table as if it were a map. Indeed, we all drew close, to study it. As if Mr. Barnum's expressive handwriting alone could tell us which direction to follow—and I truly believed, at that moment, that it could.

"If we do this," Mr. Bleeker said in his grave, considered manner, "you'll be world famous, for I know of no other troupe that has undertaken such an arduous journey. It's truly unprecedented."

"Then we must do it!" I couldn't contain my excitement; I clasped my hands together and jumped up and down, letting my dignity fall to the floor in a rumpled heap. To think of it all! The exotic scenes—Commodore Perry had returned from Japan only a scant nine years before; even during the Civil War, newspapers had been full of the strange Oriental habits and customs just beginning to be known to the West. Those long sticks they used for utensils, the way they drank their tea in small bowls instead of cups. The way they sat upon the floor to eat! How charming a custom, especially for one my size! I had spent far too many an elaborate dinner perched upon precarious cushions, my feet dangling from my chair like a child's. I couldn't wait to partake of an authentic Japanese meal seated upon the floor, where everyone would be my size.

Australia, I knew nothing about, other than that it was a wild, untamed place, much as our American West had been twenty years ago. Yet I was eager to see it; eager to see the highest mountain peaks on our own continent; eager to see the new railroad, almost finished, that linked the Atlantic to the Pacific; eager to see *everything*. That world that had beckoned to me for so long—it was not bigger than me, after all. I would conquer it by seeing every corner of it; I felt sorry for the women who had to content themselves with gazing at the globe while they dusted it, dutifully, trapped in the houses of their husbands.

"We must do it," I said once more. "Think of how famous we'll be! How much we will impress those who think our bodies are weak simply because they're small!"

"Vinnie has a point there," Mr. Bleeker said, doing his very best to keep his face neutral—he had the best poker face among us, with his drooping mustache and beard, and sad eyes; we often joked that if we found ourselves penniless, we could always send him out to win back our fortune in a saloon game. But I saw that glint in his eyes, the way he quickly licked his lips, as if tasting something tantalizing and sweet. I knew he desired to go, quite as much as I did.

He deferred, however, at least in manner, to Charles; after all, it was my husband's name upon the masthead of our stationery. In theory, Charles was the decision maker of our party.

"Mr. Barnum obviously thinks this is a splendid idea," I reminded him solemnly. He nodded—just as solemnly—and puffed upon his cigar once more. I could not look at Mr. Bleeker, for fear of spoiling the moment; we held our breaths, waiting for my husband's verdict.

"Well, if Phineas thinks it's a good idea," he finally concluded, nodding gravely. And our collective breath was exhaled, glasses raised in a toast to the new adventure. Then we all scattered like mice to write letters, pack trunks, and take the first train back north so we could buy new clothes, mend old ones, and say goodbye to friends and family.

We left New York on June 21, 1869. The newspapers trumpeted the General Tom Thumb Company's "Three Years' Tour Around the World." The company numbered thirteen, which Mama felt boded ill for our safe return. However, Mr. Bleeker quickly pointed out that he always paid full fare for each of the two ponies we brought with us to pull our miniature carriage, so that really there were fifteen in the party. I don't believe this mollified her.

"Vinnie, please take care, and bring yourself and Minnie safely home," Mama said, clinging to both of her daughters before we boarded the train from the New York and Harlem Railroad Station. This was a new, expanded station, very different from the little shack where I had first disembarked in New York, all those years ago. Yet there were rumors that an even grander, more central railroad terminal was to be constructed by Commodore Vanderbilt just a few blocks away. All those trains that came into New York from the north and east, like pins stuck haphazardly in a cushion, would now all end at the same terminus. The new depot was even rumored to have a restaurant inside for waiting passengers!

"Mama, I will, I promise! Try not to worry, and we will write whenever possible." I kissed my dear mother on the cheek and patted Papa fondly on the shoulder; both were kneeling down, although I knew how difficult it was for them, now that they were older. Age had even made Papa less stoic; he had tears in his blue eyes, which he did not even try to hide.

"I'm always saying goodbye to my girls," he said gruffly. "I don't know why that is. I always said I never knew what to do with you, Vinnie, and I have lived to see the truth in it. You never stop surprising me—all the way around the world now! I never imagined I'd leave Middleborough, let alone see my daughters off to Japan!"

"We'll bring you back glorious presents—would you like a samurai's sword? That would be handy for cutting hay!" I laughed, kissing my father lightly; he surprised me by hugging me to him so tightly I could hear his faithful heart beating against my cheek, like the faint but reliable ticking of an old pocket watch. Then he released me with the same urgency, and groaningly pushed himself upright.

Blinking up at him through my own tears, I smiled, then gently pulled Minnie out of Mama's possessive embrace. "Keep her safe," Mama whispered to me, and I nodded, pulling Minnie toward the train, where Mr. Bleeker was waiting to lift us both up the stairs. The engine was already huffing, steam billowing out from the tall chimney. I hesitated only a moment, searching the platform for a particular gold-tipped walking stick. Mr. Barnum had promised he would try to see us off. I did so want to see him once more; three years seemed like such a long time.

He did not come, however, and I could wait no longer as the conductor made his final cry of "All aboard!" I nodded at Mr. Bleeker to lift me up, and then I made my way down the aisle of the train as it lurched away from the station. Stumbling, I nearly fell, headfirst, into the lap of a woman seated on the aisle. Only Mr. Bleeker's ready hand upon my head kept me upright.

"Goodness me!" The woman laughed—and then she pulled me to her in a smothering embrace. "I declare, you are the sweetest little thing, aren't you?"

"Madam, please!" I pushed myself away from her; she smelled strongly of peppermint drops and camphor. "I beg your pardon!"

She didn't take offense; indeed, she kept beaming at me as if I were a precocious child.

"This is Mrs. Charles Stratton," Mr. Bleeker informed her. "She is on her way to tour the West."

"Oh, I knew her right away—I said to my Fred"—she poked the man next to her with her elbow; he grunted and turned away—"I said, 'Fred, that's that little Mrs. Tom Thumb, I just know it!' She looks just like her little picture, yes, she does!" Still the woman beamed, even as she continued to talk above me, as if I wasn't there. Smiling frostily, I bowed and continued down the aisle, shaking off Mr. Bleeker's steadying hand upon my shoulder.

I climbed up into my seat next to Minnie; Mrs. Bleeker had already placed a cushion there for me, so that I might see out the window. As New York fell away, I wondered how many days it would be until we reached Omaha. There, we would board the new Union Pacific railroad, some of the first passengers to do so.

I doubted that vile woman was traveling any farther than Albany; certainly she wasn't going to be shaking the hand of the Emperor of Japan!

Yet for a moment, I couldn't prevent myself from imagining how it would be to travel—even if it was just to Albany—by myself, to climb upon a train unassisted, to carry my own luggage, to take whichever seat I wanted, no cushion or stool necessary.

I imagined what it would be like to be able to walk around freely, anonymously, nothing about me remarkable in any way. Would I like it? Would I trade my fame if it meant that I never had to suffer fools hugging me to them ever again?

I honestly did not know. And I was more than a little relieved that it was a moot point, after all.

THIS BOOK IS NOT INTENDED TO BE A MERE TRAVELOGUE; MY DEAR Mr. Bleeker wrote a very fine account of our journey in *General Tom Thumb's Three Years Tour Around the World,* which I am sure you have read previously, as it was a very popular book and made quite a lot of money.

I cannot pass over this time in my life, however, without wanting to share some of my impressions. Naturally I am proud of what we accomplished, especially in such primitive circumstances compared to the comforts of today. Our planned route involved an average travel of one hundred and ten miles every day, as well as the giving of two entertainments! To those who are used to more modern ways of travel and hospitality, this may not seem much of a feat. However, the last spike had just been driven in the Union Pacific railroad only a little over a month before we embarked upon it. The West was newly open, raw and unforgiving. Cities which today conjure up images of cultured civility—Salt Lake City, Omaha, Reno—were little more than canvas camps at the time, sprouting up along the newly built railway like prairie flowers. Many more of these temporary cities—hotels, restaurants, post offices, even, made of dirty canvas flaps draped over wobbly wooden frames—have now faded from memory, vanished in the dust of the trains that roared on ahead, once the tracks were laid.

We confidently expected to see Indians, and indeed, even as the train was pulling out of Omaha, nervous passengers were looking out the windows for the red man. Mr. Bleeker packed a pistol; so, too, did Charles, although it was a ridiculously tiny one given to him by Queen Victoria, with custom bullets so small they could scarcely hurt a prairie dog, let alone an Indian on a pony. Yet he strutted about, stroking his beard with one hand, patting his breast pocket with the other, just as he saw the other men doing—acting as if he had enough firepower to take out an entire band of ferocious savages.

While sleeper cars were now in use on eastern trains—a platform could be raised to join two facing seats into one bed, while above, a bunk was lowered from the arched roof of the car—those first trains to go west from Omaha were not outfitted in this way. Hence, on extended legs—our longest was twenty-six hours of continuous travel—we had to sleep, to use the word loosely, upright upon the hard seats. Even though they were upholstered in horsehair—an improvement over those hard wooden seats from my first train trip to Cincinnati back in the fifties—they made for very uncomfortable sleeping, indeed. Although for once, we little folk had the advantage of our companions, as we could curl up easier than they could!

As always, it was impossible to keep oneself clean and tidy; even with the windows pushed up, the dust from the prairie and the cinders and grit from the tracks managed to seep inside the cars. Not to mention that it was very hot, as we left Omaha in July of 1869. While there was a dining car on the train, the food was not well prepared or even fresh, and there was never any ice for water. In the primitive water closets, where I had to lug my steps with me so that I could reach the basin, the water in it was already so gray with other people's grime that I never wanted to splash it upon my face. And the smell in that hot, stuffy little cell was intolerable.

But the scenery, as we sped across the great prairie, was always interesting, always majestic; I'd never seen a sky so big, not even upon the sea. The tall, waving grasses, undulating in the wind, were as hypnotic as any ocean waves. Prairie dogs popped up and down like children's toys, and herds of antelope raced along the train, as did immense herds of buffalo. We could see them from a distance; at first, they resembled a swarm of flies moving now away, now toward, the tracks; as we got closer, we could actually feel the thundering of their hooves through the floor of the train. At the first sighting, more than a few passengers decided to use them as target practice; with cries and whoops, men pulled out their pistols or rifles and thrust them through the windows, the ringing from the shots practically piercing my eardrums.

We reached Cheyenne, our first stop, almost exactly twenty-four hours after leaving Omaha and without having seen a single Indian, much to my disappointment. The manager of the theater there met us at the train and helped us load our belongings—trunks of costumes, trinkets and *cartes de visites* that we would sell, scenery and props—into a waiting Wells Fargo wagon; Charles and I climbed into our miniature carriage, while Rodney Nutt harnessed our two little ponies, who were restless from being cooped up, prancing mischievously against the bit. We hadn't a chance to freshen up; my traveling dress was dirty and wrinkled beyond measure, and I felt as wilted as the feather in my bonnet. But straight to the theater we went, Charles and I waving to the townspeople who spied our carriage and followed out of curiosity; Minnie and Nutt accompanying the Bleekers in the wagon. As soon as we reached the theater—really a barn, barely swept, with rows of crude benches and hay bales upon which the audience sat—we tidied ourselves as best we could. Mr. Bleeker and our agent hastily set up their concession and box office, and soon we were onstage in front of an eager audience of prairie folk. We repeated our performance later in the evening, then collapsed in a canvas tent that served as the town's hotel, before getting back on the train the next day.

This became our routine, then. Many of the hotels were merely tents. Other times we stayed in houses, usually the mayor's own, or one of his relatives'. We never ordered a meal to our own choosing; we ate what was given to us in the hotel, boardinghouse, or private dining room. Privacy was at a premium; oftentimes the men were separated from the ladies by only a thin canvas flap.

Charles and I, and Mr. and Mrs. Bleeker, as the two married couples, were sometimes accorded some privacy, but I always made sure that Minnie was with Charles and me, as she was the only other female. I knew she was very homesick on this trip, much more than she had been in Europe when she had the various infants to occupy her time.

"Vinnie, what do you think Mama and Papa are doing right now?" she would ask me several times a day, and it became almost a game; often I would answer nonsense, just to make her laugh.

"I expect Papa is baking a cake right now, wearing Mama's best apron, and Mama is sitting by the fire smoking a pipe," I might say, casually—and be grateful for Minnie's helpless giggles at the notion.

Or—

"It's five o'clock; wouldn't Papa be bringing in the cows from the pasture right now?" Minnie would muse, peeking out the canvas flap of our latest "theater," as if she could see all the way back to Massachusetts.

"No, he's just taking them out now; they like to spend the night outside, not in the barn, don't you remember? So they can look at the stars and wish upon them!"

Minnie laughed at this notion; her dimple deepened, and her merry eyes sparkled under her dark, suspicious brows. She flung her arms around me and whispered, "I'm so glad I'm here with you—I'm so glad that you're not lonely!"

"Lonely?" I laughed, holding her at arm's length, looking into her sweet, sympathetic face. "What do you mean? I wouldn't be lonely—I wouldn't have the time!"

Minnie merely smiled and hugged me again; then she walked away with such a knowing, understanding look, a sudden, sharp blade of guilt knifed itself through my heart. Was it wicked to keep her with me just because I needed her? Just because I was afraid of being left too much alone with my husband?

And did she truly understand that she was the necessary glue that kept Charles and me together, that she alone made us a family? We both clung to her, in different ways. Charles loved her dearly, as she loved him; the two of them played together, lavishing affection upon every stray dog, cat, or even the occasional chicken that wandered into our hotel or theater. Or they made up games of their own device, games that they would not teach anyone else, acting exactly like two school chums who wanted to appear clannish.

With Minnie, the three of us together at table could always find something to chatter about; she loved to listen to Charles's tales, and he was a wonderful storyteller when he had an eager audience, which I must admit I was not. On the rare occasions when it was just Charles and me, we exhausted conversation before the soup was gone.

"We'll be in Utah in the morning. I'm anxious to see how the polygamists live, aren't you? It seems more barbaric than the Indians," I said one evening as we dined alone in our hotel room—a corner of a canvas structure; the proprietor had proudly offered Charles and me "a romantic dinner for two," apart from the communal table set up in the middle of the tent. He had found a small table and two camp stools, and hung up a thin curtain to shield us from the others. Yet we were taunted by the merry dinner talk, the convivial clinking of glasses, on the other side of the curtain.

"Charles? Did you hear me?" I spoke louder, trying to drown out the guffaws accompanying Rodney Nutt as he told a story about a man who once raced a horse the wrong way around a track. "About the polygamists?"

"Oh, I'm—of course, of course, polygamists! Dreadful insects, aren't they—always buzzing around your ears! My dear, did I ever tell you about the time that I swallowed a bug? I was onstage during a sweltering heat, and a fly was buzzing about, and just as I opened my mouth to sing 'Yankee Doodle,' that creature flew into it and down my windpipe! I tell you, I couldn't sing a word after that! I coughed and coughed until . . ."

Smiling tightly, I nodded at Charles as he continued his story, and allowed my mind to wander elsewhere—along railroad tracks, over mountains, across oceans. *Dear God, please don't ever let the world stop expanding, stop sprouting new cities and railroads and passageways for me to visit, for me to dream about*—I almost prayed it out loud.

It was in Ogden, Utah, that I had the opportunity to correct Charles's impression about polygamy. For it was here that I first saw it in practice. Ogden was a town of about two thousand people; compared to the other communities along the Union Pacific, it was a model of cleanliness and order, and we could not help but attribute this to the fact that the Mormon bishop controlled the town. Neat clapboard buildings lined clean streets; there were none of the usual saloons and houses of ill repute that had followed the progression of the railroad in other villages.

The bishop offered us the use of their Tabernacle for our entertainment; I thought this very good of him, indeed, and quite surprising. I could not imagine any Baptist church doing the same! So my initial impression of the Mormons was quite favorable.

He asked that the first two rows be reserved for his family. Over fifty seats in all, and I was amused, thinking, logically, that there were far more seats than could be filled by one brood. Yet in a flash the bishop returned with his brother, followed by seven adult females and forty-two children varying in ages from three to fourteen years; then came three more females and twenty-two children, whom the bishop referred to, casually, as "my family"!

It may have been amusing at first, as we peered out from behind the curtain, sure that at any minute the endless parade of children would stop, but soon I ceased to find it so. During our entertainments, Mr. Bleeker always invited a dozen children, from the ages of three to ten, to stand with Minnie onstage to compare their height to hers. When the invitation was extended on this night, Bishop West immediately turned to his family and beckoned the requisite number to the platform. Mr. Bleeker placed the smallest of them nearest to Minnie and then requested the parents to give their ages. Pointing to the first child, Mr. Bleeker inquired, "What is this child's age?"

"Four years," replied the Bishop with a satisfied smile.

"And this?" Mr. Bleeker pointed to the next.

"Four years," the Bishop answered placidly.

"They're both your children?" Mr. Bleeker could not help himself from asking.

The Bishop nodded. A faint blush mottled his cheeks.

"How old is this one?" Mr. Bleeker pointed to the next largest.

"Four," the Bishop said, his voice becoming a bit strangled.

"Yours, as well?"

The Bishop nodded.

"And this one?"

"Four."

"Yours?"

"Yes."

"And this—?"

"Stop!" I could not help myself; I raced forward to Mr. Bleeker, tugging at the bottom of his coat, imploring him to cease this disgraceful display. Startled, that poor man could do nothing but signal to me to keep quite, and indeed, I did not know what more I could say—I only felt such embarrassment for the children, for the wives, for us all. It was *barbaric,* that's what it was, barbaric that all these children of the same age could be sired by one father in these modern times. I did not want to be here any longer; I could not wait to leave. Yet even when we returned to our hotel, I could not prevent myself from inquiring into the marital status

of the proprietor, and nearly screamed when I was told that he had ten wives!

Ten! Those poor women, having to subject themselves to one man, having to share him with others, having to raise all these other children as their own, having to lie down with him whenever he desired, never able to refuse—

"I trust the pin money won't bankrupt you!" My husband was laughing with the innkeeper, man to man, and I whirled about.

"Charles Stratton, how dare you? How dare you laugh with this man as if—as if—"

The entire company was staring at me, mouths open; they had never seen me act so strangely. I took a breath and tried to calm myself, but I could not dampen the fire of indignation that burned in my breast, searing my skin as if it had been branded from within. Why did these men disgust me so? Why could I not look any of their wives in the eye? I had seen natives by now, brown-skinned people who lived in squalor, whose men drank but whose women carried their children on their backs, proudly erect. I had not been disgusted by them. They were not God-fearing people, and so could live only as their instincts told them, and it was obvious their women were strong, stronger than their men.

But the Mormon women were different; there was something shameful and dejected about them. They did not seem to live in the same sphere as their men, except to serve and—I couldn't prevent a shudder—have relations and bear endless children. It was the same way in Salt Lake City, where we journeyed by wagon, since there was no railroad yet built from Ogden. When we arrived we were treated like dignitaries and introduced to everyone of importance, including Brigham Young. These men were cordial enough, but we met their women only during mealtimes when they served at table, their heads bowed in submission. The obsessively clean appearance of the city in general attested to a feminine hand, yet it remained hidden, as if behind a curtain—or jail—of masculine design.

I could not get out of Utah fast enough.

Finally, we continued west, to Nevada. Leaving the railroad, we decided to travel by stage to a few places, such as Virginia City; progress upon these mountain roads was perilous, beset as it was by not only unpredictable weather, steep mountain drops, and Indians, but also highway robbers. Naturally, we attracted much attention wherever we went, and my jewels and fine clothes were well known, as was the fact that we had, by necessity, to travel with large amounts of money.

One evening, our last night in Virginia City, two strangers struck up a seemingly pleasant conversation with Mr. Bleeker at the hotel, during which they urged him to take several precautions with my jewels, the cash from the box office, and other valuables.

"Cut a lining in your hat, Sir; that's always where I carry any gold," one of the fellows said.

"That's a good plan; those highway robbers always check your boots first," said the other.

"Thank you, Sirs, for the excellent advice," Mr. Bleeker said.

"You're leaving on the regular stage, then?" the first man asked as Mr. Bleeker rose to leave.

"Yes, indeed."

"Good thinking, for it has an excellent guard, always."

Mr. Bleeker left these two "gentlemen" to smoke cigars in the lobby of the hotel; he then snuck out the back door and went straight to the Wells Fargo and Company office to arrange for two wagons. We left at seven the next morning, and when we reached Reno, we heard that the regular noon stage had been held up by two masked men who, while methodically relieving all the poor passengers of their valuables, kept muttering, "Tom Thumb! Where's Tom Thumb? He's supposed to be on this stage!"

Finally, we reached San Francisco. It was such a relief to be in a cultured metropolis once more, with paved roads and gaslights and hotels made of wood, not canvas. Triumphantly, Charles and I paraded through the streets in our miniature carriage, our ponies none the worse for the trip. Three times a day we filled Platt's Hall, which held two thousand people, and were able to telegraph Mr. Barnum that the trip had been the "golden opportunity" he had envisioned, indeed.

We left San Francisco for Yokohama, Japan, on November 4, 1869; we would not return to the shores of this great country of ours until June 22, 1872. All in all, we traveled 55,487 miles (31,216 of them by sea) and gave 1,472 entertainments in 587 different cities and towns in all climates of the world without missing a single performance because of accident or illness.

We met the Viceroy of India, King Victor Emmanuele II of Italy, Emperor Franz Joseph of Austria, and assorted Maharajas and Shahs. We ate leechee nuts in China, chewed tea leaves in Ceylon, and consumed octopus in Japan. We saw the Pyramids, pilgrims on their way to Mecca, and sampans in Japan. The heat in Singapore was like being wrapped in a hot woolen blanket and set out in the noonday sun; the cold of the Australian desert at night made your bones cry. We saw women dressed scandalously, in nothing but scarves and jewels, in Madras; we observed entire families bathing together in the nude in Japan. Trains, when we could find them, were primitive: some with benches, with no backs, for seats; others simply cavernous cars in which you sat upon the floor. Ships were steamers, and often they were overcrowded, with poor people practically hanging off the deck rails. Often we would get to a destination with no clear idea how we would then travel on to the next place; maps were crude, unreadable, and unreliable.

Yet even in such places we would sometimes come across a reminder of home; of civilization. Minnie spied an 1862 issue of *Godey's Lady's Book* in a fish market in Bombay, of all places; she eagerly begged the fishmonger to give it to her, instead of using it to wrap up his eels. Somehow he understood, and she carried it with her through the rest of the tour, reading and rereading it although the fashions, of course, were long out of style even before we left home. (Such wide skirts we used to wear! And those ridiculous, enormous-ribboned bonnets!)

And one evening in Ceylon, while I was trying to read by the weak oil light in the hotel parlor (there was no reading in the primitive bedrooms, as everything was encased with thick mosquito netting), Mr. Bleeker presented me with a tattered copy of the *New York Herald Tribune*. "Look at this," he said with a sly grin. He pointed to an article with his bony finger.

"Barnum's newest sensation," I read aloud, and laughed. I checked the date of the paper; it was over a year old. But seeing Mr. Barnum's name in print, so far away from him, after having been gone so long, made my heart leap unexpectedly, almost as if he himself had entered the room. We stayed in communication during the trip, of course, but mainly with telegrams, which were always so businesslike and addressed to the troupe in general, never to me personally. And if telegrams were sporadic in the places we were visiting, letters were even more so. So it was with a hunger I hadn't even been aware was gnawing at me that I read his name.

"The old man has kept himself busy while we're away," Mr. Bleeker said with a chuckle, as he folded his long frame into an absurdly small, lacquered Oriental chair. He lit his pipe and puffed until he could get a good draw on it.

"Yes, it appears he has," I said as I continued to read the article. Mr. Barnum had begun presenting a new discovery, an Admiral Dot. Admiral Dot was "a dwarf more diminutive in stature than General Tom Thumb was when I found him," Mr. Barnum had told the newspaper.

"You've got to admire him. He loses his museum, he builds another. He sends you all off to see the world—"

"And he replaces us with someone else." Crumpling the newspaper, I tossed it on the floor. But Mr. Bleeker didn't notice, as he finally had gotten his pipe burning to his satisfaction, and was stretching his long legs out in front of him.

"He just keeps on going. 'Admiral Dot.' He has a genius for naming things, don't you think?"

"Absolutely. Almost God-like, naming all the animals."

Mr. Bleeker must have finally noticed the sarcasm in my voice, for he peered at me through the pipe smoke, eyebrows raised. Then he saw the newspaper on the ground.

"What's wrong, Vinnie? I thought you'd be happy to know that he's carrying on, as usual."

"Oh, I suppose I am, it's just—never mind." I picked up my book and tried to find my place, but suddenly Mr. Bleeker plucked it out of my hands.

"You're not jealous of that Dot fellow, are you?"

"I have no need to be jealous of another performer—especially one so unproven—thank you very much. Now, will you please return my book?"

"But that's just Barnum's way! You know that! He knows what the public wants, and he gives it to them. Truth is, he usually tells them what they want, before they know it. So the public wants to see another little man. So? That has nothing to do with you. It's not personal with him like that."

"Nothing ever is personal with him." I sniffed, then held my hand out for my book. Mr. Bleeker gave it back to me, but I still felt him staring at me. He even scratched his head, so deep was his puzzlement.

Suddenly, however, he snapped his fingers and smiled; like an eager pupil, he tugged on my sleeve. Not in the mood to hide my impatience, I closed my book with a sigh and looked up.

"But Vinnie, listen! I never did tell you what he told me after your wedding. All that day, he was proud as could be, but I tell you, Vinnie, after the reception was over, he asked me to drive back home with him. And he was sad, Vinnie—the saddest I'd ever seen him."

"He was?"

"He sure was! You know he's sometimes a crier—remember how he sobbed when the Emancipation Proclamation was announced?"

"Yes." And despite myself, I smiled; that was one of my most cherished memories, the January day when we all sat in his office and he read aloud Mr. Lincoln's Proclamation from the newspaper, tears running unchecked down his pink face.

"Well, that day in the carriage, he had tears in his eyes. Sad tears. And he said, 'Bleeker, this has been the happiest day of my life. And the saddest.' And I asked him why, and he said, 'Because I'll never have this great a success again. Those two little people, they've spoiled me. How will I ever top this?' And you know, Vinnie, I don't think he'll ever stop trying, even though he knows, deep in his heart, that he won't. But it's just in him to keep going, that's the thing you have to admire about him. You two, though—Charles and you—you brought him the greatest success he's ever known, and he won't ever forget that. Or you. The two of you, well—you're special."

I stared at Mr. Bleeker for a long moment; he stared back, that anxious, eager smile upon his face. And I couldn't help but nod, as his intentions were so obviously good.

"Yes, of course. I know that. I'm just tired from this heat, that's all."

"I'd give my favorite pipe for a cold bath tonight, but the manager said there isn't any fresh water." Mr. Bleeker nodded in agreement, and he settled back down with his pipe, content to watch an enormous moth that was determined to hurl itself, over and over, toward the oil lamp.

I opened my book again, but I found myself staring at the same page for the longest time, before finally giving up and going upstairs to bed.

As our travels continued, our clothing never seemed to be clean; the dust and dampness of travel was trapped forever within the folds of cotton, silk, and satin. We mended and re-mended until our fingers were sore; it's difficult to contemplate what to pack for three years' travel, and when clothing ripped or became worn, we could not replace it. For one thing, very few places where we traveled were adept at sewing Western fashions, complete with the new bustles and tight bodices in fashion. Sarongs and kimonos were plentiful, but of courser Minnie, Mrs. Bleeker, and I could not wear those! For another, particular items such as gloves, shoes, bonnets, etc., that had to be custom-made for Minnie and myself were impossible to come by. So we had to continually patch and repair.

In some places, such as Japan and China, where there were few Americans or Europeans, communication was impossible, if not comical; we bowed and scraped a lot. Our size, however, never failed to bring a grin or a smile even to the most dour Chinaman or round Buddhist matron; this was always our entrée into different cultures, and it always assured us goodwill and hospitality. If few of the people we met had ever seen an American, they certainly had never seen a very tiny one, and so Charles, Minnie, Nutt, and myself had to put up with much patting and touching and petting. Never did I feel there was anything sinister or insulting in it, though—and, after all, we were just as curious about their strange costumes and manners as they were about ours. So it was more of a *mutual* curiosity; we patted and touched and petted right back, free to do so in a way we were not at home—and we enjoyed it.

So used was I to seeing the world through a maze of table legs, wagon wheels, ladies' skirts, and men's trousers, I could only note, with pleasure, how much more colorful it was in these exotic lands. The vivid hues of the Orient were a welcome contrast to the more sedate—dare I say dull?—wardrobe choices of the West, such colorful silks in hothouse colors of pinks and oranges and greens!

When travel became difficult, particularly in Australia, where we had to journey hundreds of miles in the desert with only a faint pair of wagon tracks to guide us, the four of us—Minnie, Nutt, Charles, and myself—trudged through the sand just like everyone else, to give the horses a rest. The horses sank to their knees, as did Mr. Bleeker and the others; we did not, although it was difficult to get our footing, as we never reached solid ground.

Despite all the perils we faced—a typhoon on the way to Japan, pythons in Ceylon, wild kangaroos in Australia, fearsome spiders everywhere; despite the marvels we saw—the great Pyramids of Egypt, which inspired Mr. Bleeker to whisper that for once, he understood how we must feel, as he thought himself to be only about two feet tall at that moment—only once did I experience, keenly, my size and how vulnerable it made me. And that was in Nevada, before we even left our own continent.

Minnie, Mrs. Bleeker, and myself were perched in a hired wagon; it had a cover on it, but the sides were wide open to the elements. We had stopped at an inn, where the men and the driver got out to ask for directions. We were on a mountain road with drops so steep as to not be believed; as we waited patiently inside the wagon for the men to return, something startled the horses and they took off, uncontrolled, around the bend.

As the wagon careened faster and faster, the thundering of the horses' panicked hooves ringing, like a blacksmith's hammer, in my ears, Minnie and I bounced around helplessly; soon we were covered in bruises. I feared, desperately, that we would be thrown from the wagon. Our feet could not steady us, as they could not reach the floor, and our hands were too small to grip the rough wooden slats of the seats; at one point I looked down, amazed to see that my palm was cut and bleeding. Then I felt an arm around me; Mrs. Bleeker somehow managed to gather us both in her arms, grasping us tightly. And she began to pray, like the serene creature she was; she told us not to be afraid, even unto death.

Death seemed like a distinct possibility, for we could not know when the horses would stop, and sharp boulders surrounded us on all sides. Had the wagon been smashed, we surely would have perished; as it was, the horses continued their wild ride until they rounded a particularly sharp curve—all three of us were thrown, together in a prayerful heap, down to the floor of the wagon—to a suddenly flat, fenced parcel of land. One of the horses swerved, with a wild whinny, directly into the fence; for one suspenseful minute, we slowed almost to a walk.

"Quick, jump, before they take off again!" I cried, not content to pray. I grabbed Minnie and hugged her to me; closing my eyes, I pushed us both from the wagon, and we landed on a soft patch of grass, rolling over and over. Miraculously, we were mostly unhurt, as was Mrs. Bleeker, who landed only ten feet away. Gasping and blinking, we sat catching our breath until Mr. Bleeker came running up on his long, loping legs, his beard practically trailing behind him.

"Julia! Vinnie! Minnie! To see you alive—didn't think I would! You've had a providential escape!" He fell to his knees and fiercely embraced his wife.

"I did not really think any of us would be killed," his wife replied, although her lips trembled, as did her hands. "I was so busy holding the little ones so that they wouldn't go flying out, I couldn't be afraid."

"You saved us," I told her, my own limbs shaking. "You kept us inside the wagon."

That was the one time, on the entire trip, Reader, when I truly felt vulnerable. Every other danger had been equal to us all. Indians, robbers, those terrifying sudden thunderstorms in the mountains that could wash away a road in the blink of an eye—any in our party could have perished because of them, regardless of size.

But as that wagon careened down the road, and Minnie and I were utterly helpless, unable to brace our feet against anything to keep us inside, I had felt, for only the first time since my days with Colonel Wood, physically vulnerable. Even more distressing, I had felt unable to protect my sister, despite my promises to Mama and Papa—and to myself.

"Are you all right?" I finally looked at Minnie, who was still in my arms. "Oh, what a terrible blow it would be to Mama and Papa, had we both perished!"

"Yes, I'm fine," Minnie answered, with an unexpected little laugh. "I thought to myself, *Go ahead, horses, do your best; I can ride as fast behind you as you can run*." She laughed again; I stared at her as she gently but firmly unwound my arms from her shoulders and slid off my lap. She stood up and brushed her torn skirts briskly; my timid little sister did not appear to have been frightened in the least.

"You did, did you?" I asked her, amazed.

"Yes. For you see, Sister," Minnie said with a suddenly wise, ancient look in her eyes, "I am not to be killed so easily."

I laughed, surprise and relief chasing away my terror. And I believed her, all of a sudden. I believed her conviction, her defiance in the face of disaster. Or perhaps I simply *wanted* to believe her. Whatever the case, for the rest of the trip I did not worry at all for my sister's safety, and it was a great burden lifted from my shoulders. No more did I feel guilt and anxiety for keeping her with me; she would be perfectly fine.

How foolish I was! For it wasn't kangaroos or snakes or typhoons or runaway horses that I needed to fear. It was nothing nearly so dramatic as all that.

No, it was simply love, the desire to live a normal life, like any woman. This was what I myself did not have the courage to face. And so I did not think, even for a moment, that my sweet, simple sister did.

But I was wrong.

INTERMISSION

From *The Popular Science Monthly,* February 1877

Talking by Telegraph

On Sunday, November 26th, Prof. A. Graham Bell experimented with the "telephone" on the wires of the Eastern Railroad Company between Boston and Salem. . . . According to the account published in the COMMONWEALTH of Boston, conversation was carried on with Mr. Watson at Salem, by all those present, in turn, without any difficulty, even the voices of the speakers being easily recognized.

From *Scribner's Monthly,* October 1877

New and Cheap Antiseptic

Bisulphide of carbon has been recently reported as possessing remarkable antiseptic and preservative qualities, but the offensive smell and inflammable character of this substance make it both dangerous and troublesome.

FIFTEEN

A Sister Act Breaks Up

"VINNIE, I'D LIKE TO SPEAK TO YOU."

"What is it, dear?" I looked up from my writing desk. Minnie was standing in the doorway to my boudoir, a charming little picture in her bustled dress, with her hair done up rather severely, although a few curls could not help but escape. With her matronly hairstyle and sophisticated clothes, she looked like a girl playing dress-up; her solemn face with those incongruously impish eyes still looked so childlike.

"Is this a good time? It's a bit—serious."

"Serious?" I couldn't help but smile. "What's serious, Pumpkin? Oh, I'm sorry—I mean, Mrs. Newell."

I still had a difficult time saying those words—*Mrs. Newell*. It seemed incredible to me that my little sister had actually gone and gotten married. How had that happened? It was almost as if she had done it when I wasn't looking; as if I'd forgotten myself and gone to take a nap only to awake and find my sister had run off somewhere. And now, almost six months later, I still didn't know where to find her.

Yet she had gotten married in a perfectly respectable manner, to a man we met through Mr. Barnum, Edward Newell. He was not as small as we were—he was no "perfectly formed miniature man"—but he was not tall, either. He was a performer, originally from England; he started out with a roller-skating act for Mr. Barnum, and when Commodore Nutt decided to retire—and marry a normal-size woman!—Edward took his place in our troupe.

He was also a perfectly nice man who adored Minnie. I hadn't taken much notice of his affection for her at first. I simply had no expectation of romance for my little sister—even when Nutt had mooned after her, I hadn't really thought it was a possibility, more like another of his pranks. And what did True Love look like? I did not know myself, so how could I recognize it in others?

Soon after Edward joined the troupe, however, Minnie began to withdraw from me, ever so slightly. No more was it our happy threesome; even when she was with us physically, it was obvious her thoughts were elsewhere. And I had to wonder, then, if all those times when Minnie had played with Charles and peppered me with questions about home hadn't been deliberate on her part. Had she been homesick—or had she worried that I was? Had she truly enjoyed playing with Charles—or had she seen that he was lonely?

I honestly couldn't say anymore. My sister was turning into someone I didn't recognize; she was turning into a woman. A woman with sudden blushes, mysterious silences, longing sighs—a woman who did not want her sister's protection any longer. For when Edward and I walked into a room together, it wasn't me to whom Minnie turned. She no longer had any desire to hide behind her older sister; she no longer had any desire to hide, period.

Minnie and Edward had married, quietly, without Astors and Vanderbilts and Presidents, this past summer of 1877; it was now December. While Minnie and Edward made their home with Charles and me in Middleborough, they did not need our presence the way we needed theirs. I watched, both jealous and bewildered, as they took long walks together, immersed in conversation; as they sat quietly in a dark corner after dinner, content simply to be near each other; as they retired to their shared bedroom, to their shared bed, earlier than was strictly necessary. Sighs and smiles and murmurs and glances—they spoke in a language that was more foreign to me than French.

Charles watched them, too. Sometimes, he then turned to look at me, confusion and hurt in his big brown eyes. But he never spoke to me about what he was thinking, to my great relief.

"Vinnie, I have something to tell you," Minnie repeated, drawing up a stool next to me, her earnestness pulling me out of my reverie.

"Yes, something serious, I know." I could not prevent a smile from playing upon my lips; goodness, but her manner was full of portent!

"I'm afraid that I won't be able to go back out on tour, if you were planning anything for this winter. Nor will I be able to go anywhere in the summer, either."

"I have no plans at the moment, but may I ask, dearest, why?" I brushed the back of her hand—so much smaller, even, than mine!—lightly, possessively; I was always reaching for her these days, clutching her hand, tugging at her skirts—trying, perhaps, to keep her from drifting further and further away?

Still smiling, I expected Minnie to answer something innocuous, something adorable, like "We decided to get a puppy" or "Edward has a terrible cold" or "I don't like trains, they're so dreadful."

Instead, her eyes lit up with a soft glow, a glow that I had seen in her once before. I couldn't quite remember when; I knew only that I recognized it, and a troubled, vaguely shameful feeling began to stir within my breast. As I struggled to recall the circumstances—as you do when you're trying to remember a particularly terrible dream in the safe light of day—Minnie said, with a shy duck of her head, "I'm going to have a baby."

I stared at her for a long moment, the words bouncing around in my brain but refusing to fall into place, making absolutely no sense. Then, with frightening finality, they did click into meaning; my nightmare was recalled to me, that whole horrible, dreadful business of the baby, and the way Minnie had looked when she had held the French child—Cosette, wasn't it?—in her arms. That same contented, dreamy look was in her eyes now as she raised them, uncertainly, to meet mine.

"No!" I let go of her hands, as if she were contagious, as if having a baby was a disease that I could catch from her touch. "No! Impossible! No!"

"Not impossible," Minnie said with a brave little laugh. "Entirely possible, I'm quite sure. I've just had the doctor, who confirmed it. I haven't told anyone yet, not even Edward. I wanted you to be the first to know."

"But how? But, Minnie, you—and Edward?" I was shocked, sickened. Yes, my sister was married. But so was I. I knew she and Edward shared a bed, but—didn't she know the dangers of allowing a man to touch her, she who was so delicate, so vulnerable—even more vulnerable than me?

"Oh, it would be dreadful, impossible," I heard my mother's stricken voice from across the ages. *"Don't you remember the little*

cow . . ." Didn't Minnie know? Didn't she understand how dangerous it was for her to even consider having a child?

No, she didn't. Because I had never thought to tell her—not even when she married Edward. For so long, my fears were her fears, her fears were mine, and I thought I could protect us both. But Minnie had changed, Minnie had grown—Minnie had become a real woman. Not simply a woman in miniature, like me.

"But, Vinnie, of course it's a perfectly natural thing, and I know how sad you've always been that you couldn't have a child. And just think of it—we won't have to give it back! This will be *our* child—for, of course, she will be just as much yours as she will be mine, as I'm sure I will need your help. She! Isn't that funny, Vinnie? I already think of it as a girl!" And Minnie laughed, all seriousness, all gravity gone from her eyes so that they were the impish—innocent—eyes of the sister I thought I knew.

"Minnie, listen to me." I grabbed her hand again and held it tight; too tight, for she winced. "How far—how far along are you?"

"The doctor said nearly three months, he thought."

"Three months." I searched my memory, my vast storehouse of knowledge gleaned from a life so different from hers; the words *prevention powders* were recalled from some dusty, neglected corner of my brain. Carlotta—Carlotta, that poor girl from Colonel Wood's boat—she had tried to give me those prior to my first private audience. What were they again? How did one use them?

"He also admitted it's hard to tell," Minnie continued, happily unaware of my thoughts. "Of course, Dr. Mills said the child will be tiny—as tiny as me!"

"But, Minnie, you—" I stopped. Minnie looked so unconcerned, so happy—so *well.* She did not appear to recall that she herself had not been a tiny baby, and neither had I. But the doctor? Surely he knew better?

"Yes, of course," I told my sister, still holding her hand. I could not prevent myself from searching her, appraising her, top to bottom, as if she were a new broodmare Papa had decided to purchase; she was so very small, so delicate. As if made from wishes and dreams, not flesh and blood. Then I shut my eyes as a cold wave of terror washed over me: *She must not have this child. She must not.* For her, for me—giving life meant summoning death.

But I did not tell her this now; I simply sat and listened to her talk excitedly about the baby, how happy Charles would be, as he did love children so, how we all would love this child, we would all raise her together, she would be ours forever. And my heart twisted itself about in knots as guilt, recrimination, and fear all fought for possession of it. Neither one winning, but none leaving, either—each parked itself in my heart, setting up housekeeping. I knew they would never leave; I knew I would have to carry them all around forever.

She must not have this baby—the phrase repeated itself over and over, wearing such a sharp groove in my mind, I had to grit my teeth from the pain of it. I needed to talk to someone, I needed to figure this out, for that was what I did—I figured things out. I took action. I made plans. I kept my sister safe. I was all mind, not heart—

And there was only one person who understood that. There was only one person I could turn to.

AS THE TRAIN PULLED INTO BRIDGEPORT, I WONDERED HOW MANY times I had taken this journey. It was hard to keep track, for I had taken so very many journeys by now. Since returning, triumphantly and in a blaze of headlines, from our world tour in 1872, the General Tom Thumb Company had gone back out to revisit this country, telling stories of our travels; this was when

Edward joined us. However, after that tour, Charles finally put his foot down; he was tired of mimicking people onstage and now wanted to mimic our Society friends by living a life of leisure.

So he bought a yacht, and a matching captain's jacket and hat, recommended to him by Mr. Belmont; he bought horses—fast, expensive horses—and built fine stables for them; he bought me jewels, just as his friends Mr. Vanderbilt and Mr. Astor did for their wives; he ordered the finest cigars from Mr. Barnum's man in New York. He built us our grand house in Middleborough, just across from Mama and Papa's old homestead, and furnished it with the most exquisite furniture and carpets and draperies, much of it built specially for us. The stair steps were not steep, the windows were lower to the ground so that we might easily see out of them; there was even a special kitchen built with sinks and a stove only two feet off the ground.

It was all grand; it was all impressive. Middleborough twittered and preened whenever dear Caroline Astor came to visit, and even erected a sign at the town border proclaiming this the *Home of Mr. and Mrs. Charles Stratton, or General and Mrs. Tom Thumb.*

It was also less real to me than the flimsy scenery we carted around whenever we toured. I wasn't the mimic that my husband was; while I could do a fair representation of a satisfied lady of the manor, I had yet to learn how to successfully impersonate a wife offstage. While my sister looked for ways to steal even more time with her husband, I made up excuses to spend less time with mine. A quick weekend up in New York, a jaunt over to Bridgeport; my blood always stirred with excitement even as my nerves relaxed in relief each time I boarded the train out of Middleborough.

Even today; even as I still felt—physically, as if I had been clubbed repeatedly—the blow of Minnie's news. Yet I looked forward to traveling; even more did I look forward to seeing

Mr. Barnum. I reached inside my reticule and took out a piece of pink chamois, rubbing it all over my face to take the shine and dirt off, just as we pulled into the station in Bridgeport.

As I stood on the top of the stairs, my favorite porter beamed in recognition and bustled over to lift me down to the platform. "Good morning, Mrs. General! Here to see Mr. Barnum?"

"Yes." I handed him a nickel.

"I thought so—he's outside in his carriage, waiting for you."

"He is?" Mr. Barnum never came to the station himself. How odd that he had done so today of all days—but then again, perhaps it wasn't. Tears filled my eyes; I had not yet cried, so determined was I to fix Minnie's "problem." But the relief of being able to share this with someone who possessed sense and determination; the relief of being able to share my burden, period, with the one person I desired to share my burdens with—it was so unexpectedly sweet. I reached into my reticule again, this time removing a handkerchief; dabbing my eyes, I blinked away the rest of my tears.

Then I followed the porter outside to the curb, where Mr. Barnum's enclosed carriage was waiting. He was standing next to it, bundled up in a heavy coat with a white fur collar that reached to the bottom of his ears even as his white curls brushed the tops, so that his face—pink as a baby's in the cold—stood out vividly. He was heavier now, more wrinkled, a bit round-shouldered, with a tendency to lean more decidedly upon his walking stick. But his gray eyes were just as lively, just as perceptive, as ever.

"What's wrong?" he barked as soon as he saw me. He threw his cigar upon the pavement, crushed it with his walking stick, and lifted me up into the carriage with such haste that I swallowed my words of greeting before they could reach my lips. And then we were inside, Mr. Barnum rapping his hand upon the outside of the carriage, signaling for the driver to go. "Take the long way," he shouted, sticking his head out the door before he shut it quickly against the cold. We lurched away, the horses soon settling into a smooth, slow trot that caused the carriage to sway gently, the lanterns—lit in the gloom of this depressing January day—to swing to and fro, casting ominous shadows upon us.

"It's Minnie," I said breathlessly, shivering, although there were heated bricks on the floor and hidden in the corners of the seat. Mr. Barnum leaned forward and tucked a buffalo robe about me; it was so heavy that I felt pinned to the seat, unable to move. But I was warm, anyway.

"What is it? Is there trouble with her husband? I always wondered about him; he seemed too darn polite, even for an Englishman."

"No, not that. She's—she's with child." I whispered this, feeling for the first time the indelicacy of the subject.

"She is? Why, that's wonderful!" A great, crooked grin pushed across his face, and he clapped his gloved hands in delight. "How happy you all must be!"

"No!" I shouted it, frustrated that he did not immediately understand the situation. "No, it's not wonderful. It's terrible. Don't you see? She's—we must do something about it. Minnie was not—I was not—we were both normal-size babies. Mama always told us this, don't you remember? I weighed six pounds when I was born. Do you know how much Minnie weighs now? Thirty pounds, at the most. Can you imagine—well, you were born on a farm, you must know! I remember Mama and Delia saying, long ago, how I must never—and now Minnie is, and she can't, she can't, it will kill her, and we must stop it!" Somehow I had flung that oppressive robe off me, kicking it to the floor, and now I was rocking back and forth, my arms clutching my shoulders. I knew I sounded wild, unhinged, but I did not care.

Comprehension dawned upon Mr. Barnum's face; he paled,

then colored, then his eyes narrowed, as if he was squinting at some faraway point, and I took a big, crackling breath and wiped my face with the sleeve of my coat. He was thinking; the wheels in that great, perpetual-motion brain of his were turning, and I was weak with relief. I knew I could depend on him.

"Excuse me, Vinnie, for being so forward, but we must dispense with modesty. How far along is she?"

"She thinks almost three months, but the idiot doctor apparently can't tell. He told her the baby would be tiny, like her—I don't know if he's totally ignorant, or if he told her that so she wouldn't worry. I suspect the former."

"Country doctors." Mr. Barnum snorted. "I'll find the finest New York doctor and send him to Middleborough."

"Yes, that would be a relief." I nodded, hesitating—but then I decided to plunge forward, as time was of the essence. "However, would he be willing to—I know there are things you can do, if the health of the mother is in question. It's probably past the stage of any prevention powders, but—"

"What? Prevention powders?" Mr. Barnum stared at me, aghast; then he blushed. He actually blushed; I had never seen him do that, not even when the wild Circassian girl asked if she could dance bare-bodiced at the Museum. "What on earth do you know about such things?"

I met his gaze levelly. "When I was on the river. A girl—a dancer—once thought I might need something of the kind. She was quite mistaken, I'm glad to say. However, it was the first time I had heard of these things, and now I'm happy that I did, for I can think clearly about Minnie's situation."

"Vinnie, you never cease to amaze me," Mr. Barnum said, grasping my hand. "You are the most remarkable woman I have ever met."

I smiled at him, happy to hear this; it filled my soul with

gratitude and yearning and other unfamiliar emotions that I usually did not have time to miss—except when I was with him. But now was not the time to reflect upon such things.

"We need to consider the option of doing—something—so that Minnie does not carry the child to term."

"But do you think there's the possibility that the child might be tiny, as the doctor says?"

"I don't know. All I know is that Minnie and I were not. Nor was Charles, remember? That's three of us who were born normal-size that I know of—and that's enough for me. I have no idea how we'll be able to convince her, for she is over the moon with happiness—she said she's doing this for me, too." And now I was face-to-face with the hard, unpleasant truth of the matter, the factor I had tried my best to ignore but which would not go away. I looked at him and took a big breath. "All that baby business, back in the sixties. It broke her heart to say goodbye to those infants. She keeps saying how glad she'll be not to have to say goodbye to her child, how happy Charles will be, how happy I must be. She thought I mourned those children just as she did, but I did not. She says she's so glad she can do this for me! So it's all my fault!"

"The one thing you cannot do is blame yourself." Mr. Barnum shook his head. "Believe me, I know. When I lost Pauline last year, I couldn't stop blaming myself, wondering if I could have seen the symptoms earlier."

"But this is different! Pauline died of fever! I have pushed Minnie into making a decision that will cost her her life."

"You don't know that, Vinnie. You don't know if she wouldn't have done this anyway."

"She never would have met Edward if it wasn't for me!"

Mr. Barnum pressed his crooked lips together, as if trying to prevent himself from saying anything further. He did not; I think he understood that I needed to say these things. Instead, he pushed himself off his seat and lurched over to my side of the carriage; he put his arm about me and gathered me close so that I could lean my head against his broad chest. He had never touched me in this way before; always he had been proper, respectful. A kiss upon the cheek in greeting, a fond handshake when embarking upon a new venture, a pat on the back in farewell.

But never had he held me; never had any man held me like this, so completely, as if he had a right to do so. Not even my husband, who would not have attempted to unless I first instructed him how. But I would never have done so; it was not in my nature, so accustomed was I to cringing from a man's touch, fearing the intent behind it, fearing my own helplessness in the face of it. I had never before missed being held.

Until now.

I felt my limbs loosen; no longer did I feel responsible for holding them together within my skin, assembled correctly, upright and proper. At that moment, all my bones and muscles and tissue melted together, melted away, melted *into* someone else, someone strong and caring, someone just as capable as I. Someone who would keep my bones and muscles and tissue from draining away altogether, who would give them back to me, intact, when I needed them again.

But I did not need them right now; I was content to give them away. I was content to simply *be*—with another. With Mr. Barnum.

We sat like that for a long while, as the carriage indeed took the long way around Bridgeport, swaying rhythmically, hypnotically. The clap of the horses' hooves against the hard, frozen streets was muffled by the sound of my own heartbeat, Mr. Barnum's breathing, the faint tick of his pocket watch hidden beneath layers of fur, wool, and understanding. It would be all right, I thought drowsily; Minnie would be all right. I had someone to help me, someone who understood.

Someone who didn't need me to be strong. This was such a novel sensation, I didn't quite know what to do with it. But given time, I thought, as I nestled farther into Mr. Barnum's welcoming arms, I could learn.

I WAITED OUTSIDE MINNIE'S ROOM; DR. FEINWAY WAS THROUGH examining her and had stepped out onto one of the balconies with a cigar. I had held Minnie's hand as she bravely allowed him to measure her abdomen, her hips; as he listened to her heart, felt her pulse, put a strange tubelike contraption against her stomach, which had distended alarmingly in just the last couple of weeks, since my return from Bridgeport.

In that short time she had changed from a slender, delicate reed to a puffy, swollen *thing.* Her ankles and wrists were no longer separate, defined entities but rather ugly extensions of her arms and legs. Her body was already stretching to absorb this child, and to my unpracticed yet worried eyes, it looked as if it couldn't stretch much more.

But she was happy, despite her obvious physical discomfort. She smiled all the time, when she wasn't retching over a chamber pot or falling into a deep, exhausted sleep in the middle of the day.

"Mrs. Stratton." Dr. Feinway beckoned to me from the other end of the hall; I slid off my chair and followed him.

Charles suddenly popped out of his room, blocking my path. He held a stick of wood in one hand, a miniature carving tool in another. "Vinnie, I'm making a spinning top for the baby, do you want to see? Your father showed me how to carve it!"

"Later, dear." I patted his arm. "I'll look at it later. Right now I need to discuss something with the doctor."

"Oh." His face, which had been smooth and happy with his accomplishment, clouded over just a bit, which wasn't much. A lifetime of pleasing the public had ironed out most of the muscles necessary to frown. "Minnie is all right, isn't she?"

"Yes, of course. I'll tell you all about it later." I gently nudged him aside and joined the doctor, leading him down the stairs and into the library, which Charles had designed in almost perfect imitation of Mr. Barnum's own. Once the doors were closed, Dr. Feinway refused my offer of a seat; he was obviously agitated, so I could do nothing but remain standing, looking up at him with my neck at an uncomfortable angle. But he did not appear to notice how awkward this was for me.

"Where is Mr. Newell?" he asked abruptly.

Evading his piercing gaze, I busied myself with straightening a doily upon a table. "He is up in Boston for the day, on business." I did not reveal that I had sent him there; I fully intended to discuss the situation with him after I had all the facts from the doctor. But Edward believed everything Minnie told him—if she had said the sky was yellow, he would have accepted it as fact; his head, not to mention his heart, was not steady enough to hear or speak plainly.

"Well, I would have preferred to have him here. But there is no time, not even for delicacy, so forgive me, Mrs. Stratton. Your sister appears to me to be carrying a normal-size child; according to her calculations, it's still early, but she's already retaining fluid, and her pulse is rapid. There is really only one reason for this. The baby is straining her system."

"Are you sure her—calculations—are correct?" I still could not help thinking of Minnie as that shy shadow that trailed me wherever I went, except to school; surely she had made a mistake.

"It appears she kept a very detailed diary of her—womanly days. She was obviously planning this child, keeping track. So yes, I believe her calculations. She's a little over four months along."

Minnie had been *planning* this? It wasn't just one—singular—unfortunate accident? Unwanted images filled my head, of Edward and Minnie in bed night after night, clinging together, sweating, panting, loving each other as man and woman were supposed to do, but as I had never experienced, never wanted to experience—I was dizzy, nauseated, desperate to sit down so that I would not collapse. But the doctor remained standing. He was a tall, aristocratic man with impeccably shaped, buffed nails. For some reason I could not take my eyes off them; they were obviously a source of pride for him. Could a man be a good doctor and have such vanity? But obviously Mr. Barnum thought he was; I must accept him.

"Then what are we to do?" I asked, tearing my gaze away from his hands. Finally, he appeared to notice the disparity in our heights; his eyes, behind gleaming spectacles, softened, and he looked about for a chair. I gestured to one, and he took it. I had never been so glad to sit down in all my life; once relieved of their duty, my legs began to tremble. I had to press my hands upon my thighs to keep my silk skirt from rustling like aspen leaves in the wind.

"I think the only humane thing is to convince your sister to abort her child. There's no question it will be a normal-size baby if it's taxing her so early on."

"She thinks it will be a tiny, like she is. She doesn't seem to recall that she and I were both normal-size at birth, and so far I haven't had the heart to tell her. I'm afraid—if we tell her, and she refuses to abort the child, then she has to spend the next months in fear, dreadful fear. But if we don't, she won't understand the severity of the situation. I don't know what to do—oh, I don't know what to do!" And I wanted, so desperately, for Mr. Barnum to be here now; I trusted no one else to make this decision for me.

The doctor looked at me in sympathy. Then he removed his spectacles and rubbed the bridge of his nose. Placing those glasses, with his fine, manicured hands, deliberately back upon his face, he said, "There is nothing for you to do. We must tell your sister the facts as we know them, and she must decide."

"But you don't understand, I've looked after her all our lives; she's not as—as—" But I broke off, ashamed of what I was saying. Minnie wasn't as—what? Smart as me? As quick? As perceptive?

As *cowardly*?

"I think your sister is of perfectly sound mind," Dr. Feinway said gently. "But I do hope you can persuade her to see the medical facts. Even the soundest of minds grow soft at the idea of a child."

"If she were to—abort—the child, how is it done?" I was sick, sick to my stomach, sick to my spirit; I had already killed one child, and now I would soon have another on my hands. This irony fell upon me like a particularly ugly, ungainly costume; it turned me into someone else, someone I couldn't recognize in the mirror.

"There is risk in the procedure, I won't lie. The usual way is a flushing out of the uterus with special waters, although I've read about a newer practice involving scraping."

I flinched at the words; my own abdomen tightened, and I felt bile rise up in my throat.

"But if she carries the child to term?"

Dr. Feinway hesitated. "I have been present when a large child was born to a small woman; it's an impossible situation, but sometimes Providence provides a way. But I've never before seen a fully mature woman as small as your sister. There are instruments that can assist—forceps, primarily—but those would be of no use in this case. There are instances when the child can be cut from the womb, but only after—after all hope is gone for the mother."

"She must not be allowed to carry this child!" I balled up my fists, pressing them even harder against my legs. My entire body was filled with a cold, heavy liquid; it had replaced my blood, and I knew, from the bitter taste of it in my mouth, that it was terror. I had never experienced terror before, not even when Colonel Wood had tried to attack me.

Only Minnie could make me feel it; only Minnie could make me feel so many things, love and affection, and now, finally, cold, debilitating terror.

"Do your best to explain the facts, then. And don't neglect to engage her husband," Dr. Feinway said, rising. "Do you happen to have anything to drink? I could use a brandy about now."

I nodded and rose; ringing for the maid, I asked her to show the doctor to the dining room, where we had a small stock of fine whiskey in decanters. Neither Charles nor I drank spirits, but we had some on hand for guests. Although, at the moment, I had a longing to join Dr. Feinway; I had to go to Minnie now, and the temptation to have something strong in me for courage was great.

But I did not; I walked back upstairs, down the hall, past Charles, who asked me, again, to look at his carving. I didn't answer him. Instead I knocked on my sister's door and let myself inside.

"Annabelle?"

"No, too silly."

"Amelia?"

"Too serious."

"Sarah?"

"Too plain."

"Guinevere?"

"Too fancy!" Minnie laughed merrily, the shining tinkle of her laugh—like delicate bells—filling the air.

It was the only recognizable thing about her now. Her laugh, the sound of her voice—those things had not changed. Nor had her temperament: by turns serious and trusting, patience itself, always hopeful. She had borne her penance with a peacefulness I knew I could not have, were I in her place. But I could never be in her place; I had made my choice long ago.

Confined to her bed since the day that Dr. Feinway examined her, she had not complained. She had accepted it, not as her fate but rather as her privilege, almost as if receiving a benediction or blessing. So willing was she to obey the doctor's orders, she scarcely moved from her back at all, as if for fear of dislodging the life that was so obviously overtaking hers.

For of course she refused to abort her child. I knew she would, but that hadn't stopped me from dropping to my knees beside her bed and grasping her little hand, my tears punctuating my words.

"Minnie, darling, you don't understand," I began, faltering; I had never wanted to mention Uncle's little cow to my sister, as that was my own personal Gethsemane. I never wanted it to be hers. But then I took a deep breath, squeezed her hand, and looked straight into her eyes.

"The child is not tiny, not like you think," I made myself continue. "The child is most likely normal-size, just as I was—just as you were when you were born. The doctor was very certain that is the case."

Minnie's eyes widened, but she did not flinch. She absorbed the news gravely, her hand going to her abdomen, stroking it, caressing it. She remained silent for so long that I feared she hadn't understood me completely.

"You do—you do understand the way babies are born," I began, blushing. "You do understand how—how—"

"Of course I understand." Minnie's eyes blazed at me. "Honestly, Vinnie, how young do you think I am? I'm a married woman, just like you!"

I bit my lip and looked away. She was right, of course. I could have prevented this by treating her as I had always wanted to be treated myself—as a sensible adult, regardless of my size. But no, I had always wanted to protect her. And I had done my job too well.

Or had I? For after all, I had willingly snatched baby after baby out of her hands, causing her poor, tender heart to break over and over again. I had allowed her to respond to all those condolence letters. I still had them somewhere; I hadn't been able to throw them away, and I hadn't known just why. But now I did; they were portents, weren't they? Harbingers of what lay ahead.

Concentrating on a worn patch of wallpaper next to the headboard, I somehow continued. "Minnie, I—I should have told you, oh, so much! It's all my fault, and I—"

I felt a hand upon my shoulder. Steeling myself against the accusation I knew I would find in her eyes, I took a trembling breath and turned to my sister.

But there was only that now-familiar soft, hopeful light in Minnie's eyes as she smiled and hugged me to her.

"It doesn't matter, Vinnie. I'm glad you told me, but—it doesn't matter. You don't understand, you can never understand, what it is to have life within you! I'm so sorry that you haven't had this chance, but I'm so grateful that I am able to! Even if—but I know that God will find a way. I know that He will see me through this. And I promise, this baby will be yours as well as mine. You're always looking out for me—still! You're always doing things for me. Well, this is the one thing I can do for you, and I would not wish it any other way."

I had to leave the room then, coward that I was, that I now knew I always had been. I couldn't bring myself to witness the bravery in those still incongruously impish eyes, the nobility in that dimple and faint, determined scowl.

All were gone now; she lay, still so patiently, but her body was no longer her own. It was a puffy, stretched, swollen, throbbing vessel for the life within, the life that continued to grow and grow, so obviously not the "fairy child" that we all continued to talk hopefully about, regardless of the facts. Through eyes that were slits, a face too swollen to display a dimple; with hands that were so awkward and puffy, she could barely hold her knitting needles, but still she tried; over an abdomen that stretched her skin as tight as a drum and made it impossible for her to do more than allow an extra pillow beneath her head—my sister prepared for the new life expected.

"What if it's a boy?" I asked her, as I knitted an absurdly tiny cap out of the softest wool; it was all for show, the tiny layette that Mama, Delia, and I were preparing for her, to ease her mind—as well as Edward's. He refused to consider the possibility that the child would be normal-size, and forbade us from discussing it.

"She is not a boy, I know it." Minnie struggled with small knitting needles, trying to maneuver them upon her swollen belly.

"How?"

"Because she is very considerate about when she kicks. A boy would not be so thoughtful."

"What—what does it feel like?" I was hesitant to ask; I talked about the child in theory, allowing her to dream of it. But I did not like to discuss any of the practical—physical—aspects of what my sister was going through. It was almost as if I could wish them away by not giving them voice.

But by the look of relief—of happiness—in Minnie's gaze as she considered my question, I had to wonder who I was protecting in this way. Her? Or me?

"Do you remember the time I swallowed a grasshopper?" she asked me.

"Yes." I laughed; I hadn't thought of that in years. "You said you could feel it hopping about inside you, and then you started to hop, too; you hopped all through dinnertime, until Mama didn't know what to do and was about to send for the doctor."

"Well, it's like that. Only this time, it's real; I do feel something hopping about inside me. As if I've swallowed a very large, very heavy, grasshopper. Oh!" She gasped, and her hand flew to her stomach.

"What is it? Are you all right? Shall I send for the doctor?" I jumped out of my chair, my knitting falling to the floor. I was halfway out the door when I heard my sister's happy laugh beckoning me back inside.

"Vinnie—come, quick! She's kicking right now! Come feel!"

"Oh!" I turned back to her but remained where I was, in the doorway. My hands flew behind my back almost of their own accord.

"Come!" Minnie patted the mattress, one hand still upon her stomach, which twitched, ever so faintly, beneath the sheets. I stared at it in horror.

"No, I don't want to hurt you, dearest—"

"You won't hurt me! I promise—come feel her, Vinnie! Come say hello to your niece!"

"No, can't you listen to me? I said *no*!" I couldn't help it—my voice was rough with anger, and I flinched at the startled look on Minnie's face. "I mean, I will another time. Oh, will you look at that! My yarn rolled beneath the bed!" And I fell to my knees to avoid her hurtful, reproachful gaze; I was grateful for the exertion it took for me to wiggle under the bed and retrieve my knitting.

When I resumed my seat, I felt shyness and guilt, both, envelop me; I concentrated on my knitting with such intensity, the needles came close to poking out my eyes. My sister was a stranger to me now in so many ways; she had outpaced me, she who had always held docilely on to my hand while I led. Suddenly, our roles were reversed. And I knew Minnie wanted only to share her joy; I knew she wanted only to *teach* me the things she was learning with every passing day, every evidence of the child growing within.

But I was as reluctant a pupil now as she once had been. For the lessons my sister wanted to teach me were lessons not of the mind but of the heart.

"So no boys' names, then? Not even one, just in case?" I returned to a safe subject.

Minnie was silent for a moment; she turned her head away from me, staring out her window, but finally, after a soft little sigh, she replied, "No. But I do have an idea for a girl's name. A perfectly lovely girl's name."

"What?"

"Pauline," my sister said quietly.

I dropped my knitting again, tears filling my eyes once more—oh, there was not even ten minutes a day, it seemed lately, that I did not cry!

"Oh, Minnie, that's too—too sweet of you. Mr. Barnum will be so touched."

"Indeed, he will," said a familiar hearty voice. Minnie and I both looked up, startled; there, in the doorway, stood Mr. Barnum himself. A beautiful cradle, adorned with an enormous pink silk bow, was in his arms.

"Mr. Barnum!" Minnie exclaimed; with a very feminine gesture she patted at her hair and smoothed the ribbons on her bed jacket. I ran to her and tried to prop her up a bit upon her pillows, but she was too cumbersome; she smiled and raised her hands helplessly.

I glanced at Mr. Barnum; he was trying, unsuccessfully, to hide his shock at her appearance. His hands shook as he set the cradle down, and his gray eyes were misty with tears.

"We didn't expect you," I told him, rushing over to take his hat, placing my hand upon his arm to steady him. He smiled and kissed me on the cheek; one of his tears fell upon my face, and I pressed my hand to it, absorbing it into my own flesh. Then I turned away, hoping he hadn't seen.

"Would you really like it if I named her Pauline?" Minnie asked him.

"It would mean the world to me. I can think of no greater tribute." Recovering himself, Mr. Barnum pulled up a chair next to Minnie's bed and plopped himself upon it; in his shock, he must not have seen that it was a small chair, made for us. So he sat with his knees up to his chin, his fleshy body spilling over the arms; Minnie and I burst into laughter, and he had no idea why.

"What? What is it?"

"Nothing." I signaled Minnie to keep quiet, and she did, with a look of such delight upon her swollen face that my heart lightened enough so that I was not, for one blessed, fleeting moment, aware of it.

"Well, Miss Minnie, it's good to see you so cheerful, anyway."

"I have our Vinnie to thank for that. She never lets me get bored or anxious. And she tells me wonderful stories every day about all the things she's seen."

"You've accompanied her on all her travels; surely there's not much she can tell you?"

"Oh, but there is! It's almost as if I haven't been in the same places she has, for she remembers things I didn't even know happened! Like the time the Maharaja tried to give her a purse of rubies—I had no idea!"

"You were too shy, Pumpkin. You wanted to remain behind in our rooms and have your dinner with Mrs. Bleeker, remember?"

"I know. That's why I love hearing your stories; I get to live my life all over again, through different eyes!" Minnie smiled at me, and I had to look away; I didn't like to recall how long she had been in my shadow. I didn't like to hear her talk of living her life again, as if she had a premonition about the future.

"Well, I may not be as good a storyteller as your sister, but I'm no slouch," Mr. Barnum said hastily, catching a glimpse of my face as I busied myself with arranging a bowl of forget-me-nots on the windowsill; it was spring now in Middleborough. Life was bursting out all around us: flowers and tender grass and birds singing, newborn calves, foals, the first sprouts of Mama's kitchen garden. Sometimes I felt hopeful; with all the vigor and optimism of the season, how could Minnie not survive her upcoming ordeal? Surely the same pulse, the same spirit that carried the scent of new-mown hay through her window, always open now so that she might hear the birds, would see her through, safe and sound?

Other times, when I heard her moan softly as she sought a comfortable position, as I watched Dr. Feinway's increasingly grave countenance when he left her room (he came every two weeks, arranged by Mr. Barnum), I felt the cruelty of the season. It wasn't fair! Life should not come so easily to the dumb creatures of nature, when my own sister did not have the same chance.

"Have I told you about my elephant?" Mr. Barnum asked Minnie. She shook her head, her curls—dull now, changed like the rest of her—ruffling her pillow. I pulled up a chair on the other side of her; both of our faces turned, like flowers to the sun, to Mr. Barnum as he began his tale.

"Jumbo is his name," he said, shifting about uncomfortably in his tiny chair, still unaware of its proportions. "Well, he's not mine yet—but he will be! He's in a zoo in London now; he was found as a baby in the deepest, darkest jungles of Africa. He's the biggest animal of his kind, I'd swear it! Well, between you and me, I wouldn't exactly swear it in a court of law, but I'm confident the public won't hold me to that. He's really a stunner—his legs are ten feet high! One of my giants could easily pass under him! Yet he's the gentlest animal soul I've ever seen; right smart he is, they say. He can count to three by stomping his foot, and when he does, the whole earth quakes! Minnie, I would love to see you curled up in his trunk; he loves to cradle things. One time at the zoo, one of the monkeys was missing, and finally they found him sleeping in Jumbo's trunk, that elephant rocking him back and forth just like a baby!"

"No!" Minnie exclaimed breathlessly. "Didn't he hurt the poor monkey?"

"Not a bit! Gentlest animal ever—they even let children ride him! Some of those elephants can get pretty ornery, but not Jumbo. Shh, don't tell anyone yet, but I'm planning on buying him and bringing him over here. I can build an entire circus around him. I'll put him in a special train car, bright red with his name in big yellow letters, so that when we come to town he's the first thing folks want to see!"

"Oh, I'd love to see him. Can I? Can we, Vinnie?"

I believe, at that moment, Minnie had forgotten her condition; she was a girl again, about to embark upon a new adventure with me. I was so grateful to Mr. Barnum for giving her that moment of respite, for I knew, despite her cheerfulness, she was worried about her confinement. If I couldn't talk to her about it,

Mama could, at least a little; I overheard Minnie asking her once how much it would hurt. Mama told her only about as much as it hurt to have a tooth out, but that she'd forget about it the moment it was over and she held her baby for the first time. Yet when Mama left the room, she broke down sobbing in my arms, and I heard Minnie crying softly in her bed.

Mr. Barnum proceeded to tell her more stories about Jumbo; he had that same light in his eyes he used to have when he spoke of Jenny Lind, and I smiled to think of how jealous I had once been of her! Now I knew that Mr. Barnum was like a child in his affections: The newest toy was always his favorite. And Jenny Lind was across the ocean, matronly and married; Jumbo was in his zoo. I was right here, and I always had been. As I always would be.

Minnie was growing weary. She slept a lot now; it was painful to recall how she used to move, like quicksilver, such a sprite of a thing. Even when she left her bed to use the chamber pot, she moved so heavily, she reminded me of Sylvia.

I noticed her trying to stifle a yawn.

"Mr. Barnum, it's time for Minnie to rest now," I interposed gently but firmly, for he was not used to having his stories interrupted.

"Oh! Well, listen to me going on and on. I'm sorry, Miss Minnie. You must store up your energy, for when that baby comes, you will surely need it!" He spoke lightly, looking directly at her as he said this. Then he tried to rise from his chair and became stuck; standing, the chair clung to his behind like a burr, and Minnie giggled at the sight.

Finally, after much turning about, he managed to remove it, and so it was with cheerfulness and humor that he and Minnie said their farewells. Just as he bent over her bed to shake her hand, however, Minnie's face grew serious; she tugged upon his sleeve, pulling him closer to her. She tried to whisper, but I could hear her, anyway; didn't she know that I could always hear her? Her voice was ever in my thoughts, ever in my memories.

"Mr. Barnum, please look after Vinnie for me, won't you? Sister worries too much, and I know that you're the only person she'll listen to. Try to amuse her—and just—take care of her, please? She's always taken care of me, but nobody ever takes care of her."

Mr. Barnum's forced smile froze. He looked into my sister's eyes and I suddenly feared what he would say.

"Come, let Minnie get her rest," I said briskly from the doorway, pretending not to have heard—although my voice was suddenly unpredictable; I couldn't quite stop it from quavering. "I'll be back soon, dearest."

Minnie turned her head away from me, but I saw her lips tremble as she nodded.

Resolutely, I led Mr. Barnum out into the hall, as Delia curtsied shyly to him and took my place by Minnie's bed. Together we walked down the stairs; as always, he slowed his pace to match mine, without seeming to think about it.

Still not speaking, we walked through the front door; he didn't have to ask if I wanted some air. We walked until we were far from the house, with all its open windows, and could speak freely. An iron bench, nestled among a patch of daffodils, beckoned, and we sat down upon it. I took in as much air as I could, breathing in greedy gulps, as if I were suffocating. Despite her open windows, Minnie's room was growing unbearably stuffy, the air stagnant, full of sickbed smells; sweat and urine and vomit, and, most pervasive of all, fear.

"You look like something the cat dragged in, chewed up, and then spit back out again," Mr. Barnum finally remarked, and I had to laugh. I had no idea how I looked—me, the perfectly groomed little Queen of Beauty! But it had been ages since I had spent any time dressing my hair, and I couldn't remember the last time I looked in a mirror. I rose every morning, donned whatever dress was handy, did my hair up in a simple knot, and went to Minnie's room. Edward always greeted me with a quick update—usually, she had spent a restless night, unable to lie comfortably, and now bedsores were becoming a worry—before stumbling off to Charles's sitting room, where he might shave and bathe, but more often than not, collapsed on a settee and slept like a dead man. Edward was suffering, too; a good soul, so devoted to Minnie that he appeared unable to think ahead to the outcome of this ordeal. But I could not like him. I was jealous, jealous of his right to spend the nights with her, angry for his inability to keep himself away from her, for giving in to his animalistic urges and putting her in this situation. I knew it wasn't fair to think of him that way—as a heathen who couldn't control himself, just like a *polygamist*—but I did. He was a man, after all. And I knew what men were like.

I patted my hair, knowing that it was in a lifeless knot at the back of my neck, and agreed with Mr. Barnum. "I'm sure I look a fright."

"You should think of yourself some, and take rest whenever you can."

"I've spent my entire life thinking of myself. It's a privilege to spend this time thinking of her," I replied, speaking the truth.

"If you won't think of yourself, then I will—shall I ask Charles to return to Bridgeport with me? I haven't seen him nearly enough, and would enjoy a little bachelor vacation myself. Nancy will be in England visiting her family." Nancy was his second wife; he had remarried following Charity's death in 1873. I was no more fond of his second wife than I was of his first. Nancy was younger than I, vain and cold, interested only in the many material benefits of being Mrs. Phineas Taylor Barnum, for she spent no time with him.

"That would be good of you. I know Charles would enjoy it, for he's been somewhat lost in all this. He's beside himself with worry for Minnie—he spends some time with her each day, reading stories, but mainly he's been left to his own devices."

"I imagine this might lessen your own load a little, too. Charles is my good friend, but I know he requires a fair amount of handling."

"Yes," I admitted, again feeling the blessed relief of plain speaking; it was as if my stays had been loosened, as well as my tongue. I hadn't been able to indulge myself like this in such a long time; for months, we all tiptoed about, not talking about the one thing that was on all our minds. It hovered in the air, unspoken, like smoke lingering from a burnt pot on a stove. And none of us made a move to clear it.

I was so grateful to Mr. Barnum for allowing me to speak what was in my heart; it was the desire to prolong this moment that caused me to blurt out, "She's going to die, you know. It's so obvious, I want to scream, but we all pretend and pretend not to see what we see. This child is not a tiny little fairy sprite. It's a normal flesh-and-blood baby, and Minnie will not be able to survive its birth. We can't *pretend* anymore."

Mr. Barnum, to my everlasting gratitude, did not try to persuade me otherwise. "What will you do if the child lives?"

"I—I don't know," I sputtered, stunned. I had not thought of this possibility. I had not given the thing within my sister any identity or thought beyond its destructive nature. That was the only way I could see it: as the likely cause of Minnie's death. It wasn't a baby to me; it was a poison or a tumor or a fatal condition.

"You should prepare yourself, Vinnie. It's a possible outcome, you know. I don't imagine Edward will be in any position to care for a child alone. You must talk to Minnie and determine what she would wish. Most mothers," he continued gently, seeing the horror upon my face, "give some thought to this, you know, regardless of their condition."

"I can't!" I shook my head; it felt as if the sun had just disappeared behind a cloud, so chilly was my soul. But the sun still shone brightly; I could see our shadows spilling across the lawn at our feet, one long and one short but so close together there was no space between.

"You must try. She might even be hoping that you do. It is my experience that the dying wish us to speak more plainly with them than we think—you heard what she said to me when I left. She's trying to prepare us—she's trying to prepare you."

"No, you're wrong. She's hopeful—" I faltered, remembering the time—*times,* if I was being truthful—I had overheard her crying. But I shook my head, erasing them from my memory. She was not afraid, for the simple reason that I couldn't bear for her to be. "What she said back there, she just meant for the present. She's been knitting for the child, *naming* it—you heard! And you know Minnie. She's always been so simple. She doesn't understand what's truly happening."

"Vinnie, if you've ever done your sister a disservice—and I believe you think you have—it's only in this: that you have persisted in thinking of her as younger and simpler than she really is."

"I don't know what you're talking about." I shifted uncomfortably on the hard bench; suddenly our shadows appeared to me to be too close.

"Your sister is a woman, Vinnie. A woman who has chosen her own fate. You haven't done it for her, no matter what you think. She was more than capable of doing it for herself."

"What do you know of fate? Of choices? You're just a man—

and men never have to pay for their choices like women do." I started to rise, as did my voice, but Mr. Barnum reached for my arm. He continued to speak in a low, soothing tone, which maddened me; I was not a child.

"Vinnie, you can't possibly mean that. We all have to pay for the choices we make—but come, let's not quarrel. There's no need for anger, especially on such a beautiful day."

"Oh, beautiful day be damned." I kicked at a daffodil, to make my point.

"Vinnie!"

"Do I shock you? Well, good. I want to. I want to shock God, too. Can't you see I *am* angry? I'm angry with God—I'm angry with myself," I muttered, still kicking at innocent daffodils, so mocking in their vivid, irrepressible cheer.

"Why on earth? It's simply God's—"

"*Will?* Oh, how sick I am of hearing God talked about in this house! I'm glad He gives Minnie comfort, but I'm not so easily tricked."

"Call it Providence, then—but you're still not responsible."

"Oh, yes, I am! Do you know why? Let me tell you—let me finally tell someone!" Jumping to my feet, my hands clenched, I stood before him as honest as I had ever been with anyone—and as vulnerable. His hand was still upon my arm, but I felt it loosen its grip, recoiling as my confession spilled out of me.

"It's not as if I *couldn't* have children—the truth is I didn't *want* to. I told Charles, I told you, I even told Minnie that I couldn't, when the truth was, I was too terrified to try. So I never explained to Minnie about the dangers of childbirth for the two of us. And now look what's happened!"

"But you—afraid? I don't understand."

"Of course you don't—you never have." I rushed on, desperate to unburden myself—even more desperate, for some reason, to burden *him*. "If you had, you never would have thought up that whole baby business. I'm angry with you, too!" I finally wriggled out of his grasp—or, rather, he let go.

"Me?" Mr. Barnum's expression suddenly became alert and watchful; before my eyes, his soft, uneven features began to harden.

"Yes, you! Oh, if I'd only been honest with you about Colonel Wood! That was my fault, but then you—you *forced* me to bring Minnie along to pay my debt. And then that ridiculous *humbug* about the baby!"

"That baby business made us both a small fortune, if you'll recall. All those *cartes de visites* sold! We made thousands. And you accepted the money, if my memory is to be trusted, without any hair tearing or breast beating." The gray in his eyes turned to steel, and he clutched his walking stick as if he was trying not to use it as a weapon.

"I—well, we needed the money, the way Charles spends, but that's not the point. It hurt people—it hurt Mama, because I'd told her I'd never let you do anything in my name that I didn't approve."

"Then why are you scolding me?"

"Because! Mama feared I'd lose my soul if I went with you, and I told her I wouldn't, but now I have. But I don't care about myself. I'm willing to accept my punishment, but, oh, that it has to be Minnie who pays! That's what I can never forget or forgive, either of us."

"Lavinia Warren Stratton, the conceit in you! I knew you had an ego, m'dear, but I had no idea you thought so much of yourself that you could buy and sell souls." He barked a hard, withering laugh that set my teeth on edge.

"Talk about ego—is there anything in New York or Bridgeport that you haven't plastered your name all over?" My eyes narrowed, considering him. We glared at each other for a long moment; everything else—the flowers, the bees, the lazy neighing of a horse in a nearby pasture—faded away until I was aware of only the rasp of his breathing, the pounding of my wrathful heart.

"Let's not continue this line of discussion," Mr. Barnum said with maddening calm. "Minnie would not be happy to know we were quarreling."

"Oh, you have no idea what Minnie would like," I snapped. I would not be soothed. "You don't know her at all. You only want to make money off her, just like you do with everything and everyone. You know frauds and hokum and cheats and scoundrels—and I include myself in all that!—but you do not know goodness! So don't try to tell me what to do or how to think about my sister. She's mine, she's me—the very best and only true part of me! The only true part I have left! You're a sham, and you expect everyone else to be a sham, too!"

"I don't know *goodness*?" He threw his stick down in disgust. "Or truth? What do you know? Have you ever asked me—I watched my wife suffer all her life, saw two of my daughters die. I know truth from lies, Vinnie, and I see the truth in Minnie and I see the truth in you, although right now you don't want me to—and maybe you never did, at that! For if we're speaking of friendship and goodness, let me ask you this: Why do you only come to me when you need something—money or advice or even, yes, my *name* when it suits your needs? Why do you never visit me, just because? It's always under the pretense of some piece of business. And furthermore, I would like to know something else." He pushed himself off the bench with determination, turning away from me so that I could not see his face. "Why, in all the years we have known each other, have you never once called me by my given name?"

"I—what?" Stunned, I stopped my wild pacing; so unexpected

was his question, his obvious hurt, that for a moment I forgot my anger.

"I have called you Vinnie almost since the first day I met you. Charles calls me Phineas, Bleeker does, all my friends do. But you persist in calling me 'Mr. Barnum.' You always keep me at arm's length, and I would like to know why. Do you only think of me in terms of business, then? Do you have no room for true friendship or affection in your life?"

"'True friendship'? Oh, don't talk to me about what's true!" I resumed my pacing, disgusted by his blatant attempt at manipulation. I'd heard him put that quaver in his voice many times before, usually when he was trying to negotiate the terms of a new contract. "We've only ever been a meal ticket for you. Just like all your other toys and curiosities—*your* giant, *your* elephant, *your* dwarfs. That's all we've ever been to you, and you know it!"

"I do not, and I'm offended you'd even think such a thing!"

"Really?" I spun around. "You're saying we'd be friends even if I wasn't what you persist in calling, in all my advertising and even in your latest autobiography, a *dwarf*?"

"Oh, for heaven's sake, Vinnie! Remember, *you're* the one who first contacted *me*. You sent that note calling my attention to a certain Miss Lavinia Warren Bump, whose dainty height and symmetrical proportions were much admired along the Mississippi. When I sent that first telegram, you answered so fast the wires were still singing! You yourself know that no one would pay a dime to see you, otherwise. And I always admired you for knowing that—I always admired you for your honesty and good sense. But lately, I'm not so sure—"

"*You're* lecturing *me* on honesty? And as far as good sense—"

"Yes, good sense. Look at all your Society friends, all your lavish spending, all the airs—it's almost as if you've forgotten how it all began. But these people, Vinnie—they don't see you! Not really, not beyond being a novelty, and you're going to get hurt if you don't watch yourself. And the thing is, *I* see you—I see beyond the perfect little woman in miniature; I see the real person, but you don't want me to. That's why you always keep me at arm's length—you're afraid of me. You're terrified of what I might see."

"I'm not terrified of anything," I said hotly, even as I knew it wasn't true.

"Yes, you are." Mr. Barnum was reading me, reading my face, as he so avidly read an audience before a show, predicting exactly where they would applaud. I looked about, desperate suddenly for a place to hide, but there was nowhere to go.

"That's it," he continued, circling me, peering at me, *trapping* me, even as I tried to squirm and duck. His eyes were gleaming with an interest that was almost scientific. At that moment, I was more intriguing to him than the biggest elephant in the world; once more, I was his newest discovery. "That's what all this is! You're afraid of what you see in the mirror every day, aren't you? Afraid, and ashamed. And so you've hidden behind it, hidden behind your size, even as you've tried to convince yourself no one sees it but you."

I gasped; it was as if all my clothing had just been torn from me and now I stood, naked and defenseless, beneath his perceptive gaze. Oh, how did he know? How did he always see straight to the heart of me?

"And Minnie—she's different than you, no matter how much you try to convince yourself otherwise. She isn't you, because she's happy. And you're not."

"'Happy'?" Finally, I found my tongue, and it felt strong and supple in my mouth, a weapon I could expertly use against him. "What do you know about happiness? You're just as miserable as you think I am, marrying the wrong woman over and over!"

"By God, if you were a man—" He wheeled and strode away

from me, reaching down to grab his walking stick, swinging it like a scythe as he lopped off the heads of dandelions and daffodils, both. "You are the most extraordinary female I've ever—I knew this day would come. We have usually been on the same side of an issue, but I always knew that there would be trouble between us if ever we were not."

"Trouble? Is that all you think this is? My sister is dying and it's my fault and your fault both, and you call it *trouble*? I can never forgive you for this!"

"If that is what you believe, then you are not the person I thought you were!" He turned. We stood like two warriors at the end of a battle; carnage lay at our feet, but it wasn't bodies we had slain. It was our history.

"No, I'm not. I'm not the person *I* thought I was," I said through a clenched jaw. "No, I'm not brave—not like Minnie. But then, neither are you. The only chance you ever take is with your bank account. The only chance I ever take is with a train schedule. Neither one of us has ever been brave enough to take a chance with his heart."

"And back we come, to the crux of the matter. Because Minnie took risks. Minnie fell in love. Minnie didn't need you, after all."

I opened my mouth to deny it but could think of nothing more to say. He was right. But so was I—oh, none of it mattered. Not now, not with Minnie—

Suddenly, I began to shiver; I was aware of a creeping, numbing chill threatening to overcome me, confusing my thoughts. I realized that I hadn't slept in days, that the back of my neck was gray with dirt and sweat, that my stomach was empty. And I ached all over, not just within my heart. A lifetime of looking up, of climbing stairs too steep for me, of using doorknobs and pens and brushes and utensils, even water glasses, that were too large for my hands—it was just this summer, this summer of dread, that it was beginning to take its toll on my once-elastic body. My right hip was cold and stiff in the mornings; my neck had a permanent kink to it, even while I lay down. The knuckles on my hands were beginning to knot up.

For the first time in a very long time, I felt *small.*

"I want you to leave now," I said, recovering some remnant of rational thinking. "Although if you will allow Minnie to continue in the care of Dr. Feinway, I would appreciate it. But as for me, I would prefer not to be under any further obligation to you."

"You don't mean that," Mr. Barnum said, and I could see, across the chasm between us, the flicker of hurt in his eyes even as he bravely set his mouth in that familiar crooked smile.

"I don't? Why is that—because I'm only a dwarf? A '*novelty,*' as you put it?"

His smile turned into a grimace. "Vinnie, I didn't mean that—you're too tired to know what you're saying."

"Then we're agreed on something." I shrugged. "I am tired. And I don't have time for your showmanship anymore, Mr. Barnum. Now, if you'll excuse me, my sister needs me."

"Vinnie, wait—" He took a step in my direction, but I spun around and began to walk toward the house, to my sister. Away from him.

"Vinnie, don't leave like this," he called, and there was sadness in his voice now, the genuine sadness of an old man, for that was what he was. I didn't usually think of him that way, and I wished I hadn't allowed myself to do so now. I did not want to feel sympathy for him.

So I picked up my skirts and began to run; if I could put enough distance between the two of us, I would never be tempted to go back.

My hair came undone from its bun; it streamed down my

back, heavy and tickling as it hadn't done since I was young. Since Minnie and I were girls, running around the barnyard hand in hand, laughing and searching for hidden treasures, for rocks and eggs and anthills, four-leaf clovers, fairy wings.

Objects that only the two of us, so close together, so close to the ground in a way that no one else was, could see. Objects that Minnie had always found beautiful, and that she had persisted in trying to share with me.

But I never could see them, not then, not now.

I was always too busy looking for the man in the moon, instead.

THE TWENTY-THIRD OF JULY STARTED OUT LIKE ANY OTHER SUMMER day; it dawned bright and warm, with the promise of midafternoon heat in the pale morning sun. The house seemed airless by eight a.m.; after bringing Minnie her breakfast, which she could not eat except for a little nibble of dry toast, I went outside, hoping to cool off.

Papa's cow pastures were almost all sold off by now, divided up among my brothers, who had built houses of their own. But one pasture remained untouched, just big enough for the small herd he still kept; I headed out there, careful not to step in cow patties or gopher holes. Up ahead, on top of a little hill, was an enormous, leafy tree that was sure to provide nice, cool shade. I was eager to reach that restful spot; I walked faster, as if in a race against time and sun. I knew I could not linger, for Minnie was due any day now. Yet I so wanted to spend a little time sitting against the trunk, maybe even taking off my shoes and stockings to let my feet play in the tall, cool grass; I hadn't done that since I was a child.

Finally, I reached the shade; pausing to collect my breath, I unbuttoned the top of my bodice so that some of the heat, trapped within the folds of my dress, could escape. Then I took a closer look at the tree; it had been so long since I had tramped outdoors, but this tree looked familiar.

Creeping closer to the trunk, I pushed away some of the tall grass, and there it was, like a long-forgotten friend—my name. My name, and the line marking my height, which was still just an inch or two below where I stood now. I looked up, seeing all the other familiar names—*James, Benjamin, Delia* . . .

But where was Minnie? For the first time, I realized her name had not been etched in the rough, gnarled bark. I couldn't remember why that was—had she even been born then? Was she just too timid to romp about that day? Had I abandoned her, as I sometimes did, impatient that she didn't want to run after the others, annoyed that she was so content to sit in the kitchen with Mama, playing with her dolls? I honestly could not recall. However, it wasn't right that her name was not here with the rest of us; how could I have not noticed it before? Anyone looking at this tree would think she hadn't existed at all—

Like a thunderclap, the panic startled me, overcame me; I had to scratch her name right here, right *now.* I had to record my sister's life on this tree this very instant, capture it somehow. And if I did, surely, like a gypsy's charm, everything would be all right. I looked about, but of course there was no handy knife or tool nearby; I grabbed a stick, but it snapped against the rough bark. Finally, I tried to use my fingernail, scraping until my finger bled, but it was no use. There wasn't even a faint outline of her name; I hadn't made a dent.

Breathing heavily, hot and perspiring even under the shade, I sat down for a moment to think. I could run over to Mama's—their house was closer. I needn't tell her why I required a knife; it would only upset her. I could just take one from the rack in the kitchen, slip back outside and run back here before—

"Vinnie! Vinnie!" There was a figure far down the hill, jumping up and down, waving its arms. Standing, I shaded my eyes from the sun with my hand, and recognized it as Charles. "Come quick—Edward sent me to fetch you. Minnie needs you, Vinnie—do you s'pose it's about the baby?"

There was uncertainty in his voice. Uncertainty as well as fear. My legs began to propel me down the hill before I could fully realize what they were doing; I shot past Charles in a blur. I was much faster than he was, as I ran just as I used to as a girl, forgetting about my corset, my train, my straw hat, which flew off my head at some point. Charles must have retrieved it, for later I found it on my bed, crumpled but not torn.

I also forgot about the tree; I remembered only when Dr. Feinway asked me why my fingernails were torn. By then, all the men were banished from the house, sent across to Mama and Papa's; Edward did not want to leave, but Minnie, between gasping and writhing, insisted.

How do I write of what happened next? I've never been able to speak of it: not to Charles, not to Mama, not to anyone. Yet Minnie's story cannot be told without describing the hell of that day, beginning with the sweltering July heat that soon turned the room into a sauna. It was captured in the sheets, in the curtains, within the folds of my clothing, rivulets flowing into rivers of sweat plastering my undergarments to my skin, turning my cotton dress into a velvet shroud, stifling my pores until I felt as if I were being boiled in a covered pot.

When the pains started, Minnie was so hot that she kept tugging at her nightgown, complaining that it was too heavy; by the end, she had lost so much blood that she was shivering uncontrollably, her skin icy to the touch.

The blood! Oh, so much blood, such a defiant crimson, soaking the sheets, sticking to her legs, covering Dr. Feinway's arms, stringing, like ropy spiderwebs, between his fine, tapered fingers. The child simply could not emerge, although nature tried to take over, tearing my sister, wracking her with pain. Her piteous cries pierced the air, pierced my ears so that they still ring with them, all these years later. She started out whimpering, smiling apologetically between the pains; as they came closer and closer, more furious, unrelenting, she stopped apologizing. Her pupils dilated like a wounded animal's as she waited for the next, and then the next, and then the next. Soon her entire body was being wrung with the force of the infant desperate to be born; her limbs flailed, her back arched off the mattress, as the doctor tensely held her legs down. Even as she was in the primitive throes of her torture, he was still able to overpower my diminutive sister. Minnie was helpless against everything, everyone, in that room—except me.

"Can't you give her some ether?" I pleaded with Dr. Feinway, as her eyes glazed over and she bit her lip so hard that now there was blood there, as well.

"Not yet, not while there's still a chance she can expel the child," he barked. He had lost his kind, professional demeanor and was now in his shirtsleeves, spattered with blood, looking more like a butcher than a doctor. He grunted and groaned nearly as much as Minnie, and ran to the window to spit outside and curse his frustration before returning to the bed and the nurse he had brought with him. She was a woman so methodical, so practiced, as to be an automaton. She did not react to Minnie's cries; she did not blanch at all the blood. She merely stood, silent and efficient, waiting to do whatever Dr. Feinway needed.

I hovered near the top of the bed, near the only part of her that was not being torn apart. I mopped her brow but could not do it easily; she had been moved to a guest room, placed upon a regular-size bed so that the doctor could better attend to her. I had to use my wooden steps, standing awkwardly, but by the end I simply crawled into bed with her, holding her to me as she begged me, in the most heartbreaking whisper, to "Rock me, Sister, rock me." And I tried to do just that; I maneuvered my body around hers as best I could, and cradled her shoulders in my arms.

"Little drops of water, little grains of sand," I began, unable to recall any song but the ones I used to teach in school. All the popular songs I had sung onstage to Kings and Queens escaped my mind at that moment; only the simplest ones, the ones I had taught to children, remained.

But it didn't matter; no angelic smile, no whisper of relief, greeted my singing. I don't think she heard me, and I wondered, later, if she asked only because she knew I needed to do something at that moment.

I remained there, half sitting, half reclining, rocking my sister for the longest time, crooning softly into her tangled mat of hair for hours, it seemed. I was still rocking, still crooning, my voice hoarse and dry, when I felt a hand upon my shoulder. Looking up, it took me a long moment to recognize Dr. Feinway; I was almost surprised to see him there, so fiercely had I tried to block out everything but the blessed weight of my sister in my arms.

But now that weight was motionless, cold. Minnie was no longer moaning or thrashing. Her eyes were shut, her long lashes coal-black against the marble white of her cheeks.

"Vinnie, she's gone," Dr. Feinway said gently but urgently. "The child still might have a chance, but we have to cut it from her. You need to leave now."

"Leave?" I looked at Minnie, lying limply against my arms, peaceful for the first time in such a long while. "Rock me, Sister," she had whispered, and I had. I had rocked her, finally, to sleep.

"Leave," the doctor said, lifting me roughly off the bed so that

I had to release my sister. She fell back, like a marionette whose strings had been cut, against the pillow that was soiled and drenched from her sweat, her blood.

I allowed Dr. Feinway to push me out of the room—until I caught a glimpse of the instruments the impassive nurse was laying out upon a table; there was a knife, with gleaming, sawlike teeth.

"No!" I wailed, wanting to run back in and warn Minnie. But Minnie wasn't there anymore, and Dr. Feinway shut the door in my face; the handle turned until it locked. Then I heard a soft moan behind me. Spinning around, I saw Mama, who had been sitting sentry in the hall the whole time, slide off her chair and onto the floor, where I dropped to my knees just in time to catch her. Not a muscle moved on her kind, careworn face as she uttered only one cry, but it had all the love and worry of a lifetime in it.

"My baby," she moaned, burying her face in my chest—only those two words, but there was no need for more. Then she started to weep, softly, as she clung to me. And I held my mother; I rocked her, too; I sang softly, scraps of songs that Minnie loved. Songs that I knew I would never sing again.

I had no sense of how much time passed, but when Dr. Feinway opened the door and said, "We could not save her daughter," the windows were dark and someone had turned on the gaslights in the hall. I was surprised to see a tear roll down his patrician face; I had imagined him to be above emotion. That my sister had touched him so, in the short time he had known her, moved me beyond words.

"Do you want to see the child?" he asked.

"No! I don't want to see that—that *thing* that killed my sister! Take it away! Take it away from here—"

"Vinnie, please." Mama clutched at my sleeve with trembling hands, her face irrevocably old; I knew that from this moment on, she would look forward only to death, not life. "Please, for me, because I'm not strong enough. But you are."

I hadn't the heart to tell my mother she was wrong. So I gently nudged her off my lap, and rose on unsteady legs, and followed Dr. Feinway into the darkened room, still stuffy, but now a chill wind was blowing in from the window; the heat had broken and the air was cool, fresh, like spring. The nurse was methodically folding bloodstained linens and stuffing them in a wicker basket, the crimson faded to rust; despite the wind, the metallic smell of blood was everywhere. I thought, oddly, that I must replace the carpet and wallpaper in here; the smell would never come out otherwise.

The only light in the room was from two oil lamps on either side of the bed upon which Minnie was lying, her eyes closed, her skin already turning waxen.

"I've never known such courage," Dr. Feinway said softly.

Someone had brushed her curls so that they were no longer tangled and damp; miraculously, they looked like they used to, silky black, no longer that dull, coarse texture of these last months. She almost appeared as if she were sleeping, and perhaps she would to someone who did not know her. But I—who had slept with her so many nights, held her close, watched her dream—knew she was not. I knew it because her red rosebud lips, usually slightly parted, the tip of her pink tongue between them, were blue. Her chest, which always rose and fell so trustingly, was still. Everything about her was so still, so empty; there was no life in this room.

And in her arms was a doll, just as there had been so many times. But it wasn't a doll; it was her child, her daughter—"Pauline," I said, christening her. She was cleaned up, bathed by the nurse, I presumed, but there were bruises and cuts about her pale, lifeless face; no rosy cheeks and lips, only scrunched-up eyes that had never opened, making her look angry, frustrated. But she had black hair, just like Minnie's.

My little wooden steps—now so worn, so distressed, from being bumped, dragged, and dropped across continents and oceans—were still by her bed. I could have climbed them, had I wished, to touch her, kiss her once more. But I did not. I felt almost in awe. This was not my sister; this was a holy shrine, an icon apart from the horror and pain of the earthly world, the deception, the dishonesty—the sin.

And I wondered, in that moment, if the enormity of my guilt was in inverse proportion to my size. Had I been bigger, would my sins on this earth be less significant—just like my hopes and dreams?

"I imagine so," I whispered, although Minnie could not hear. "I dreamed too big, dearest, for you and me. And you were the one who had to pay. Forgive me, oh, forgive me!"

And then I backed out of the room, unable to look away until I closed the door softly, as if afraid to wake her up. Leaving Mama sobbing quietly in her chair, I ran down the stairs, out the door, and toward the old homestead, pausing in the middle of the road to catch my breath, surprised to feel the night air sweet and refreshing upon my aching brow. Then I gathered up my skirts, as well as my courage, and continued across the road.

I knew I would find Papa in the barn; he didn't turn around as I came in. He simply continued to work, planing a soft pine log, sanding it to the smoothest surface; smooth enough for a cradle, smooth enough for a coffin.

Tears rolled down his craggy face as he began, for the last time, to craft something beautiful, something practical, something that would ease life's journey, for one of his two little girls.

INTERMISSION

A Song and Chorus dedicated to the worldwide friends and admirers of Minnie Warren, entitled "Rock Me Sister," composed by Horatio C. King (published 1878 for voice and piano)

Summer echoes gently stealing Oe'r the meadow, through the grove,
Bore the sighs of loved ones kneeling, By the death bed of their love,
There with face of pearly whiteness, Failing pulse and fainting breath,
With a gaze of heavenly brightness, Minnie Warren smiled on death
(Chorus)
"I am going, rock me, sister," so the little mother sigh'd,
Then as tearfully they kissed her, Fairy Minnie smiled and died.
Set the chimes of elf land ringing, Let each tiny fairy bell,
On the air sweet music flinging,
Whisper gentle Minnie's knell.

From *The Popular Science Monthly,* April 1878

ON EDISON'S TALKING-MACHINE, BY ALFRED M. MAYER

Mr. Thomas A. Edison has recently invented an instrument which is undoubtedly the acoustic marvel of the century. It is called the "Speaking Phonograph," or, adopting the Indian idiom, one may call it "The Sound-Writer who talks."

[SIXTEEN]

The Curtain Falls, Between Acts

At first, I did not know how I could go on without her.

When Minnie died, part of me died with her. For I had lost not only the sister whom I loved more than anyone else in the world; I also lost the one person in my life who had ever looked up to me. She and I had shared things that no one else could imagine; for so much of our lives, we had shared a chair at table, shared a bed, shared a train seat, shared clothing, even. How often had Mama cut up one of her old dresses and made it over into two smaller ones, just for Minnie and me? There was so much in this world that was too big for one of us alone, but that, together, we could just about fill. Except for hearts, that is; Minnie, alone, was big enough to fill up the hearts of everyone she met. And now my own heart was so empty I decided to put it away for good. There was only one other person who might have had some use for it, but I was no longer speaking to him.

Eventually, however, I did go on, in a fashion, without my sister. For the alternative was to stay home, alone, with my husband.

Edward moved away to New York, although I did not urge him to. Witnessing his grief upon seeing his wife and child lying together in their tiny coffin thoroughly changed my attitude toward him. Perhaps I could not have taken care of Minnie's child, but I found myself softening toward her husband, allowing that he had truly loved her in a way no sister ever could. I was as in awe of his love as I had been of Minnie's.

I was also envious, just as Mr. Barnum had so infuriatingly observed. For now that it was just the two of us, I could not help but look at my own husband through skeptical, disappointed eyes.

Oh, Charles was kindness itself, tiptoeing around me as I fiercely gathered the black veils of that first grief and wrapped myself within them. I would not allow anyone to tell me that I must carry on, that I must be strong, that I must remember that Minnie and her daughter would be waiting for me in Heaven. "I don't care!" I shouted in response. "I want her here! Now!"

Charles did not say such things to me, but it was only because they were not in his repertoire. He had not been taught by Mr. Barnum how to behave with a grieving wife. So he did not recite platitudes and proverbs, and at first I was grateful for that. He was the one person who spoke honestly and plainly about his feelings; possessing none of the stoicism that ran through the male line of my family, he wept along with me. Many nights he crept into my room, climbed into my bed, and slipped his hand in mine as he cried softly into my pillow; I cried into his shoulder. I thought, then, that perhaps we had at last achieved the emotional intimacy of a married couple; perhaps I even allowed myself to wonder if we could achieve physical intimacy, as well.

But my sister's death—the blood, the suffering—was too fresh, too horrible, for me to reach out to my husband in that way. And Charles, ever the devoted pupil, trained first by Mr. Barnum and then by me, had long stopped reaching out to me. My husband fell asleep on my pillow but not in my arms.

Soon, however, I began to be irritated by his tears; it was almost as if he was imitating my grief, although not in a malicious way. I finally acknowledged that my husband had no personality of his own; he was merely an imprint of everyone around him. As soon as I stopped crying, he did; the only time I ever saw him read a book was when I had one in my hands; the only time he went for a stroll was when I proposed one. He went to bed at the same time that I did every night; his favorite foods were mine. The only things he did that I did not were smoke cigars and drink an occasional glass of brandy—the two vices Mr. Barnum enjoyed.

He was so very good at imitation, at mimicry, that I suspected he did have a quick mind. But by now—he was forty—it was rusted over, for the most part unused.

He was also very portly. New clothes were required constantly, and he came to me one day with a tailor's bill in his hand and a worried shadow crossing his usually cloudless eyes.

"Vinnie, dear, do you remember that necklace of yours, the one with the sapphires and diamonds that you hardly ever wear?"

"Yes." I was kneeling next to a trunk, folding some of Minnie's dresses away into it. I hugged one particularly dear white frock to me, remembering how sweet she had looked in it, just like a painting I had seen in France of a little girl carrying flowers in her apron.

"Where is it?"

"The necklace? With the rest of my jewels, in the safe, of

course. Why?" I turned my best schoolteacher's gaze upon my husband; he reddened and hung his head, just like a naughty student.

"I suppose you wouldn't mind selling some of them? It seems that we're a little out of money, at least this month."

"'A *little* out of money'?" I rose, shaking out my skirts. "Be more specific, please."

"Well, the yacht, you know . . . and then the interest on the cottage's mortgage increased, and some of my buildings in Bridgeport are no longer quite as desirable as they once were, and of course I do need some new clothes, you yourself said so the other day."

"You wouldn't need new clothes if you pushed yourself away from the table now and then," I scolded. "I wouldn't mind selling some of my jewels, I suppose—I have so many. But, Charles, you can't let this happen again."

"I know, I won't!" He smiled, so grateful to be let off the hook; he ran back down the hallway to his study, and I went back to my packing. Two weeks later, when the clothes arrived, he showed off the two new top hats he couldn't help himself from adding to the order, and made me a present of a silver fox muff, "to take the place of the jewels!"

Mollified, I did not inquire further into our finances. But I did suggest we consider touring again, not only to bring in more money but because I simply could not bear to be in this house, so empty without Minnie and Edward. I couldn't bear to remain in Middleborough, with all the memories. And I could not bear to be alone with him any longer.

To get back out on the road, with Mr. and Mrs. Bleeker in their old familiar roles, with trains to catch and performances to make, new people to meet, distance to cover every single day—I almost wept at the thought of it! Then I gathered up my train schedules and hotel listings and repaired to my room.

"What about Phineas?" Charles asked me one evening, as I pored over my maps. How easy it was, these days, to plan a tour! So many train routes were now connected, and there were books that listed hotels by city—imagine! I could telegram reservations ahead of time, not take my chance on a letter getting lost or delayed. There were even rumors and rumblings about a new "standardized time" that would organize the country by geographical region; no longer would each individual village or town set its own clock by the sun. How much easier it would be, then, to arrange train schedules!

"What about Mr. Barnum?" I asked, bewildered. I licked the tip of my pencil and raised my arm, hovering over the map before me, ready to draw out a route. "He's no longer our partner—heavens, Charles, don't you remember? He resigned his partnership ages ago, after the world tour."

"I know. I just thought that he could come for a visit and help us plan things. You know how much he enjoys that."

"I'm quite capable of planning it myself. He's very busy with his circus, you know, and that new Madison Square Garden, where he puts on those ridiculous shows. He has no time to visit."

"But he does! He says so in his latest letter!" And Charles's face lit up as he produced this letter; he had obviously been carrying it around in his pocket for all of five minutes. The paper was hardly creased.

"I don't need to read it," I murmured, looking down at my map, wondering if it was up to date. So many new states had joined the Union lately! So many new cities were still sprouting up, cities that had never before greeted General and Mrs. Tom Thumb.

"Vinnie, but he says to tell you, especially, that he could do with a good chat in front of the fire, just like old times."

"How nice for him."

"He said you'd say that! He wrote it, see here? He calls you Mrs. Stratton—why is that, Vinnie? He never did before! But he writes, 'And if Mrs. Stratton says something along the lines of "how interesting" or "how pleasant," tell her that her old *friend*'—and he underlined that, Vinnie; why, do you think?—'says, "Hogwash," and that she needs to forgive some people, starting with herself.'" Charles looked up from his letter, flush with the success of his reading. "What does he mean by all that, Vinnie?"

"It's nonsense. He doesn't know what he means," I replied, trying to keep my voice even and pleasant, returning to my maps as if I wasn't seething on the inside. Seething and longing, both—how dare he put Charles in the middle of our quarrel! Yet my fingers also itched to tear the letter away from Charles, pick up my pen, and answer it immediately, restoring our friendship, speaking my mind. Perhaps even locating my heart, if I could recall where I had placed it—probably in the trunk with all of Minnie's things.

Minnie. Oh, how could I even think of going back to him, to the way things were before? Minnie might still be here if it wasn't for him, and I knew that were I to be alone with him for just two minutes, he would make me forget that. He would sell me a new memory, for that was what he did. With P. T. Barnum, memories and dreams were available for only a quarter—unless you were smart enough to find your way to the Egress.

I must not have succeeded in hiding my turmoil, for Charles dropped the letter, wringing his hands in worry. "Oh, why are you two quarreling? I don't understand! No one tells me anything, not you, not him! I miss him, Vinnie. Let's go up to Bridgeport tonight and surprise him!"

"You can if you wish, dear." Frowning, I drew a big circle around Middleborough; then I began to trace the rail lines leading away from it. "I'm busy."

"You know I can't go without you," Charles said, pouting. "I don't *want* to go without you!"

I sighed, dropping my pencil upon my desk; I would get nothing done as long as he was standing here. "Do you want me to read to you, then? You're getting agitated. See what Mr. Barnum does to you? That man!"

"Oh, would you read to me?" And just as quickly as a summer storm moving across the countryside, my husband forgot about any quarrel. Together, we walked to one of the small library tables in the study, where he happily echoed the titles that I suggested to him—*Black Beauty, The Water Babies, Through the Looking Glass.* In the end, we settled on *The Adventures of Tom Sawyer,* recently published.

It was such a charming book. It reminded me so much of my days upon the river, when I could wake up every day to a new town. And I was quite fond of the character of Tom, who was such a smooth talker, able to get all the children to whitewash the fence for him—even eavesdropping at his own funeral! I felt I knew him intimately, even if he was just a character in a novel.

More jewels were sold, along with the yacht and the cabin, as we told friends that we simply didn't have the time to put them to good use. Yet when we were in New York, we stayed at the finest hotels and dined with our dear friends the Astors, the Vanderbilts, and the Fisks, although sometimes it took them several days to realize we were in town. The newspapers did not always trumpet our appearances as they once did, so often I had to drop a note informing them of our presence.

The younger generation, the children of dear Caroline and dear Julia and dear Mittie, were no longer the admiring little boys and girls who shyly hid from their parents so that they might steal a peek at us. They were now young men and ladies swept up in a new frenzy of balls and parties and dinners, all part of what Mr. Twain had named the Gilded Age. Charles and I were not part of this crowd; rather, I sensed these young people viewed us as relics, odd pets of their parents, leftovers from a simpler, less smart time.

Once I overheard Mrs. Astor's youngest daughter, also called Caroline, whisper to her dinner partner about how "amusing it was when I was a child, when Mother used to dress little Mrs. Stratton up like a miniature Mrs. Astor. She even had her hairdresser give her the same hairstyle! Imagine—how we all laughed!"

I did not let on that I had heard; instead, I smiled brightly at my dining companions and told the story of how Queen Victoria had invited us to tea at Windsor and given us a beautiful grand piano, which we still displayed in our library.

But I remembered that remark; I remembered also that Mr. Belmont had once presented Charles with a nautical jacket and cap identical to his own. Charles had been so pleased, so proud; he had worn it every time the Belmonts invited us onto their yacht.

Finally, I remembered that Mr. Barnum had not liked that jacket; nor had he ever accepted any of our invitations to go sailing with the Belmonts.

I did not drop a note to dear Caroline the next time we came to town.

Naturally, we could not avoid Mr. Barnum altogether. We encountered him at occasional dinner parties, where he and Charles always greeted each other so fondly, I did feel guilty for keeping them apart. I sometimes caught Mr. Barnum looking wistfully at me from across the table, leaning forward, as if he could scarcely contain some thought or idea and was eager to share it. And it wasn't only my grief and loyalty to Minnie that kept me from returning his gaze. I had bared my soul, shared my dark secret and even darker emotions with him—and now I was afraid of who I would see reflected back to me in those glittery, knowing eyes.

And so he would subside, hunching over his cigar. I would stir uncomfortably, and suggest to Charles, far too soon, that we think about going home.

Only when we took our leave would I allow myself to look at him; his shoulders were more stooped with every passing year, and at times I noticed his hands trembled when he lit his cigar. But his mind was as sharp as ever. He was filled with plans for this circus of his, talking boisterously of combining it with others, making it "the greatest show on earth," he told all who would listen, and in fact I was not surprised the day I saw it advertised so in the newspaper.

I was surprised, however, to receive an invitation to join it in 1881. Our finances were at their lowest point; we were discussing letting out the house and moving in with James and his wife. I couldn't exactly say what had happened; we toured, but our audiences were smaller than they once were. We were popular but no longer made headlines. Charles invested but saw little return. Yet we had to keep spending—new wardrobes as the fashions changed, new ponies as the old ones died. Without Mr. Barnum investing in our tours, we had to front the money ourselves, which wasn't always easy.

So it was in desperation that I tore open the letter, the envelope embossed with the seal of "The Barnum and London Circus Company." And I nearly fainted with relief at the amount he was proposing to give us for a season's work; it would more than cover the stack of second notices piling up, alarmingly, on Charles's desk. I telegrammed our acceptance right away; then I dashed off a letter to Mr. and Mrs. Bleeker, asking if they could accompany us.

Then, and only then, did I remember to discuss it with my husband.

INTERMISSION

From *The New York Times,* November 5, 1880

Mrs. Astor Entertains Gen. Grant

Mrs. John Jacob Astor entertained Gen. Grant last evening at her residence, No. 388 Fifth avenue. A dinner was given, and the company, consisting of both ladies and gentlemen, was very select. The occasion was purely a social one. Gen. Grant remained until about 11 o'clock. He was in the best of spirits, and, while making no speech, engaged freely in conversation with those who approached him.

From *The Manufacturer and Builder,* May 1881

Electric Illumination

It is daily becoming more and more evident that the near future will decide the question of the practicability of illumination with electricity in competition with coal gas. Never was there such widespread public opinion manifested in the subject as at the present time. . . . The indefatigable Edison has announced that he has at length solved all the practical difficulties that had hitherto threatened the success of his electric lamps for the household, and has taken the field in person to superintend the work of introducing his system.

[SEVENTEEN]

Ladies and Gentlemen, in the Center Ring . . .

After the second American Museum burned down in 1868, Mr. Barnum effectively retired from the show business, aside from his partnership in our around-the-world tour and the occasional discovery, such as Admiral Dot. He claimed he chose to concentrate on traveling, politics, and philanthropy. But in 1871 he bought a small circus; then he bought another—and then another. And soon the whole thing had exploded into what he called "P. T. Barnum's Grand Traveling Museum, Menagerie, Caravan & Hippodrome." Now, instead of having the public come to him, Mr. Barnum was back to his roots, when he had first traveled the New England countryside with Joice Heth forty years ago. He was bringing the world of P. T. Barnum to the public.

But true to form, he reinvented what was an already established tradition. He was the first to move his circus by railroad, on his own train—an endless stream of cars all emblazoned on the side with his name, just like the old American Museum. While other circuses had to rely upon unpaved roads and unpredictable ferry crossings, Mr. Barnum's circus chugged steadily along all the new streamlined tracks that linked the country together. In the winter, he parked the show in Bridgeport; in the spring, he launched the new season in New York, in the giant Hippodrome at the Madison Square Garden, which seated thousands.

In 1881, when we joined his circus, he had partnered with so many other circus owners, consolidating everything into one grand show, that I had difficulty keeping them all straight—there was a Mr. Bailey, a Mr. Hutchinson, a Mr. Sanger; the show now was called the Barnum and London Circus. We arrived at the cavernous, roofless Madison Square Garden—formerly a train station until the new Grand Central Station was built, when it became an outdoor arena for spectacles—in the spring. The colossal tents were going up, over the three immense rings of the circus; the place was a madhouse of sawdust and people upon wires and animals forever being exercised and trained. Awed, and not a little intimidated, by the enormity of the operation, Charles and I were overjoyed to see Mr. and Mrs. Bleeker once more; their friendship and familiarity were more welcome than the practical assistance they would provide in helping us navigate the usual difficulties of travel—getting on and off trains, managing luggage, reaching hotel beds, opening windows, etc.

However, from the moment we boarded the vast circus train, after the last performance in New York, I thought we had made a mistake. While our accommodations were, by far, superior to everyone else's, they were far from luxurious. Charles and I did not have a private car, only half a car, to ourselves. An entire circus company is gargantuan; I was reminded of that canvas city of soldiers we had visited just after our marriage. There were stagehands and construction workers and animal handlers; publicity men, ticket takers, popcorn sellers; wardrobe girls, prop men, barkers; an army of men responsible for raising and lowering the tents and packing them up; cooks, laundresses, boys whose jobs were just to take care of the animal waste; wagon drivers. And that's not even counting the performers! Trapeze artists, specialty riding acts, jugglers, dancers, a woman who gyrated upon a pyramid of chairs, gymnasts, wrestlers, high-wire acts, Japanese acrobats who balanced upon their fingertips—not to mention all the animals!

Even though I had grown up on a farm, the overwhelming odor of all those captive creatures made my nostrils close up and my eyes water; I couldn't bear to walk past the animal cars after a long night's trip. Mr. Barnum had to have special cars built for the giraffes, elephants, lions, and tigers; all the rest, the zebras, peacocks, goats, sheep, all the many horses and ponies—some of the most magnificent trained creatures mixed up with dull draft horses that pulled the wagons—managed with regular animal cars. The dogs used in specialty acts traveled with their owners.

Similar acts traveled together. Those in the center ring were closest to the front of the train (the first cars were reserved for the advance men—publicity people, managers in charge of erecting everything); then the other rings were parceled out in cars farther and farther down, with the sideshow acts coming after all the other performers. They were then followed by the band members, then the workers, like the roustabouts and seamstresses and cooks, and then finally the animals and their handlers.

Charles and I, and the Bleekers, were given the best car, right behind the advance men. We had to share it with two European bareback riders, ladies both; they spoke no English, so we communicated with smiles and grunts. I could not complain about our accommodations on the train; we had seats that turned into bunks, and our own washroom, and the walls were freshly painted, the gaslights gleaming. We could retreat there and be somewhat private, apart.

Why did I not enjoy this life? I was on a train again, traveling once more through the night so that I awoke every morning in a new town. Compared to the primitive conditions under which we crossed the continent thirteen years earlier, we were traveling in the most modern manner. No Indians to worry about; no hair-raising wagon rides on treacherous mountain roads; no journeys across a scorching desert, fearful that we might sink into the sand. Not once did we ever have to get out and travel on foot.

But when we were introduced as *"General and Mrs. Tom Thumb, those beloved Lilliputians!"* we were not alone; this was not our show. In the circus parade that began every new engagement (we would hurry off the train each morning at dawn, drive in wagons to the site where the tents were being pitched, then dress in costume and assemble for the parade through town), our miniature carriage, while given a prime spot, was just one in a never-ending line of colorful wagons and rolling calliopes. And at the beginning of each performance, while we were featured in the center ring, we were merely the first of a very long procession of other entertainers who marched around, waving at the audience. We had to be exceedingly careful not to step in animal droppings.

Then we were ushered out of the big top, to a noisy line of tents and booths that made up the sideshows: the acts that were too intimate to be viewed in the vast expanse of the rings. These included many of the kinds of acts I had first encountered on the river—sword swallowers, tattooed ladies, specialty dancers. While our tent was very tastefully decorated, and we performed the kind of dignified entertainment we had given for Presidents, Kings, and Queens, there was no ignoring the somewhat low quality of our surroundings. Just outside, the barkers were always shouting out a patter, the cheap music—usually just a banjo or a trumpet—from the other tents nearby produced a cacophony, and the puppet shows across the way were always eliciting shouts of childish laughter.

Upon our temporary stage, in a tent full of townspeople whose excited eyes, reflecting all the color and sights still to be sampled, could scarcely be induced to linger long upon him, Charles stood, top hat and cane in hand, and began to sing, as he had for years—

"I should like to marry, if only I could find
Any pretty lady, suited to my mind,
I should like her handsome, I should like her good,
With a little money—yes, indeed I should.
Oh! Then I would marry, if I could but find
Any pretty lady, suited to my mind."

I then twirled out to meet him in my beautiful gown, my last few jewels blazing under the oil lamps and torches, which was all the illumination possible in these tents. I curtsied, he bowed, and we began to dance about the rickety stage as our pianist segued into the "Tom Thumb Polka."

But no Kings and Queens smiled and asked us to tea; no natives gaped in awe at the sight of us, so elegantly clad. The audience murmured a bit, clapped politely, and soon hurried on to one of the other attractions. It was an endless, rolling sensation, watching them move in and out of our tent, eagerly but dutifully. There was so much for them to see. They didn't want to waste any time.

One day I left our tent, looking for Charles. He had taken to disappearing between performances, but I knew where he went—the Punch and Judy show, about five tents down from ours. My husband never tired of watching the antics; he laughed heartily whenever the crooked-nosed Punch, in his red jester's cap, hit one of his foes with a stick and a cry of "That's the way to do it!" Charles was also attracted by the children; he watched them wistfully as they held tightly to their parents with one hand, sticks of rock candy in the other.

"Vinnie? Vinnie Bump?" a voice called out behind me. "I thought it was you! See, I told you I knew *her*!"

Turning around, I saw a stout woman standing before me, her hands upon her hips. Next to her were two small women, about my height. But they were not like me—not at all. I glanced uneasily at them, then looked up at the woman who had spoken.

"Excuse me? Are we acquainted?"

"'Are we acquainted?'" the woman mimicked me, then gave a low, admiring whistle. "You haven't changed one bit, except for all the fine clothes! Don't you remember me?"

"I'm sorry . . ." I began to apologize, automatically; I'd met so many people in all my travels. This happened quite often; someone who had shaken my hand on one tour would appear on the next, asking if I remembered him. Usually, I nodded and said I had, and that sufficed. But I did not think it would with this woman, who stood there, smiling so strangely down at me, her bright yellow hair so badly dyed that a line of gray arched above her forehead, like a sad crown.

"Carlotta?" The words flew out of my mouth before my brain had finished identifying her. "Is it you?"

"It sure is! Oh, Vinnie, Vinnie, it's so good to see you!" And she dropped to her knees, holding out her arms; with a smile, I walked into them. I hugged her tightly; it *was* good to see her!

"I can't believe it's you! Did you ever marry your young man on the river?" I stepped back so that I could get a better look; her hair, of course, was the same, a riot of yellow piled atop her head in blowsy curls, but her face was no longer so desperately made up. In fact, she wore no paint at all; with her soft, malleable features, a few missing teeth, and wobbly chin, she looked like any country woman. She was wearing a plain beige dress, homespun but not patched; it was clean and pressed.

"Oh, no. No, he was killed at Chickamauga." Her pale blue eyes blinked, but there were no tears.

"Oh, I'm so sorry!"

"That's all right, it was a long time ago. Lawd, I ain't the only woman who lost her man in the War. So I'm still in the business, same as you!"

"You are?"

"I'm traveling with the company as a seamstress. I always was good with a needle! It's been a spell since I could kick the way I used to—oh, remember, Vinnie? How high I could kick! But I still can't stay in one place, I guess. Same as you!"

"Well, yes, I suppose—did you know I'm married now?"

"Married? For God's sake, do you think I live under a rock? Of course I know all about you and your little General! I been reading about you in the newspapers for years! Look at you, little Vinnie, all dressed up, a married woman! And all them places you've seen! Oh, I'm sorry about your little angel, though. And your sister."

"Thank you." My voice wobbled a little; how ironic that Carlotta, of all people, was offering her condolences for my "child" and my sister. After all, she was the one who had spoken so plainly to me about the dangers of relations with men; I remembered those awful gray "prevention powders" she tried to give me. How long ago it was now!

"Curious, isn't it?" Carlotta mused, pulling me back into the present. She still remained on her knees before me; those eerie women hung back behind her, eyeing me suspiciously. The eager, pushing circus crowd bustled about in both directions, undeterred—ignoring the four of us as if we were ghosts.

"What is?"

"We all thought you were going to be famous, Vinnie, and you are! Do you ever talk to any of the old company?"

"No, not really—I write to Sylvia; she's in Maine. She gives spiritual readings, and seems quite happy. But that's all."

"Me either. Billy's still performing around with his minstrels; I hear of them now and again. Colonel Wood, remember him? What a mean man! I always worried about you and him, Vinnie. I never liked the way he looked at you."

"Yes, well, he was an awful man." And still haunting me, in so many ways, I didn't add. "I need to fetch my husband, Carlotta, as we have a performance. You should come by our car one night, and I'll introduce you to him."

"That's mighty nice of you, Vinnie! I will!" Carlotta—I had such a difficult time reconciling the name with this matronly, staid-looking woman—rose to her knees with some difficulty. "But before you go, I wanted to introduce you to these two. They didn't believe me when I said I knew you, but see?" She turned to them, a triumphant smile creasing her leathery face. "I do! I told you!"

"Oh." I stared at the two women, uncertain how to react to them. For I had seen them before—and done my best to avoid them.

They were part of a troupe of other small people that performed with the clowns. Almost from the first day we joined the circus, I had seen them hanging about wherever we went, trailing Charles and me like shadows, whispering and pointing. But they weren't like us. They had large heads on small, barrel-chested bodies, oddly proportioned arms and legs. They truly looked like the pictures of dwarves in fairy tales—like Rumpelstiltskin, like jesters. They were tossed around by the larger clowns, mute and wild-eyed. They looked simple, in their heads.

They made me uneasy; they made me ashamed, for how the audience howled with laughter whenever they jumped up and down, flapping their grotesque arms, rolling their bulging eyes! I did not wish to make their acquaintance.

"This one here is Miss Humphries, and the other one is Miss Mary," Carlotta told me, nudging them. They each curtsied, still staring at me with round eyes, taking in my silk dress, tightly drawn up over a bustle, in the latest fashion. Both were clad in rough homespun shifts that dropped straight to the ground. Then Miss Humphries extended her hand.

It was odd, ugly, disfigured, with short stumps for fingers and a very fleshy palm. I placed my own delicate, perfectly formed hand—my nails buffed a pretty pink—in hers.

"How—how very nice to make your acquaintance," I said with a smile that I hoped hid my shudder.

"Yes, Ma'am," Miss Humphries said, and stepped back behind Carlotta.

"Have you been with the circus long?"

"All my life, me and my sister both," she said.

"Oh, you're sisters?" They did look alike, upon closer examination. "How nice. I have—I used to travel with my sister, too."

"We know," the younger one piped up. "We've read all about you."

"Oh? Well, isn't that nice! You've *read* about me, you say? Isn't that wonderful!"

"Yes." The older one scowled at me. "We can *read*."

"Of course, of course, I didn't mean—well, naturally!"

"I thought you all might get along." Carlotta beamed down at us, lumping me with those two—two—oddities, to my horror. Did she not see how wrong she was? Did she not see that I was nothing like these two?

And nothing like the others, the other grotesque, misshapen little people who found themselves all under the same sweeping circus tent. I had done my best to ignore their existence. Dressed up like pygmies, some were used in the flame thrower's act; others were dressed up like ugly babies and rolled around in rickety prams as part of another clown routine. They all traveled together in a car far, far down the line from ours. There was no need for me to ever utter one word to any of them, and I hadn't. Until now.

"I really need to find Mr. Stratton," I repeated to Carlotta, desperately; the challenging, slightly resentful yet also envious way the two lumpen girls kept staring at me filled me with unease. "I'm sorry to be rude—"

"Of course, now, you go on and fetch your little husband. But isn't it interesting, Vinnie?"

"What is?"

"Just that—you and I ended up in the same place, after all this time! It just beats all, don't it?" She chuckled, shaking her head, gesturing to the other two. "Here we are, all together, in Mr. P.T. Barnum's circus!"

"Yes, isn't that interesting? Good day, ladies." Pressing my lips tightly together, I turned and hurried off—doing my best not to run, so very much did I want to get away. I pushed along the crowded passageway, hemmed in on all sides by booths and tents and dancers and giants and men in black vests and red-and-white striped pants yelling out, "Come see the *bearded* lady, freshly shaved just yesterday but *already* with a beard *two feet long*!"

And other men in black vests and red-and-white striped pants countered back with "Come see the world-famous General and Mrs. Tom Thumb, those *diminutive darlings* of royalty, those *wee world travelers*—*intimate* friends of *Mr. P. T. Barnum himself*!"

"We really are!" I wanted to cry out to the crowd, some of whom were pointing to me and smiling—laughing, even—others of whom were simply ignoring me, having already seen their share of oddities—Isaac the Living Skeleton, George the Armless Wonder. I'm sure there was a two-headed kitten around somewhere as well. "We really are world-famous! We really do know Queen Victoria! Mrs. Astor came to our wedding! We're not like the rest of these—"

But I didn't know what to call them. Because I didn't know what to call myself. Dwarf? Tiny? Perfect woman in miniature? None of them, all of them; had I ever been simply Lavinia Warren Stratton? To anyone—even myself?

Oh, good heavens—I was late! We were going to be late—and where was Charles? I pushed my way through the crowds until I spied him. Clad in his top hat and frock coat, Charles was nevertheless upon his knees in front of the Punch and Judy show, playing marbles with a pack of dirty children. I hauled him up by his arm and dragged him back to our tent, brushing the dust off his clothing and scolding him. Five minutes later, we were back onstage; he was singing, I was twirling, we were dancing in front of the restless crowd as the pianist played the "Tom Thumb Polka."

Once, I remembered, closing my eyes as if I could wish myself back in time, this very tune had been played in our honor at Royal Albert Hall. We were the guests of the Prince and Princess of Wales. We rode in the Royal carriage, accompanied by a regiment of palace guards, the Princess of Wales and Minnie both too shy to wave to the crowds.

It really had happened, I whispered to myself fiercely. *It wasn't just a dream.*

"What isn't just a dream, Vinnie?" Charles whispered back. I shook my head and allowed him to lift me up by my waist in time to the music. Someone in the audience clapped; someone else tittered.

When the season was over in November, I wrote a short letter to Mr. Barnum informing him that we would not be returning in the spring.

For once, he did not try to change my mind.

INTERMISSION

From the *Brooklyn Daily Eagle,* May 2, 1882

William Godfrey Krueger, the inventor of a flying machine, and who had spent many years of thought and restless toil over it committed suicide yesterday at his boarding house, No. 186 Forsyth Street, New York. He was out of money and was in daily expectation of getting the first installment of a pension due him from the Government. It came yesterday morning after he had killed himself. Krueger was a native of Prussia, and had been in this country twenty-three years. For fifteen years he has been entirely absorbed in studying out the great problem of his flying machine, and did little more than to write an occasional article for the newspapers. The secret of the flying machine died with him.

From *The Century,* January 1883

Women's Wages by Janet E. Ruutz-Rees

I have been looking for some clue to the unsatisfactory relation of women's work to women's pay. There are, in reality, two distinct classes of women who are in the field of remunerative employment: those who desire to add to an insufficient income, and those who depend upon themselves absolutely for bread. Both classes call for consideration, and yet the fact of their existence is precisely that in which the difficulty we are considering has its rise.

[EIGHTEEN]

A Terrible Conflagration

"Oh, who is that little girl?" Mama cried, pausing in her rocking. She leaned forward and peered at me, as if trying to remember my name. "Little girl? I spoke to you—who are you?"

My heart squeezed up until my entire chest ached, even as I patted her arm and pushed the rocking chair, lulling her back into silence. How many times had I been mistaken for a child? But to hear my own mother do so hurt me beyond reason—even if it was only the result of a sick, muddled mind.

Charles and I had moved into the old homestead with my brother James and his family, this December of 1882, after letting out our house. Papa had died in 1880, but Mama was still alive. Infirm, growing deaf, content to rock in a chair all day, her hands were now idle, as was her reason. Even as I was glad that she could no longer remember Minnie, and so could no longer mourn her, I grieved that she could not recognize me. I was a stranger to my mother, to my entire family, really—and in a way, hadn't I always been? James and his wife were kindness itself, but I felt they were always defensive about the simplicity of their life, comparing it, too often, to what Charles and I had grown accustomed to.

"I don't suppose the Queen served sassafras tea when you all went calling there, did she?" my sister-in-law would say as she prepared for callers.

"No, Mary, but I've always liked sassafras tea," I would reply.

"Well, it's what we're used to around here," she would say, resentment flavoring the tea almost as much as the sassafras.

Or—

"I reckon they take wine with their meals in France," James would remark at dinner, passing around platters of good boiled New England beef.

"They do," Charles would agree.

"Well, we don't go in for that around here, you know," James would scold, mildly—as if we had asked for wine, demanded wine, threatened to lock ourselves in our rooms unless we were served wine.

I don't mean to be ungrateful; my brother and his family did us a great kindness in allowing us to stay with them. But it was uncomfortable, nevertheless. So I did what I always did; I plotted my escape. If my family didn't know what to do with me, my audience did; they smiled, they clapped, and in the spotlight, up on a stage so that all I could see were faces, not legs, I felt big. As big as my dreams.

But never as big as Minnie, who, after all, had been large enough to carry two beating hearts within her. Next to her memory; next to my sister-in-law, with her brood of children and happy domesticity; next to my mother, who, even in her confusion, often caressed the finger upon which her plain gold wedding band still resided—I felt insignificant; I felt small; I felt *less.*

So we were going back out on tour again; this time with just the Bleekers. No more circus trains for us! Just a genteel entertainment, singing, dancing, stories of our travels; we were even introducing a new feature, a stereopticon, to project images of the places we had seen. Mr. Bleeker was quite excited about it; it had been my idea. I couldn't wait to try it out.

"Little girl! Do I know you? Are you Delia's daughter?" Mama stopped rocking again; she was growing agitated, shrugging off her shawl, kicking at her skirt.

"No, Mama," I said, placing her shawl back upon her shoulders. "I'm Vinnie. Remember? Vinnie—your daughter."

"Vinnie?" She tilted her head like a parrot; she was very birdlike these days, the way her hands incessantly plucked at her clothing, and her eyes blinked constantly in any light stronger than a candle. "Vinnie? I used to know a Minnie, once. Whatever happened to her?"

"Minnie died, Mama."

"Died? How?"

"I killed her," I replied. Then I ran upstairs to finish packing.

THE FIRST STOP ON THIS LATEST TOUR WAS MILWAUKEE. WE arrived there on January 9, 1883, a gray, wintry day, although we barely saw it, getting in late, as usual, and driving straight to our hotel. Starting with our circus travels, it seemed to me that we spent less and less time in a particular city, so that I truly had no sense of place. Milwaukee, Minneapolis, Davenport, Sioux City—they all looked the same to me. All had bustling, well-lit train stations, paved streets, new electric wires going up next to all the commercial buildings in the center of the city. Even the smallest towns had tall buildings now, for elevators were becoming commonplace.

Of all the many marvels of the modern age, the elevator was the one that most changed our lives. Maybe others were talking about telephones and electric lights, but Charles and I never tired of gushing about elevators. A lifetime of taking stairs meant for normal-size legs had taken its toll on both of us; Charles was now forty-five, I, forty-one. Our hips ached, as did our backs. Oh, the convenience—the bliss!—of walking into that wonderful little iron cage, watching the lift boy, clad in a smart uniform with a cap, move the handle, and then miraculously rising up, up, up, past all those awful stairs and landings!

Never before had Charles and I ever stayed above the first or second floors of a hotel, until elevators came into vogue. And so we were particularly excited to find that, upon checking into the Newhall House Hotel, we had rooms on the sixth floor—imagine! The very top floor, and we could get to it easily. Surely there would be a very fine view of the city from there!

This somewhat made up for the fact that the Newhall House was not the nicest hotel in Milwaukee. We could no longer afford to stay in the newer gilded palaces of stone and marble; the Newhall House was twenty-five years old, one of the few wooden structures left in that city just north of Chicago, which had suffered the infamous fire twelve years before. But still, the hotel was clean and bright—new electric lights were in every room—and we were happy to see other theatrical folk there, as well.

"Old troupers, all of us," Mr. Bleeker said as he waved at one of the members of the Minnie Palmer Light Opera Company, seated across the lobby. "We'll all die in the harness. It's a sickness."

"Speak for yourself, Sylvester," Mrs. Bleeker said fondly.

We were all four seated in one of the parlors after dinner; it was particularly cozy on this night, as it was frigid outside, but inside, we had the warm familiarity of flocked wallpaper, worn carpet, chipped hotel dinnerware. That was the life we knew, the four of us, and we had shared it for so long. The few times we saw one another out of such surroundings—not on a train, or in a theater or a hotel—it seemed odd; we always acted stiff, uncomfortable, overly formal. *This* was where we belonged—in anonymous hotels, in cities we never saw save from a train window or from a stage door. It may sound depressing, but it was not; rather, the bland anonymity of our surroundings served only to sharpen our identities, making us dear and recognizable to one another—making us a family.

The first stop on a long tour was always particularly full of warmth and laughter, like the first Sunday dinner after a long absence from home. And this night, we were all especially happy, for some reason. Mr. and Mrs. Bleeker sat close together on a plum-colored velvet settee; Mr. Bleeker's lean face relaxed until it almost looked merry. He had his arm around his wife, who nestled her head against his shoulder without her usual reticence. Generally, Mrs. Bleeker conducted herself so modestly as to be ignored by those too busy to observe her gently mocking smile, her soft brown eyes that were quick to notice the most unusual details—the one man whose topcoat wasn't buttoned properly, the one flower that poked its nose up through the grass ahead of the others. But tonight she appeared not to care who might see her playing coquettishly with the buttons on her husband's vest; if I hadn't known her better, I would have thought she had taken wine with dinner!

Charles and I sat close together, as well—the other couple's playfulness seducing Charles into trying something of the same with me. And tonight, for a change, I allowed it; I allowed my husband to hold my hand in his, tucking it under his arm with proud ownership. I even sighed, playing my part, and inched closer to him.

To the casual observer, we were simply two old married couples, happy in one another's presence, perhaps on holiday together. I enjoyed thinking that was how others might see us tonight, this restful, contented night.

"What do you mean, Julia?" Mr. Bleeker looked fondly down upon his wife, who blinked up at him with eyes that crinkled at the edges, like a fine piece of lace.

"I mean, I don't want to spend all the rest of my life on the road. I love you all, but I want a little farm, up in Albany near my family. You may be an old trouper, Sylvester, but I'm not. I only married one."

"You've been talking about that farm for years," Mr. Bleeker scolded, but his eyes kept smiling.

"You've been promising me you'd give it to me for years," his wife retorted.

"You know we could never go on without the two of you," I interposed, but not anxiously; I could not take this talk seriously. Mrs. Bleeker often mentioned that farm but always stood ready, her worn portmanteau in hand, the next time we met at Grand Central Station. "Why, who would ever change my costume so quickly as you? Who would lace me into my corset? And who would keep track of us all?" I turned to Mr. Bleeker. "Remember how calm you were back in sixty-nine, when you outsmarted those bandits in Nevada?"

"Why, sure, don't you remember?" Charles squeezed my hand excitedly. "How you told them we would be on the stage, and then you got us all out of there early?"

"Oh, that was a time!" Mr. Bleeker laughed. "I do wish I'd seen those varmints' faces when they held up the coach and we weren't there!"

"That was a lovely trip," I said, remembering. "All the places we went!"

"It was a tiring trip," Mrs. Bleeker insisted. "I just wanted to get back home safe and sound!"

"But the things we saw—the Pyramids! The temples in Japan!" I closed my eyes, as if I could conjure up those long-ago sights. They were fading from memory, little by little; I could no longer recall the entire settings—I didn't remember how we got to the Pyramids, for example, but I did remember, vividly, how it felt to stand in their ancient shadow. Unreal, almost, as if we were standing in front of a flat backdrop painting of them, instead—until I noticed the clouds moving across the sky, throwing gently changing patterns of light across them, making the rough, uneven surfaces suddenly stand out, almost reaching toward us. Only then did I know they were real.

"Remember, Vinnie, how I said to you that I knew exactly how you must feel, for the first time in my life?" Mr. Bleeker chuckled. "Because I felt about two feet tall next to those things?"

I was about to reply, but to my surprise, Charles answered first. "I do," he declared, decidedly. "I heard you say that to Vinnie, and I wanted to tell you, old fellow, that you couldn't possibly know how we felt. Because none of those desert chaps, the ones working there digging in the sand at the bottom, were pointing to you and laughing."

I was stunned. I remembered that—I remembered thinking *exactly* that. I was nodding to Mr. Bleeker but watching those brown men pointing at our party, holding their hands down to the ground to approximate our size, and doubling over with laughter.

What I didn't remember was that Charles saw them, too—and that he felt the same way. I studied my husband now; he was older, his face so puffy, his beard still rather ridiculous. But there was something in his eyes that I'd never even bothered to look for before—and that I recognized, for I saw it in my own in those rare moments when I paused long enough to stare into a mirror. Hurt and determination, both: That's what it was. Hurt at the cruelties the world sometimes threw at us; determination not to let anyone notice.

Perhaps I had also recognized it in the eyes of those misshapen little women from the circus; perhaps I hadn't wanted to, and so made myself forget I'd seen it. Until now.

I shook my head, even as Charles looked at me with a new, understanding smile. I did not know what to say—so I squeezed his hand and smiled back. For a moment, we were miniature reflections of Mr. and Mrs. Bleeker, seated opposite.

For a moment, it didn't even feel as if we were pretending.

We passed the rest of the evening like this, four friends reminiscing about old times. When the clock struck ten, we all rose and took the elevator up to the sixth floor. Mrs. Bleeker knelt down to give me her usual good-night kiss, and Mr. Bleeker shook Charles's hand. Then we turned and went to our respective rooms—theirs farther down the hall than ours—shutting the doors behind us.

Once Charles and I changed clothes and climbed my steps up to bed, he immediately rolled over to the far side, leaving me the space I always desired. But I did not roll over; I lay upon my back, conscious of his presence in my bed in a way I never had been before. His warm, steadily breathing presence; the way his nightcap got twisted about, even before he closed his eyes; his feet sticking out of his nightshirt, pink and sturdy as a child's but with little tufts of hair upon his toes—like a man.

I had never felt my husband's bare feet against mine. We had never slept that closely; our bodies had never been so entwined. There was always so much distance between us, and I had put it there, from the very beginning. Charles, ever-pleasing, ever-pliable, had not once questioned why I had. Neither had I—until tonight.

Holding my breath, I stretched my right hand toward my husband. Yet I could not reach him; the bed was too big, and I was too small; suddenly, delicately, *femininely* small. Afraid to disturb him, afraid not to, I inched even closer and reached out again.

Sighing with a soft, unexpected snort, Charles rolled over in his sleep and moved tantalizingly closer toward me.

That wasn't what I expected; I snatched my hand back as if he were a hot coal, something dangerous, something that could hurt me. Rolling away onto my own side, my heart racing so that it was pounding in my ears, I held my breath, waiting to see what he would do next. But he did nothing; he simply continued to sleep, unaware of my turmoil on the other side of the deep, linen-covered—and dream-littered—chasm between us. I almost laughed at the absurdity, the feminine timidity, of my behavior—why, I was forty-one! I had been married for twenty years now. I was behaving like a blushing virgin—

Which, of course, I was. I wouldn't have known what to do even if I had touched my husband's shoulder, turned him to me, welcomed him with a smile. Beyond that, I couldn't imagine; my horror of everything that had happened to Minnie would not allow me to think further than an embrace, perhaps maybe a kiss.

I plumped my pillow and told myself, sternly, to get to sleep; we had three performances on the morrow, and we had to get to the theater early to try out the stereopticon. Even though I tossed and turned and couldn't get comfortable, my nightgown unusually hot and heavy against my tingling skin, I did finally go to sleep that night.

And when I did, I later remembered, I was thinking of my husband. For only the first time in our marriage; also, as it turned out, the last.

"VINNIE! VINNIE!"

A hand was upon my shoulder—my husband's hand. I snuggled down into my pillow and smiled; hadn't I just fallen asleep, imagining this, his hand upon me?

"Vinnie! Wake up!" He was shaking me, not tenderly but forcefully. "Wake up! I hear people in the hall! I smell smoke!"

I opened my eyes; Charles was kneeling beside me, his nightcap all twisted about, his eyes, even in the darkness, wide with fear. I yawned—and swallowed a faint trace of smoke.

Then I heard the footsteps in the hall, the confusion. Someone was banging on our door; someone was banging on all the doors in our hallway.

Someone was yelling, *"Fire!"*

I sat straight up, my heart pounding. Charles continued to hover over me, wringing his hands. "Oh, what do we do, Vinnie? What do we do?"

"Get dressed!" I barked, jumping out of bed—forgetting to use the steps, so that I fell with a thud to the floor. Scrambling up, I threw on a dressing gown; Charles did the same. Then I ran to the door and opened it with my usual difficulty, the doorknob large for my hand, and too high; I felt my shoulder strain as I wrenched it open.

The hallway was filled with people, frightened people, their faces still creased from sleep while their eyes were blank with panic. Everyone was in dressing gowns or nightshirts, some with shoes on, most in bare feet. It was utter pandemonium as people ran to and fro like confused mice, simply following their instincts. And their instincts told them to get out—for there was smoke, hazy right now in this part of the hall, but someone shouted, "It's coming up the elevator shaft! The smoke is coming up the elevator shaft! We can't use it!"

And over and over, on everyone's lips, the one word— *"Fire!"*

My instinct was to run to the Bleekers' room: Did they know? Were they awake? But I took one step out of the doorway and was nearly knocked off my feet; there were so many people, now some of them were carrying portmanteaus, or dragging trunks that were much bigger than I was. One almost smashed me even as I stood in the doorway. Everywhere I looked were legs, legs running back and forth, dragging things, holding things—sharp things (umbrellas, walking sticks, even one man with a sword), heavy things. There was no possibility of pushing myself through that stampede without being trampled to death. I couldn't even shout my presence; the din was far too great, as the air was filled with panicked cries and shouts of confused directions: "The elevator must be working!" "No, the flames are coming up the shaft!" "I think the stairs are this way!" "A man said we must be prepared to jump!"

Quickly I leaped back inside our room, banging the door shut behind me. Charles was standing in his dressing gown, uncinched so that it hung loosely, his belly, in his nightshirt, protruding; he was still in his bare feet.

"Put your shoes on!" I told him, as I sprinted to do the same thing. "Gather up anything of value—take my steps, and I'll get my jewel case!" I ran to find the case, but a maid had put it high on top of a bureau, so I could not reach it. Cursing her stupidity, I grabbed the steps out of Charles's hand and dragged them to the bureau; standing up on my very toes, I was able to reach the case.

"Now!" I jumped off the steps and thrust them back to

Charles. "We can't go out in the hall—we'll be trampled to death! We'll either have to wait for people to clear it, or—or—"

"Or what? Get burned to death?" Charles cried. His face was an alarming red; his breathing was labored, and he was shaking from head to toe. He did not look at all well, but I couldn't allow myself to worry about that; first, I had to get us out of this room.

Something was rattling; it sounded like dice being shaken in a cup. I looked down, and it was the jewel case; my hand was trembling so, all my jewelry was bouncing around inside. Later, I realized how ridiculous it was to worry about that case; I had forgotten that everything in it was imitation now.

My entire body was shaking, with fear and energy, both; my heart was racing but only to stir my blood, stir my mind, so that I might come up with a way out. That I would was never in doubt; I knew I could not rely on Charles, and I did not want to die here, consumed by flame and smoke. So it was up to me.

"We can—we can tie bedsheets together!" I looked around, realizing we should probably dampen them first, in case the flames reached our room, but there was no water in the pitcher. "Quick, take the sheets off the bed!"

Charles and I both ran to the bed and began to remove the sheets; it was difficult for us, as they were so heavy and the mattress so huge, the top of it just about level with our eyes; even the pillowcases were cumbersome in our arms, as we could not quite reach all the way about them. In the end, I held on to each pillow while Charles tugged at the cases, both of us falling flat on our bottoms in the effort.

Meanwhile, the commotion outside our door grew even more deafening; the temperature began to rise, and as the early-morning light began to fill our room, we could see that the air was beginning to turn hazy. The smell of smoke stung the inside of my nostrils.

Oh, where was Mr. Bleeker? Why had he not burst into the room to save us, as he always did? But maybe he needed to be saved, for a change; what if they were sleeping, incredibly, through all this? I dropped the sheet I was holding and ran to the door once more—but the hallway was now thick with smoke, with even more people covering their eyes, choking, running, and still crying that one word—*"Fire!"*

I shut the door, knowing I couldn't open it again unless we had no choice but to try to make our way out through that teeming, terrifying hallway. But I couldn't let any more smoke inside our room; while Charles was trying to knot the sheets together, I shoved two of my dresses beneath the doorway to try to keep the smoke out. The Bleekers couldn't save us, and I couldn't save them; we were all on our own, now. I could only pray that we would see one another, safe and sound, when all was over.

"Vinnie, it's so hard—my hands are too small!" Charles protested, massaging his wrist. I ran to help him; it *was* difficult, knotting those heavy hotel sheets together; I didn't know how we'd get them secure enough to hold our weight.

"Here, tug on this," I told him, grabbing one end of two knotted sheets and handing him the other. "Tug hard!"

He did, I did—and the sheets slid apart. We stared at each other; Charles sat down upon the floor, as if he simply had no more will, and began to cry.

"Vinnie, we can't do this! Where's Bleeker? We can't save ourselves! We're too little!"

"Don't say that!" I longed to shake him; I detested his weakness at that moment, for I was too close to giving in to my own.

Kicking at the sheets, I ran to the window, but of course it was too high, the sash far above my head. I needed to stand upon something solid in order to open it, and my steps were too wobbly. "Help me," I yelled at Charles, as I spied a heavy chair next to the bed; we managed to inch it—oh, so excruciatingly slowly!—across the plush carpet, until it was in front of the window. Climbing upon it, throwing all dignity to the wind—my nightgown was now twisted about my waist, exposing my legs—I tried to unhinge the lock on the sash; it was big, slippery in my sweating palms, and at first I didn't think I could move it. But finally it did loosen, and I tugged on it until it released; leaning my shoulder against the sash, I pushed with all my might, praying that it might move. It did, enough so that I could then jump down and put my hands in the opening of the window; Charles joined me, and we were able to push it up enough so that we could lean out.

The scene before us was unreal. The street was full of people, some running, some crying—some lying broken and still. Oh, how wonderful it had seemed yesterday, to be on the very top floor of the hotel! But now it simply meant that we were a very long way from the ground. Smoke rolled out of windows on either side of us, and below, terrifying fingers of flame indicated that the fire must have started on one of the lower floors. I felt the heat rising all around me, as if from the very depths of hell. Horses were neighing, people were sobbing and shouting, bells were clanging—fire bells, from fire wagons; there were many already in the street below, and others coming; you could hear the clatter of horses' hooves, the squeal of careening wagons, echoing between the buildings several streets over.

The hotel was surrounded on all sides by other buildings, but it was also surrounded on all sides by wires. All those new electric wires cities were installing these days—they were like a lethal spiderweb just outside the hotel windows, close enough that a normal-size person could touch them in places. Even as I registered their presence, I saw someone jump from a window on our floor, hit a wire with a sizzling sound, and bounce up and then down to another wire before finally falling to the street below.

I turned away, sickened; there was nowhere to look any longer, no escape to try—all was hopeless. Sliding to the floor, I buried my face in my hands because I couldn't bear to look at Charles. For the first time in my life, I was all out of ideas. Charles slid down next to me and, like a loyal, trusting puppy, laid his head on my lap. Automatically, I began to smooth his brow.

My heart, which had been racing so fast, fueling my fear and desperation, began to slow down, and I was painfully aware of it, wondering how much longer it would continue to beat, wondering what would come first—the smoke, or the flames. Oh! A great cry almost tore my heart open right then; I did not want to die! Not in this way—smoke was beginning to snake in beneath the closed door, despite my wadded-up dresses. But we could not jump—not six floors! That was too high for even a normal-size person; for us, it would be like jumping from an even greater height.

Had Minnie known, just before her heart stopped beating, that it was her last breath? Oh, Minnie! Had she forgiven me? Had she even blamed me, in the first place? Before she died—and she must have known that she was dying; she must have known she could not keep losing so much blood—had she been angry? I was angry now—I was furious! To think that I would die here in this way—why, if there had been someone nearby whom I felt was responsible, I would have yelled, I would have screamed, I would have accused and blamed.

But Minnie hadn't done that, and so, as I strained to see her dear face one more time—but the smoke was so thick it was obscuring my memories as well as my vision—I had to believe that she wasn't angry with me, that she didn't blame me. If only I could forgive myself—

And then my eyes flew open wider as I peered through the smoke, trying to see one last image; my heart, with one final, mighty burst of energy, opened up and flooded my sinking spirits with one last thought. It was of a face; it was of an apology. It was of an acknowledgment that there was one person I would miss—and one person that I hoped would miss me. But that could happen only if I forgave us both.

Charles was coughing, his head still buried in my lap. So was I—my chest was already aching from the effort, although I hadn't realized it. My throat was burning, as were my eyes; perspiration was running down my neck, between my breasts, my thighs.

But I had strength enough left to whisper, "I'm sorry, I was wrong, I forgive us both, I forgive you—" His name was upon my lips; that name I had withheld, for no reason. For every reason.

I was just about to utter it, wondering if it would be the last word I ever spoke, when I heard a voice cut through my fading consciousness.

"Hello?" it said, in a brogue almost as thick as the smoke filling the room. The wall behind my back shuddered, and an enormous thud was heard in the window above my head. "And would there be anyone in here now?"

I leaped up, knocking Charles to the floor; there, in the window, was the tip of a ladder, and a round, beautiful, blessed Irish face, covered in grime and wearing a fireman's hat, staring at me.

"Oh! Thank Providence!" I burst into tears; I couldn't believe that he was real. I climbed upon the chair just so I could touch his face; without a word, he grabbed my arm and started to haul me over the windowsill.

"Wait! I can't—" I gazed down at the ladder; there was no

way I could traverse it, for the rungs were far too widely spaced. "I can't climb down! And my husband is here!"

"Your husband?" The fireman blinked, just as Charles scrambled up on the chair next to me. The three of us stared at one another for an almost comical moment, considering the circumstances. "Ach—you're wee! Both of you!"

"Yes, and we can't climb down the ladder ourselves!"

"Then I'll just have to take you down, then, one at a time. Who's first?"

Charles and I looked at each other; I don't know what he was thinking, but all I could wonder was what if something happened—the ladder collapsed, or the flames broke through, before the man could climb back up? Having just absolved myself of Minnie's death, I could not bear to think of either of us having to live with that burden.

"No, can't you—please, take us *both*?"

"How much do ye weigh?" The man was so calm, standing upon a ladder hundreds of feet above the ground with electrical wires humming not five feet behind him, flames licking below him, people screaming and hanging out of windows on either side.

"Not much—maybe eighty pounds, total?" I tried not to look at my portly husband.

"All right, climb aboard!" The fireman was cheerful about it, as if he was offering us a ride upon his favorite horse. As we hesitated, not sure what to do, he simply reached with one hand and grabbed me about the waist; I was hauled out the window and instructed to climb on his back, which I did, pressing myself tightly against him, trying to make myself even smaller so as not to touch those hissing electrical wires. He yanked Charles out the window by the back of his nightshirt and tucked him under one arm, like a ham. Then he started to climb down, but I called out, "Oh, wait—my steps!"

"Your what?"

"My steps—please, my father made them!"

"Sorry, Miss—no time!" And we began to inch our way down the ladder.

I couldn't look, but I couldn't shut my eyes, either; I wanted to be aware of every moment. I wanted to be able to convince myself I had really survived. So I concentrated on the fireman's back; his heavy coat; the sweat running, in neat little rivers, down the back of his red neck; his matted brown hair curling out from under his black fireman's helmet.

Yet I couldn't shut out all the rest—the bodies that fell on either side of us, landing with the sickening thump of a ripe melon being thrown to the ground; the people hanging out of windows, waving, screaming, holding towels and handkerchiefs up to their faces to block out the smoke, which was boiling out of every window now, thick and black, bits of paper and fabric swirling within it. The air began to cool as we continued down the ladder; I had the oddest thought that Charles must be feeling quite a draft, as the entire lower half of his body was sticking out, uncovered, for all the world to see.

Finally, we reached the ground; the fireman tossed Charles, unceremoniously, to the street and knelt down so that I could slide off his back, muttering, "Eighty pounds, my arse." He then grabbed the ladder and moved it over to the next row of windows, and began to climb back up.

"Charles, Charles!" I bent down, shaking him; I was overcome with joy, with relief—I could have danced a jig, right then and there. "We're safe!"

But to my surprise, my husband was crying. Lying on his side in the street, while people stepped over us, shouting for us to get out of the way, he hid his face in his arms. His shoulders were shaking; he was sobbing more wretchedly than he had at any time during the ordeal.

"What? What's wrong? We're saved!"

"Oh, Vinnie! To have to be lowered down that way, that awful, mortifying way! Like a—like a sack of something—just hauled out like that! It's so humiliating—I couldn't do a thing for myself, I couldn't save you or me, it's so awful!"

I stared at him, unable to believe what I was hearing. I suppose my heart should have softened toward him, for he was a man, after all. And men did have their pride.

But we were alive! I was so grateful for that, I couldn't understand his shame.

I rose; all around us were people sobbing, yelling, running about. There were broken bodies, arms and legs at unnatural angles, littering the street; even as I registered this, another fell just ten feet away from us.

"We need to move away from here," I told Charles, gripping his arm. "Come, let's find a place to stay, and we'll look for the Bleekers."

Sniffing, rubbing his eyes, Charles rose and allowed me to guide him through the carnage, across the street to a bakery that had opened its doors to the survivors. Someone was handing out blankets, and one fell across my shoulders, as if by magic. The warm, homey smell of fresh bread and pastry was an odd counterpoint to the horrible stench—of burning flesh as well as burning wood—outside.

Already there was a coroner's wagon on the scene; stretchers were being removed from it, filled with bodies covered with sheets, and then placed back inside. Hospital wagons were also being loaded with the wounded, and every few minutes the driver would slap the reins as a wagon sped off, full of broken, burned occupants. Mothers were searching for children, crying out their names; children were screaming for parents. Everywhere there were people walking, looking, seeking.

But also, people were simply sitting, on curbs, in the street, still in their nightclothes which were now torn and streaked with ash and dirt; some were dripping wet, as if they'd doused themselves with water to protect against the flames. All were staring at the scene before them, eyes glazed over, as if they simply could not process the carnage, as if they simply could not understand how they had escaped it.

"You stay here. I'll go out and see if I can help, and find the Bleekers," I told Charles, who dutifully nodded and sat down upon an upturned bucket. Someone had placed a blanket around his shoulders, too, but he was shaking, his face still that awful red, his breathing labored. But I couldn't stay inside with him, waiting to be told what to do next; I needed to move, to fill my lungs with air, to remind myself that truly, I was alive.

So I moved among my fellow survivors as the hotel continued to burn; occasionally, there would be a fresh cry as pieces of it came crashing down. But soon there was no one left inside to scream; the flames continued to crackle, the bells to clang, but from within the flames there was only deathly silence.

"Please, let me help." I tugged on the skirt of a woman in a white dress, a blue cape around her shoulders; she carried a basket of blankets and a bucket of clean water with a ladle, and was moving among the survivors, giving them drinks and warmth.

"That would be a blessing." She smiled down at me, not betraying any surprise at my size, and handed me an armful of blankets. The heat from the fire was still blazing hot but only if you were facing it; otherwise, the January air was relentlessly cold. As the sun continued to rise, people's wet garments began to sparkle as if fine diamonds had fallen upon them—but after a closer look, I saw that they were ice crystals. Shuddering in sympathy, I was grateful for the blanket across my shoulders, the warm shoes upon my feet—for many survivors were barefoot.

"Do you know where—is there a place where the wounded are being taken? Where we might be able to meet up with our friends, to see if they survived?"

"I believe there's a man writing down the names of the survivors—over there." She pointed to a man carrying a pad of paper and a pencil, near the largest fire wagon. "You can check with him and give him your name."

"Thank you." I headed that way, handing out blankets; a few people recognized me and smiled weakly, calling out, "Mrs. Tom Thumb! What are you doing here?"

"My husband and I were staying in the hotel," I replied. "We were rescued by a fireman." I scanned the crowd in all directions, searching for the Bleekers—surely Mr. Bleeker, so tall, with his distinctive long gray beard and sad face, would stand out? Surely they escaped, just as we had?

And then I heard my name again—"Vinnie!" But it was a moan; about twenty feet away, I saw Mr. Bleeker kneeling over a broken body in a nightgown.

"Mr. Bleeker!" Picking my way across what now resembled a battlefield, I fell to my knees beside him; he was holding his wife's hand, shaking his head as tears rolled down his face.

Julia Bleeker was still alive; her eyes were closed, and her breathing was shallow. But her face was pale, her nightgown was plastered to her body in bloody patches, and her leg was turned out from the hip at an unnatural angle.

"What happened?" I picked up her other hand; it was cold,

and I was reminded of Minnie. But then she squeezed it, and I had hope. "Mrs. Bleeker! It's me, Vinnie! Charles and I are fine—we were rescued from our room."

She didn't reply, although her eyelids fluttered; I looked over at Mr. Bleeker, who took a big, shuddering breath.

"She jumped—we both jumped from our room to a balcony about two stories below. I landed just fine, but Julia, she—she hit the fencing, the iron fencing, and her head—it just hit it. This big post. I was able to get her down a ladder, but—I don't know, Vinnie. I just don't know."

"Oh!" There was no bruise visible on her face, but it was so deathly pale.

"I tried to get to you and Charles, I did, but it was impossible." Mr. Bleeker now looked at me anxiously. "Gosh, I'm glad you got out. I was worried sick; so was Julia. She kept crying, 'Oh, Sylvester, those dear little souls! How frightened they must be!' But then—" And he couldn't go on.

"I know. Don't think about it."

"That farm," he said, a great tear rolling down his face.

"What?"

"That farm. She always wanted that farm up in Albany. 'Sylvester,' she said, but never in a scolding way—oh, no! 'I surely would like to have that little farm.' But I never gave it to her. I'm the one with the show blood in my veins, not her. But she never once complained, she always followed me, and now—"

"Shhh," I said, for I believed Mrs. Bleeker could hear us, even if she couldn't speak. "You'll give her that farm, I know it. You'll have all the time in the world."

"Do you think so, Vinnie?"

I looked at him; his eyes were round with both hope and fear.

"I do," I lied, as all at once, two men and a stretcher made their way through the crowd toward us. Much too roughly, they loaded Mrs. Bleeker upon it and trotted off toward a hospital wagon; Mr. Bleeker had to sprint to catch up, shouting, "Where are you taking her?" It all happened so fast, I didn't get to say goodbye—to either of them.

I continued to pass out blankets until the sun rose high in the sky; it must have been noon before I realized I was still in my nightgown. But then, so were many other people. Eventually, policemen rounded everyone up and directed them to other hotels; we were told not to leave Milwaukee for at least two days, as they needed to take down statements from us all.

Somehow, I managed to get Charles more or less upright and moving again, and at my urging, over the next few days we gave two benefit performances for the victims of the fire. And we dedicated each performance to our good friends Julia and Sylvester Bleeker. It was the first time we had performed without them, and it felt wrong; neither of our hearts was in it, but we were happy to help a good many people, a number of whom feared being stranded now that all their money was in ashes.

After the benefits, Charles and I left for home, this time for good; there was no question of continuing the tour. And so, after traveling the globe, crossing the country countless times, traversing up and down and through rivers, deserts, and mountains, the General Tom Thumb Company came to its sad end in the ashes of a hotel in Milwaukee, Wisconsin. Minnie was gone; Nutt had died in 1881 of Bright's disease.

And now, too, was Mrs. Bleeker taken from us; she died twelve days later from her injuries. After staying in Milwaukee to give testimony at one of the inquests, Mr. Bleeker retired to a niece's home in Brooklyn—still agonized because he had not been able to get to Charles and me.

Although, oddly, many news reports and articles began to surface saying that he had—that he had saved Charles and me from the flames himself, depicting him as a grieving, but heroic, husband and friend.

And while I don't know exactly how that rumor began, I could not help but suspect that an old friend of ours might have had something to do with it.

INTERMISSION

From the *Brooklyn Daily Eagle,* June 11, 1883

It is not open to dispute that the Brooklyn Bridge is the most wonderful work of its kind on the globe. . . . There is no instance in the world save that afforded by the Brooklyn Bridge of a span of nearly 1,600 feet sustained entirely by cables.

From *The New York Times,* December 27, 1884

A Brilliant Christmas Tree—How an Electrician Amused His Children

A pretty as well as novel Christmas tree was shown to a few friends by Mr. E. H. Johnson, President of the Edison Company for Electric Lighting, last evening in his residence, No. 189 East Thirty-sixth-street. The tree was lighted by electricity, and children never beheld a brighter tree or one more highly colored than the children of Mr. Johnson when the current was turned and the tree began to revolve. Mr. Johnson has been experimenting with house lighting by electricity for some time past, and he determined that his children should have a novel Christmas tree.

[NINETEEN]

Finale, or—the Curtain Comes Down

AND NOW IT WAS JUST THE TWO OF US—GENERAL AND Mrs. Tom Thumb, Mr. and Mrs. Charles Stratton. The perfect couple, a love story in miniature, the sweethearts of a country torn apart by war but united in good wishes for our happiness: we were never supposed to end up like this. Diminished, unnerved, hiding in the house I had been so determined to leave all those years ago.

Quite bluntly, Charles was never the same after the fire. Shaken to the core by his inability to save himself, humiliated by the manner in which he was saved, he refused to ever again appear in front of an audience.

"Charles, you're being ridiculous," I told him, time and again. "Can't you just be grateful that we survived?"

"No." He shook his head, his breathing even more labored these days, his body not merely large but puffy, his skin clammy to the touch. "I can't forget the fireman hauling me down the ladder like that. I couldn't do a thing to help myself, Vinnie! You don't understand. You don't know what that's like!"

I pressed my lips together and shook my head. I did know what that was like—but now our roles were reversed. My husband was not inclined to look into my eyes for understanding or recognition. He was not inclined to look into anyone's eyes, lest they see him for what he believed he was—a coward.

He was only forty-five, but until that night, he had never faced any real physical danger. The worst was probably the time when he was a child and Queen Victoria's dog had tried to bite him, a story he told over and over to anyone who would listen. And his pride had suffered; this was the man who had stomped around with a tiny pistol in the West, confident he could slay any number of Indians with it. He had laughed along with everyone else at the notion, but deep down, I knew that he thought he could. He may have been imitating people all his life, but what made Charles such a gifted mimic was his conviction; he believed in every single role he had ever played—including that of husband.

And now he thought he had failed in that as well; suddenly he could not meet my gaze or even enjoy being in the same room with me. I didn't have the courage to tell him that he was wrong; he had never been given the chance to succeed in that role. For hadn't I made sure of that, long ago?

So he holed himself up in Mama's parlor, where he read over old newspaper clippings and hauled out tarnished medals and yellowing citations, reliving his past instead of facing the future. Charles had been a Mason for years, attending elaborately secret meetings (I knew they were secret because he always made a point of telling me they were); soon after we were married he had been made a Knight Templar in the Bridgeport order. And now I often found him looking over all his various hats and plumes and swords from that organization; it meant a great deal to him these days. I think he felt it bestowed the last measure of dignity he had left.

We both slept badly after the fire; we moved from my old upstairs room to one on the first floor, and could not go to sleep unless one or both of us checked to make sure the windows and doors were unlocked, and there was a bucket of water close at hand.

And never again did I reach for him in bed, as I had that night; my desire had been quenched, along with the flames.

"Charles, I'm taking the train down to New York to see Mr. Bleeker," I told him one morning in July. "Would you like to join me? I'm sure it would do him good to see you."

"No, no." My husband waved a plump hand in the air, as if brushing the very notion away.

"Charles, why won't you see him?" I sat in one of our little chairs; we had moved what pieces of our miniature furniture that we didn't sell into this house when we let out our own. It looked as if there were whole families of furniture living together, mother and father chairs spawning baby chairs.

"I just—I just can't, Vinnie. That's all." Charles, who was seated upon the floor, paging through an old scrapbook, looked up at me; even that small effort seemed to tax him. His breathing was so rapid, I could hear it across the room.

"You don't blame him for the fire, do you?" This suspicion had crossed my mind, as Charles refused to even write a sympathy letter to his old friend.

"No," Charles said, too quickly.

"That's absurd. Mr. Bleeker tried to come to our aid—remember, I told you? But for pity's sake, Charles, he had his own life to save, and that of his wife! We were not Mr. Bleeker's responsibility, you know. Why can't you be glad that we're alive?" Suddenly furious with him—as I was so often these days; I suppose he was not the only one changed by the tragedy—I ran to him and took his hands in mine. "We must get out of this house—we must get back to work! If we don't, we'll—we'll—we'll simply rot! We don't know any other life, the two of us. It's all we have."

"Vinnie, I just can't. I can't face anyone." Charles pulled his hands away; he wouldn't meet my gaze.

I sighed. There was only one other thing I could think of to try; there was only one person I could think of who might be able to talk some sense into him.

"I might stop in Bridgeport on the way back," I said, keeping my voice casual. "To see Mr. Barnum. Wouldn't you like to come with me, then?"

Charles hesitated; I could see the struggle in his once-merry eyes. But then he shook his head violently. "No."

"Well, why don't I stop to see if he would like to come to you, then? It's been such a long time since he's been to Middleborough."

Again, that hesitation; again, his negative response. "No, no—why won't you leave me alone, Vinnie? For pity's sake, that's all I want—to be left alone, finally! All my life I've been surrounded by people! Leave me in peace, for once!"

I sighed, then rose—stiffly, my right hip uncooperative. "Well, maybe I'll just stop in on my own!"

"Do whatever you want." Charles shrugged. "Take your time. Enjoy yourself."

"I'll give Mr. Bleeker your love. And Mr. Barnum, too—that is, if I do decide to stop in Bridgeport. I haven't made up my mind."

I turned to go, but Charles abruptly cried, "Vinnie!" before I could leave.

"What? What is it?" I spun around in alarm. He had jumped

up, his arm full of clippings, a morose figure in his dressing gown and worn slippers. The shades were drawn, but I could still see the stumps of cigars in every ashtray, the papers and photographs and citations and ribbons and, above all, memories; remnants of memories, threadbare, worn almost to shreds from a lifetime of use, lying in tatters at his feet. The room smelled like sadness, like stale breath and cheap cigars and musty papers that hadn't seen light in decades. It reminded me of a deserted, desolate circus tent long after the crowd had gone.

"You're not mad at me, are you?" He looked so pathetic, his soft brown eyes almost quivering with tears.

How easy it would be to tell him I was not—I considered it, for a tempting moment. My approval was the one thing left that I could bestow upon him without guilt. But then I realized that approval would do him no good this time; indeed, it would probably harm him. He needed to be shocked out of his torpor. He needed to be reminded that he was lucky he wasn't dead, so that he could get back to living.

"Yes, yes, I am," I said briskly—coldly. "I'm quite mad at you, if you want to know the truth."

Then I turned to go, before I could see the effect my words had on him. I didn't want to be late for my train.

The telegram arrived at Mr. Bleeker's house the next morning. We were having breakfast in his niece's narrow dining room; it was odd, just the two of us. I wasn't sure we had ever taken a meal alone together before.

Mr. Bleeker's sad face was even sadder; it was only now, with his wife gone, that it was obvious how much warmth and light she had given him. But he was not like Charles; he did not live in the past. He was doing his best to enjoy life with his niece, who had two small sons, and for the first time, I wondered why he and Mrs. Bleeker had never had children of their own.

"Julia couldn't," he said frankly, over toast and eggs. "I think that's why she enjoyed traveling with you all, even though she did long for that farm. But you and Minnie, especially—you were like daughters to her. You were our family."

"Odd, isn't it?" I sipped my coffee—the cup was large for me, so I had to use two hands.

"What is?"

"We all pretended to have children we didn't, in a way. Except for Minnie. She wasn't like us; she wasn't content just to pretend."

"Yes, except for Minnie. She would have been a wonderful mother."

"I know. It's been five years," I said softly, wonderingly. "Almost exactly—it was July, I remember it so well. Five years, too, since I last spoke—well, five years."

"Vinnie, what happened between you and Barnum?" Mr. Bleeker asked, and I was reminded that no matter how sad his face was, his eyes were ever sharp, ever perceptive. "I've always wondered. Goodness knows plenty of people have fallen out with him over the years, but I never thought you would."

"I—that is, it's hard to put into words. We both said things that hurt, and—that whole baby business." I shook my head. "It was the one thing my parents warned me about when I first met him. They warned me not to get caught up in one of his humbugs. Well, I did, and I brought Minnie along with me, and see what happened? Minnie's gone. I can't forget that."

"Just like I can't stop thinking that I was responsible for Julia," Mr. Bleeker whispered. "How do we live with that? How have you gone on?"

"By being so angry with Mr. Barnum, I sometimes forget to be angry with myself," I replied, smiling ruefully. "But ever since the fire . . ." I stirred my coffee and shrugged.

Ever since the fire, I had not stopped thinking about him.

That horrible moment when I thought I was about to take my last breath and form my last thought—it had been of him. I knew I wanted to see him one more time. I knew I wanted to tell him things—just what, I couldn't say. But inside my soul, in addition to the great burden of guilt I carried with me about Minnie, was a greater burden of things unsaid.

"Ever since the fire?" Mr. Bleeker prompted.

"I've been thinking it would be good to see him again."

"He is in Bridgeport now, I understand," said Mr. Bleeker, ever the organizer, ever the manager.

"I was hoping he was," I replied, wondering if I should wire him that I was going to stop on my way back. Or should I simply surprise him? He always did like surprises. Maybe I could stop into a shop and buy a stuffed elephant to bring him—he would like that; he would laugh, throwing back his head, and then motion for me to pull up a chair and sit with him.

Or maybe I should wire, after all. What was the best way to end a rift like ours? I smiled, thinking that if it were left to him, he probably would take out an ad in *The New York Times* proclaiming his apology and selling tickets to our reunion for twenty-five cents each.

And so it was that I was thinking about someone else, his moods, his quirks; wondering how I might reach out to him again over the morass of all the years, memories, and misunderstandings—

When the telegram arrived informing me of the death of the man whom I constantly had to remind myself to think about. The man whose name I eagerly took but whose heart I had never wanted, in the first place.

* * *

Charles Stratton, better known as General Tom Thumb, died of apoplexy, some said, the inevitable conclusion to a lifetime of cigars and rich foods. Others said he never recovered from the devastation of the Newhall House fire, of witnessing the tragedy of so many unfortunate souls.

They were all mistaken; I knew better. I knew he died of shame. He had played the hero, the leading man—the perfect man in miniature—onstage for as long, literally, as he could remember. The realization that he was not built to be a hero in life was too much for him to bear; he could never play that role again, and so he simply—stopped. Like a child's windup toy, used too often, the spring finally broken.

We buried him in Bridgeport, Connecticut, the town of his birth. Years before he had done a benefit for a brand-new cemetery, and had arranged his own plot at the time; he had even posed for a statue he wanted placed upon his monument—a life-size statue.

Ten thousand people attended his funeral. He would have been so pleased—a packed house! I smiled, safely veiled in my widow's weeds, thinking of how he would have shaken the hand of every man and kissed the cheek of every woman here. Charles did so love to meet people.

Two plumed Knights Templar stood at attention at the foot of his casket; upon the lid was his own small, plumed Knight Templar hat and miniature sword. Among those in attendance were Astors, Vanderbilts, and Bleekers; also the tattooed man he became quite fond of while touring with the circus, and many, many children, which would have touched him immeasurably. Queen Victoria sent a wreath, as did President Chester A. Arthur. The largest floral display of them all said, simply, "Friend"; it was given by Mr. P. T. Barnum, who sat several rows behind me in the church.

Minnie's service had been so small, I remembered, watching the throngs file past Charles's coffin, the reporters scribbling down every detail. Just in Mama and Papa's parlor. How Charles had sobbed! As if she were his own sister, and truly, I knew he thought of her that way. Whatever my husband was or wasn't, there was no denying he was genuinely giving of his love and affection. Charles had no enemies at all; he was the only person I knew of whom I could say that. No, Reader, I take that back. Minnie didn't, either.

And there was genuine grief at his funeral, too; I saw it in the faces that passed me. I heard it in the sob coming from several pews back, the sob of an old friend, the man who had taken a five-year-old boy and turned him into a miniature adult—and together, they had conquered the world. There would have been no P. T. Barnum without Charles Stratton, and there would have been no General Tom Thumb without P. T. Barnum.

I longed to go back there and comfort him, for I alone knew of the genuine affection between the two. Others saw only a business partnership; I saw a friendship. Mr. Barnum's sobs tore at my heart in a way that my own husband's death did not; my tears would not fall, and so I appropriated his. He could cry over Charles, for the both of us, just as I had cried over Minnie.

But I did not go to him. I sat in my pew, upon a cushion so that I would be visible to all, and I adjusted my thick black veil so that it hung with dignity down my back. And I tried to remember the things I loved about Charles. For this day, of all days, I did not want to pretend; I did not want to feel as if my mourning dress was a costume, as my wedding dress had been. I closed my eyes, and I remembered Charles as he was with children: warm, openhearted, all pretend dignity tossed aside, almost always on his knees, even though he—alone of all adults—did not have to bend down to be on their level.

I remembered Charles as he was with Minnie: the two of them co-conspirators, impish, playing pranks, sharing confidences, sharing a chair, the back turned to the rest of us, as they whispered together.

I remembered Charles as he was the last time I saw him: tear-stained, asking for my approval—because he had given up asking for my love. And I had refused him. It seemed to me I spent our entire married life refusing him, he who asked for so little of me. He had died alone, in our bed; even if I had been there with him, he would have died alone. For I had never allowed love to join us there, and without it, the two of us could not begin to fill up all the empty spaces between us.

His coffin looked so small in this great church, the stained-glass windows looming over it, those tall Knights Templar dwarfing his tiny plumed hat, perched so jauntily upon the top. I thought I should go and stand by him, so he wouldn't be so lonely, as he had always stood by me—

And that's when I realized what I would most miss about him. For I had lost the person who shared my view of the world, the person who had stood by me as I traveled continents, met Queens, shook hands with Presidents. I hadn't stood alone in over twenty years; always I had someone by my side whose eyes saw the world as I did. Through a maze of legs, of wheels, of barriers large and barriers small.

Barriers of hearts, and barriers of minds.

I bowed my head, tears finally trickling down my cheeks. And I found a way to mourn for my husband.

INTERMISSION

From *The Humbugs of the World,* by P. T. Barnum

And whenever the time shall come when men are kind and just and honest; when they only want what is fair and right, judge only on real and true evidence, and take nothing for granted, then there will be no place left for any humbugs, either harmless or hurtful.

[TWENTY]

One Last Encore

AFTER THE FUNERAL, I WENT BACK TO MIDDLEBOROUGH—back to my family. It was unspoken, but I knew they assumed that I would finally settle down, once and for all, within their bosom. Henceforth, I would be "Aunt Vinnie" to my various nieces and nephews, so numerous I honestly could not remember all their names.

"Aunt Vinnie, who used to be in show business"—I could just imagine how it would be. On Sundays the children would be forced to come into my parlor and visit with me, giving me a dutiful peck on the cheek while I rocked in my widow's weeds and told them stories they would not believe until they were older. It would only be after I was gone that they would believe me, after someone inherited a trunk full of scrapbooks and costumes and handbills—probably intended to be thrown out, but for some reason, someone thought to open it first. Then, imagine the surprise!

Aunt Vinnie had told the truth; she wasn't just a dotty old lady after all. Who would have believed it?

Oh, this was but one of many elaborate scenarios I envisioned for myself as I sat, brooding, in the house of my childhood. Sometimes the trunk was opened by an eager niece who wanted to go into the theater herself; she had always believed me, even though her brothers taunted her. Sometimes the trunk was sold, unopened, only to be discovered at an estate sale a year or two later.

And sometimes the trunk was simply thrown out. And no one remembered me at all, until I died and my will was read, stipulating I was to be buried next to my husband. That little man, that General Something-or-other; hadn't he been famous first?

Yes, he had. And now, without him, with only his name, who was I, anyway? Who would want to come see the widow of General Tom Thumb, all alone? What could she do on her own, other than tell stories that nobody believed anymore? Stories of Kings and Queens and Mormons and old Civil War generals? Who would pay money for that? *I wouldn't,* I thought to myself as I tried, unsuccessfully, to fall asleep in the room I had shared with Minnie as a girl.

Only I was all alone now; Minnie was gone, and even though at times my chest still ached with the memory of her head nestled against it, it had been five years since I had rocked her, finally, to sleep.

And Charles—I had never imagined that I would miss my husband as much as I did. I even missed his solid warmth in bed next to me, even though we never touched. But still, his snoring, his movement in the night, for he was a restless sleeper—I missed it now as I lie, once and for all, alone. Alone in my little bed, the one I used as a girl. The elaborate carved bed I had shared with Charles was gone; I put it in storage, for I could not bear the reminder of my failure as a wife.

And just as I had, so long ago when I heard Mama weeping softly over my lonely fate—how prescient she had been!—I lay in my virginal bed, and tossed and turned, longing for something else, something more. And just like then, I didn't know what it was.

I knew only that at age forty-two, after almost twenty-five years of running—running to catch trains, running to make performances, running to the next city, the next country, the next continent—

Running away, from my husband, from my family, from my name scratched in a tree, destined always to be smaller than everyone else's—

I still hadn't found what I was looking for.

Why was I, alone of everyone I knew, always still seeking? Still searching? Why did everyone else seem content enough, *brave* enough, simply to—live? Minnie, for all her timid ways, her shyness, was braver than I had ever been. She had been brave enough to live the life that I had only pretended to, the life that I had done my best to avoid yet somehow had ended up impersonating all over the world. That of the perfect wife and mother, the embodiment of the feminine ideal—in miniature. Always, in miniature.

There was only one other person I knew who never seemed satisfied. There was only one other person I knew whose dreams were as immense as the ones I had dreamed so long ago. There was only one other person who, though larger than me, had never allowed his shadow to completely obscure my own.

I picked up my pen and wrote another letter. I even walked into town to the post office myself, as I had done all those years ago; I even worried, just a little, about his reply.

But I didn't worry too much. For I knew I had found my way back from the Egress, after all.

* * *

"I WAS GOING TO COME ANYWAY, WHETHER YOU WANTED ME TO OR not," he said grumpily—although he couldn't completely prevent a crooked smile from spreading across his face.

Those lips were thinner now, the bushy eyebrows completely white, along with his curls. He did not use his gold-tipped walking stick as an accessory—punctuating sentences with it, outlining imaginary train routes, twirling it like a magician. Now he leaned heavily upon it, especially when going up stairs.

His voice, so much higher than one would think it should be, was still the same, as was his mind; closing my eyes, I could almost hear it whirring and turning, just as before. And, of course—that barely checked glimmer behind the gray eyes; I knew it was still there, just waiting for the perfect opportunity to mesmerize, beckon, delight.

"You were not, for you are afraid of me," I told him, just as grumpily. I had received him in Mama's parlor, now updated with gaslights instead of oil lamps, although there was a rumor that in the next few years, electricity would be run to all in Middleborough. My sister-in-law had redecorated everything, so that the plain, homespun braided rugs and simply carved furniture were gone, replaced by more ornate, heavy chairs, plush carpets. It looked like every hotel parlor I'd ever visited, but I didn't tell Mary that. She was very proud of this room.

"Afraid? I don't know what you mean," Mr. Barnum replied. "I am afraid of no one."

"You are afraid of women, and you always have been. You were terrified of Jenny Lind, you know. Why else would you let her slip away so soon and go back to Europe? And you're afraid of your wife now. Why else did you leave her in London while you came back home?"

"Why, that—" He began to stir; it had been such a long time

since we had sparred, and I don't believe he quite remembered how. I almost apologized, for I did not want to spoil the visit—but then he relaxed and allowed that glimmer in his eyes to wink at me. "Well, Vinnie, I see your tongue has not dulled with time. No one ever has spoken to me the way you do."

I smiled, pleased. But then an awkwardness fell over us. There was still so much left unsaid, so much I wanted to tell him—too much, in fact. For I didn't know where to begin.

"So why did you ask me here?" Mr. Barnum finally said, pulling his spectacles out of his pocket, putting them on, as he always did when he was preparing to talk business. "I heard—well, dash it, Vinnie, I heard that Charles left you in the lurch and that you're practically destitute. Is that true?"

I hesitated; it felt disloyal to talk about Charles in this way so soon after his death. But finally I nodded. "It's not so bad, though, as you see. I have a home, a roof over my head."

"Not fitting for you," he answered, shaking his head. "I know your family is dear, but Vinnie, you can't be happy living here, can you?"

"No, but that's not why—oh, I don't know. Yes, that's it—that's why I asked you here, to see what you advise for the future. For you always know what to do."

"Oh." Now his eyes hardened. "That's the only reason you asked, then? Because you needed something? I should have known. That's the only reason anyone ever calls for Mr. Barnum."

I looked away. I did not know how to apologize to anyone, let alone him. I was quite sure he didn't, either. The room was so silent, of a sudden, only the sound of his breathing, my sigh; his foot jostling, my skirt rustling. Our hearts, too rusty, both of them, from disuse—but suddenly now I could hear them both pounding, roaring in my ears.

Or was it just mine, alone?

"Minnie," I finally said in a whisper, not looking at him. "Minnie."

"I know," he replied, so gently. I was reminded of his gentleness at other times in my life: when he found out about Colonel Wood, for instance. When he heard of Minnie's plans to name her child after Pauline.

When he said my name, as I left him outside on the lawn, before Minnie died.

"We both—that is, I don't blame you, anymore. We both were equally responsible, for it all—the baby hoax, taking Minnie out, away from here. I wanted her with me, just as much as you wanted her in the troupe. I could have said no—I knew that, for you always listened to me. But I didn't. I can't blame you anymore."

"You shouldn't blame anyone. Vinnie, I've never in my life apologized for anything—not for Joice Heth, not for taking one nickel from the public, not even for the Feejee mermaid. I never made a person do anything he didn't want to. I'm not going to start apologizing now, either. But I am—I do regret—the thing is, Vinnie, dash it, Minnie was *happy,* you know! She could find the beauty in quiet things in a way I never could, and she should be envied for that, not mourned. She was happier than you and I will ever be and ever were, God bless her soul. We just don't have it in us to be content like that—but your sister did." He was excited now; he had inched his chair closer and closer to mine, until, before either of us could fully register it, we were sitting knee to knee.

I looked away, still loyal to Minnie's memory; it was hard to forgive him. It was harder still to forgive myself. I missed her so much, missed her joy, her trust, her touch—

Suddenly I felt my hands being picked up and clasped with warmth and understanding. I couldn't help it; a quick sob escaped my burdened heart and a tear rolled down my cheek. I tried to brush it away, but my hands were held captive.

"She did find beauty here, in this home, and she always tried to open my eyes to it," I whispered. "But I can't be content with it, even now, because you were right. Being content with home would mean being content with myself, just as I am, and I've never been able to be that. Yet I've lived such a little life, compared to my sister."

"Who said such a thing? I'll thrash 'im within an inch of his life!"

"Nobody—just me."

"Well, I'll thrash *you,* then!"

I looked up and smiled. "No, you won't."

"No, I won't," he said agreeably. Still holding my hands, he gave them a stern little shake. "But I won't hear such talk. Mercy Lavinia Warren Bump Stratton—even that name isn't as big as you are! You've traveled the world, met everyone worth knowing! Whatever I said—and who can remember, anymore?—the plain truth is that you were never meant to stay at home on a farm, and it has nothing to do with your size. Imagine you, selling eggs at the kitchen door, or getting excited about baking pies for the church bazaar!"

"I'll have you know, my pies are exceedingly light and delicious," I replied primly.

"Who cares if they are? I can have any kind of pie I want, anytime I want. But if you had decided you were content with that accomplishment only, I would never have had the privilege of your friendship. And that, my dear, would be a tragedy."

"No, it wouldn't. You'd still have Jenny Lind, and Charles, and Jumbo, and your circus. You wouldn't miss me at all."

"Then why am I here, then? Why'd I come all the way from Bridgeport to godforsaken Middleborough, at the first sight of a letter from you? I hardly even opened it before I was packing my bag!"

"I don't know," I mumbled, my tongue tied, for once. I felt as if I were on the edge of a grand discovery, something that would change the world—or, at least, my life.

"Because I missed you, you fool! I was wrong about something just now. I have been content, you know. Would you like me to tell you when?" Mr. Barnum's voice was softer—shy, almost.

I nodded, unable to meet his gaze.

"Remember when you first came to New York? And we used to sit together in Caroline's parlor and talk? Then I thought I was happy. I wasn't used to talking over my plans and schemes with anyone else, but somehow—I just found myself talking them over with you. And I was happy."

"So was I," I whispered.

"And I've missed that, I've missed that so much. So don't go talking about not living a big enough life, for you were big enough for me to miss, terribly. And that's saying a lot, as I own an elephant. Several of them, in fact."

"Me, too—oh, I've missed you, too!"

I couldn't say more; he didn't try. He acted, for the first time in his life, as if words truly were no longer necessary. I simply *felt* his understanding in the way he continued to hold my hands; the warmth of his grasp made its way somehow to my heart—which filled with satisfaction. Looking up, gazing into his eyes, I thought I recognized his heart, too; it was the light that I always saw there, finally revealed, fully, to me. I smiled in its illuminating glow, and the name that I had carried within me, for so long, finally found its way out of my suddenly open heart, and rushed toward that light.

"Phineas," I whispered.

His eyes grew wide; a great, satisfied grin broke crooked

across his face. And in that moment, I found what I had been searching for all my life. I saw happiness; I saw respect.

I saw love.

"So," he said after a moment; he released my hands, and we settled into our respective chairs, knee to knee, eye to eye.

Heart to heart.

"Let me tell you about my latest idea." He took out a cigar from his breast pocket. I reached for the matchbox on the table beside me, struck a match, and lit it for him. He leaned back in the chair and puffed away, satisfied.

"Is there a role in it for me?"

"It's all about you. Opera, that's the thing. Hear me out. A perfect, miniature opera company—what do you think about that?"

"Opera? That would take a lot of people, wouldn't it?"

"It would, indeed. Have you heard of the little women over in New Hampshire? Sisters, they are; genteel, ladylike, although they can't hold a candle to you. But they sing—that's what I hear."

"Opera," I mused, mulling it over. Opera was all the rage now—and, of course, I could sing. I had always been told I had a lovely voice. "Tell me more."

"You'll be the leading lady. But imagine headlining your own troupe! I've even picked out a name, the Lilliputian Opera Company, starring Mrs. General Tom Thumb. What do you think?"

"I like it," I said, nodding, turning it around in my head, waiting for it to click into place, to make sense—to get my heart racing again, wondering where all my train schedules were. Had I packed them away, like everything else? Oh, I certainly hoped not!

"I like it," I repeated, smiling up at him. "I like it a lot, Phineas."

"I knew you would, Vinnie," he said, with a satisfied smile, as he puffed away on his cigar—just like a man. I got up then, pausing to rest my hand upon his shoulder, as I began to walk around the parlor, turning on the lights—just like a woman.

For outside, the dusk was falling.

And I knew we would talk well into the night.

CODA

From the *Brooklyn Daily Eagle,* April 7, 1878

Professor Edison, the inventor of the most marvelous instrument of modern times, has already hit upon a scheme in which millions seem to lurk, namely, the publication of a cheap phonographic library, by means of which a five hundred page novel can be sold in electrotype sheets to be adjusted to the phonograph. The instrument will then be adjusted and the novel will be read aloud to the listener by machinery. Fortunately this instrument has only just come into fashion, otherwise we should never have come into possession of that exquisite mine of Oriental fancy the Arabian Nights.

AUTHOR'S NOTE

I first encountered Lavinia Warren Stratton in the pages of one of the masterpieces of historical fiction, E. L. Doctorow's *Ragtime*. She appeared, briefly and near the end of her life, in a scene with Harry Houdini.

She didn't make much of an impression on me then. However, a few months later I was searching for the subject for my next novel, noodling around on the Internet, reading books, histories, lists of notable people—anything that might help me find that one person whose story I just had to tell. On one list, the name "Lavinia Warren Stratton" leapt out at me; I remembered her from Doctorow's novel, did a basic search on her name, and was immediately entranced.

Lavinia—known as Vinnie—was born on October 31, 1841, in Middleborough, Massachusetts, to a family of good standing. All of her siblings, as well as her parents, were normal-size, except for her younger sister, Huldah, called Minnie. Both Minnie and Vinnie had a form of proportionate dwarfism, probably caused by a pituitary disorder; had she been born in more modern times, she would have been given human growth hormones. But at the time, she—and her future husband, Charles Stratton (or General Tom Thumb, as he was more widely known)—were highly prized "curiosities" in an America that was just beginning to be linked. With the advent of the railroad, steamships, photography, and the modern press, people could now experience a world outside their own small villages; most people had never seen, nor really ever heard of, little people. And the fact that Vinnie and Charles and Minnie were "perfectly formed people in miniature" made them palatable and interesting to the public; those who had disproportionate dwarfism were, tragically, considered distasteful, and often used in circuses and sideshows to depict savages or idiots.

Vinnie had a very loving and normal childhood, and was engaged as a schoolteacher in her town. However, a Colonel Wood—purported to be a cousin, although that was never proven—showed up at her door one day with an invitation to appear on his "floating palace of curiosities" out west. To the great shock of her pious New England family, Vinnie leapt at the chance. In her autobiographical writings, she admits to a desire to travel, to see things, to experience a wider world than she could in New England.

She doesn't admit that her fate, were she to remain at home, would likely be a dismal one. A woman in mid-nineteenth-century America had few options; either she married, or she remained dependent upon her relatives for the rest of her life. She could not have a career (beyond that of modest schoolmarm) of her own. It's unlikely Vinnie or her family ever thought, given her size, that she would marry. However, after her cousin's visit she had another option. She could leave Middleborough; she could travel, she could have a career, and she could do this as a single woman precisely *because* of her size. For a man named P. T. Barnum had just introduced the public to General Tom Thumb; suddenly there was great interest in the "curiosities" of the world, and Vinnie was only too quick to take advantage of this opportunity.

After spending almost three years upon the Mississippi—her travels were interrupted by the outbreak of the Civil War—Vinnie returned home to Middleborough. A year or so passed before, somehow, P. T. Barnum "heard" of her, and sent an agent to interview her. Her parents were skeptical; they did not wish to have their daughter caught up in any of Barnum's infamous "humbugs." But somehow, Vinnie and Barnum persuaded her parents to let her go, and it was only a matter of weeks before Vinnie was capturing the hearts of the New York press with her stately levees; she was heralded by all as the "Little Queen of Beauty."

It made sense—not only to Barnum but probably to Vinnie herself—that the Little Queen of Beauty should marry a King, and the perfect candidate happened to be close at hand. Charles Stratton—Barnum's great discovery and greater friend—made her acquaintance; Barnum wasted no time in fanning the flames of love and most important, the press, and in February of 1863, the two were married.

Their marriage was the nineteenth-century equivalent of the wedding between Prince Charles and Lady Diana; every paper in the land covered it, relegating the Civil War, for a few days at least, to the back pages. From that point on, Vinnie and Charles, along with her sister Minnie and another little person, Commodore Nutt, performed as the most famous quartet in the world. They traveled the globe; they met Brigham Young, every president in the White House, Queen Victoria; they were among the first passengers on the new Union Pacific railroad linking the country and among the very first Americans of any size to travel to the new colony of Australia.

In 1878, Vinnie's beloved sister Minnie died in childbirth. Commodore Nutt had already retired from their troupe, and suddenly the most famous quartet in the world stumbled upon hard times. Vinnie and Charles continued to perform, but tastes were changing; the country was more sophisticated, and their venues were becoming smaller. Hard-up financially—for they had believed they had to live the life their society friends could more easily afford—they even traveled with Barnum's great circus for a season, performing as part of the sideshow.

In 1883, Vinnie and Charles were touring once more, staying at the Newhall House in Milwaukee when that hotel caught fire, resulting in one of the worst hotel tragedies in history; Charles apparently never recovered from the shock of that experience and died only six months later. Retreating to her childhood home, her finances in ruin, Lavinia was on the verge of retiring when Barnum encouraged her to keep going, to keep appearing before the public.

Of course, she did. In 1885 she remarried—to another little person, Count Primo Magri of Italy—and formed the Lilliputian Opera Company. She continued to tour, even appearing in vaudeville and early silent pictures; ever short of funds, the couple opened up a roadside stand near their home called "Primo's Pastime," where they entertained anyone who would stop and buy a souvenir. They also spent a sad couple of summers as part of the "Midget City, Dreamland" exhibit at Coney Island.

In researching Lavinia's life, the challenge was always to separate the humbug from the truth. P. T. Barnum looms large over everything written about her. Many articles and even a book or two, written not only at the time but much later, appear to accept as fact everything that Barnum ever put forth, including the blatant falsehood that Vinnie and Charles were the parents of a daughter who died in infancy.

Even Lavinia's own writings left much to the imagination. She had hopes of publishing an autobiography in her lifetime, but didn't; several incomplete chapters were discovered after her death, however, and edited and published by A. H. Saxon in 1979. She also published a couple of essays in the *New York Tribune Sunday Magazine* in 1906 that purported to be part of her autobiography. But there is so much missing from all of these pages! She never mentions details of the death of her sister, for instance. She doesn't discuss the baby hoax. She doesn't discuss much of anything, actually; her writings are really a rather uninspiring travelogue, listing the places she traveled and the people she met. And she freely borrows from Sylvester Bleeker's published account of their world tour.

She also doesn't discuss her feelings. She never shares any disappointments, any frustrations about her size, her physical discomforts. She presents a determined, sunny face always. You have to read very carefully to find the disappointments and frustrations.

For example, she gives her time with Barnum's circus in 1881 only a couple of paragraphs and concludes by saying, "It was not to our taste." Similarly, while writing about some of the dangers of her life upon the river with Colonel Wood, she admits, "It cannot be denied that these occurrances (*sic*) were a little disquieting."

And she makes no mention of her "child," the humbug she and Barnum perpetuated concerning a baby Thumb. Accounts vary as to whether Lavinia was barren, or she chose not to have children. I have to think that, as intelligent as she was, she was very aware of the dangers to one her size. And when Minnie became pregnant, apparently Barnum's doctors tried to convince her to have an abortion, which she refused. So obviously, while press accounts of Minnie's death mention her "fairy child," Vinnie was only too aware of the risks.

How she felt, then, having deceived the public into rejoicing over the "birth," and then mourning the "death," of her own child can only be imagined; likewise, the guilt and grief she must have felt in watching her own sister die in childbirth. She discussed the hoax once in public, in an interview given to *Billboard* magazine in 1901, explaining the procedure of obtaining "English babies in England, German babies in Germany." But she also takes pains to say that "Mr. Barnum was a great man."

As I researched Lavinia's history, her great intelligence and drive were the characteristics that spoke to me. There seemed to be only one other person in her life who even came close to matching those characteristics, and that person was, of course, P. T. Barnum himself.

Lavinia's story is so big—there were times when I feared turning her into a nineteenth-century version of Woody Allen's *Zelig*—that it threatened to get away from me at times. Yet I found that whenever I turned back to Barnum, a story came into focus. I believe that every novel is either a mystery, a tragedy, or a love story—some are all three—and it became clear to me that this is a love story. An unusual love story; an affair of the mind rather than the body. P. T. Barnum was always the light she was seeking; whether, as at first, he was just the means to bring her to a wider audience and take her away from the dangers of working with shadier characters or, ultimately, the companion, the true partner, she could never find in Charles Stratton or even her beloved sister Minnie.

I chose to end my novel, then, a good forty years before Vinnie's death. To me, the story had to end with Barnum; he was the great love of her life, I came to believe, and everything she did began and ended with him. Even in her own autobiographical chapters, Lavinia only devotes four pages to her life after the death of Charles Stratton.

Did Vinnie marry Charles Stratton only for the fame she had to know it would bring her? Most accounts record their marriage as a happy one. Yet he does not loom over her life in the way that Barnum does. It is difficult to imagine that Vinnie wasn't aware of the enormous fame that would result in marrying a fellow little person—the most famous little person in the world, in fact. The novelty of the perfect little couple in miniature was too much to pass up. Most accounts also record Charles Stratton as being somewhat of an innocent, an intellectual weakling—although a very genial man, one who would not have caused Vinnie any grief. He also would not have excited her mind in the way someone like P. T. Barnum would have.

Barnum died in 1891; somewhat like another larger-than-life character, Tom Sawyer, he arranged to have his obituary run a few days prior to his death so that he could read it. His last words were, "How were the receipts today at Madison Square Garden?"

Lavinia died on November 25, 1919; she was buried next to her first husband in Bridgeport, Connecticut. Despite her second marriage, she signed her name, until the end of her life, as "Mrs. General Tom Thumb."

Yet when she was asked, after Charles Stratton's death, if she was preparing his biography, she answered no. However, she assured the questioner, she was confident that "My own autobiography I hope to have published and put out to the public before long."

In some way, I hope I have fulfilled that ambition; I can't help but think Vinnie would be pleased to see her name in print, once more.

ACKNOWLEDGMENTS

One of the delights of telling Vinnie's story was learning not only about her life and that of P. T. Barnum, but also about a colorful, exciting period in our nation's history. Some of the most helpful books I read were *The Lives of Dwarfs* by Betty M. Adelson; *The Life of P. T. Barnum* by P. T. Barnum; *P. T. Barnum, the Legend and the Man* by A. H. Saxon; *Freak Show* by Robert Bogdan; *Barnum Presents General Tom Thumb* by Alice Curtis Desmond; *General Tom Thumb's Three Years Tour Around the World* by Sylvester Bleeker; and, of course, *The Autobiography of Mrs. Tom Thumb (Some of My Life Experiences)* by Countess M. Lavinia Magri, formerly Mrs. General Tom Thumb, with the assistance of Sylvester Bleeker, edited by A. H. Saxon.

There is a delightful website called The Lost Museum, which reconstructs Barnum's American Museum in an interactive fashion, and also provides much history about Barnum and his various performers: www.lostmuseum.cuny.edu/intro.html. Another website, The Disability History Museum (www.disabilitymuseum .org), introduced me to Lavinia Stratton's autobiographical essays published in the *New York Tribune Sunday Magazine* in 1906.

Two sites were very helpful in providing color commentary on the period: www.sonofthesouth.net is a wonderful resource for *Harper's Weekly* magazines of the Civil War period, and Cornell University Library's "Making of America" website is a treasure trove of nineteenth-century periodicals: dlxs2.library.cornell .edu/m/moa/.

I am indebted, as always, to Laura Langlie for her insight, support, and savvy. Thanks, of course, to everyone at Random House: Kate Miciak, my wonderful editor; Gina Centrello, Libby McGuire, Jane von Mehren; Susan Corcoran and the tireless publicity team; Sanyu Dillon and the amazing marketing team; Robbin Schiff for her brilliant cover art; and Denise Cronin, Rachel Kind, and Donna Duverglas. Much gratitude to Randall Klein for answering my endless questions, and Loyale Coles.

And as always, I could not have done this without the support of my family, especially Dennis, Alec, and Ben Hauser.

THE AUTOBIOGRAPHY OF

Mrs. Tom Thumb

MELANIE BENJAMIN

[*A Reader's Guide*]

Family Album

One of the great pleasures of publishing is the ability to revisit a book with each new edition. As an author, I have time to learn from readers and hear what they want to know more about or what they don't quite understand about the book or the time period. With this edition of *The Autobiography of Mrs. Tom Thumb,* I decided to share with you some photographs that helped me better understand the character not only of Vinnie, but of our young country in the middle of the nineteenth century. In this novel, I truly came to see the United States as a major character, one that starts out a bit naïve but grows up alongside Vinnie, ever optimistic, ever expanding, sometimes learning from the past but more often not. I think these photographs are a kind of family scrapbook of our nation during its youth!

This image delights me so much! In Vinnie's time, there were many songs and dances composed in honor of her and Charles—"The Tom Thumb Polka," for example. I think this sheet-music cover perfectly encapsulates that era—an era when popular music was enjoyed in the home, sheet music passed around from house to house. There was no radio, no iPod, no Victrola, even. Every young woman knew how to play; almost every household, however poor, had a piano. And for every "Battle Hymn of the Republic" or "My Old Kentucky Home," there was a silly novelty piece as well—just like "The Hippopotamus Polka"!—sung by the family in the evening, or played at the local barn dance, just for fun.

The caption of this photograph simply reads, "Unidentified Drummer Boy in Union Uniform." I think this is a heartbreaking photo. While Vinnie's life played out as if the Civil War was merely background noise, the country, of course, was torn in two. At least two of Vinnie's brothers fought for the Union. Vinnie spent most of the war in New York or touring Canada and Europe; meanwhile, the South was decimated. While a visitor to a northern city might not have even realized there was a war at all, the fighting was happening in the backyard of every southerner. And by the end of the war, young boys and old men were being drafted, as an entire generation of southern men had already been used up. But there were very young men in Union uniform, as well; perhaps even some of Vinnie's pupils from her schoolteacher days.

Vinnie mentioned in her autobiography that her schoolroom had one long table that went around the perimeter of the room. For some reason, I could not get a proper image of this in my head, until I found this painting by Winslow Homer: "The Country School," painted in 1871. I love how it depicts the different students all in one room; some with proper shoes and stockings, others barefoot. Vinnie grew up on a farm, and while I'm quite certain she never went to school with bare feet, I imagine some of her pupils might not have been so fortunate. I also love the image of the schoolteacher, tall and commanding, in charge; I try to imagine how Vinnie managed, being smaller than her youngest pupil.

The Booths were the most famous acting family in America in the 1800s. I've always been fascinated by them, especially Edwin, who was generally acknowledged to be the greatest actor of his time. In one of the newspaper articles about Charles and Vinnie's wedding, one item caught my eye: a list of wedding presents. On that list, amid all the Tiffany plates and jewels, was a pair of slippers, handmade by Edwin Booth. How delightful! The most famous actor in America hand-worked a pair of slippers for Vinnie! And yet, how tragic that two years later this endearing man's brother would assassinate Abraham Lincoln. Edwin was haunted by his brother's act for the rest of his life, but it's a testament to his talent and character that the public never seemed to associate him in any way with it, and his popularity never waned.

This is a photograph of the docks in St. Paul, Minnesota, in 1858, which is when Vinnie was performing on her cousin's "floating palace of curiosities." While her description of the boat makes it clear it wasn't anything like as grand as these, still, this photograph helped me imagine how busy and bustling those river towns were. The Mississippi River was the major highway of the West in those years; it was crowded with steamboats, flatboats, even canoes as people and goods made their way north and south. And how exciting it must have been when the showboats and floating palaces docked! I can well imagine farmers and their families all flocking to the dock to see the entertainment—the minstrels, the specialty dancers, and of course, the curiosities such as Vinnie and her roommate, Sylvia Hardy, the Maine Giantess. What color these people brought to otherwise drab, staid lives!

THE DRIVE IN THE CENTRAL PARK, NEW YORK, SEPTEMBER, 1860.

This is another Winslow Homer piece, depicting the drive through New York's Central Park in September 1860. When Vinnie first came to New York in late 1862, the city was far different than we know it today. While it was the largest city in the United States, there was still somewhat of a bucolic air about it; pigs might be rutting in a lot adjacent to a store. Horses were stabled, of course, throughout the city. And Central Park was brand new. It first opened in 1857; sixteen hundred citizens, many of them free African Americans, had to be evicted from the parcel of land designated for the park. In 1858, Frederick Law Olmsted won a competition to design and expand it. This wood engraving, which first appeared in *Harper's Weekly,* shows how well-heeled New Yorkers used the park, probably on a typical Sunday drive. Note how different the park looks, how few trees have yet been planted. And sheep actually grazed in the Sheep Meadow up until 1934!

The caption for this reads, "The new American railroads, anonymous, 1860s." I think this image of a typical trestle railroad bridge is terrifying! The railroad was Vinnie's salvation, in a way; without it, she could never have had the career she did. But this photograph depicts how truly primitive and sometimes hair-raising the conditions under which she traveled were, especially once she traveled to the West. There were numerous fatal accidents on the railroad: engines blowing up, trains derailing, switches malfunctioning. Travel, period, was risky in the 1800s. Stagecoaches were regularly held up, or horses got spooked and ran away; steamboats blew up or were torn apart by hidden underwater dangers (like the sunken remnants of other blown-up boats!). It took a lot of courage for anyone to travel far from home in those days, even if she wasn't thirty-two inches tall!

Reading Group Questions and Topics for Discussion

1. What are the parallels between Vinnie's celebrity and the definition of celebrity today?

2. Why did Vinnie determine to communicate only her optimism? What was she trying to hide behind, or hide from herself, by choosing not to dwell on the many obstacles in her way?

3. What in Vinnie's family life prepared her to be so strong and independent, and so determined to make her own way in the world?

4. Why did Vinnie go along with Barnum's humbug concerning the infant?

5. Which is the true love story of the book: Vinnie and Barnum, Vinnie and Charles, Vinnie and Minnie, or Vinnie and the public?

6. Why do you think the notion of the Tom Thumb wedding so swept the nation that even today, children reenact it?

7. Why do we now remember Barnum mainly for his circus?

8. What was the most interesting historical fact in the book for you? Which was the most startling?

9. The "intermission" snippets between the chapters are actual news articles from the era. How are they different from articles today? Or are they?

10. " 'Vinnie,' my mother was fond of telling me (Lavinia being the name by which I was called, shortened within the family to Vinnie), 'it's not that you're too.small, my little chick, but rather that the world is too big.' " (page 11) Does this turn out to be true for Vinnie?

11. How do you see Vinnie's experience as a teacher influencing her work as an entertainer?

12. Compare and contrast Colonel Wood to Barnum. Do you think either man has Vinnie's best interests at heart? Why or why not?

13. Vinnie takes to heart her father's admonition to not bring shame upon the family. How does Vinnie try to avoid being shameful? Is she successful?

14. Sylvia points out a photograph of P. T. Barnum in the window of a store. "I was surprised and, I confess, a little disappointed; the man in the photograph looked so very . . . *ordinary.* Curly hair parted on the side, a wide forehead, a somewhat bulbous nose, an unremarkable smile. He resembled any man I might have passed in the street; he certainly did not resemble a world-famous impresario. Colonel Wood, I had to admit, looked much more the part than did this man." (page 78) Vinnie is used to people making immediate assumptions about her based on her appearance. What assumptions, though, does Vinnie make about people for the same reasons? Are preconceived notions about people ingrained in us?

15. "Ever since we'd stepped foot in that magnificent carriage, I had instinctively known how to behave among such riches. My

parents, however, did not; never had I seen them so unsure of themselves. I could not imagine either of them happily living in a mansion; Mama would wear herself out scrubbing all those marble floors, for she would never trust anyone else to clean them!" (page 142) How does class separate people in this novel, especially Vinnie from her family, Vinnie from the performers on Colonel Wood's boat, and Vinnie from Charles?

16. What does it mean to Vinnie that she is descended from the "first Americans"? What does that mean to you?

17. What part of the American Museum would you be most entertained by? Does such a thing still exist today, in one form or another?

18. Is Charles Stratton a tragic figure? Why or why not?

19. Compare and contrast Vinnie and Charles's wedding to a modern-day spectacle, like a royal wedding or a wedding between two actors.

20. What do you think it means to live one's life in the public eye, as Vinnie and Charles did? How would you react to being scrutinized by the press for your every action? Compare how you may have felt in Vinnie's day compared to today's twenty-four-hour news and gossip cycle.

21. For Vinnie, what do you think was the best part of being famous? What was the worst?

22. Is Vinnie a role model for people of small stature? Do you think she helped to open people's minds and educate them?

23. Barnum says to Vinnie, "Vinnie, if you've ever done your sister a disservice—and I believe you think you have—it's only in this: that you have persisted in thinking of her as younger and

simpler than she really is." (page 325) Do you agree? Do you think you could treat a sibling the way Vinnie views Minnie? Is there anything Vinnie does that you would not do?

24. Were you surprised by Minnie's decision to have her child?

25. Vinnie says about Charles, "I finally acknowledged that my husband had no personality of his own; he was merely an imprint of everyone around him." (page 344) Was Charles his own man, or was he a creation of the act?

26. Toward the end of her stage career, Vinnie asks herself, "Had I ever been simply Lavinia Warren Stratton? To anyone—even myself?" (page 363) Do you think Vinnie chose this life for herself, or did she essentially hop on a ride that she couldn't get off? Was the price she had to pay for her fame and fortune her own chosen identity?

27. What role in life do children serve for Vinnie? For the Bleekers? For Barnum? For Charles?

If you loved Melanie Benjamin's

The Autobiography of Mrs. Tom Thumb,

read on for a sample of

her bestselling debut novel,

Alice I Have Been,

available from Bantam Books Trade Paperbacks.

[CHAPTER ONE]

Oxford, 1859

OFF WITH THEIR—LEGS. THAT WAS THE CURIOUS NOTION I had as a child.

That certain people—queens, generally—lost their heads was understood to be a historical fact.

But in my world, legs were missing with alarming regularity as well. The men in their long academic robes, the women in their voluminous skirts; everyone skimming, floating, like puffs of cotton in the air—that is the first, and most vivid, memory of my childhood.

I knew, of course, that children possessed legs; yet the legs seemed to disappear as their owners grew up, and if I never questioned the logic of this it must be because, even then, I understood that Oxford was a kingdom unto itself. It was different from, and superior to, the rest of the globe (which of course meant Britain, for those were the years when the sun never set on

Victoria's empire), complete with its own rules, language, and even time; all the clocks in Oxford were set five minutes ahead of Greenwich mean time.

Naturally, it follows that if Oxford was its own kingdom, then I was its princess—one of three, to be precise—because my mother was, as everyone knew, its queen.

Remarkable for a woman who bore ten children—one would have assumed she was perpetually in a state of bearing a child, or waiting for a child, or getting over a child—Mamma made certain that the Deanery was the social center of Christ Church, which was of course the social center of Oxford. No one dared give a party or a bazaar or a dance without her approval. At times she even graciously made room for other queens; Victoria herself once stayed with us, although not even her plump, imperious personage intimidated Mamma.

Papa was merely the Dean of Christ Church, responsible for the education and religious upbringing of hundreds of gentlemen, including the sons of that same queen. Even when I was so young that the only place I could look was up, for I was all too well acquainted with the ground, I knew that he was quite important. Instructors would bow to him, scholars would pale in his presence, princes deferred to him; entire halls full of young men would rise upon his entrance, as well as his departure.

While at home he could scarcely make himself heard; he was entirely eclipsed by Mamma, and entirely happy to be so. There was even a silly rhyme that made the rounds of Christ Church in those days—

I am the Dean, and this is Mrs. Liddell
She plays the first, and I the second fiddle

This did not reach my ears, however, until much later. For as the daughter of the Dean and Mrs. Liddell, I was sheltered, at least for a time, from most of the gossip that was the chief occupation of some of the finest scholarly minds of the age.

Privileged was how I would describe my early years, if only because I was told that they were such. I knew no life before Oxford, although Papa was, even then, a rising academic: domestic chaplain to Prince Albert, headmaster of the Westminster School in London. I was baptized in the Abbey, the fourth child, second daughter.

Ina was not baptized in the Abbey. I may have reminded her of this with some regularity.

While we still lived in London, an older brother, Arthur, died of scarlet fever. Papa had difficulty speaking of him later; his kind face, with the aristocratic nose and decided chin (which I, unfortunately, inherited) would grow quizzical, his brow furrowing, as if he—such a learned man—could not understand the simplest, most frequently asked question of all:

Why?

I don't recall that Mamma ever spoke of it one way or another. Although surely that can't be true.

When I was scarcely four—in 1856—we arrived in Oxford, upon Papa's appointment as Dean of Christ Church. By then the family included Harry, the eldest, followed by Lorina, myself, and Edith—the three princesses. Ina was three years older than I, Edith two years younger. All of us—along with servants, fine china, heirloom silver, imported linens, and all the other necessities of a distinguished household—moved into the Deanery, which Papa had arranged to be enlarged and remodeled to accommodate our growing family. Even so, it was never quite large enough for Mamma's ambitions.

It was in this world, this Oxford, that my first memories were made. It was a peculiar world for a little girl, in many ways; there were few children my age, as all the students and dons at the time were supposed to be celibate. Only the deans, the senior members of the college, were allowed to marry, and most of them were of an age where children weren't possible. Papa was rather the exception to the rule, and I believe that he was proud of the fact.

Perhaps that was why there were so many of us.

Each night, after I was snug in bed, Old Tom, the bell in the imposing tower that was the centerpiece of Christ Church, tolled one hundred and one times (signifying the original number of students at the college); even as I struggled to remain awake for the first chime, I rarely made it all the way through to the end. Our home, the Deanery, was opposite the tower, our front entrance part of the pale stone fortress of buildings bordering the flat green Quad; we also had a private entrance opening up to the back garden. Quite literally, we lived among the students; I remember walking with Ina and Edith—three little maids all in a row, always dressed exactly alike, crisp white frocks in summer, rich velvets in winter—in the Quad with our governess, Miss Prickett, as young men removed their caps and bowed low, exaggeratedly, at our approach.

People in Oxford spoke in solemn, measured tones. Centuries-old traditions demanded to be followed, whether or not they made much sense. To me, still coddled in the nursery world of a proper Victorian childhood, they often did not; that is precisely why I wouldn't have changed them for the world. I was no ordinary little girl, I fervently believed, and Oxford only reinforced this notion. Every year on the first of May, we all gathered at dawn on the gray stones of Magdalen Bridge, sheltered by huge trees in the early burst of bloom, listening to the whisper of the river Isis down below. Magically, just as the first glow of sun painted the sky from purple to pink, a choir of pure, young male voices would float down upon us, singing ancient hymns to welcome summer.

My birthday was on the fourth of May; I cannot deny that as a child, I secretly believed this hallowed ceremony was somehow in honor of me.

Pricks—Miss Prickett—did not share this belief. She adored Edith, as did everyone; Edith was the most compliant creature on earth, and her swirls of russet red hair only helped endear her to everyone she met. Yet Pricks practically worshipped Ina; as the eldest, the most refined, she could do no wrong.

As for me, in the middle—the only one with pin-straight hair; Mamma deplored how it hung on my neck like seaweed, so she chopped it off, short with a heavy fringe that made me feel as vulnerable as a baby bird before it grows feathers—I must admit, Pricks tolerated me. Barely.

"Alice, what on earth did you do to your frock? Look at your sisters—they haven't managed to get awful dirt stains on their hems! Whatever were you doing?"

"I was playing in dirt," said I, frustrated by my need to state the obvious.

"Playing in dirt? On your knees? In a white frock? Who would do such a thing—white *stains* so!"

"Then why do we wear it, when you know we're going out to the garden to play? Why don't we wear brown frocks, or green, or perhaps even—"

"Brown? Who ever heard of wearing brown in May? You'll wear white, as your mother wishes. Brown. What can I do with such a child?" Whereupon Pricks would throw up her hands to the heavens, as if God alone could tell her what to do with me.

I suspected He couldn't. I had once overheard Papa say that

"God Himself broke the mold when it came to that one," and I knew, somehow, that he meant me. Even in a house full of children, I was the only one ever referred to in such a singular way.

I was rather proud of that, to tell the truth.

Pricks was prickly. That's why I named her Pricks; it had nothing to do with her last name. Pricks exclaimed a lot; she threw her hands up a lot. She bristled when I asked her the most natural questions, such as why the wart on her face had a hair growing out of it whereas the wart on her hand did not.

"Alice," Ina would murmur, patting her long brown curls. Oh, how I longed to have curls! The greatest tragedy of my life, at age seven, was that I had short black hair exactly like a boy. "That's simply not spoken of."

"What is?"

"Warts. Pricks can't help it. It's not very nice of you to talk about it."

"Do you think she slept with a frog when she was little?"

"I—well, perhaps." I could tell Ina was interested in spite of herself; she relaxed her pose—sitting on the windowsill of the schoolroom, hands folded properly in her lap, head bowed in perfect ladylike composure—and actually swung her feet to and fro. "Still, ladies don't talk of such things."

"You're not a lady. You're only ten."

"And you're seven. I'll always be older than you." She clapped her hands with delight, while I scowled and longed to pull her hair. How unfair, how *tragic*, the world was; I would always be younger than her.

"But you'll always be older than me," Edith whispered, sliding her moist little hand in mine. I gave it a squeeze, as thanks.

"Oh, look, there's Mr. Dodgson!" Ina jumped up and pressed her face against the windowpane; Edith and I joined her, although

Edith had to climb up onto the cushioned window seat in order to see.

The three of us watched—the windowpane, warm from the sun, smooth against my forehead—as a tall, slim man, dressed all in black from the top of his hat to the toes of his leather boots, wandered into view. He was strolling, hands in pockets, across the generous garden that separated the Deanery from the library. Stopping to examine flowers, hedges, he refused to walk in any sort of straight path, altogether acting like someone hoping to be discovered.

Just then Papa ran into the picture, gown flapping behind him like giant insect wings. He consulted his watch, dangling precariously on its gold chain, with a shake of his head; a huge book was tucked under his left arm. Papa was always running late. I held my breath as he nearly ran Mr. Dodgson down; fortunately, at the last possible moment he swerved around him, not even noticing when Mr. Dodgson raised his hat and bowed.

Mr. Dodgson looked up, then, and saw us in the window; Ina gasped and ducked out of sight, mortified to have been caught spying on him. Ina always behaved so oddly in his presence; she basked in his attention, schemed of ways to encourage it, and then, at the very last minute, always pulled back. Yet whenever I pointed this out to her, merely trying to be helpful, she had a tendency to pull my hair or pinch my arm.

That didn't prevent me from continuing to comment upon it, however. If she didn't want my help, that was her misfortune.

I shook my head at her and then tugged on the creaky sash of the window until it opened enough for me to stick my head out.

"Hullo, Mr. Dodgson!"

"Hullo, Miss Alice, Miss Edith." He bowed in his usual stiff way. I had recently informed him that he walked as if he had a poker stuck down the back of his jacket. He had thought about this, considered it gravely, and agreed that he did, but that he couldn't help it.

I thought this was a reasonable response and left it at that.

"Alice!" Pricks bustled over—no doubt summoned by Ina, who was standing well away from the window, her arms crossed over her chest, glaring at me. "What on earth are you doing? Young ladies do not shout out of windows like monkeys!"

"Oh, I do wish I was a monkey!" I forgot about Mr. Dodgson for a moment; monkeys were my favorite animals, along with kittens, rabbits, hedgehogs, mice, and lizards. "Wouldn't that be smashing?"

"Alice! Wherever did you hear that word? Young ladies do not say 'smashing.' " Pricks reached over my head to push down the window. However, when she saw Mr. Dodgson smiling up at us, she hesitated. "Oh!"

"W-w-w-ould the young ladies like to join me for a pleasant st-stroll around the Quad?" He doffed his hat. "Accompanied by you, of course," he added hastily. I shook my head in sympathy; his stammer was worse than ever. Poor Mr. Dodgson! (Or—Do-Do-Dodgson, as it sounded coming from him.) Still, he never appeared too upset about it, unlike Pricks and her warts; she was always trying some new cream or lotion to be rid of them.

"Oh, well." Pricks smiled in that unexpected, scary way of hers; she bent slightly at the waist and twisted her face up almost as if she was going to be ill, but then, at the last minute, a smile appeared, a wide, snapping smile that revealed most of her teeth.

Patting her hair, smoothing her skirts, she swung around and surveyed the three of us, frowning at my dirty hem. "Alice, go ask Phoebe to change you at once. All three of you will have to change, I suppose—I might as well do the same."

"But why? I'll only get dirty again." Once more, I did not see why I had to remind her of the obvious.

"Because your mother will have a—will be quite disappointed, if I allow you out looking like that."

I was forced to admit that she had a point. Mamma would certainly make a fuss if she saw me, the Dean's daughter, outside in anything other than a stiff, freshly laundered white frock, the more frills, the better.

Pricks turned back to the window and whispered loudly, "We would be happy to accompany you, thank you so much, Mr. Dodgson. We'll join you directly."

"He can't hear, you know," I reminded her. "He doesn't hear out of his right ear. You have to shout."

"Oh, but I—oh, go ahead, Alice, but don't shout. Just—speak loudly."

I shook my head. Pricks was so exceedingly proper all the time, except when it came to Mr. Dodgson. Only he could make her behave in such a manner that I could almost, if I scrunched my eyes and tried very hard, imagine that she had once been a real little girl, like me.

"We would be happy to accommodate you," I said loudly, slowly, my voice as deep as Papa's when he gave a sermon. "We shall join you directly." Then I bowed.

Mr. Dodgson looked up at me, opened his mouth, and laughed. He was still laughing as he sat down on a bench to wait, after first taking care to pull his trousers up at the knees; men did this, I knew, to keep their trousers from creasing. I wasn't altogether sure why I knew that; it was one of the many bits of useful information I was just now aware that I possessed. When I was six, I had known nothing. Now that I was seven, however, I couldn't help but be impressed by how very wise I was growing.

"Come, girls!" Pricks clapped her wide brown hands. "Change quickly!" She bustled us out of the schoolroom, looking back at the blackboard with a sigh. "We really should get back to geography—it's such a lovely afternoon, though. We'll study botany instead. That will be a pleasant change." And she smiled, violently, suddenly, to herself.

I wondered again at the ability of adults to turn every single pleasurable experience into a lesson. Did they do this only for our benefit? Or when they were alone, at the dining table or gathered for one of Mamma's musical entertainments, did they, even then, stop to say, "This tea is very delicious. Are you aware that it comes from India, the subcontinent, which has been a part of the Crown since the rebellion of 1857?"

I believed I was on the cusp of discovering the answer, for I was starting to be included in some of the entertainments held here at the Deanery. Only a month ago, Mamma had allowed Ina, Edith, and me to perform "Twinkle, Twinkle, Little Star" for her guests. Mr. Ruskin, in particular, had pronounced himself impressed; he reached out to pat my hair as I walked past him, after we had curtsied good night.

Although he patted my hair, he had actually gasped at Edith's—"Look at those titian curls!" he exclaimed. I remembered to ask him what "titian" meant, during our last drawing lesson; he sucked in his breath and informed me my education was appalling but never did answer me. Not even after I pointed out that he had just missed an excellent opportunity to improve it.

"Alice, do hurry!" Ina grabbed my arm and pulled me down the wide gallery, lined on one side with the oil paintings of the English landscape that Papa so admired, on the other with an ornately carved banister crowned with ferocious lions at either end, as finials. "We mustn't leave Mr. Dodgson waiting!"

"Why ever not? He doesn't have anything else to do." I fervently believed that; while I knew, vaguely, that he taught mathematics at the college, I understood that this was not his chief occupation. No, he was ours more than the students'. He was our playmate, our guide on many excursions, our galley slave (he often took us rowing on the Isis, where we loved to pretend that we were Nelson and his men, while Mr. Dodgson did his best to maneuver us about as if we were at the battle of Trafalgar).

It was only recently so. My brother, Harry, along with Ina, had been his favored companions since the day he first made our acquaintance by seeking permission to photograph the Deanery from the garden; Mamma was fond of saying Mr. Dodgson showed up one day with his infernal camera and never really left. Edith and I were only summoned occasionally from the nursery, most often to be photographed. Harry went away to school this year, however, and Mr. Dodgson appeared, finally, to notice Edith and me, and to ask for us, along with Ina, when he called.

Ina did not appreciate this development, I knew. There was nothing she could do about it, and she never let Mr. Dodgson notice her resentment; she was, I had to admit, absolutely brilliant at presenting a sweet, simple face to the world, no matter her true feelings. Just as a lady should, Pricks never wearied of reminding me.

“You silly little girl. Of course Mr. Dodgson has other things to do. Loads and loads of things. He’s a very important man.” Pulling me into the nursery, Ina started unbuttoning the back of my dress, while Phoebe, our nurse, flew about, opening up cupboards until she found three identical white frocks, flounced with pink satin ribbons, the buttons covered in the same pink satin.

“I don’t think so,” I replied, remembering how Mamma had referred to Mr. Dodgson as “that nuisance of a mathematics tutor, a more obtuse man I have never met.” Even though Papa corrected her—“Now, my dear, he is a *don*”—he had done it mildly. Papa was capable of standing up to Mamma, I knew, when he felt strongly about something. But evidently he did not feel strongly about Mr. Dodgson.

"Oh, Alice, why did you have to go and muddy your frock?" Ina was now stepping out of her own; her petticoats swayed to and fro as she crossed her arms over her chemise and glared at me. The way her eyebrows angled, high and disapproving, and the way her small mouth pursed, as if she was sucking on a lemon, made her almost always look cross, to be perfectly honest. "Those blue stripes on the bodice suit me so well! I despise the pink."

"I'm sorry." I genuinely was; I disliked getting dressed more than once a day. It was too much of an ordeal, what with all the buttoning and fastening and layer upon layer of stiff, scratchy underclothing. Chemise, pantalets, not one, not two, but *three* petticoats, stockings that I never could coax into staying smooth and high; my garters *always* came undone.

It would only get worse, I thought gloomily. One day I would have to wear a corset.

"C'mere, lamb," Phoebe said to Edith, who was kneeling in front of her dollhouse, a headless rag doll in her hand. "Let's get you into your fine feathers."

"It's so much fuss, simply to go outside." I raised my arms; Mary Ann, one of the maids, dropped the beribboned dress over my head.

"Are we ready?"

I turned toward the door; Pricks was standing there, in her new blue silk dress with yellow piping down the bodice that did not go well with her brown complexion, not at all. Still, she looked quite pleased with herself; she had even managed to add a pouf of false hair to the back of her head, so that it stuck out from behind her straw hat like the fuzzy tail of a bumblebee.

"Yes, Pricks," I said as Mary Ann buttoned up my last glove. Phoebe handed me a pink parasol. "Although what if Mr. Dodgson wants to take us to the Meadow? Perhaps to allow us to roll down a hill? I'll only stain my dress again, in that case."

"Mr. Dodgson won't do any such thing. He's a gentleman," Pricks said with a sniff.

Again, I wondered just what part of him Pricks and Ina could see that I could not. It was almost as if we knew two different people, both with the name Charles Lutwidge Dodgson. That was his full name; he had told it to me, after I confided that mine was Alice Pleasance Liddell, which I found rather a long name to write. However, he pointed out that his was longer by one letter, and that cheered me immensely.

I suspected, in a deep, serious part of me no one else knew I possessed, at least so far, which was somewhat worrisome, that Mr. Dodgson was the kind of person who *would* allow me to roll down a hill. I felt he was the only person on earth, actually, who would; he was my one chance to do this, to do other things that I desired, even things I did not yet know but somehow, I felt *he* did.

I felt it most when he looked at me as he stood behind his camera, holding the cap to the lens, counting slowly, his eyes never moving from mine as he exposed the plate. There was something about his eyes—the color of the periwinkle that grew at the base of the trees in the Meadow, such a deep blue—that made me feel as if he could see my dearest wishes, my darkest thoughts, before they made themselves known to me. And that simply by seeing them, he was also giving me permission to follow them. Perhaps he was even showing me the way. For I wasn't very comfortable with the dark thoughts—muddled, nameless thoughts—that sometimes came to me when I relaxed my watchfulness.

I was always on guard, you see. One had to be vigilant; for what, I did not know.

"Alice, come!"

Pricks, Ina, and Edith—predictably clutching her parasol too high, in the middle of the handle; she was such a baby!—were already at the end of the gallery, descending the staircase; I ran after them and immediately felt my right stocking start to sag down my shin.

"Miss Prickett!"

The three of them froze; I took advantage of this moment to sneak into my rightful place, between Ina and Edith.

"Yes, madam?" Pricks turned, her eyes cast down. She curtsied as my mother walked slowly from the library down the front hall, confronting our little group at the bottom of the stairs.

"May I ask where you are taking my daughters?" Mamma smiled as she said this, but the smile did not make it up to her eyes; they were wide, wary—not inclined to believe what they saw, I knew from experience. Such as the time I broke the china shepherdess that always perched, much too nervously, near the edge of the library mantel. Even though I had the foresight to pick up a shard of china—the faded pink china bow of the shepherdess's apron—and plant it in Ina's shoe that night, hoping to incriminate her instead, I did not fool Mamma.

Perhaps there would be an advantage to having such a sharp mother someday; that's what she said, after she punished me by making me take my meals alone in the schoolroom for a week. Still, even for a child so prone to daydreaming, I could not imagine the circumstances under which this could ever be true.

"We're going out for an expedition, madam. A little botany expedition. It's such a lovely day." Pricks raised her gaze to meet my mother's; she was always a trifle nervous around her but, unlike the rest of the household, had so far avoided being reduced to trembling tears. There was some hint of steel in her character, I had to admit, although she was careful to act completely obedient, always, to Mamma.

Mamma dabbed her upper lip with her handkerchief; it was warm for late May, and despite being tightly bound, a few strands of her black hair had escaped, lying damp and flat against her high forehead. She was fatter than usual because soon another baby would join us. I wasn't precisely sure what her being fat had to do with a baby, but that was how it was explained to me, and when I asked what the one had to do with the other, she would not say. She told me only that young ladies weren't supposed to ask such questions.

Still, I couldn't help but suspect that one very important piece of information was being withheld; I vowed, someday, to discover just what it was. Perhaps Mr. Dodgson would tell me.

"I don't suppose Mr. Dodgson has anything to do with this?"

I jumped; had Mamma read my mind? But no. She was talking to Pricks.

"Mr. Dodgson suggested it, yes," Pricks said without apology.

"The girls already took their exercise this morning, did they not?" Now Mamma singled me out with her black-eyed gaze; I felt her look me over, head to toe, searching for stains and tears as evidence.

Pricks could have lied, given how neat I looked now, but she didn't. "Yes," was all she answered, choosing to leave the rest up to Mamma.

Suddenly Mamma looked so tired; she closed her eyes, pressed her handkerchief against her forehead. I felt sorry for her. Babies must be very trying to get ready for.

"Oh, do go ahead. Just don't let the girls romp—and Alice, please try not to get dirty."

"I'll try, Mamma."

She smiled then, her eyes still closed. "Good girl." Then she slowly climbed the stairs, her wide skirts, in the jeweled red she favored, whispering as she brushed past us. As she went by me, she patted the top of my head.

"Now, girls." Pricks pulled her left glove up as high as it would go; it was rather a habit of hers, as she was always anxious to conceal that wart. Personally, however, I would have been more concerned about the one with the hair growing out of it.

Mary Ann held the door open for us, and we walked outside. Adjusting my parasol, I blinked at the sudden brightness of the sun; inside the Deanery everything was so gloomy and muted, with heavy sculpted carpeting and oppressive flowered paper, dark wood paneling and banisters. It was always a shock to go outside.

PHOTO CREDITS

Page 429: commons.wikimedia.org/wiki/File:Hippopotamus-polka-early1850s.jpg

Page 430: "Unidentified young drummer boy in Union uniform" from the Liljenquist Family Collection at the Library of Congress, Washington, D.C., 20540

Page 431: commons.wikimedia.org/wiki/File:Winslow_Homer_-_The_Country_School.jpg

Page 432: commons.wikimedia.org/wiki/File:Edwin-Booth-Hamlet-1870.png

Page 433: commons.wikimedia.org/wiki/File:Stpaulboats.jpg

Page 434: commons.wikimedia.org/wiki/File:The_drive_in_the_Central_Park,_New_York,_September,_1860_%28Boston_Public_Library%29.jpg

Page 435: commons.wikimedia.org/wiki/File:Railroad1860.png

Melanie Benjamin has written the *New York Times* bestselling historical novel *The Aviator's Wife*, the nationally bestselling *Alice I Have Been*, *The Autobiography of Mrs. Tom Thumb*, and *The Swans of Fifth Avenue*. She lives in Chicago with her husband, and far enough from her two adult sons not to be a nuisance (she hopes). When she isn't writing, she's reading.

melaniebenjamin.com
Look for Melanie Benjamin on Facebook.
@MelanieBen

To inquire about booking Melanie Benjamin for a speaking engagement, please contact the Penguin Random House Speakers Bureau at speakers@penguinrandomhouse.com.